D1272320

Woman and the Feminine in Medieval and Early Modern Scottish Writing

Woman and the Feminine in Medieval and Early Modern Scottish Writing

Edited by

Sarah M. Dunnigan

C. Marie Harker

and

Evelyn S. Newlyn

First published 2004 by
PALGRAVE MACMILLAN
Houndmills, Basingstoke, Hampshire RG21 6XS and
175 Fifth Avenue, New York, N.Y. 10010
Companies and representatives throughout the world

PALGRAVE MACMILLAN is the global academic imprint of the Palgrave
Macmillan division of St. Martin's Press, LLC and of Palgrave Macmillan Ltd.
Macmillan® is a registered trademark in the United States, United Kingdom
and other countries. Palgrave is a registered trademark in the European
Union and other countries.

ISBN 1–4039–1181–9

This book is printed on paper suitable for recycling and made from fully
managed and sustained forest sources.

A catalogue record for this book is available from the British Library.

Library of Congress Cataloging-in-Publication Data
Woman and the feminine in Medieval and early modern Scottish writing /
    edited by Sarah M. Dunnigan, C. Marie Harker, and Evelyn S. Newlyn.
        p. cm.
    Includes bibliographical references and index.
    ISBN 1–4039–1181–9 (cloth)
        1. Scottish Literature—To 1700—History and criticism. 2. Scottish
    literature—Women authors—History and criticism. 3. Women–
    –Scotland—Intellectual life. 4. Feminism and literature—Scotland.
    5. Women and literature—Scotland. 6. Femininity in literature. 7. Sex
    role in literature. 8. Women in literature. I. Dunnigan, Sarah, 1971–
    II. Harker, C. Marie, 1963– III. Newlyn, Evelyn S.

PR8546.W66 2004
820.9'3522'09411—dc22

                                                    2003064653

    10   9   8   7   6   5   4   3   2   1
    13 12 11 10 09 08 07 06 05 04

Transferred to digital printing 2005

For Anna and Matthew – aon turas eile, le gaol

For Rowan Lindley-Harker

For Janet Elizabeth Robinson

Contents

Part Two: 'Writing Women'

Part Three: 'Archival Women'

Acknowledgements

We would like to express our gratitude to the Research Committee of the School of Literatures, Languages, and Cultures in the College of Humanities and Social Sciences, University of Edinburgh, for the award of a grant which enabled the publication of this book. Randall Stevenson of the English Literature Department offered generous and invaluable guidance for which we warmly thank him. Professor Cairns Craig also gave vital advice and support in the early stages of the book. Sarah Dunnigan would personally like to thank Dr Sarah Carpenter, Head of Edinburgh's English Literature Department; Professor Colm Ó Baoill, Head of the Celtic Department at Aberdeen University, for kindly and unstintingly providing information on the Gaelic material; and Dr David Salter, who has been a thoughtful reader, in all ways, at all times.

We are immensely grateful to Rhona Brown, doctoral student in the Department of Scottish Literature, University of Glasgow, for compiling the Index and to Jill Hamilton, honours student in the Department of Language and Literature, Truman State University, for her assistance with copy-editing.

We would also like to acknowledge the tireless patience and advice of Emily Rosser and Paula Kennedy, and the kind assistance of Tim Kapp, at Palgrave; and to express our gratitude for the insights given by the book's external readers.

List of Abbreviations

ASLS – Association of Scottish Literary Studies
BL – British Library
DOST – Dictionary of the Older Scottish Tongue
EUL – Edinburgh University Library
GUL – Glasgow University Library
IR – Innes Review
NAS – National Archives of Scotland
NLS – National Library of Scotland
NDNB – New Dictionary of National Biography
SBRS – Scottish Burgh Record Society
SHR – Scottish Historical Review
SLJ – Scottish Literary Journal
SSL – Studies in Scottish Literature
STS – Scottish Text Society

Where unambiguous, citations to university presses have been abbreviated accordingly: e.g. 'Aberdeen: AUP'; 'Toronto: UTP'; but 'Ithaca: Cornell UP'. As applicable, scribal abbreviations have been expanded, as indicated in italics: e.g. *'tha*t' for 'ᵇt'. The graph thorn has been normalized; yogh has been retained. Middle Scots orthographic convention as to interchangeable vocalic i/y (e.g. Lyndsay/Lindsay) has been retained. Lowland Scots terminology has been translated, throughout, thus: first references to terms in each essay, e.g. 'quhilk' as [*which*], subsequently untranslated.

Editorial practice throughout this volume has been respectful of the disciplinary distance between our varied contributors. Although the collection as a whole adheres to Modern Humanities Research Association guidelines for scholarly work in terms of both accidentals and substantives, we have chosen in certain instances to respect our contributors' preferences as to style in expression and citation.

Contributors

Gordon DesBrisay is Associate Professor of History at the University of Saskatchewan, Canada. Currently writing a book on seventeenth-century Aberdeen, he has published on topics including Scottish Quakers, wet-nursing and illegitimacy, Aberdeen in the civil wars, and the fate of women under 'godly discipline'.

Sarah M. Dunnigan is Lecturer in English Literature at the University of Edinburgh. She has published on Scottish medieval and Renaissance literature and is the author of *Eros and Poetry at the Courts of Mary Queen of Scots and James VI.*

Garrett P. J. Epp is Professor and incoming Chair of English at the University of Alberta, Canada. He studies and teaches late medieval and early modern drama, especially in relation to queer theory and gender studies. He is currently working on a new edition of the Towneley Plays, while continuing his research on the staging of masculinity and sodomy in early English theatre.

Deanna Delmar Evans is Professor of English at Bemidji State University, Minnesota. She has published on Scottish literature, medieval biography, medieval folklore, and women writers. Her most recent work is an edition of 'The Babees Book' in *Medieval Literature for Children.*

Elizabeth Ewan is Professor of History and Scottish Studies at the University of Guelph, Ontario, Canada. She is the author of *Townlife in Fourteenth-Century Scotland*, co-editor of *Women in Scotland c.1100-c. 1750*, and currently co-editor of *The Biographical Dictionary of Scottish Women.* She is also preparing a study of defamation and gender in late medieval and early modern Scotland.

Morna R. Fleming is Depute Rector, teaching at Beath High School, Cowdenbeath, Scotland, and secretary of The Robert Henryson Society. She has published articles on the poetry of James VI and his courts in Scotland and England, and on the teaching of the works of Robert Henryson.

Janet Hadley Williams is Visiting Fellow in English and Theatre Studies at The Australian National University. Her publications include

Stewart Style 1513-1542: Essays in the Court of James V and the recent edition, *Sir David Lyndsay: Selected Poems.*

C. Marie Harker is Associate Professor in English Literature at Truman State University, Missouri. She works on late-medieval English book production and has published on late medieval and early Modern English and Scottish literature, with a critical focus on feminist and gender-theory.

Kevin J. McGinley teaches part-time at Glasgow and Edinburgh Universities. He has co-edited *Of Lion and Of Unicorn: Essays on Anglo-Scottish Literary Relations in Honour of Professor John MacQueen*, and has written on Robert Henryson, Sir David Lyndsay, and James Boswell.

Inge B. Milfull is Lecturer in the department of English and Comparative Linguistics at the Catholic University of Eichstaett, Germany. She works on Old English and Scottish cultural studies as well as lexicology, dialectology, and stylistics. She has also written on *The Wallace* and is preparing *The Wallace: Stylistic and Lexicological Studies.*

David George Mullan is Professor of history and religious studies at the University College of Cape Breton in Sydney, Nova Scotia. He is the author or editor of several books on early modern Scottish Protestantism, including *Scottish Puritanism, 1590-163*, and *Women's Life Writing in Early Modern Scotland: Writing the Evangelical Self, c.1670-1730*. He is currently writing a book tentatively titled *Lively Memories and Useful Lives: Scottish Religious Narrative, 1660-1725.*

Evelyn S. Newlyn is Professor of English at the State University of New York at Brockport. She has published on Middle Scots poetry, early Scottish manuscripts, medieval literature, and the Middle Cornish drama.

Colm Ó Baoill is Professor of Celtic at Aberdeen University, where he will be retiring. His research interests were initially linguistic, especially the dialectology of the Gaelic world, but he is also interested in the Scottish Gaelic verse of the seventeenth and eighteenth centuries.

Jamie Reid-Baxter is Honorary Research Fellow in Glasgow University's School of Scottish Studies and a translator in Luxembourg. He publishes on, organises, and performs in presentations of Scottish music, poetry, and drama, particularly of the sixteenth and seventeenth centuries, and has produced and/or sponsored several CDs. He is currently editing *Elizabeth Melville: Poems and Letters* (forthcoming), and (with Regina Scheibe) *The Poems of John Burel*.

Suzanne Trill is Lecturer in English Literature at the University of Edinburgh. Her publications include *Voicing Women: Gender and Sexuality in Writing, 1500-1700* and as co-editor with Kate Chedgzoy and Melanie Osborne, of *Ladies, Take the Pen: Writing Women in England, 1500-1700*. She is currently preparing an edition *of Lady Anne Halkett's Memoirs and Selected Meditations* for Ashgate (forthcoming 2005/6).

Introduction
Sarah M. Dunnigan

'*Graunt me your favours I requeist to end this worthelie*'
Mary/Marie Maitland (d. 1597)

'*the Lord knows I never loved to make appearance this way...*'
Elizabeth West (fl. 1680)

'*Bithibh cuimhneach air na tha mi 'g ràdh'* [Don't forget what I say]
Sìleas na Ceapaich ('of Keppoch'; c.1665-c.1729)

This book is about medieval and early modern Scottish women as the subjects of writing. The definition of 'subject' is twofold: women as the subjects of literary and other discursive forms of representation, and as the authorial subjects, or creators, of texts themselves. It is the first book of its kind to explore women and literature in Scotland during this period. While it is impossible to pinpoint the exact source of a book's inception, especially a multi-authored volume, the idea was properly mooted in August 1999 at the triennial Medieval and Renaissance Scottish Language and Literature conference at St Andrews University. There the importance of bringing together increasingly diverse work on early Scottish women writers, and on the representation of women within early Scottish literature, was realised by the three editors of this book. While *Woman and the Feminine* crystallises that shared vision, the necessity for its existence may not be obvious to those outside the field of early Scottish studies. This Introduction explains why we have assembled essays on women's representation and female creativity from the fourteenth century to the early eighteenth; from the island of Skye to the Scottish Borders; from the female subject in heroic epic, humanist

xiv

history, political allegory, courtly romance, and satirical burlesque to the female subject as translator, manuscript compiler, lyric poet, epistolary writer, autobiographer, and spiritual memoirist. Our volume redresses the prevailing critical neglect of early Scottish women writers, and presents a range of new theoretical feminist approaches to texts and writers both established within the early Scottish canon and newly discovered. We hope that the volume challenges and redefines the received literary and cultural history of medieval and early modern Scotland and, in so doing, contributes to the well-established body of feminist scholarship in medieval and early modern English and European literatures. We begin by discussing the exclusion of medieval and early modern Scottish literature from 'mainstream' scholarly work, and the relationship of the volume to feminist theory and feminist readings of the early period in general.

Within the context of 'British' early modern studies, the notion that there might have been 'renaissances' other than the dominant English and largely Elizabethan Renaissance has gathered strength. Under contemporary intellectual pressures such as critical revisionism, a politicised New Historicism, and postcolonial studies, the English Renaissance has been 'decentred', or at least questioned. Questions have fruitfully been asked of the relationship between early modern national and literary identities.[1] In spite of this, the idea of an autonomous literary and artistic culture existing in the northernmost part of the British archipelago has still to grow firm roots within 'British' Renaissance studies as a whole.[2] Work on medieval and early modern Scottish literature is fertile but tends to be published within important but 'discrete' collections.[3] There are possible reasons for Scotland's neglect within wider Renaissance studies: perhaps a (misplaced) perception of the 'smallness' of the early Scottish canon; or reticence in the face of its linguistic differences. Unlike early modern Ireland, for example, early modern Scotland is less easily accommodated under postcolonial critical wings since, after all, James VI entered his nation into a union of supposed parity with England in 1603; although a contentious issue, Scotland was never oppressed or subjugated in the ways that Ireland was.[4]

Though these debates may seem far removed from the subject of early Scottish women's literature, they are part of the reason for its 'invisibility'. As other critics of Scottish women's writing have pointed out, it has suffered from a 'double marginalisation': as writing by women, and as writing which is Scottish.[5] We will return to this apparently thorny point later. In the context of the debate about why

Scottish literature is still elided from current critical impulses within Renaissance studies, the present volume may place the period in general in a more focused critical light. It does not offer a comprehensive or inclusive history of Scottish women's writing pre-1800. Nor is its scope conceived as irrefutably 'Scottish'. While the material which our contributors discuss arises from cultural and linguistic environments, sufficiently distinctive to merit allusion to the corpus of 'Scottish women's devotional writing', an inflexible national 'boundary' is not imposed. The degree to which the women writers explored here *explicitly* identified themselves, or their writing, as 'Scottish' is debatable. Yet what the Irish poet Seamus Heaney calls the 'frontiers of writing' are crossed in the collection since the essays explore literature composed in Scots, Scottish Gaelic, and English, and from a variety of oral and written sources.[6] Our desire to reveal new sources and new readings has been paramount, but we acknowledge the need for further comparative research on the provisional oeuvre of early Scottish women's writing delineated here. Because of its linguistic and cultural diversity (arguably in comparison to English women's writing of the period), this literature questions notions of homogeneity or uniformity;[7] its very 'marginality' invests it with the power to re-evaluate conventional paradigms of culture.

For the reasons suggested above, Scottish medieval and early modern literature occupies a peculiar position in relation to theoretical developments within the broader scholarly field. This also holds true of its relationship to feminist literary theory, and to the significant number of publications in the last two decades which bring feminist methodologies and analyses to medieval and early modern English literature. It is impossible to do justice within the space of a bibliographical endnote to this prolific area of scholarship. Few of the works combining an interpretative or theoretical 'feminist' practice with new archival discoveries or evaluations of early women's writing include Scottish material.[8] Three qualifications should be made. First, there are exceptions: Louise Olga Fradenburg's theoretical work on Margaret Tudor and the court culture of James IV; the growth of articles on gender and representation in the poetry of Robert Henryson and William Dunbar; Priscilla Bawcutt's work on early Scottish women as book owners and collectors; explorations of Renaissance representations of women by Evelyn S. Newlyn and Sarah M. Dunnigan; and readings of gender and sexuality in relation to James VI and Anna of Denmark.[9] Second, the volume of Renaissance women poets edited by Jane Stevenson and Peter Davidson was the first to make significant inclusion of Scottish writers.[10] Third, the work of the historian, Elizabeth Ewan, is important: the interdisciplinary essay collection edited by Ewan and Maureen M. Meikle, *Women in Scotland c.1100 - c.1750* (1999) constitutes a new vision of pre-1800 Scottish history in its discovery of the economic, legal, political, and cultural roles played by medieval and early modern Scottish women.[11] Ewan and Meikle's account of the omission of 'female histories' from orthodox narratives of Scottish history reveals affinities with the omission of early Scottish women's writing and feminist criticism from conventional narratives of Scottish literature.[12] The present volume develops and intensifies the revisionist work of Ewan and Meikle's collection. It explores women's literary and textual 'culture' within the period in the widest sense: the writing arises out of distinct social, religious, and political environments. Unlike the earlier collection, the main concern of these essays is with artistic or literary culture. As Part Two illustrates, some of these women write with a more consciously 'aesthetic' purpose than others; for many, writerly (self) expression is subsumed within the larger purpose of spiritual and political expressiveness. The concepts of the medieval and early modern woman writer are often contrary to modern understandings of creativity.

The first and most extensive account of Scottish women's writing appeared in 1997: *A History of Scottish Women's Writing* edited by Douglas Gifford and Dorothy McMillan. In their Introduction, the editors acknowledged the difficulties of the enterprise: 'the whole notion of Scottish women's writing is itself open to a continuing questioning which constantly produces redefinition, a process reflected in the construction and edition of this History which at times turned the dream of recording women's achievement into nightmare in its conjunction of need and difficulty'.[13] They concede that the endeavour to 'construct a version of the history of Scottish women's writing is not wholly revolutionary and certainly far from innocent. It is very much a function of its place and time'.[14] So too is this volume, in its particular combination of feminist practice and interpretive methodology, a consequence of Scottish literature's often tangential relationship to the achievements of feminist literary criticism over the last thirty years. Such criticism has questioned conventional notions of 'canonicity' and authority, and assumptions informing judgements of literary and aesthetic value; and explored the nature of female political agency, identity, and subjectivity. What is known as first, second, and third wave feminism has seen the development, and subsequent revision, of a reconstructionist 'history' of women's writing or of a 'female tradition'. The undesirability of an autonomous tradition of women's literature and a unified female/feminine/feminist reading practice has also been exposed. How does one read as a woman? In whose name does one speak? Against this background of the intellectual richness and internal self-questioning of current feminist theories our book emerges. We agree with Ruth Robbins' assertion that 'feminism' can no longer be 'a single category with clear limits, fixed in a single semantic space' but, rather, is 'multiple';[15] we acknowledge that our volume offers a combination of new and 'established' feminist approaches.

The title of the collection demands explanation. Our choice of the apparently essentialist category 'Woman' may contradict Julia Kristeva's assertion that 'Woman can never be defined'.[16] Our use of the term 'feminine' evokes Helene Cixous's questioning of the category *féminin* (and indeed *masculin*) in the context of defining writing practice.[17] Yet we intend to draw on the ambiguous resonances of these terms. In dividing the contents into 'Written Woman' and 'Writing Women', we seek to convey movement from a 'passive' to an 'active' female subject. The essays in Part One explore how the nature of the feminine as an abstract category ('Woman'), shaped by medieval and Renaissance philosophical, ethical, and religious understandings of womanhood, is adhered to, qualified, and subverted by the imaginative literature of the period. Some essays explore the female characters of romance epic and of mythological allegory, others the literary or fictive transmutations of 'real' women such as Madeleine de Valois and Black Agnes.

Part Two fulfills Kristeva's desire that 'Woman' transcends 'nomenclatures and ideologies' by exploring a number of 'real' writing women: early Scottish women who wrote professionally and privately. Though the seven essays encompass a temporally, geographically, and thematically wide range of women's writing, and differ in their interpretive approaches, the essays are bound by a shared concern with whether and how such women articulate a specifically female or gendered identity. Is these writers' endeavour to create a writerly 'selfhood' enabled or frustrated by the historical constraints of gender? In the writing of the extraordinary seventeenth-century Quaker woman, Lilias Skene, we witness her oscillations between explicitly gendered and non-gendered identities being put to precise rhetorical effect: poetic acts of self-abnegation or self-advocacy serve different spiritual purposes. The creativity of late seventeenth- and early eighteenth-century Gaelic women writers courted the risk of association with witchcraft and enchantment. As Colm Ó Baoill's title, 'Neither Out nor In' (a haunting phrase from Uist oral tradition) suggests, such women poets were clearly absorbed and accepted within their culture, distinguishing their position from that of women poets in Lowland culture, yet their creative 'power' could also exile them symbolically, if not literally. Several essays examine how the female subject, or the concept of the feminine, is represented by such women writers. The early seventeenth-century poet, Anna Hume, translated the *Trionfi* of Petrarch with sensitivity to the role of the angelic Laura and the panoply of female characters from mythology and classical history which adorn Petrarch's allegory. Despite the disparate nature of the material and the critical approaches in Part Two, the essays are all individually attentive to what Kristeva calls the 'work of language'.[18] The words of these women, whether erotic, spiritual, political, or other, speak for themselves.

Accordingly, there is a natural link between Parts Two and Three of the book. Much of the material discussed in the essays of Part Two is not easily accessible; some of it, as in DesBrisay's and Mullan's essays, is published here for the first time; we have tried to allow as generous quotation as possible from these sources. Since this book cannot be comprehensive in its account of early Scottish women's writing, we would like it to serve as a resource for further research. Since Sarah Dunnigan carried out a preliminary investigation of early modern Scottish women's writing in 1997,[19] new writers and archival sources have come to light. A testament to such recent and ongoing research is Suzanne Trill's investigation of manuscript holdings of women's writing in the Scottish archives and registers. In Part Three, she presents a checklist of some of her findings. Here, for the first time, one glimpses the diversity and range of types of surviving women's texts. In her preface to the checklist, Trill explains some of the reasons for the predominance of certain textual forms, such as letters and 'auto/biographies'. Not all the documented texts are by Scottish women; Trill explains the insights that can be gleaned from the inclusion of material by English and European women on Scottish cultural and political issues. Another example of current archival research is Jamie Reid-Baxter's discovery of a manuscript collection of poems which he persuasively ascribes to Elizabeth Melville. Baxter's discovery transforms Elizabeth Melville's poetic corpus into the most substantial of all known early modern Scottish women writers and presents new material which enriches our understanding of her increasingly recognised poem, *Ane Godlie Dreame*, here analysed in detail by Deanna Delmar Evans. In the remainder of this Introduction, the essays comprising Parts One and Two are described in more detail.

The essays in Part One examine manifestations of the feminine in a range of late medieval and early sixteenth-century Scottish texts, encompassing poetic, prose, and dramatic genres. They explore how the figure of Woman serves as sign, metaphor, and 'performance', and is often imbued with other aesthetic, cultural, and political meanings. The approaches of individual essayists differ, making varied use of theoretical and feminist analyses, attentive rhetorical readings, and new historical and cultural contextualisation. Some of the writers examined, such as Robert Henryson and Sir David Lyndsay, have already elicited a substantial body of critical literature. The three essays devoted to their work (Hadley Williams, Epp, McGinley) view it through different critical lenses. For example, Hadley Williams draws attention to the conspicuously 'feminised' nature of Lyndsay's political and allegorical poems; Epp draws out the bawdy and political *jouissance* of Lyndsay's play, *Ane Satyre of the Thrie Estatis*, by a combination of feminist and queer theory; and McGinley chooses Henryson's poem *Orpheus and Eurydice*, and not the well-known *Testament of Cresseid*, to illustrate the former's importance for an understanding of the 'feminine' poetic subject in the larger Henrysonian canon.

Within the period from the mid fourteenth-century to the 1550s, Scotland shared the orthodox view of Woman perpetuated by the variety of theological, intellectual, philosophical, and cultural discourses in western Europe. While these should not be taken to constitute an absolute antifeminist edifice, any late medieval or early modern cultural representation of Woman may seem to work within confined boundaries. Scottish texts such as the *Spectakle of Luf*, composed in the mid-1400s and found in the Asloan Manuscript, vigorously attest a familiarity with the well-established conventions and tropes of medieval misogyny.[20] The *querelle des femmes* tradition is sustained in the 1560s by the series of poems preserved in the Bannatyne Manuscript which 'debate' the nature of womanhood.[21] This particular Scottish manifestation of the *querelle* is lent a contemporary political significance by coinciding with the reign of Mary Queen of Scots.[22] Yet what these essays reveal is that the antifeminist version of Woman provides a 'template' in which the rhetorical and cultural complexities of individual texts and writers wrestle. Works such as the medieval carnivalesque poems which Harker identifies as 'insistently gendered' are placed alongside the 'dissolv[ing]' antifeminism, in Hadley Williams's term, of some of Lyndsay's poems, which must be understood through the specific matrices of genre and literary convention. All six essays are attentive to the linguistic and generic intricacies of the texts which they discuss, texts which are themselves transformed by incorporating female protagonists, and by the changing ideological meanings of the nature of Woman.

The first illustration of such 'transformative' power is Elizabeth Ewan's essay, 'The Dangers of Manly Women: Late Medieval Perceptions of Female Heroism in Scotland's Second War of

Independence', which explores the representation of Lady Seton of Berwick and Agnes, Countess of Dunbar, in a range of historical chronicles. Both these women offer examples of medieval female heroism, that are far less well-known than those of their male heroic counterparts in the First War of Independence, William Wallace and Robert the Bruce. Where male heroism is obviously bound up in the conventional chivalric ethos, the presentation of female heroism, Ewan contends, challenged male chroniclers. In emphasising the dignity, wisdom, and intellect of these women's words, they also praised the women's 'courage' which was at once to render them 'manly'. The discomforting 'manliness' of the redoubtable Black Agnes was deliberately 'feminised' by being made to serve the preservation of domestic and familial virtue. The ideological tampering of chroniclers with the compelling narratives of these two women culminates in the early sixteenth century. In Sir Richard Maitland's version, her importance is greatly diminished because a woman's courage 'should not be glorified at the expense of a man's'. As Ewan notes, the appearance of this history coincides with the publication of John Knox's *First Blast* against female supremacy. The idea of 'Woman' within this range of texts is therefore unstable, perpetually transformed by the pressure of political exigencies until her 'excessiveness' is contained.

This idea of 'containment' is mirrored in C. Marie Harker's essay, '*Chrystis Kirk on the Grene* and *Peblis to the Ploy*: The Economy of Gender', which re-examines two well-known poems of the fifteenth-century, 'Chrystis Kirk' and 'Peblis'. Harker reveals how both poems, usually celebrated as fairly transparent carnivalesque, displace contemporary social anxieties and burghal politics 'onto the interpretive gridwork of misogyny'. Focusing on the recurrent topos of Woman as the dangerous and subversive Other, Harker demonstrates how the poems satirise the polemical figure of the peasant-girl who challenges established mores of class and sexuality. What seems 'merely' the transgressions of an 'ahistoric' female sexuality are brought into sharp focus by Harker as articulating anxieties about the riotous and troubling figure of 'the burghal woman' which are expressive of the increasing class hostilities of late medieval Scottish urban life.

Inge B. Milfull's essay, 'War and Truce: Women in *The Wallace*', echoes Ewan's essay in exploring the representation of Woman in the medieval epic, *The Wallace,* in which the idea of male heroic supremacy (and, one might suggest, a chauvinistic and bloody nationalism) prevails. Contrary to expectations, women are not marked by their absence from the text. Milfull's detailed analysis of the text's female protagonists demonstrates their association with sexual and emotional conflict and, as a corollary, with aspects of the hero's physical and moral vulnerability: Wallace must preserve himself from the 'transfer' of feminine fragility and pain. Milfull reveals that not only is the realm of the feminine seen as the antithesis of the heroic, martial code but also that female sexuality is conceived as a direct and dangerous threat to the 'patriotic project'. Her reading of the courtship narrative between Mistress Braidfute and Wallace suggests that this apparent verse romance can be regarded as an anti-romance since the courtly love paradigm, as with any suggestion of illicit or immoral desire, is rejected. Feminine and masculine desires are irreconcilable in the aesthetic and political terms of this text.

In 'The Fenʒeit and the Feminine: Henryson's *Orpheus and Eurydice* and the Gendering of Poetry', Kevin J. McGinley examines the representation of gendered desire within Henryson's poem, *Orpheus and Eurydice*. Henryson's allegorical reworking of the Greek mythological narrative, which depicts Orpheus' 'vayn' quest to rescue his 'quene' from the Underworld after she trod 'barefut' upon a serpent in fleeing the lustful Aristaeus, reflects on the nature of poetic art. The poem appears to draw on the traditional medieval condemnation of poetry's artifice as dangerously corporeal and sensual. The fictional poetic text is accordingly gendered feminine, subordinate to masculine reason and intellect embodied by the 'moralitas'. Yet McGinley's reading demonstrates how Henryson's 'sensual' and 'feminised' narrative resists this orthodoxy. In presenting a positive and consoling image of earthly 'lufe', the 'affective' text ironically comments upon the moralitas' perspective of 'parfyte reson', which is incapable of providing understanding of suffering and loss. 'Feminine' interpretation is ultimately rendered superior.

Janet Hadley Williams's essay, 'Women Fictional and Historic in Sir David Lyndsay's Poetry', explores how the poems of Sir David Lynday, court poet to James V, represents the feminine allegorically and historically, focussing on the contrasts between Woman as rhetorical effect and as historical subject. Hadley Williams takes issue with the prevalent view of Lyndsay as a cynical misogynist and argues that attention to the previously unexplored role of women in his writing has important literary implications. Women, both fictional and historical, are integral to the contexts of the courtly, political, and cultural relationships which inform Lyndsay's poetry. Poetic allegory, astute politicisation, and strategies of praise suggest the courtier's vested interests in depicting the feminine. In making the allegorical bird of the *Testament of the Papyngo* female, for example, Lyndsay emphasises her vulnerability but also 'the corrupt and acquisitive representatives of the church' whom she accuses of the sexual misuse of power.

Lyndsay's treatment of power, gender, and sexuality in his famous allegorical drama, *Ane Satyre of the Thrie Estatis*, engages Garrett Epp in his essay, 'Chastity in the Stocks: Women, Sex, and Marriage in *The Satyre of the Thrie Estaitis*'. Epp demonstrates how critical commentary, in its preoccupation with the play's ethical and political concerns, has ignored the way in which bawdy, sexual play is inseparable from such concerns. Why is Woman in Lyndsay's drama reduced to a 'spectre that haunts and disrupts the proper realm of masculinity, even as it defines that realm'? Epp analyses the implications of the playing of female roles by men and boy-actors, and what such cross-dressing might have signified to Lyndsay's audience: the 'masculinised' nature of the ostensible female characters ('male bodies beneath female garb') and the 'feminisation' of ostensibly 'manly' men. Exploring the comic debacle between the Taylour, the Sowtar, their wives, and Chastetie, and the infamous mutual 'kiss' of divorce between the Sowtar and his (masculine) Wife, Epp suggests that the play overall presents Woman as 'a threat to masculinity'. In restoring the visibility of sex in Lyndsay's play, both theatrically and ideologically, Epp reveals the manifold forms of sexual and political orthodoxy at its heart.

In Canto 37 of Ariosto's *Orlando Furioso* (1532), the narrator pays homage to the abundance of contemporary Italian women writers. In medieval and early modern Scotland, such abundance seems to be lacking. Only in 1571 is women's writing first printed with the attribution of the 'Casket' sonnet sequence to Mary, Queen of Scots. One can debate the nature of what constitutes 'writing' since there are manuscript letters which survive from before this period. One might also claim, with qualification, that the *Life* of St Margaret of Scotland constitutes the earliest example of female textual expression in Scotland.[23] There is also considerable evidence of late medieval female book ownership and patronage.[24] But it is the Scottish Gaelic tradition which offers the earliest and richest examples of late medieval women's writing. As Anne C. Frater has indicated, the earliest surviving poem by a woman in vernacular Gaelic, *Cumha Mhic an Tòisich* [the lament for Mackintosh], stems from the early sixteenth-century.[25] The *Book of the Dean of Lismore*, compiled between 1512 and c. 1526, contains poems in classical Gaelic by aristocratic women, probably composed in the previous century, notably Aithbhreac nighean Coirceadail's elegy for her husband, and the exquisite courtly love lyrics composed by Iseabail Ní Mheic Cailéin.[26] In contrast, until the post-Reformation period, very little material composed in Lowland Scots survives. The reasons for such an absence can only be conjectured: why is there virtually no evidence of production or creation at Scottish nunneries, for example?[27] Is the material destruction of the Reformers to blame for the paucity of archival and textual traces? Have we simply not discovered the evidence for medieval women writers in Scotland? What *can* justly be asserted is that the seventeenth-century sees a prodigious output of women's writing: for example, in 1603, Melville's *Ane Godlie Dreame* is the first religious text by a Scottish woman to be published (subsequently reprinted many times in both Scotland and England); later, in 1644, Anna Hume's *Triumphs* is the first printed secular work; a substantial amount of vernacular prose in manuscript is found; and new genres such as autobiography and devotional memoirs emerge.

That it should be seventeenth-century devotional or spiritual writing which offers the richest source of vernacular Scottish women's writing is not surprising (and not untypical of English early modern women's writing as well). Nor is it unexpected that women write from the faiths which institutionally and culturally are either persecuted or beleaguered at this time: these women are radical Presbyterians, Covenanters, and Quakers. Often their very act of writing is also an act of direct political intent as well as spiritual self-expression, exemplified by Elizabeth Melville's printed consolatory sonnet to an imprisoned Covenanting minister; by Katharine Collace's autobiography which reveals her associations with radical Covenanters in the north; and by Lilias Skene's prophetic sermon of 1677, 'A Word of Warning to the Magistrats and Inhabitants of Aberdene'.[28] As David Mullan observes, one explanation for this period's small amount of women's writing in print may stem from the real threat of persecution; circulation in manuscript was therefore mandatory. Deanna Delmar Evans' essay reveals the passionate political mission of Melville's *Godlie Dreame*. Evans argues that the visionary allegory expounds the Reformed doctrine of 'justification' and that, in composing the poem, Melville simultaneously 'lay[s] claim to her own justified state'. In so doing, she transforms herself into a 'bold female preacher', interweaving her poetic text with Knoxian allusions, and exhorting and comforting her religious community in a period of persecution. The 'passionate' aspect of her mission is rhetorically mirrored in the incantatory and exhortatory rhythms of her writing. In her poem, Melville is at once female narrator, dreamer, preacher, and prophet.

Collectively, the essays by Evans, DesBrisay, and Mullan illustrate how different doctrinal and theological traditions foster the nature of these women's writerly self-expression: how spiritually, creatively, and intellectually they found a voice. DesBrisay argues that Quakerism offered Skene 'a liberating discourse to shape her thoughts and words, and a community of fellow writers to encourage and critique her work'. Yet as his essay illustrates, the assurance of the 'collective' and 'community' identity of Quakerism brought conflict to Skene and her writing: a gendered conflict between the desire for self-assertion and yet conformity; between the need to 'extinguish the self', in DesBrisay's phrase, yet to make that self speak eloquently (an eloquence well attested by her poetry). Mullan's and Evans's essays also invite reflection upon how these women regarded their spiritual mentors and the orthodox Presbyterian clergy: it was a relationship which could be both tender and enabling but also one of dissent and contradiction. The pressure of orthodox clerical authority seemed to provide women, such as the visionary Elizabeth Cairns, with the justificatory impulse to write.

The 'tradition' of extant religious women's writing in Scotland (with the marked exception of Skene's) derives from Protestant evangelism. Female textual voices from the Roman Catholic tradition seem not to have survived (if we exclude the religious sonnets in French by Mary, Queen of Scots), though there are a number of 'conversion' narratives, such as Helen Livingston's.[29] Blame may be imputed to post-Reformation dangers of persecution and destruction; sensitive material may be deposited in Catholic archives abroad. Examples of pre-Reformation female spirituality are best found in Scottish saints' lives.[30] It is only the Gaelic tradition which offers rich examples of Catholic female sensibility in the poetry, for example, of Sìleas na Ceapach.

Seventeenth-century Gaelic women's songs also offer the greatest range of 'secular' themes. The lyrical poetry of the four most important female song-writers from the period discussed by Colm Ó Baoill is diverse in subject: the poetry of Sìleas alone embraces the Jacobite cause, the death of her daughter, Anna, and advice on 'boga-bhriseadh' [love-making'] to the 'nianagan bòidheach' [lovely young girls] of Glencoe.[31] Ó Baoill uses the South Uist description of the female poet, 'cha robh i muigh is cha robh i staigh' [she was neither out nor in] to convey the cultural 'threshold' status of early Gaelic women poets but other 'thresholds' exist within their songs. One such threshold is that between 'public' and 'private' expression: the 'voice' of Mairi nighean Alasdair Ruaidh mirrors the heroic and panegyric codes of clan poetry; Sìleas' brokers a transparent interiority that is rarely found in the slender body of Lowland women's secular lyrics. Gaelic women's songs embody a different, and bolder political quality than the other 'politicised' poetry explored here in Scots and Anglo-Scots. Composing within and for the clan system, many songs are exhortatory, intended to 'uphold' that society 'through formal praise of its leaders', as Ó Baoill shows. Adherence to its codes is not always sustained, however; tradition records that Mairi was exiled from Skye, having offended MacLeod of Dunvegan with one of her songs.

The 'dark [...] silences' of literary history of which the American writer Tillie Olsen wrote have been increasingly 'voiced' by a feminist criticism which 'listens to' what has been elided, concealed, or suppressed from women's writing. Evelyn S. Newlyn's essay, 'A Methodology for Reading Against the Culture: Anonymous, Women Poets, and the Maitland Quarto Manuscript', seeks to 'listen to the silences' of Renaissance Scottish manuscript culture. Using as illustration the Maitland Quarto manuscript of the 1580s which belonged to Mary (Marie) Maitland, Newlyn proposes a detailed methodology of reading practice that may be used to hypothesise evidence of female authorship in early manuscript collections. Arguing that many anonymous or unsigned poems may have been composed by women (or Mary herself) associated with the manuscript's social and cultural circles, Newlyn explores how textual arrangement within a manuscript, thematic choice, and poetic language, structure, and strategy can suggest female authorship. Such a methodology necessitates the adoption of a 'transgressive perspective', alert to the 'ideologies' which govern both 'self and text', and to recognition of 'the value not only of the "objective" but also of the subjective'. Newlyn's essay uncovers the rich potential of the Maitland manuscript but also delineates possible interpretive approaches to the many other manuscript collections of late sixteenth- and seventeenth-century Scotland, enacting the volume's desire as a whole to render articulate the conventionally silenced or unvoiced feminine.

The other two essays in this section, Sarah M. Dunnigan's 'Daughterly 'Desires: Representing and Reimagining the Feminine in Anna Hume's *Triumphs*' and Morna J. Fleming's 'An Unequal Correspondence: Epistolary and Poetic Exchanges between Mary, Queen of Scots and Elizabeth of England', address the question of female reading and interpretation, exploring how this activity is adopted by the woman writer herself. Dunnigan's essay considers how the gifted but unknown Hume 'read', and recreated, Petrarch. In adopting the Renaissance metaphor of the original, fatherly, or patriarchal source text to conceive the relationship between Hume and her symbolic literary 'father', and between the source and translated texts, Dunnigan reveals the *Triumphs'* relationship of 'fidelity' and 'disobedience' to the *Trionfi*. 'Daughterly' rebellion is most apparent in Hume's portrayal of Petrarch's beloved Laura, and in her witty, 'proto-feminist' commentary upon the poem's mythological and historical female protagonists. In being dedicated to Princess Elizabeth of Bohemia, *philosophe* and correspondent of

Descartes, Hume renews Petrarch's 'great work' within a literary, cultural, and intellectual framework of feminine meaning.

The subtleties of interpretation acquire pointed political significance when two rival queens are engaged in writing and reading each other, as Fleming's essay attests. While much recent scholarship has been conducted on Mary Queen of Scots' writing,[32] Fleming newly explores the letters which she wrote to Elizabeth, 'ma bonne soeur', in the decade of her Scottish rule. Fleming illustrates the rhetorical and psychological oscillations of her epistolary discourse, poised between states of artfulness and artlessness. She shows how her poetry to Elizabeth served as a 'document' of political import. Both queens portray their own sovereign femininities through the art of letter-writing. In demonstrating the emotional and linguistic intricacies of their rhetorical conversation, Fleming portrays the intense political and personal relationship between two powerful female rulers who encountered each other only through their tangled web of words.

Woman and the Feminine is the beginning, and not 'the end', the present summative point reached in an ongoing exploration of women and literature in medieval and early modern Scottish writing. We hope that this book will demonstrate vital ways of 'reading against the culture', and convey the power and pleasure of texts which are newly transformed when the significance of Woman is understood. This collection reveals 'writing women' who shunned the process of exposure or discovery (evident in Elizabeth West's disavowal cited in this essay's epigraph), who desired the realisation of their creativity (Mary Maitland's request), or who exhorted that they be remembered (Sìleas na Ceapaich's command). Aiming to fulfil Sìleas's desire, this book begins the process, in Cixous's words, of 'pushing back forgetfulness'.[33]

---

[1] See most recently, for example, *British Identities and English Renaissance Literature*, ed. by David J. Baker and Willy Maley (Cambridge: CUP, 2002).

[2] For other discussions of the elision of Scottish literature from Renaissance or early modern critical narratives, see R.D.S. Jack, 'Translating the Lost Scottish Renaissance', in *Translation and Literature*, 6 (1997), 66-80, and 'Introduction' in *The Mercat Anthology of Early Scottish Literature* ed. by Jack and P.A.T. Rozendaal (Edinburgh: Mercat, 1997; 2000), pp. vii-xxxix; Theo van Heijnsbergen and Nicola Royan, 'Introduction', in *Literature, Letters, and the Canonical in Early Modern Scotland*, ed. by Theo van Heijnsbergen and Nicola Royan (East Linton: Tuckwell, 2002), pp. ix-xxx. Of relevance also is Gerard Carruthers, 'The Construction of the Scottish Critical Tradition', in *Odd Alliances. Scottish Studies in European Contexts*, ed. by Neil McMillan and Kirsten Stirling (Glasgow: Cruithne Press, 1999), pp. 52-65.

[3] Cf. most recently van Heijnsbergen and Royan, eds; *The European Sun*, ed. by Graham Caie and others (East Linton: Tuckwell, 2001).

[4] For recent examples of work on early modern Ireland, see Patricia Ann Palmer, *Language and Conquest in Early Modern Ireland: English Renaissance Literature and Elizabethan Imperial Expansion* (New York: CUP, 2001); Joan Fitzpatrick, *Irish Demons: English Writings on Ireland, the Irish, and Gender by Spenser and his Contemporaries* (Lanham, Md: UP of America, 2000).

[5] Marilyn Reizbaum, 'Not a Crying Game: The Feminist Appeal. Nationalism, Feminism and the Contemporary Literatures of Scotland and Ireland', *Scotlands*, 2 (1994), 24-31.

[6] The poetry ascribed to Mary, Queen of Scots is composed in French, Italian, and Latin (cf. Fleming's essay in this volume).

[7] Cf. Sarah M. Dunnigan, 'Undoing the Double Tress: Scotland, Early Modern Women's Writing, and the Location of Critical Desires', in *Feminist Studies*, 29.2, (2003), 1-21.

[8] The collection *Women, Writing, and the Reproduction of Culture in Tudor and Stuart Britain*, ed. by Mary E. Burke and others (Syracuse, N.Y.: SUP, 2000), notably includes an essay on Mary, Queen of Scots (Mary E. Burke, 'Queen, Lover, Poet: a Question of Balance in the Sonnets of Mary, Queen of Scots', pp. 101-18). The volumes *Women and Gender in Early Modern Wales*, ed. by Michael Roberts and Simone Clark (Cardiff: University of Wales Press, 2000); *Women in Early Modern Ireland 1500-1800*, ed. by Margaret MacCurtain and Mary O' Dowd (Edinburgh: EUP, 1991); and *'The Fragility of Her Sex?': Medieval Irish Women in their European Context*, ed. by C.E. Meek and M.K. Simms (Dublin: Four Courts, 1996) illustrate how recently historical and cultural work on early Scottish women has been published.

[9] Louise Olga Fradenburg, *City, Marriage, Tournament. Arts of Rule in Late Medieval Scotland* (Madison, Wis.: UWP, 1991); on Dunbar, for example, see Elizabeth Ewan, 'Many Injurious Words': Deformation and Gender in Late Medieval Scotland', in *History, Literature, and Music in Scotland, 700-1560*, ed. by Andrew R. McDonald and Edward J. Cowan (Toronto, ON: UTP, 2002), pp. 163-86, and on Henryson, see Felicity Riddy, 'Abject Odious': Feminine and Masculine in "The Testament of Cresseid" ', in *Chaucer to Spenser: A Critical Reader*, ed. by Derek Pearsall (Oxford: Blackwell, 1999), pp. 280-96. On Renaissance literature, see Evelyn S. Newlyn, 'The Political Dimensions of Desire and Sexuality in Poems of the Bannatyne Manuscript', in *Selected Essays on Scottish Language and Literature*, ed. by Steven McKenna (Lewiston, Queenston Lampeter: Edwin Mellen, 1992), pp. 75-96; 'Luve, Lichery, and Evill Wemen: The Satiric Tradition in the Bannatyne Manuscript,' *SSL*, 26 (1991), 283-93; 'Images of Women in Sixteenth-Century Scottish Literary Manuscripts', in *Women in Scotland c1100-c1750*, ed. by Elizabeth Ewan and Maureen M. Meikle (East Linton: Tuckwell), pp. 56-66; Sarah M. Dunnigan, *Eros and Poetry at the Courts of Mary, Queen of Scots and James VI* (Basingstoke: Palgrave, 2002); 'Female Gifts: Rhetoric, Beauty and the Beloved in the Lyrics of Alexander Montgomerie', *SLJ*, 26.2 (1999), 59-78. On James VI, see *Royal Subjects. Essays on the Writings of James VI and I*, ed. by Daniel Fischlin and

Mark Fortier (Detroit: Wayne State UP, 2002), and further bibliographical references therein; on Anna, cf. Clare McManus, *Women on the Renaissance Stage. Anna of Denmark and Female Masquing in the Stuart Court 1590-1619* (Manchester: MUP, 2002).

[10] *Early Modern Women Poets 1520-1700: An Anthology*, ed. by Jane Stevenson and Peter Davidson (Oxford: OUP, 2001). For the first outstanding endeavour to assemble poetry in Scots, Gaelic, and English, including material by medieval and early modern Scottish women, cf. *An Anthology of Scottish Women Poets*, ed. by Catherine Kerrigan, with Gaelic translations by Meg Bateman (Edinburgh: EUP, 1992).

[11] See, for example, Elizabeth Ewan, 'Women's History in Scotland: Towards an Agenda', *IR*, 46.2 (1995), 155-64; 'A Realm of One's Own? The Place of Medieval and Early Modern Women in Scottish History,' in *Gendering History: Scottish and International Approaches*, ed. by Terry Brotherstone, Deborah Simonton, and Oonagh Walsh (Glasgow: Cruithne, 1999), pp. 19-36.

[12] On this point, see Dunnigan, 'Undoing the Double Tress', pp. 8-15.

[13] *A History of Scottish Women's Writing*, ed. by Douglas Gifford and Dorothy McMillan (Edinburgh: EUP, 1997), 'Introduction', pp. ix-xxiii (p. x).

[14] 'Introduction', p. xiv.

[15] Ruth Robbins, *Literary Feminisms* (Basingstoke: Macmillan, 2000), p. 3.

[16] 'In "woman" I see something that cannot be represented, something that is not said, something above and beyond nomenclatures and ideologies': 'La femme, ce n'est jamais ça' (1974), in *New French Feminisms. An Anthology*, ed. and intro. by Elaine Marks and Isabelle de Courtivron (New York: Harvester Wheatsheaf, 1980), p. 137.

[17] See *La Jeune Née* (1975) (written with Catherine Clément) for Cixous's early meditation on *écriture féminine*.

[18] Cited in Toril Moi, *French Feminist Thought: A Reader* (Oxford: Basil Blackwell, 1987) p. 115; discussed by Robbins, p. 120.

[19] Sarah M. Dunnigan, 'Scottish Women Writers c1560-c1650,' in Gifford and McMillan, eds, pp. 15-43.

[20] Cf. *The Asloan Manuscript: a Miscellany in Prose and Verse*, STS, 2 vols (Edinburgh: Blackwood, 1923-5), I, 271-98.

[21] See Newlyn's articles cited in n. 9; Dunnigan, *Eros and Poetry*, ch. 2.

[22] See David J. Parkinson, ' "A Lamentable Storie": Mary Queen of Scots and the Inescapable *Querelle des Femmes*', in *A Palace in the Wild: Essays on Vernacular Culture and Humanism in Late-Medieval and Renaissance Scotland*, ed. by L. A. J. R. Houwen, S. L. Mapstone, and A. A. MacDonald (Leuven: Peeters, 2000), pp. 141-60.

[23] Cf. also 'Prayer in St Margaret's Gospel Book', in *The Triumph Tree. Scotland's Earliest Poetry, 550-1350*, ed. by Thomas Owen Clancy and others (Edinburgh: Canongate, 1998).

[24] Priscilla Bawcutt, ' "My Bright Buke": Women and their Books in Medieval and Renaissance Scotland', in *Medieval Women: Texts and Contexts in Late Medieval Britain: Essays for Felicity Riddy*, ed. by Jocelyn Wogan-Browne and others (Turnhout: Brepols, 2000), pp. 17-34.

[25] Anne C. Frater, 'The Gaelic Tradition up to 1750', in Gifford and McMillan eds, pp. 1-14 (p. 1).

[26] Cf. Kerrigan, ed., pp. 53-61.

[27] Cf. D.E. Easson, 'The Nunneries of Medieval Scotland', *Transactions of the Scottish Ecclesiological Society*, 13. 2 (1940-1), 22.

[28] See Gordon DesBrisay's essay in this volume.

[29] On Livingston, see Dunnigan, 'Scottish Women Writers', p. 38; on the devotional politics of Mary's Catholic sonnets, see Sarah M. Dunnigan, 'Sacred Afterlives: Mary, Queen of Scots, Elizabeth Melville and the Politics of Sanctity', *Women's Writing*, 10.3 (forthcoming 2003).

[30] See Audrey-Beth Fitch's excellent chapter, 'Power Through Purity: The Virgin Martyrs and Women's Salvation in pre-Reformation Scotland', in Ewan and Meikle, eds, pp. 16-28.

[31] 'An Aghaidh na h-Oba Nodha', ll. 49, 54 in *An Lasair. Anthology of 18th Century Scottish Gaelic Verse*, ed. by Ronald Black (Edinburgh: Birlinn, 2001), pp. 22-9.

[32] See most recently, Lisa Hopkins, *Writing Renaissance Queens: Texts by and about Elizabeth I and Mary, Queen of Scots* (Newark: University of Delaware Press, 2002); *Reading Monarchs Writing: the Poetry of Henry VIII, Mary Stuart, Elizabeth I, and James VI/I*, ed. by Peter C. Herman (Tempe, Ariz.: Arizona Center for Medieval and Renaissance Studies, 2002); Dunnigan, *Eros and Poetry*.

[33] Hélène Cixous, 'Coming to Writing', in *'Coming to Writing' and Other Essays*, ed. by Deborah Jenson, with an introductory essay by Susan Rubin Suleiman (Cambridge, Mass.: Harvard UP, 1991), p. 3.

Part One

_____

'Written Woman'

1

The Dangers of Manly Women: Late Medieval Perceptions of Female Heroism in Scotland's Second War of Independence

Elizabeth Ewan

William Wallace and Robert Bruce, heroes of the First War of Independence, are known throughout Scotland and beyond, but other heroic figures from the tales of the Second War of Independence (1333-41) are less well known. According to historians writing in late medieval Scotland, just as Wallace and Bruce defied Edward I and II, so Lady Seton of Berwick and Agnes, Countess of Dunbar, defied Edward III. Lady Seton was the wife of Sir Alexander Seton, captain of Berwick, when it was besieged by Edward in 1333; Seton, giving his son as hostage, agreed to render up the town if it were not relieved by a certain date. On the approach of a Scottish army, Edward threatened to execute his hostage if Seton did not surrender, but Lady Seton's courageous words to her husband kept him from yielding. Similarly heroic, Countess Agnes, in her husband's absence in 1338, successfully defended the castle of Dunbar against the English for five months. The vast expenditure England required for that siege helped convince Edward to withdraw from Scotland.[1]

These two stories were told repeatedly in medieval Scotland, although they have disappeared from most twentieth-century histories.[2] In the case of Lady Seton, the historian Lord Hailes in 1797 concluded that her speech was an invention, as her husband had lost his command and could

3

not surrender the town.[3] However, the tale was accepted for centuries and, along with the story of Black Agnes, was used by historians from the Middle Ages to the nineteenth century to inspire pride in the Scottish past. This essay examines the depiction of these two women's actions by historians from the late fourteenth to the mid-sixteenth century and the way in which those histories reveal how medieval male writers negotiated the complex issue of female heroism when it was displayed in the masculine world of warfare.

Most of these histories were characterised by pride in Scottish independence, loyalty to the king, and a belief in history's role in providing examples of admirable behaviour; the male heroes of the Wars, for example, were models for later kings and noblemen. Female heroism, however, was a more difficult topic for writers steeped in the late-medieval ethos of chivalry,[4] which emphasised the masculine attributes of military prowess, knightly accomplishments, and honourable devotion to king and country as well as to women, attributes traditionally associated with men. Historians therefore found female heroism difficult to fit into such a model, especially since medieval society commonly associated women with words and men with deeds. Although historians used a variety of approaches, most portrayed Lady Seton and Black Agnes as expressing their heroism through speech. Lady Seton, always appearing with her husband, used words to encourage bravery in her spouse. Black Agnes, who acted alone, used speech to demonstrate defiance to her enemy. Historians also stressed the women's intellect and wisdom, a wisdom which their words demonstrated and which led others to act. In another approach, because courage was generally associated with men, historians often described courageous women as 'manly'. But manly women could pose a danger to a social order which enforced strict gender roles, and women's 'manliness' thus needed to be softened. In the case of Lady Seton, who was described by some historians as 'of greater courage than men', this danger was mitigated by focusing her speech on the necessity for men's bravery and chivalric values, including honour, duty to one's king and country, and maintaining the reputation of one's family.

Black Agnes presented historians with a different problem, because she acted as well as spoke. Their solution was to make her 'manliness' more feminine by associating her actions with traditional feminine virtues concerned with the upkeep of home and family. She could then be portrayed as keeping her home safe for her absent husband, who would resume his authority when he returned. Historians rarely mentioned honour in their versions of Agnes's story but, significantly, when they did, they associated it with traditional ideas of 'feminine' honour.

Medieval historians of course gathered material from many sources; their debts to earlier histories are often clear, but their other sources, especially oral traditions, are harder to identify.[5] Recent work has emphasised the role of women as tradition-bearers and highlighted the strong and assertive role women played in ballads, which may possibly be due to female authorship. Women have also been shown to be especially interested in preserving stories about their own families.[6] The accounts of Lady Seton and Black Agnes probably represent a survival of such traditions and perhaps of female voices. However, since the extant histories were written by men, the portrayal of women in them is mediated through the male voice.

No surviving Scottish chronicle was contemporary with the sieges involving Lady Seton and Black Agnes, but chronicles from England and France described them.[7] None discussed Lady Seton, but the *Chronicon de Lanercost*, written in England, in a section probably dating to 1338-46, mentioned Agnes. The chronicle relates that besiegers threatened to execute her captive brother, the earl of Moray, if she did not surrender. Agnes responded that they could do so; since her brother had no heirs, she would become countess of Moray.[8] Interestingly, this tale did not appear in any medieval Scottish tales of Agnes; perhaps it was seen as English propaganda detracting from the nobility of the Countess, since it suggested an unfeminine lack of sisterly affection. Ironically, the threat of the execution of kin was also central to the story of Lady Seton.

Both women first appeared in Scottish sources in the vernacular verse *Orygynale Chronkil of Scotland of Androw of Wyntoun*. Prior of St Serf's monastery, Wyntoun wrote this work for a local laird, completing it shortly after 1420.[9] Wyntoun explained that for the period 1329-90 his material came from a friend's history. This history, written c.1390, apparently drew 'on eye witness accounts or family traditions provided by important aristocratic families from Scotland south of the Forth'.[10] The stories of Lady Seton and Black Agnes were probably among these accounts and traditions.

Late fourteenth-century material added to the Latin history known as *John of Fordun's Chronicle*[11] described Thomas Seton's hanging before only his father, but Wyntoun (or his source) said the hanging was witnessed by his father and his mother also (l. 3673), thus introducing Lady Seton. In Wyntoun's account, she reminded her husband they were still young and could have more sons; moreover, she said, he should not be swayed by his son's suffering for he died in the defence of the town, to his own and his family's great honour. She urged her husband instead to act for the safety of his country, emulating his brave ancestors.

Wyntoun's Lady Seton thus emphasised for her husband and son the chivalric ideals of bravery in the face of death, honour, family reputation, and loyalty to one's country and king. Her own contribution would come through the uniquely female action of bearing more sons: 'Thus wes this lady of comford, / Quhen scho disesit saw hir lord' (ll. 3695-6). Her brave words persuaded her husband to sacrifice their son for the greater good of the country, and their defense against the siege continued.

One reason Wyntoun told Lady Seton's story might be found in another episode which both he and his near-contemporary Walter Bower described. About 1347 Alan de Winton (or Wyntoun) took the young heiress, the Lady of Seton (probably a kinswoman of the Berwick Setons, although the Seton genealogy is obscure at this time)[12], and made her his wife. According to Bower, this marriage followed an abduction, something at which Wyntoun only hints. Details in Bower which resemble a folk-motif, and the existence of a ballad 'Alan of Winton and the heiress of Seton', suggest an oral source for this episode.[13] If Wyntoun felt embarrassment about this act by a man with his surname, perhaps recounting the bravery of Lady Seton of Berwick helped assuage it. Moreover, since heiresses had particular reasons to preserve the histories of their families, in order to safeguard their inheritance, possibly the younger Lady Seton was the source of the story of her brave ancestress, and passed it on to her children; her son, William Seton, who died between 1408 and 1416, may have known Wyntoun personally.[14]

Wyntoun had no similar reason to write about Agnes except, perhaps, that he knew a good story when he heard one. He explains that William Montague, earl of Salisbury, was ordered to besiege Dunbar:

> Bot gud Dame Agnes of Dunbar,
> Withe the gudmen that with hir ware,
> Defendit it full douchtely.

> (ll. 4647-9)

Most of Wyntoun's chapter, 'Off the assegeing of Dunbare, And of Dame Annes wis and ware', was devoted to Agnes. When Montague's catapult hurled stones at the wall, Agnes responded by sending to the battlements a beautifully-dressed damsel with a towel to wipe off the spots where the stones had hit, 'at thai mycht se, / To gere [*make*] thaim mare anoyit be' (ll. 4661-2). In describing this action, Wyntoun ascribed both feminine and masculine attributes to the countess. Agnes used what were seen as 'feminine' preoccupations, concern with dress and the cleanliness of the family home, to demonstrate the 'masculine' attribute of active defiance in the face of a military threat.

As the siege continued, Wyntoun indicates, Montague acquired a grudging admiration for his opponent, although he used courtly language and feminine imagery rather than the language of masculine bravery. When a soldier was killed by an arrow from the castle, Montague commented "'This is ane of my ladyis pynnys [*pins*]; / Hir amouris to my hert thus rynnis'" (ll. 4677-8), his ironic courtliness acknowledging his 'feminine' opponent's strength and abilities. Finally, Montague tried bribery, paying one of Agnes's soldiers to let his men in secretly; however, the man took the money and warned the countess, who wisely arranged an ambush. When the gate was raised, and Montague about to enter, John of Coupland, suddenly suspecting a trick, pushed Montague back just as the portcullis came down, trapping several men inside (ll. 4729-48). The different Wyntoun manuscripts record variations on this story, implying that it circulated orally, and the wording of one version also suggests a ballad source: Agnes's men called out to Montague as he fled, "'Faire wele, fallowis, faire wele, fayre, / Faire wele, Montague, for euermaire'" (ll. 4952-3 alternate)[15]. Wyntoun relates that soon after the failed bribery attempt, Alexander de Ramsay managed to supply Agnes's garrison, which continued to hold out until Edward recalled Montague. Concluding his tale, Wyntoun records an English 'carpynge' which emphasised Agnes's active role in successfully resisting the besiegers:

'I wow to God, scho beris hir weill
The Scottish wenche with hir ploddeill [*band of thieves*]
For cum I airly, cum I lait,
I fynd ay Annes at the yait [*gate*].'

(ll. 4793-6)

Agnes's heroism and her active role in the castle's defence were thus recognised not only by Scots, but also by her opponents. However, the heroine's courage was in being always at her door, rather than venturing forth, which might have been, for Wyntoun, an action impossibly unfeminine.

In the 1440s, around twenty years after Wyntoun's work, Walter Bower, abbot of Inchcolm, completed a Latin history, *Scotichronicon*, described by its author as a continuation of John of Fordun's chronicle. In the *Scotichronicon*, Lady Seton appeared only as a passive witness when Edward 'executed Thomas de Seton in the sight of both his parents' (p. 91). Bower rejected any story of Lady Seton, perhaps because he had no connection with the Wintons or Setons. Indeed, he may not have regarded Alan de Winton's abduction of the younger Lady Seton as reprehensible, since the patron of Bower's own history, David Stewart of Rossyth, was involved in a similar episode when he seized the heiress Janet Fenton to marry her to his son.[16] Moreover, Bower's attitude to women was clearly less charitable than Wyntoun's. In a passage which is probably Bower's own composition, he launched into a passionate diatribe about the evils of wicked wives (pp. 333-59). Although this is the only passage by Bower which includes such blatant misogyny,[17] telling the story of the virtuous wife, Lady Seton, at length, would have lessened the effect of his moralising.

Bower seems to have felt happier with the countess of Dunbar, and his various stories about her probably reflect the oral nature of his sources. Bower was, moreover, the first to refer to her as 'Black Agnes', although the nickname was probably widely known.[18] In relating the John de Coupland story, Bower also ascribed the taunting of Montague to Agnes, rather than to her men; the words in Bower differed from those given in the Wyntoun manuscripts, perhaps again reflecting a story which survived in many versions. When describing the countess, Bower states 'it is said that she was very active and cautious, showing manly feelings as she zealously incited her people to defend [the castle]' (p. 127). However, although reporting the description of Agnes as 'manly', Bower, like Wyntoun, used feminine and female imagery in his tale. The maiden whom Black Agnes sent to the battlements was in Bower's account even more feminine, being 'adorned like a bride for her husband' (p. 127). Bower also included a new story which associated Agnes with birthing imagery. He states that Montagu attacked the castle with a powerful weapon called a 'sow', an enormous wooden platform on wheels, with soldiers hidden beneath:

> At this the countess Black Annot shouted in a strong voice, saying 'Montague, Montague, beware for your sow will farrow!' With that, she caused an ingenious machine inside the castle to be drawn back for discharging a missile, and a large heavy stone, almost like a millstone, came down from a high trajectory, struck the sow [?] fiercely like lightning and dashed the heads of many inside to pieces.
>
> (p. 128)

Here Agnes's traditionally masculine military action is feminised by the use, in her words, of birthing imagery inextricably associated with women.

Bower's approach to Agnes thus acknowledges that a woman could act courageously and in a masculine fashion when exceptional circumstances, such as the absence of her husband, demanded courage and action. Bower's own career required him to recognise this for, in the aftermath of James I's assassination in 1437, Bower and his patron were supporters of the widowed Queen Joan, and David Stewart was closely involved in the affairs of the queen's party in the 1440s. Sympathy for the Dunbar family has been detected in both Bower and Wyntoun,[19] and this attitude may have led Bower to choose an example from the Dunbar family of a courageous woman acting on her own as a model for his queen, since in 1444 Joan herself was besieged in Dunbar Castle.

The *Liber Pluscardensis* (*Book of Pluscarden*), one of many Latin abridgments of Bower's *Scotichronicon*, was produced 1455-61.[20] The sieges in which Lady Seton and Black Agnes figured were described in detail similar to Wyntoun's, but Agnes was presented as more forceful and, as Wyntoun had said, wise. The anonymous *Pluscarden* author notes that Agnes 'defended the besieged castle admirably; for she was a very wise and clever and wary woman'. Moreover, the woman on the battlements was not a maiden but Agnes herself, who 'would, in the sight of all, wipe with a most beautiful cloth the spot where the stone from the engine hit the wall' (p. 215). Perhaps thinking that Agnes was not a woman to bother with beautiful clothing, the *Pluscarden* author gave her instead a beautiful cloth, but had Agnes use it to express her disdain for the attackers, by putting the cloth to 'practical' use.

Although the *Book of Pluscarden* was an abbreviation of the *Scotichronicon*, oral traditions about the Countess made her too well-known to pass over quickly, and the author attributed to Agnes a slightly longer and more aggressive speech in the scene where she told Montague she would make his sow farrow against the sow's will. In an ironic inversion of traditional rape imagery, a woman threatened sexual assault against a man whose military machine was 'pregnant' with warriors. Moreover, after the sow's destruction Agnes was said to have acted quickly and 'captured and brought into the castle all their gear, engines, and provisions, and slew many' (p. 216). The author of *Pluscarden* also offered a new story that played on women's traditional feminine role of providing food for their household and guests: after Ramsay had resupplied the castle, 'Black Annes ordered a great quantity of her provisions, namely, wheaten bread of fine corn flour and excellent wine, to be presented to the said earl [Montague], who was himself in great want of provisions' (p. 216), an action by Agnes which led Montague to attempt to bribe an entry to the castle. Clearly, for the *Pluscarden* author, Agnes was a woman of deeds as well as words.

Five or six decades after *Pluscarden* appeared, John Mair (or Major) in 1521 wrote in Latin his *Historia Majoris Britanniae, Tam Angliae Quam Scotiae* (*A History of Greater Britain, as Well England as Scotland*).[21] Because he supported peace with England, in discussing the siege at Berwick, Mair downplayed Edward III's villainy by saying that the agreed-on time for Berwick's surrender had arrived. Mair states further that the townspeople, however, refused to yield, and this led Edward to threaten the hanging of Seton's son, 'thinking that his parents, and *most of all, his fond mother*, would be moved, by the death of their son and heir, to the surrender of the town' (p. 272; my emphasis).

Mair nonetheless stressed Lady Seton's exceptional courage in this incident: 'this brave-hearted woman preferred the safety of the town and the liberty of her country to the life of her son' and she thus said to her husband, 'We are young -- we have other children -- let us patiently bear the death of one' (p. 272). Lady Seton's response reflects Mair's conception of honour; writing during the faction-ridden minority of James V, Mair emphasised that honour came from a person's actions, not merely from aristocratic birth, and Lady Seton thus makes no reference to the chivalrous value of reputation based on lineage and the deeds of ancestors.[22] For Mair's Lady Seton, honourable action took the form of patiently enduring suffering, which left the realm of action safely to men.

Mair's account of Agnes similarly attested to women's potential for bravery. Although the besiegers 'made their attacks with engines of war marvelous to behold', Mair records that the castle 'was defended by a brave woman' (p. 280). Agnes' verbal powers obviously made a strong impression on Mair: 'She spared no tempting words to entice the Scots to make stand against the English king; and in time of truce she took her place upon the walls and began to banter the Englishmen, for of raillery and manly intellect she had no lack' (p. 280). The silent maiden on the walls in the earlier accounts is in Mair's history replaced by a very vocal heroine, although one who, when necessary, used the stereotypical womanly arts of tempting and enticing. At other times, however, her powers of speech were more 'manly', consisting of defiance and mockery. For example, Mair notes that when the sow appeared, Agnes, bantering, said that 'unless the English took good care of their sow, she would find a way to make her farrow'. Her way was to pour boiling pitch, sulphur, logs, and stones on the machine, and thus Agnes 'made an end, not of the sow only, but of all her litter' (p. 280). Echoing Bower,

Mair shows Agnes ironically using reproduction and birthing imagery, to a very non-maternal and unfeminine end.

Mair portrays Agnes as a more aggressive woman than had earlier writers. When Ramsay brought supplies, Agnes did not then offer food to Montague, as in earlier accounts, but 'exhorted her people to turn the attack upon the Englishmen. And the soldiers answered to her call, and slew no small number of the English' (p. 280). When Montagu narrowly escaped her ambush in the portcullis, Mair depicts Agnes as making 'use of this raillery with him, saying "Fare thee well, then, Montagu; methought thou wert coming to sup with us, and help defend the castle against the English king"' (p. 281), a barb which, in attributing to Montague the possibility of his treachery to his sovereign, was much more pointed than the simple 'Adieu' reported by Bower. The taunt also, of course, played ironically on women's traditional responsibility for feeding guests.

Approximately six years after Mair's history, Hector Boece's *Scotorum Historiae* was published in Paris in 1527; this Latin history was then made accessible to a larger audience by John Bellenden, who, at James V's request, translated the work into Scots as *The Chronicles of Scotland* in 1531 and again, with Boece's advice, c.1540.[23] While Bellenden's versions of Boece were not literal translations, and in several places departed quite markedly from the original,[24] in the two episodes concerning Lady Seton and Black Agnes, Bellenden stayed fairly faithful to his original, although there were certain differences in the words attributed to Lady Seton.

Boece, strongly influenced by humanism with its use of classical historians as models, emulated Livy in creating long speeches for his characters.[25] Reflecting this influence in his translation, Bellenden divided Boece's work into chapters and highlighted Lady Seton's speech with his title for Book 15, chapter 4: 'Of the "orisoun" made by Sir Alexander Seton's wife, and how his sons were slain by tyranny of King Edward' (p. 303). Bellenden indicates that, on the approach of a Scottish army to Berwick before the agreed-upon date for the town's surrender, Edward threatened to hang Seton's sons; that a second son is threatened suggests that Boece had a source other than Wyntoun, Bower, or Mair. Seton asked the king to keep his faith, but Edward refused. Boece believed Seton would have surrendered the town, had he not been dissuaded by his wife, 'the mother of their common sons' (fol. 326ᵛ). Although Bellenden described Lady Seton as 'superior to male nature in the courage of her soul' (fol. 326ᵛ), her heroism largely took the form of exhorting men, both husband and sons, to behave nobly in accord with chivalric values. She had raised her sons to be noble, and sacrificing them would greatly increase the family's and the sons' honour, but if Seton surrendered, betraying his faith and bringing his people to servitude, he would be disgraced forever, and both of their sons, although saved from the gallows, would live out their lives stained with cowardice and shame. Lady Seton's honour was linked with that of her husband, although she said that if given the chance to sacrifice herself for the town, she would gladly do so. However, she also cited from the Old Testament examples of male and female bravery on which she, her husband, and her sons (and Boece's audience) could model their behaviour. In particular, Lady Seton drew specific attention to the mother of the Macabees who had first witnessed her sons' torturous deaths and then given herself up to similar punishment, thus suggesting a pattern of female courage (fol. 327^r). Bellenden, in his translation, downplayed the model somewhat by making the mother suffer death at the same time as her sons, so that her courage was not singled out from theirs (p. 305).

Boece also treated childbearing as another female form of courage, a way for women to make their own unique contribution for their country, both bearing and, even more importantly, raising children of noble spirit. Boece emphasised the pain and trouble associated with childbearing, an unusual emphasis in medieval histories, and one which may suggest the possibility of a female source for at least part of the story.[26] However, Boece notes that Lady Seton felt that her efforts in raising her children to be noble were well rewarded, for her sons were paying the debt they owed their country. Her final comment that she could yet bear more children was in Boece's account offered almost as an afterthought; children could be replaced, but honour, once lost, was gone forever.

Boece used Lady Seton's words to emphasise the loyalty to king and country which all subjects owe. He may have wanted to inspire James V's magnates, who had not been conspicuously peaceful during the minority, with the type of true nobility evident in Lady Seton, who preferred to die a noble death rather than live a long but dishonoured life. Her story could also serve as a warning not to listen to the blandishments of English kings such as Henry VIII, who was actively meddling in Scottish affairs in the 1520s, which could lead to servitude. Boece additionally emphasised Edward's villainy in breaking the truce, and his Lady Seton demonstrated her wisdom by returning to this point and explaining that even if she and her husband saved their sons, the treacherous tyrant was unlikely to keep his word: after the town was surrendered it would be sacked, virgins and matrons violated, and all the people massacred. Her description of this likelihood reflected traditional rhetoric but also recalled the earlier, vicious sack of Berwick by Edward I in 1296. Lady Seton then followed her words by action as she took her husband to her chamber to prevent him attempting any last minute surrender. In Bellenden's translation of 1531, Lady Seton's move from words to deeds leads to the author describing her as a woman of greater courage than her husband or other men.

Boece and Bellenden said little about Black Agnes, reporting only that the castle of Dunbar was defended with such spirit by the countess commonly called 'Blakanna', that the English were forced to leave (fol. 333ʳ, p. 433). Given Boece's liking for stirring speeches, his silence on this episode is surprising, since Agnes' story would have provided him with excellent material. Were such models of female military action becoming less acceptable in the sixteenth century?

William Stewart also translated Boece into verse between 1531 and 1535, apparently at the request of a court lady. Because Stewart was part of the court circle of poets, and popular with the literate elite, his translation probably had a wider audience than the survival of one manuscript suggests.[27] Trying to stress the bravery of both Setons, Stewart relates that Seton replied to Edward's threat with a defiant speech: 'Syne do his best, cum on, I him defy' (l. 52, 628), a speech that balances that of Seton's wife. However, when Edward set up the gallows, Seton wavered, as a father's natural love for sons in distress began to affect him: 'For verra deddour trymlit and he shuke, / Sic aw he stude on that gallous to luke' (ll. 52, 647-8). Lady Seton, described as a woman at 'that tyme quhilk moir curage hed' (ll. 52, 649), feared her husband's love for his sons would lead him to surrender. She drew him away from the wall and addressed him 'with greit wisdoume' (ll. 52, 660-94). As in Boece's version, she emphasised the everlasting nature of reputation and the importance of honour, but her focus was much more on male honour as she indicated that wives and children should be sacrificed, if necessary, for fame is dearer than human life.

Stewart's Lady Seton thus had a more passive role than she had in Boece's account, where she actively offered to give up her own life. Her examples also differed, as Stewart's translation omits the Old Testament model of a mother's courage; instead, Lady Seton advised her husband to model himself on God who gave up His only son. The stress on female nature also disappeared in Stewart's account, where Lady Seton made no mention of her ability to bear more children, or of pregnancy or childrearing. Stewart's Lady Seton showed an essential passivity when, although she drew her husband from the wall, it was not she but Seton himself who sought a quiet place to wait out the execution. Perhaps, to balance his earlier statements about Lady Seton's having 'moir curage', Stewart wished thusly to restore to Seton his bravery.

Drawing material from different sources, Stewart also said more about Agnes than did Boece, stating for example that Agnes defended her house 'richt manfullie'(l. 53, 861). However, along with the manliness, and for the first time in these histories, Agnes is accorded characteristics traditionally associated with female honour. Agnes was a model for all, Stewart said, 'Ane trew ladie without blek or blame / Ay to her prince, bot ony falt or cryme' (ll. 53, 858-9). Agnes might be manly in her actions, but, in her chastity and honesty, she had also become a model for virtuous womanliness.

Even though Stewart may have emphasised the bravery of Alexander Seton, this did not prevent one later outraged reaction to Boece's *History*. In 1559, at the request of his Seton kinsman, Sir Richard Maitland of Lethington, poet and government official, wrote a Seton family history.[28] Maitland objected fiercely to Boece's depiction of Lady Seton as being 'superior to male nature in the courage of her soul'; Maitland saw Lady Seton's reported speech and its effect as a deep insult to Alexander's honour. Asserting that Seton was a noble knight who defended the town 'very valiantly' (p. 22) and defied Edward, Maitland states that when Edward raised the gallows, Seton, fearing fatherly pity should make him change his mind, on his own initiative went to his chamber. As Stewart had done before him, Maitland reduced Lady Seton's active role.

Maitland reports that in Boece's history, Lady Seton, seeing her husband's great sadness, 'by the commoun custome of wemen, layit by hir moderlie sorow, and began to comfort hir husband, desyrand [him] to leif his dolour' (p. 23). This was in keeping with the stereotypical idea that such comforting was to be expected of women. However, she then 'shew him gude and stark ressonis quhy he suld do the samin' (p. 23), reasons which Maitland said Boece described at length in his 'Croniclis'. Maitland reproved Boece, arguing that attributing such words to Lady Seton, 'partlie defacies and minissis the honour of the said Alexander' and charging that Boece did this 'in ane manner wald gif the gloir to the woman' (p. 23). Maitland also objected to Boece's report of Lady Seton's action following her speech. His argument was based on 'dyvers of the auld croniclis of Scotland' (p. 23) where, he said, Lady Seton made her speech after the execution. However, apart from Boece and his translators, the only surviving references to Lady Seton are in Wyntoun and Mair; Wyntoun's description of events could be read in Maitland's way, but Mair also placed her speech before the execution. If the 'divers old chronicles' existed, they would seem to imply that the tale of Lady Seton was more popular than the extant histories suggest.

Maitland's history was intended, he says, to make future generations of the family 'the mair layth to do ony thing that may be the hurt or the decay of the samyn' (p. xi). In his view, it was wrong that a woman's courage should be glorified at a man's expense. Misogynistically assuming that women's courage was inherently of lesser quality than men's, Maitland argued further that Seton would not have been made governor if he was not 'appeirandlie of gritar curage nor ony woman culd be' (p. 23). Clearly, Maitland saw Boece's story as challenging traditional patriarchal authority, and in consequence pointed out that Seton would not have listened to his wife, if she had counselled him to act against his wishes. Maitland's motive was to redeem the glory of his ancestor, but his arguments about women, power, and courage fit well with disparaging attitudes towards women expressed in his own poetry.[29]

In those attitudes Maitland was, of course, representative of his culture. At almost the same time as Maitland's history appeared, John Knox published *The First Blast of the Trumpet Against the Monstrous Regiment of Women* (1558). Responding to the proliferation of female rulers in mid-sixteenth century Scotland and England, Knox raised pointed questions about women's capacity to rule, and thus to defend the realm. The tract led to furious debates on women's abilities to govern and command.[30] From this time on, the topic of female heroism would be a new and more immediate concern among political theorists. But much of the groundwork for discussion of this topic had been laid by the medieval historians who transmitted such stories as those of Lady Seton and Black Agnes.[31]

Notes

[1] Bruce Webster, 'Scotland without a King, 1329-1341', in *Medieval Scotland: Crown, Lordship and Community*, ed. by Alexander Grant and Keith Stringer (Edinburgh: EUP, 1993), p. 233.

[2] Michael Lynch, *Scotland: A New History* (London: Century, 1992); A. D. M. Barrell, *Medieval Scotland* (Cambridge: CUP, 2000). But see Bruce Webster, *Medieval Scotland: The Making of an Identity* (Basingstoke: Macmillan, 1997), p. 83.

[3] David Dalrymple, Lord Hailes, *Annals of Scotland* (Edinburgh: W. Creech, 1797), III, 96-105; Ranald Nicholson, *Edward III and the Scots* (London: OUP, 1965), pp. 123-7.

[4] Carol Edington, 'Paragons and Patriots: National Identity and the Chivalric Ideal in Late Medieval Scotland', in *Image and Identity. The Making and*

Remaking of Scotland through the Ages, ed. by Dauvit Broun, Roger Mason, and Norman MacDougall (Edinburgh: John Donald, 1998), pp. 69-81; Roger Mason, 'Chivalry and Citizenship: Aspects of National Identity in Renaissance Scotland', in *People and Power in Scotland*, ed. by R. Mason and N. MacDougall (Edinburgh: John Donald, 1992), pp. 50-73.

[5] See Walter Bower, *Scotichronicon*, ed. by Donald E. R. Watt, 9 vols (Aberdeen: AUP, 1987-96), IX. References in text are to volume 7.

[6] Catherine Kerrigan, 'Reclaiming History: The Ballad as a Woman's Tradition', *Etudes Ecossaises*, 1 (1992), 343-50; Elizabeth van Houts, *Memory and Gender in Medieval Europe, 900-1200* (Toronto: UTP, 1999), pp. 84-92, 147-9.

[7] For example, *The Anonimalle Chronicle 1333-81*, ed. by V.H. Galbraith (Manchester: MUP, 1970), pp. 1, 13; *The Scalacronica of Sir Thomas Gray*, trans. by Sir Herbert Maxwell (Glasgow: J. Maclehose, 1907), pp. 94-6, 105; *The Chronicle of Froissart translated out of French by Sir John Bourchier Lord Bernars 1523-25* (New York: AMS Press, 1967), I, 86-7.

[8] *Chronicle of Lanercost* 1272-1346, trans. by Sir Herbert Maxwell (Glasgow: J. Maclehose, 1913), pp. 304, 311-15. See *Anonimalle Chronicle*, pp. xxvi-vii.

[9] Wemyss and Cottonian MSS in *The Original Chronicle of Andrew of Wyntoun*, ed. by F. J. Amours, STS, 6 vols (Edinburgh and London: Blackwood, 1903-14). A third MS is in *The Orygynale Cronykil of Scotland by Androw of Wyntoun*, ed David Laing, 3 vols (Edinburgh: Edmonston and Douglas, 1872-9). References are to the Wemyss Manuscript, unless otherwise stated.

[10] Stephen Boardman, 'Chronicle Propaganda in Fourteenth-century Scotland: Robert the Steward, John of Fordun and the "Anonymous Chronicle"', *SHR*, 76.1 (1997), p. 26.

[11] Dauvit Broun, 'A New Look at *Gesta Annalia* attributed to John of Fordun', in *Church, Chronicle and Learning in Medieval and Early Renaissance Scotland*, ed. by Barbara Crawford (Edinburgh: Mercat, 1999), pp. 17-21.

[12] Monsignor Robert Seton, *An Old Family or The Setons of Scotland and America* (New York: Brentano's, 1899), pp. 38-49; J. Balfour Paul, *The Scots Peerage*, 9 vols (Edinburgh: D. Douglas, 1904-14), VIII, 569-72; Richard Maitland, *The History of the House of Seytoun to the Year MDLIX* (Glasgow: Hutchison and Brookman, 1829), pp. 21-4, 27-8.

[13] Wyntoun, VI, 190, 191; *Scotichronicon*, VII, 159, 248-9; Seton, *An Old Family*, p. 44. See Juliette Wood, 'Folkloric Patterns in Scottish Chronicles', in *The Rose and the Thistle*, ed. by Sally Mapstone and Juliette Wood (East Linton: Tuckwell, 1998), pp. 116-35.

[14] van Houts, *Memory*, pp. 73, 88; *Scotichronicon*, VII, 248.

[15] The edited text provides an alternate reading from the manuscript; quotation is from the alternate version.

[16] *Scotichronicon*, IX, 358-62.

[17] *Scotichronicon*, VII, xxi-ii; Sally Mapstone, 'The *Scotichronicon*'s First Readers', in *Church, Chronicle and Learning*, p. 42, and n.81.

[18] Dorothy M. Owen, 'White Annays and Others', in *Medieval Women*, ed. by Derek Baker (Oxford: Blackwell, 1985), p. 332; *Scotichronicon*, VII, 230-1.

[19] Michael Brown, '"Vile Times": Walter Bower's Last Book and the Minority of James II', *SHR*, 79.2 (2000), 165, 175-80; Stephen Boardman, *The Early Stewart Kings* (East Linton: Tuckwell, 1996), p. 228.

[20] *The Book of Pluscarden*, trans. by Felix Skene (Edinburgh: Edmonston and Douglas, 1876-80). See Mapstone, '*Scotichronicon's* First Readers', p. 34 n.23; *Scotichronicon*, IX, 193-8.

[21] John Major, *A History of Greater Britain as Well England as Scotland (1521)*, trans. by Archibald Constable, STS (Edinburgh: Constable, 1892).

[22] Roger Mason, 'Kingship, Nobility and Anglo-Scottish Union: John Mair's *History of Great Britain* (1521)', *IR*, 41.2 (1990), 197-8, 203.

[23] Hector Boece, *Scotorum Historiae* (Paris: [n. pub.], 1527); Bellenden (1531), *The Chronicles of Scotland translated into Scots by John Bellenden 1531*, ed. by Edith C. Batho and H. W. Husbands, STS, 2 vols (Edinburgh: Blackwood, 1936-41); Bellenden (1540), *The History and Chronicles of Scotland*, trans. by John Bellenden, ed. by Thomas Maitland, 3 vols (Edinburgh: W. C. Tait, 1821-2). Textual references to Bellenden are to the 1936-41 edition. My thanks to Dr. Padraig O'Clerigh for his help with the Latin text of Boece.

[24] Nicola Royan, 'The Relationship between the *Scotorum Historia* of Hector Boece and John Bellenden's Chronicles of Scotland', in *The Rose and the Thistle*, pp. 136-57; Sally Mapstone, 'Shakespeare and Scottish Kingship: A Case History', pp. 160-8 and notes 12-15.

[25] Nicola Royan, 'The Uses of Speech in Hector Boece's *Scotorum Historia*', in *A Palace in the Wild: Essays on Vernacular Culture and Humanism in Sixteenth and Seventeenth-Century Literature*, ed. by L. A. J. R. Houven, and others. (Leuven: Peeters, 2000), pp. 75-93; Kenneth D. Farrow, 'The Substance and Style of Hector Boece's *Scotorum Historiae*', *SLJ*, 25.1 (1998), 16-17.

[26] Although Boece gave the poor woman a ten-month pregnancy, Bellenden revised this to nine months.

[27] *The Buik of the Croniclis of Scotland or a Metrical Version of the History of Hector Boece by William Stewart*, ed. by William Turnbull (London: Public Record Office, Rolls Series, 1858), p. vii; Alasdair A. MacDonald, 'William Stewart and the Court Poetry of the Reign of James V', in *Stewart Style 1515-1542*, ed. by J. Hadley Williams (East Linton: Tuckwell, 1996), p. 190 n.58; Carol Edington, *Court and Culture in Renaissance Scotland* (East Linton: Tuckwell, 1994), pp. 97-9, 125-7; Theo van Heijnsbergen, 'The Interaction between Literature and History in Queen Mary's Edinburgh: The Bannatyne Manuscript and its Prosopographical Context', in *The Renaissance in Scotland*, ed. by Alasdair A. MacDonald, and others. (Leiden: E. J. Brill, 1994), pp. 220-2.

[28] Maitland, *The Historie*; Maurice Lee Jr., 'Sir Richard Maitland of Lethington: a Christian Laird in the Age of Reformation', in *Action and Conviction in Early Modern Europe*, ed. by Theodore K. Rabb and Jerrold E. Seigel (Princeton: PUP, 1969), pp. 117-9.

[29] Evelyn S. Newlyn, 'Images of Women in Sixteenth-century Scottish Literary Manuscripts', in *Women in Scotland c.1100-c.1750*, ed. by Elizabeth Ewan and Maureen Meikle (East Linton: Tuckwell, 1999), pp. 60-1. Cf. Alasdair A.

MacDonald, 'The Poetry of Sir Richard Maitland of Lethington', in *Transactions of the East Lothian Antiquarian and Field Naturalists' Society*, 13 (1972), 8-11.

[30] Amanda Shepherd, *Gender and Authority in Sixteenth-Century England: The Knox Debate* (Keele: Ryburn, 1994).

[31] I would like to express my great appreciation to Evy Newlyn whose care in editing and excellent suggestions helped this historian to tread in the somewhat unfamiliar waters of literary criticism. This essay was completed too soon to benefit from the excellent conference paper by Nicola Royan on literary images of Scottish medieval heroines, presented at the Leeds International Medieval Conference, July 2002.

2
War and Truce: Women in *The Wallace*
Inge B. Milfull

The verse romance on the life of William Wallace, the hero of the First
Scottish War of Independence, was composed in the 1470s by one Blind
Hary, about whom little is known except for his political affiliation with the
Scottish opponents of James III's pro-English policies.[1] To a large extent,
Hary's *Wallace* is preoccupied with war; an intensely nationalistic poem, it
identifies Scottish patriotism with a militant enmity towards the English.
Wallace embodies the war against the English in two kinds of narrative: in
outlaw or guerilla exploits, which predominate in William Wallace's early
career, and in pitched battles, which predominate in his career's second half.
Both types of narrative centre on masculine concerns, and primarily on
relations between men. In the context of *The Wallace*, therefore, women
and the feminine are, *a priori*, marginalised. However, as King has pointed
out, a remarkable number of significant female characters figure in *The
Wallace*, and their repeated introduction into the patriotic narrative raises
the following question.[2] What is the role of the feminine -- reaffirming or
critiquing -- in relation to the work's overtly masculine agenda?

Undeniably, direct forms of female opposition or support appear not to
interest the poet. Only one female character in *The Wallace*, the treacherous
English wife of William Douglas,[3] is in direct opposition to Wallace and the
Scots, and only one female character, the countess of March, supports the
Scottish side in a strictly military role by commanding troops against the
English.[4] Both the villainous Englishwoman and the Scottish Amazon
remain entirely marginal and are used by Hary merely *ad hoc* to explain the
actions and fate of their respective husbands.

Hary's more important female characters are all either supporters of the
Scots but not directly involved in military action, or are personally

interested in Wallace himself, or both. Significantly, this kind of personal support for Wallace, although non-hostile, could still threaten his role as the protagonist in the war against the English. Those women uninvolved with Wallace personally, particularly if they are independent of male kin, are unambiguously supportive of him in his campaigns, but the women intimately involved with him are associated with his physical and moral vulnerability. The risk to Wallace appears acute if the relationship is a (potentially) sexual one, even more so if conceived of in courtly terms. Wallace's relationships with women, from impersonal to intimate, from supportive to subversive, are this study's focus.

While Hary does not envisage women actually taking the field for the sake of Scotland, many women undertake for Wallace tasks requiring both cleverness and courage. Acting in subservient roles as witnesses, messengers or spies, they also repeatedly assist Wallace in escaping his enemies; these escapes thus belong with the outlaw stories. Wallace's mother, nurse and wife all undertake activities in such stories.[5] However, many of the women involved are anonymous and apparently of relatively low social rank;[6] some are widows (V. 320, X. 619, X. 688), which explains why they are, comparatively speaking, free agents.[7]

Of these anonymous women, the most impressive witnesses the treacherous hanging of the Scottish noblemen in the Barns of Ayr (Book VII) and warns first Wallace's men and then Wallace himself of the trap. Wallace addresses her as 'der nece' (VII. 275), presumably an honorific term rather than one designating relationship. When she reports the death of 'our trew barrouns' (VII. 271) and of Ranald of Crawfurd, Wallace's uncle, her language is characterised by passion and a stark rhetoric:

> 'Out off ȝon bern', scho [*she*] said, 'I saw him born,
> Nakit, laid law on cald erd me beforn.
> His frosty mouth I kissit in that sted [*place*],
> Rycht now manlik, now bar and brocht to ded!
> And with a claith I couerit his licaym [*body*],
> For in his lyff he did neuir woman schayme.
> His systir sone thou art, worthi and wicht [*strong*].
> Rawenge thar dede for goddis saik at thi mycht.
> Als [*also*] I sall [*shall*] help as I am woman trew!'
>
> (VII. 277-85)

She abides by her offer of assistance, directing Wallace's men to his hideout, organising provisions for them, spying on the English, and reporting their drunken state to Wallace. When he then sets out to burn the English in their beds, Wallace sends her before him, to mark the billets of the intended victims with white paint (VII. 407-23). Clearly, this Scottish nemesis is as fully integrated into the plan for revenge as any of Wallace's men, yet she, unlike Wallace's more prominent supporters, remains anonymous, her appearance confined to that single episode. Her lack of indicated family ties places her outside the naming system by which Hary draws his noble male contemporaries into identifying with the deeds ascribed to their ancestors, while her seeming social marginality allows her to achieve a quasi-mythic status, powerful but vague in its appeal.

The role of Wallace's former nurse in his rescue after imprisonment in Ayr (II. 258-369) is perhaps more striking, although non-aggressive and nurturing, since the nurse's actions more directly affect our reading of the hero himself. As his foster-mother, this likewise unnamed woman, apparently a widow, has a kin-like relationship to Wallace. When he is left for dead on the dung heap in front of his prison, she removes him for burial, discovers he is barely alive, and nurses him back to health, while pretending in public to mourn over his dead body. Hary plays with maternal imagery as the nurse, in reviving Wallace, assists in his second birth; moreover, he is again suckled, but by his foster-mother's daughter.[8] Unusually, Wallace is altogether helpless while the old woman appears robust and active. A touch of uneasy Bakhtinian grotesquerie seems evident in this episode with its reversal of expected roles for youth and age, masculinity and femininity, which are only righted when, completely recovered, Wallace undertakes to protect his nurse and her family, thereby demonstrating his renewed virility (II. 366-9). However, the description of Wallace's second nursing has more power to disturb, associated as it is with a crisis in Wallace's heroic career, a temporary eclipse which requires not only a miraculous recovery but also a reaffirmation of Wallace's heroic destiny by traditional masculine authority both secular and clerical.[9]

However troubling the image of Wallace returning symbolically to the womb, the nurse herself is not a threatening figure but fully supportive. As in the episode of the burning Barns of Ayr, the nurse rescuing and protecting Wallace displays considerable initiative and guile. Protecting Wallace and furthering the Scottish cause are thus congruent objectives. Yet one may ask if they are necessarily completely congruent, since it is Wallace's dedication to the war against the English that continually endangers his life. Underscoring this equation of nationalism and personal risk early in his career, his mother, having fled with him from the English to Gowrie, laments his determination to confront them and accurately predicts it will eventually lead to his death (I. 264). Her attitude in this regard is apparently not so much feminine but rather that of an older and protective family member. Although the good of Scotland in *The Wallace* is predominantly conceived in terms of the well-being of the noble Scottish families, tension is still seen to arise. Thus William Wallace's devotion to the interest of Scotland partly conflicts with his family's interest in preserving its members, a point of view that may be articulated by a female voice as well a male one. Nevertheless, Wallace's reaction to the eventual death of his mother is remarkable (X. 832-54). He is, in fact, described in part as grateful because she died from natural causes and can no longer be persecuted by the English. Her vulnerability had perhaps made her into a liability.

Wallace's single-mindedness is endangered, if not by his mother, by his encounters with women who, unlike the characters discussed above, figure as (potential) objects of sexual desire. These encounters question the compatibility of heterosexual love with the demands of war and hint at a deeper division between masculine and feminine concerns. The women of these encounters are an anonymous mistress, Wallace's wife, and the queen of England. Only when he is about to marry does Wallace, briefly, consider laying down his arms and retiring from the struggle; later the queen persuades him to conclude a truce. Since he strongly anticipates his enemies' breaking it, however, this truce is both more and less significant than his doubts at the time of his marriage: although it is a formal act rather than mere thought and public rather than private, the perceived risk of its affecting the ultimate outcome is much lower.

Wallace's wife is due especial attention on several accounts. The only woman from Hary's surviving historical sources, she appears in a short narrative that Wyntoun incorporated into his account of Wallace in the *Orygynale Chronykil*[10] where, as Wallace's mistress, she is killed by the English sheriff of Lanark for helping him to escape. Wallace's subsequent killing of the sheriff of Lanark is explained as revenging the death of his mistress. Thus Wallace's first major exploit, which sparked a successful rising against the English, is explained as vengeance stemming from the destruction of a private relationship.

If we accept Wyntoun's account as representative of the versions of the story known to Hary, then the poet has introduced a number of changes in *The Wallace*.[11] For example, Hary included the history of the woman's association with Wallace, beginning when he first saw her in church. After some doubts, he arranged to meet her in private, later deciding to marry her; this presents a remarkable difference, for in Hary's version of the story the woman is Wallace's wife, not his mistress. His later decision to marry her represents a significant shift and not simply poetic amplification: Hary casts the woman as wife not mistress, the relationship licit not licentious. Hary's text thus suggests a vital unease with the elements of the earlier story. Following the literary frame, Hary could have interpreted the relationship between Wallace and the murdered woman as a courtly love affair.[12] Yet he pointedly rejected the courtly love paradigm: the descriptions of the woman's character, of her interactions with Wallace, and of Wallace's attitude to her are all counter to courtly love.

Hary names the young woman but identifies her not by her first, or Christian, name but by her father's. The father's respectable social position defines his daughter's status since the name cited, Hugh Braidfute of Lamington, suggests that the father was a land-owner[13] who is similarly characterised by the social position of his noble ancestors and relations (V. 584-86). The young woman therefore functions as a representative of a social group, the Braidfutes, which is defined by patrilineal descent within a traditional local hierarchy, and her own view of herself is strongly conditioned by membership in that family.

At this time in her life the Braidfute family had weakened: Hugh Braidfute and his wife are dead as is their son and heir, killed by Hesilrigh, the Lanark sheriff whom Wallace later kills to revenge Hugh's daughter. Therefore Mistress Braidfute, young and unmarried, lacks the protection of a close male relative or even a widowed mother. In spite of being a member of the gentry, she is, as an orphan, particularly vulnerable to English oppression and must pay them to leave her alone. Thus loss of political power and economic loss go hand in hand. That Mistress Braidfute lives in the town can be taken to indicate that she has had to move there from the family seat at Lamington because of these pressures.

Mistress Braidfute clearly feels that this loss of political and economical status has badly affected her status and particularly her eligibility for marriage. Consequently, when, during their first private meeting, Wallace asks her for her *quentance*, 'familiar acquaintance', she expresses doubt that her *quentance* is worth having:

> 'War my quentance rycht worthi for till pryse [*worth valuing*]
> 3he sall [*shall*] it haiff, als god me saiff in saille [*happiness*],
> Bot Inglismen gerris [*make*] our power faill
> Throuch violence of thaim and thar barnage [*barons*],
> At [*who*] has weill ner destroyt our lynage'
>
> (V. 674-8)

Hary characterises this answer of hers as modest and prudent (V. 673). Throughout, in fact, the positive traits that Hary emphasises most in

Mistress Braidfute may be summarised under the categories modesty, prudence, and politeness,[14] and these virtues are exemplified by her conduct during the conversation with Wallace.

Her answer to his request for *quentance* can be interpreted in two ways. On the one hand, her answer can be seen as a polite way of expressing reservations about Wallace's request. On the other hand, Mistress Braidfute may be addressing her problematic situation quite literally since she later ponders the possibility that Wallace may consider her too far beneath his status for marriage. In spite of her sensitivity to her altered circumstances, however, she is not willing to lower her personal standards of behaviour, specifically for sexual conduct. She appeals to Wallace to respect those standards, because her loss of status is due to English transgression and in particular because she has already made sacrifices to maintain those standards:

> And I trast [*trust*] 3he wald nocht set till assaill [*to undertake*],
> For 3houre worschipe, to do me dyshonour,
> And I a maid and standis in mony stour [*am in repeated danger*]
> Fra Inglismen to saiff my womanheid,
> And cost has maid to kepe me fra thar dreid [*threat*]
> (V. 688-92)

Mistress Braidfute's sense of self-esteem is thus determined both by inherited social status and by her own efforts to live up to it. Together, she claims, these standards and her efforts outweigh her actual straitened circumstances, a claim not maintained without difficulty, although Hary also states that her reputation in the town was high (V. 601). Mistress Braidfute and her *womanheid* are embattled on two fronts: as a Scotswoman she must defend herself and the inheritance of the Braidfutes against Heselrig and the English,[15] and as a noblewoman she must defend herself against the possibility of Wallace's forcing a non-marital relationship upon her. Her defensiveness is thus rather different in emphasis from a courtly mistress's *danger*, although such a woman is also defending her reputation.

Mistress Braidfute's predicament, partly comparable to that of male Scots under England's oppressive rule, in some ways parallels Wallace's since early in life he, too, lost his father and elder brother, both killed by the English (I. 319-25); the Wallaces are also portrayed as a family counted among the gentry for generations (I. 27-32). Developments under English rule also forced Wallace to leave his paternal seat at Elderslie (I. 147-50), but there the resemblance ends, since Wallace never resorted to paying extortion to the English. Rather, he encourages active resistance from those Scots previously acquiescent to the enemy. For Mistress Braidfute, however, Hary clearly did not envisage the possibility of active resistance although later on the physical bravery of her delaying action would allow Wallace to escape from Lanark. Indeed, she pays for her activity with her life, as he will eventually pay with his. In suffering and defensive action, Wallace and Braidfute are well matched.[16] As Wallace's feminine counterpart, Mistress Braidfute lacks the strong impetus to attack and revenge that governs her future husband, his hyper-masculine aggressiveness marking him as a hero.

Initially, Wallace's courtship of Mistress Braidfute resembles a courtly love affair as he first notices her in church and then attends mass in Lanark so as to further a private meeting; courtly love affairs in medieval literature often begin with a meeting in church.[17] Hary gives us no insights into Mistress Braidfute's impressions of Wallace, except that she is apparently aware of Wallace's towering reputation as a Scottish war hero, which explains her willingness to arrange a private meeting. The use of a female dependent as a go-between and the garden through which Wallace is led to his beloved are likewise reminiscent of the courtly love affair. However, Hary justifies these romantic motifs, using them as tactics to escape English attention. Moreover, the ensuing conversation sharply contrasts with a conventional first interview between courtly lovers as Mistress Braidfute, in a reversal of courtly convention, offers Wallace her *service* (V. 686). That polysemous term can imply both more or less intimacy than *quentance*; potentially embracing politeness between equals, the subservience owed to a social and legal superior, the marital subservience of a wife, and the humility born of passionate love.[18] Mistress Braidfute is not concerned with disambiguating the term altogether, but she definitely wishes on principle to exclude one possible interpretation, service as a mistress (*leman*, V. 693). Only afterwards, when Wallace has decided to marry her, are we clearly, if briefly, told her emotional state: 'scho be chos has bath hyr luff and lord' [*for she has her beloved and her lord according to her wish*] (VI. 51). In short, Hary makes Mistress Braidfute a wife, instead of a mistress, highlighting her traits of modesty and prudence that are least consonant with traits of a mistress, and, in reporting her conversation, emphasising her determination not to become a mistress.

However, the focus of attention throughout this courtship remains firmly on Wallace, and the major emotional conflict is not between the two lovers but within Wallace himself. In contrast to Wyntoun's version, in which vengeance for his lover first impels Wallace to outright war against the English, Hary's Wallace is already so dedicated to the war that other passions and desires are not easily accommodated in his plans. Wallace's falling in love with Mistress Braidfute has been preceded by a negative mirror image of the later affair, an aborted Dalila story. While his wife eventually saves Wallace and his men from the English (VI. 119-23), the previous lover (in Perth), an anonymous *leman* and apparently of lower social status, allowed herself to be threatened and bribed into betraying Wallace. He barely escaped and only because she repented at the last moment (IV. 705-96). The lesson Wallace derives from that episode is that love makes a military leader vulnerable. His faithful follower Kerle, continuing to encourage him, points out that Mistress Braidfute's character, reputation, and social status preclude a repetition of the earlier betrayal and recommends marriage (V. 619-24, 658-9), causing Wallace first to seek and then to marry Mistress Braidfute. Their marriage constitutes a short-lived compromise between Wallace's determination as a warrior and the strength of his sexual desire, yet love does not significantly distract him from the war since its loss gives him an added incentive. His association with Mistress Braidfute has made some of her feminine vulnerability his own and the consequent pain increases his drive towards (masculine) aggression.

In his battles against the English, Wallace is motivated not only by hatred but also by his obligations towards his men, which may explain the significance of Kerle's approval of his love affair. This sense of obligation becomes even more obvious in the scene when he learns of his wife's death. Although his emotions are violent, not only shame but also the need to console and encourage his followers impel him to suppress his feelings, cut short lamentation, and channel grief into aggression (VI. 200-24). In contrast, when his friend John the Graham dies in the Battle of Falkirk, Wallace temporarily loses his mind with pain and rage and later utters an unashamedly emotional lament over the dead body (XI. 393-413, 566-82). Apparently, under the conditions envisaged by the poet, the homosocial bonding of male warriors is less liable to be subjected to rigorous emotional control than heterosexual bonding, which is essentially opposed to the warriors' necessary priorities.

Mistress Braidfute is mentioned one more time after the Lanark slayings, in the account of Wallace's negotiations with the queen of England (VIII. 1139-44, 1355-8). While courtly love is then openly denounced, Wallace's past courtship of his wife is invoked to confirm that he is in principle qualified to act as a courtly lover if he chose to do so. Defending his cause against another woman, however, Wallace recalls his courtship of his wife as youthful folly because it made him vulnerable to attack. Hary thus matches Mistress Braidfute posthumously against a living rival, contrasting Scottishness with the foreign and exotic, gentry with royalty, and modesty with courtly flirtation. The living woman advocates peace; the memory of

Wallace's wife demands war. As with Wallace's mother, the death of a woman close to the hero serves to strengthen him.

Wallace's encounter in Book VIII with the queen has no known source and can be regarded as Hary's own invention since, historically, Edward I's queen was Eleanor of Castile, while this unnamed queen is said to be of French extraction. However, in the later Middle Ages, many English queens, including Edward II's queen Isabella, were Frenchwomen, and this queen's French blood has a narrative function beyond historical identification. Although she is affiliated with Wallace's enemies, her native country of France is Scotland's ally against England, which gives her an independent point of view; she can be used to voice criticism of English treatment of Scotland, a criticism more telling than that of outright enemies of England such as Wallace.[19] Consequently, she is less afraid of Wallace than the English magnates and is willing to undertake an embassy to him at a critical point of his invasion of England.

The queen, as Hary hints with deliberate ambiguity (VIII. 1137-48), may not be acting as a peacemaker for purely political reasons. She may have fallen in love with Wallace through hearing of his reputation, in the manner of a courtly *amour lointain*. If so, her motives in seeking Wallace are therefore mixed, which may make her more dangerous. Wallace, Hary makes clear, is certainly worthy of the love of a queen, because of his military exploits and not only because of them. In contrast to the courtship scenes in Book V, Wallace on the morning of his meeting with the queen is shown from an outside point of view as a physically impressive figure in his shining and elaborate armour and allowed to demonstrate that he has mastered the grand courtly manner. In a ritual greeting, Wallace's attitude towards the queen is as contradictory as her motives in approaching him. During the council he summons immediately after the queen's arrival, he issues his men a warning to approach the ladies with extreme caution while declaring that he believes the queen's intentions to be good (VIII. 1253-4). Perhaps, in accord with conventional misogyny, he regarded the queen and her ladies as dangerous in spite of themselves.

The ensuing negotiations between Wallace and the queen take the form of the verbal duel, organised in two parts with a coda wherein Wallace's defeat of the queen is reversed. During the first half of their conversation, the queen repeatedly asserts the moral desirability of peace, in a speech rhetorically reinforced by her insistent repetition of that term. Opposing, Wallace lists both general Scottish grievances and his own losses, including the murder of his wife. Although the queen expresses sympathy and suggests these grievances can be compensated by a payment of reparation and English prayers of gratitude, Wallace insists on vengeance, his aim being a pitched battle against the English king himself. When the queen sees that bribery will get her nowhere, she changes tactics. Her second attempt at diplomacy employs courtly love strategies, and she appeals to Wallace as her supposed lover to do her service by concluding a peace treaty. Wallace rejects these courtly love rituals, and particularly 'spech off luff' (VIII. 1411), as an English ploy, for the moment including the queen among the English. Again, and this time more explicitly, courtly love is renounced and even characterised as non-Scottish.

When the queen admits defeat, Wallace at once becomes more conciliating. His final speech (VIII. 1431-42), however, although much more polite, seems to reject a role for women in diplomacy because they have no military role at all. Thus, women cannot make peace because they cannot make war. Everyone present agrees, and the queen's official diplomatic mission has failed. Yet the gold with which she failed to buy peace serves the queen well when, having retreated into a more private or semi-official function, she begins generously and freely giving gold to Scottish heralds and minstrels. While the attempt to bribe Wallace himself only offended his dignity, her giving gifts to his retainers puts him under a chivalric obligation that he finds himself unable to reject. Hary probably intends the queen's generosity to the minstrels and heralds to be taken as genuine and not designing, and Wallace's comment that even the wisest succumb to the temptation of women does not indicate the contrary (VIII. 1455). While Wallace was a match for the queen when she was trying to out-manoeuvre him, when she begins exercising her own virtue of largesse for itself (an aristocratic prerogative, feminine as well as masculine) Wallace succumbs against his better judgement and concludes the truce, which the king promptly breaks. Indeed, the queen is dangerous in herself, apart from her dangerous designs. Still, she has only temporarily weakened the hero; in the long run, his resolve never breaks.

The Wallace contains a great number of Scottish women who do not have a personal relationship, whether familial or sexualised, with the protagonist, and whom he experiences as fully supportive and, although potentially formidable in themselves, as non-threatening. However, the two linked episodes concerning Wallace's courtship and his negotiations with the queen clearly show that, in an environment so strongly determined by military obligations and patriotism, sexual passion and the feminine sex are felt as intrusive, whether the woman is a staunch Scottish patriot or an advocate of peace. Yet, there is something inevitable about the intrusion of the feminine into the world of men and the hero's resultant emotional vulnerability. The conflict of love and war, the woman and the warrior, cannot be resolved without tragic loss. Together, these two episodes express a coherent, considered view by *The Wallace*'s narrator of woman as the object of male desire.

Notes

[1] The edition used is *Hary's* Wallace: *Vita nobilissimi defensoris Scotie Wilelmi Wallace militis*, ed. by Matthew P. McDiarmid, STS, 2 vols (Edinburgh, 1968-9); see McDiarmid's introduction (I, pp. xiv-xxvi) for the dating of the poem and Hary's political affiliation. A new edition of the *Wallace* is being prepared by Anne McKim.

[2] For a discussion of the role of women in the Scottish War of Independence, focussing on Barbour's Bruce, see Roy James Goldstein, 'The Women of the Wars of Independence in Literature and History', *SSL*, 26 (1991), 271-81.

[3] X. 872-88, 1140-3.

[4] VII. 1111-15; cf. also XI. 99-101. These were both originally historical figures (see McDiarmid's notes, II, 215, 251, and 258).

[5] Cf. I. 277-96, II. 258-369, VI. 182-90.

[6] To be female, known by name, and known to associate with Wallace is apt to be dangerous. Cf. below and also the predicament of Crawford's wife (XII. 385-96).

[7] As widowed mothers, women also are able to command their sons to assist Wallace (cf. V. 349-51, also X. 677). The marital status of other women (V. 751-2, V. 1080-99, VI. 839, IX. 740) is not clarified.

[8] This, surely, is a scene not entirely free of the sexual titillation of quasi-incest and somewhat reminiscent of a story reported by Valerius Maximus, cf. *The Actis and Deidis of the Illustre and Vailzeand Campioun Schir William Wallace, Knicht of Ellerslie by Henry the Minstrel, Commonly Known as Blind Harry*, ed. by James Moir, STS, 3 vols (Edinburgh and London: Blackwood, 1884-89), II, 391, l. 273n.

[9] The prophecy of the famous seer Thomas the Rhymer concerning Wallace is witnessed by the Church, represented by the Trinitarian minister of Fail (cf. McDiarmid, II, 148).

[10] Book VIII, chapter xiii, ll. 2029-116, in the Cotton MS version (*The Original Chronicle of Andrew of Wyntoun*, ed. by F. J. Amours, STS, 6 vols (Edinburgh and London: Blackwood, 1903-14), V. 299-305); see McDiarmid, I, lxviii-lxix.

[11] For a brief discussion of this episode of *The Wallace*, see Elizabeth Walsh, 'Hary's Wallace: The Evolution of a Hero', *SLJ*, 11 (1984), 5-19 (pp. 11-14).

[12] As Sir David Lyndsay was later to do with the story of Squire Meldrum and the Lady of Gleneagles ('Squyer Meldrum' in *Sir David Lyndsay. Selected Poems*, ed. by J. Hadley Williams [Glasgow: ASLS, 2000], pp. 128-74, esp. ll. 851-1510.)

[13] cf. McDiarmid, II, 177, 183.

[14] They are described extensively in a catalogue of her virtues in the introductory portrait (V. 569-601), whereas her physical beauty (V. 607) is merely mentioned.

[15] In a position comparable to Mistress Braidfute's, a male Scottish character in *The Wallace*, William Douglas, is similarly shown buying off the English, until Wallace frees him of the necessity (VI. 771-5).

[16] On the same lines, it should be noted that there is a potential ambiguity in the word *our* in V. 676 and V. 678, quoted above. What Mistress Braidfute is saying is true of her own family, of Wallace's family, and of Scottish noble families in general (V. 679-81).

[17] For example, Troilus first sees Criseyde during the pagan equivalent of a mass (Geoffrey Chaucer, *Troilus and Criseyde*, I. 162-321, *Riverside Chaucer*, 3rd edn, ed. by Larry D. Benson (Boston: Houghton Mifflin, 1987), p. 1026).

[18] Cf. the description of the satisfactory resolution of the affair as 'that scho was maid at his commaund to bid' (VI. 45), when Wallace marries her.

[19] For a similar use of a male English character, cf. I. 430-3, III. 28-34.

3

Chrystis Kirk on the Grene and *Peblis to the Ploy*: The Economy of Gender

C. Marie Harker

> Na marchandis uncouth [...] may by ututh burgh woll na hydis or ony othir marchandyse, [...] bot gif it be fra burges.[1] [*No foreign merchants may buy wool nor hides nor any other merchandise outside the burgh, [...] unless purchased from a burgess.*]

> Na burges dwelland a landwart suld have lot nor cavill with burgesses dwelland within burgh.[2] [*No burgess living outside the burgh should speak or do business with burgesses living within the burgh.*]

> Gif ony man wytandly dois falset in mesurande or weyande of ony thyng suilk as woll [...] or swine [...] he sall pay amerciament [...][3] [*If any man does falsehood in measuring or weighing of any thing such as wool or pork he shall pay a fine.*]

Such detailed fifteenth-century Scottish parliamentary and burgh council legislation points to the pervasive trade/status-based anxiety which characterised late-medieval Scottish urban life. At the top of the burgh pyramid were the merchants, empowered to carry out national and international trade, legislators of communal behaviour, and increasingly *de facto* gentle. Throughout the fifteenth and sixteenth centuries, exigencies of the national economy served to augment their influence both nationally and locally,[4] while resistance to the increasing hegemony of that waxing merchant elite also punctuated the period.[5] Thus the Scottish burgh community was a permeable site of both social climbing and social discipline, and conflict both within those communities and between the burgh-dwellers and inhabitants of the local hinterland seems to have been endemic. Yet, oddly, two anonymous alliterative satires of the early fifteenth century,[6] 'Peblis to the Ploy' and 'Chrystis Kirk on the Grene', works insistently situated in this contested space of the burghal market, are marked more by a pervasive misogyny than any evident attention to class politics.

Most often treated as straightforward burlesques of the conventions of courtly romance, these Middle Scots companion works[7] present the spectacle of rude-mannered Lowland commoners aping the cultural practices of the nobility. In both, a festal market day offers the opportunity for non-merchant locals to array themselves, gather, flirt, dance, and fight. 'Peblis' presents the mock-heroic spectacle of rustic labourers gathering to the Peebles market from outlying villages, whilst 'wooing' and contending for their offended 'honour'. Likewise, in 'Chrystis' the activities of burghal craftsfolk, lesser indwellers of the unnamed burgh attached to the possibly fictive Christ's Kirk, are satirically transformed into a mock-romance wooing and combat of bumpkin 'champions'.

At surface, these works illustrate a wasteful and overreaching array of common folk, both rural and burghal, unsuccessfully modelling their appearances and behaviour after gentle practice. Strangely, however, these are insistently gendered works, in which sexualised *female* misbehaviour figures strongly. This seeming disjunction between the class concerns of context and the gendered concerns of text masks an underlying homology. Discursive acts of social discipline need not directly represent the sources of their concerns: rather, grounds for censure may be rendered allusively, the objects of the containment at least partly displaced. In these companion pieces, concerns anent the threat of both craftsmen newly resistant to the merchant-dominated burgh councils and a fractious rural labour force are gendered as the determinately feminine and, in particular, *sexual* misconduct of the *women* of the lower orders.

Scholarship over the past twenty years has amply demonstrated the discursive traces of misogyny as a thematics and a mode characteristic of the 'medieval'; that is, both as specific expressions and as a habit of expression, misogyny typifies much of medieval discourse. The peculiarly ahistoric, monologic quality of authoritative statements concerning women's nature and practice throughout the first fifteen centuries of the Christian West has been well described by such critics as R. Howard Bloch.[8] From the earliest patristic writers to the later scholastics, Woman exists as a defining term, the differential by which

Man is *not* of the unreasoning, the bodily, the excessive. This apparently uniform discursive tradition conditioned the abstraction of specific expressions of misogyny from the historic and contingent, rendering the discourse beyond the local and conditional, according it the status of transhistoric essence, immutable, hence beyond dispute.

However, as Michel Foucault reminds us, though discourses are constituted by histories, such a history may be subjected to deliberate erasure: most instrumental in power relations, 'sexuality is [...] capable of serving as a point of support, as a linchpin, for the most varied strategies' of social constraint.[9] Yet this 'sexuality' describes a carefully mystified *history* of its own conceptual naturalisation. We should inquire as to a discourse 'appearing historically and in specific places [...] what were the most immediate, the most local power relations at work?'(p. 97): to describe the displacement of specific and local concerns onto the essentialised and essentialising discourse of misogyny and the interests this serves. In these Scots works, so does 'misogyny', constituted by such a *constructed* sexuality, seek to erase its own history, a history of *specific* deployments in the service of specific and local interests.

Misogynist cultural production less reflects the Real than disguises it, rendering lived tensions through discursive proxies. The ready-made butts of misogynist critique serve beleaguered hegemonies, fantasising containment of such anxieties as economic pressures and changing class relations. Late-medieval Scotland's emerging market economy and reorientation of estates' relationships illustrate one such historic moment and occasion for discursive occultation. Specifically, by the early 1400s, the impact of the royal burgh, particularly its increasingly independent and restrictive merchant middle class, on class relations had become significant; resultant burghal politics are displaced onto the interpretive gridwork of misogyny in 'Peblis' and 'Chrystis Kirk'. The *ahistoric* scandal of transgressive female sexuality serves as proxy for and thus contains, if only momentarily, the distinctly *historic* class hostilities of late-medieval Scottish urban life.[10]

The settings of both works are distinguished *as* burghs by the occasion of a market day/fair no less than by references to trade, commerce, and explicitly urban dwellers.[11] Burghs, characteristically Scottish forms of urban centre which enjoyed special rights of trade monopoly and self-government,[12] are noteworthy as sites of social discipline throughout the later medieval period. The exercise and control of these privileges was the purview of the burgh council of 'free burgesses', entry to whose ranks was strictly constrained by financial and social considerations; this control enabled the emerging merchant class to amass wealth and consequent national influence.[13]

Despite such economic success, the burgh was felt to be a space under threat: its inhabitants obliged to maintain physical burgh boundaries, its visitors' entry restricted to ocular control at scrutinised gates.[14] That the majority of medieval Scottish burghs were not walled cities but at most modest berme and fosse constructions[15] must have contributed to a perception of burghal vulnerability.   The threatening entry of non-residents was thus particularly a subject of legislative concern.[16] Fears of strangers, variously described as 'vagaboundes and incomers', 'sturdie beggars or others', 'beggars and idle men', 'sornares [*beggars*], fenȝeit fooles and vagabounds', typify statutes throughout the century.[17] Significantly, it seems that such danger was associated with the necessary evil of the market: 'considdering the great evill that may fall out in the tyme of the enschewing fair'.[18] The *skathe*, or harm, represented by the outsider was concomitant with the very market through which the burgh existed.

As the physical space of the burgh was ever subject to the threat of illicit permeation, so too was the social space of caste. Burgesshood was highly contested, fraught by challenges both from within, the non-burgess craftsmen, and from without, strangers and 'uplandis men'.[19] In particular, legislation throughout the period voices fears of the unsettling liminality of the 'craftsman burgess': gradually a defining characteristic of burgesshood was the exclusion of those who worked with their hands.[20] Similarly, the penetration of burgess status by 'outlanders' also elicited anxiety.[21] Indeed, a repeated condition of burgess status was stable and demonstrable residence within the burgh walls.[22] The contradiction of a non-resident burgess threatened to unravel the definitional distinctions of the social fabric.

Thus inherent in this contested medieval Scottish burgh were contradictions and tensions which the representations of a gender/class nexus in 'Peblis' and 'Chrystis' seek to resolve. The burgh in these poems is not a site of national community, of an enabling mercantile plenitude, but rather represented as a contested site of exclusion in which varied outsiders are figured as destabilising forces. The very space which conditioned the burghs' existence and national influence — the market itself — is thus rendered as a dangerous threshold / fenestration through which the boundaries between inside and outside, self and other are made permeable. Thence the plenitude of unrestrained female sexuality is rejected as similarly labile and dangerous. The women of these two poems — penetrating boundaries of both space and class, and themselves unpredictably penetrable — serve to figure the anxieties of threatened burghal privilege.

Such women embody threats to burghal boundaries in several ways. Figured as outsiders spatially and socially, they enjoy the transient licence accorded by the disciplinary liminality of the market itself. They enter the burghal space unbidden and uncontrolled, their economic role as labourers contaminated both as wasteful, ill-judged consumers and, allusively, as retailers — the role so jealously guarded by the merchant burgess — of themselves. With satiric contempt, these poems seek to expel the outsider, conveniently configured as transgressively *feminine*.

In both texts, transgressive and consequently disciplined femininity is heralded by Pride, as the absurd and contextually resonating spectacle of the third estate expending itself in sartorial emulation of the second. This sumptuary violation serves to introduce a nexus of wilful female sexuality, pretension in dress, and class-transgression. Economic waste merges with sexual waste in a texture which offers the lower orders as Riot, loosed temporarily from social constraint by the liminal occasion of a market-fair.

The unruly peasant band tumbles into 'Peblis' under the contemptuous gaze of the indwellers, figuring contemporary concerns with specular control of burghal entry; however, the fear of the outsider is represented by the entry of transgressive women. Although rural men and women both have readied themselves for the occasions, in both poems it is *women's* dress that particularly figures pretentious excess. For example, in 'Peblis', while it is first a neuter *'thay'* who 'graythit thame [*arrayed themselves*] full gay' (l. 6)[23] in preparation for the occasion, it soon appears that it is rural *women*, the 'wenches of the west',[24] who are taking such (inappropriate) pains with their appearance. In the first of several brief character-studies in the poem, one such satiric butt is embarrassed by her unpressed kerchief, her shame an obvious social pretension.[25] The text points such nicety as self-evidently risible when, as the rustics arrive at the fair, foolishly proud to cut such figures, they elicit mockery from the watching burghal inhabitants:

> He befoir, and scho befoir,
> To se quha [*who*] wes maist gay.
> All that luikit thame upon
> Leuche [*laughed*] fast at their array.
>
> (ll. 83-6)

Although here both 'he' and 'scho' are subjected to this criticism, this class transgression is still primarily configured as feminine error, as, in the following lines: 'Sum said that thai wer merkat folk, / Sum said the Quene of May / Was cumit' (ll. 87-9). Since these rustics are explicitly not 'market folk' in the sense of merchants or craftsmen, this line must suggest either the insult of satiric inversion or, possibly, that they are 'market folk' in the sense of the beggars and tinkers, 'vagaboundes and incomers', whom the markets inevitably attracted. Yoked to the mockingly gendered May Queen reference, this class-based critique reminds us of the opening line of the work, 'At Beltane', hence the submerged fertility symbolism of the Mayday festivities -- alluding both to the evidently laughable 'finery' affected by these rural women and their ill-contained sexuality.

In 'Chrystis', the gendering of affected *superbia* is even more marked. *Women's* dress alone occupies the text's sartorial critique. '[O]ur kitteis', washed and arrayed in 'new kirtillis of gray', 'gluvis [...] of the raffell [*roe-fell*] rycht', 'schone...of the straitis',[26] and 'kirtillis [...] of lyncome licht, / Weill prest with mony plaitis', illustrate the same expensive imported goods which contemporary sources note as characteristic of the Scottish nobility and wealthier merchants. These details mirror contemporary concerns anent the ongoing inflow of imported manufactured goods, eliciting a net trade imbalance and loss of bullion, matters of considerable contemporary concern.[27] This display is presented by 'kitteis', a term frequently left unglossed and which seems to intimate a certain flirtatious, even indiscriminate, sexuality.[28] These companions of shoemakers, millers, and herdsmen (ll. 171, 181, 191) are identified by such marked names as Towsy, Mald, and Dowie (ll. 44, 54, 62), arguing sartorial pretension.[29] This representation not only satirises the absurd over-reaching of the lower members of the third estate, but enables a transference of blame for the financial excesses of the self-promoting merchant class. The topos of Woman as Waste only partly occludes that of commoner as ungoverned, a threat to the economic commonweal.

Further, the disjunction of appearance and essence which such women embody offers a sexualised reflection of burghal concerns with deceptive marketing, particularly the partial or misleading display of goods, which reappear in varied statutes throughout the period. The false representation of goods might not simply be numerical; goods could be dressed up to disguise their true quality. 'Item statutum est si contigerit quod emptor alicuius rei viderit aliquod mercimonium quod bonum sit supra et deterius subquam emendare debeat venditor rei' [*Also it is ordained, that if it happens that the buyer of any thing shall discover any of his purchase to be good above and worse below, the seller of the thing ought to amend it*].[30] The spectacle of *kitteis* in luxury apparel is likewise scandalously *bonum supra*.

Through implied luxury expenditure, feminine self-satisfaction and wastefulness merge in traditional misogynist association with wilful feminine excess of a sexual kind. In 'Peblis', the nameless woman concerned with her untidy headgear receives advice from one 'Meg' to wear a 'hude' instead (ll. 15-18). The significance of this decision proves both sexually seductive and class-marked: ensuring that the hood's 'tippet' hang down elicits the seeming *non sequitur* from an unspecified male companion, 'Thy bak sall beir a bend' (l. 23). Both a literal *ribbon* and/or a metaphoric, sexual *blow* or tightening/flexure,[31] this 'bend' promises/threatens rude sexual congress. Unable to disguise her true class-status, she is thus suggestively better fit for a rustic lover. Accordingly, her rejection, 'We meit nocht', generally glossed as a flirtatious sort of *catch me if you can* rejoinder, is multiple. The word *meit*, pronounced [meːt],[32] offers a variety of punning meanings, both recognising the male interlocutor's sexual threat and negating it with the woman's social pretension: *we are not matched* ('we are social unequals, you are below me'),[33] thus, by figurative extension, *we mate not* ('we will not have sex').

With other objects in mind, this country girl rejects her rural would-be lover. This sketch concludes with the woman distressed, unable to go to the market fair, 'amang yon merchands', on account of her sunburned appearance, another mark of both social pretension and, allusively, selfwilled and illicit feminine sexuality:

> I dar nocht cum yon mercat to,
> I am so evvil sone-brint.
> Amang yon merchands my errandis do,
> Marie, I sall anis mynt [*once mean/determine to*]
> Stand of far and keik thaim to [*peer at them*],
> As I at hame was wont.
>
> (ll. 33-8)

The class-affectation of shame at a sunburn, the mark of a rural labourer, is here combined with a specular concern lest she be seen *by the merchants*; rather, she wilfully plans to gaze on *them* without their knowledge, *as her usual practice*.

These peculiar lines have elicited little critical comment; they bear attention. She had planned to attend the market apparently to display herself to merchants, the source of burghal influence. Her appearance marred by the mark of her true status, however, she refuses to reveal herself. As her previous rejection of her peer's sexual invitation, this suggests that the 'errand' she had intended was the *marketing* of herself to an upscale clientele. Such a retail depended upon a misleading presentation; once revealed as a labourer, the peasant woman withdraws herself from display. Further, she offers a scandalous inversion of the specular balance: she would 'keik thaim to', gazing upon the unknowing merchants, rendering *them* objects of appraisal, allusively merchandise. This instance of sexualised social advancement as a species of false marketing, merchandise dressed up to disguise its true quality, again echoes issues of anxiety in the medieval Scottish burghal polity; the very activity by which the merchant-burgess was defined and from which his local and national hegemony derived, retailing, was subject to violation and discipline.[34]

Yet this figure of the peasant woman marketing herself as fit for burgess consumption speaks also to contemporary anxieties of a necessary class contamination. Though jealously protected, merchant-burgesses' membership was subject to depletion and threat from burgesses themselves. Late-medieval Edinburgh legislation points to merchants' failure properly to protect their positions by providing for heirs: several statutes attempt to prevent burgess alienation of the inherited burghal land upon which burgess status ultimately depended.[35] Similarly, burghal records attest a regular pattern of familial exhaustion by which various burgess lineages are without issue by roughly the third generation;[36] some degree of suppletion from without, including outdwelling labourers configured as the licencious women of 'Peblis' and 'Chrystis', must have been essential.

Still impugning rural femininity, the text then goes on to intimate considerably less selective female sexuality. Halfway to Peebles, 'the madinis come upon *thame*' (l. 62): the country men. This line suggests, oddly, that the crowd was separated by gender, despite the previous clear interactions between the men and women. Either this represents a *new* band of girls, or that 'come upon' indicates rather different behaviour, seemingly a wilful, sexualised voracity on the part of the 'maidens'. Nevertheless, this enthusiastic female desire occults female passivity: *male* voices offer to 'dispone' (l. 64), or *dispose,* of the women. This sexual hostility presents the overdetermined figure of the lower class woman, her sexuality scandalously wilful and simultaneously thus liable to serve uninvited masculine desire, hence will-*less*, subject to male disposal. In a burlesque treatment of romance diction, one of these men claims the 'fairest', urging his fellows to enjoy the remaining girls: 'Ane said, "The fairest fallis me; / Tak ye the laif and fone [*fondle*] thame"' (ll. 65-6). 'The fairest' is merely a sexual prize, the object of masculine agency; appropriately, the term 'fone' carried connotations not simply of physical play (i.e. fondle, tease sexually), but also of deceitful trickery.[37]

The speaker's suggestion meets with sexualised masculine approval in another countryman's rejoinder, eagerly urging his fellows, '*On* Tweddell syd, and *on* thame [the women] / Swyth! [*right away*]' (ll. 68-9). The punning instability of the preposition signals the multiple interests of the text: '*Onward* [men of the] Tweedale side, and *upon* [the women]'. Here again, the diction of romance is burlesqued by the incongruent rustic setting, but it is the diction of romance violence, of armed combat between men, rather than that of wooing fair maidens. An afternoon's dalliance simultaneously displays a displaced aggression.

The text retreats from this gendered discursive violence, returning at this point to an evenhanded sexual license, 'he to ga and scho to ga' (l. 71) and insisting that none were reluctant: 'never ane bad, "Abyd ye"' (l. 72).[38] Yet this assertion of equal desire is unconvincing against the hostility to the feminine which characterises the following scene. In a moment of sheer bawdry, 'ane winklot', which term one editor has unhelpfully claimed as a diminutive form of 'wench', another as 'a young girl',[39] falls, evidently exposing her genitals in the process, to censure by one of her female companions:

> 'Ane winklot fell and her taill up,
> 'Wow,' quod Malkin, 'hyd yow!
> Quhat neidis you to maik it sua?
> Yon man will not owrryd you'.
>
> (ll. 73-6)

This seeming modesty of the speaker seems thus to stem from feminine jealousy, with male sexual interest as the prize: '*no point in such open advertisement of sexual availability: he'll not over-ride [have intercourse with] you regardless*'. The fallen girl's response continues in a similar vein, criticising Malkin's nicety: 'Ar ye owr gude [...] / To lat thame gang besyd you [...]?' (ll. 78-9). She points her peer's sexual restraint as a symptom of the same exaggerated self-worth and class-pretension exhibited by the earlier Meg: both self-determined feminine sexuality at the service of a hoped-for social advancement.

At the conclusion of the Peblis market, the drinking and dancing done, a final passage infused with class commentary draws together these twin themes of an overdetermined female sexuality, satirised for both the overeasy access of the peasant wench and an affected fastidious resistance marking class-pretension. A final character, a miller eponymously 'Will Swane', thus explicitly a *wilful*, even sexualised, 'swain' or parodically bucolic lover, calls indiscriminately to 'the wenschis' (l. 205), 'Gude gossep, come hyn your gaitis' (l. 207), a line recently glossed as *come hence your ways*.[40] Additionally, however, this invitation points social class: 'hyn' suggesting the substantive, 'hyne', from the OE *hine*, or domestic / farm-worker, thus a direct address to the 'wenches' in terms of economic position.   The miller, on the other hand, is implicitly of a relatively elevated class status as suggested by his face freckling in the sun (l. 212), the beneficiary of an occupation less exposed to the elements than field labour.

His invitation meets with success, as Will Swane is seized by 'Tisbe', or the parodically inappropriate *Thisbe*.   A labourer in the flax trade, 'new cuming fra the heckill' (l. 213), i.e. *hackle* or flax comb, she abandons her role in the rural economy, leaving her work in order to take advantage of the miller's offer, thus enacting the nexus of class overreaching, sexual licence, and economic wastefulness.   The burghal economy depended upon a regular supply of both retail goods from the *uplandis,* or hinterland, and labour from within the burgh.   Consequently, craftsmen who attempted to find alternative employment were subject to burghal discipline: for example, such labourers as Thisbe were warned, 'Gif ony kemestaris [*combsters*] levis the burgh [...] havand sufficient works to occupie thaim within burgh, thai aw to be takyn and prisonyt'.[41]

Here again, the rural woman's wilful sexual availability is compounded with an overnice and class-affected compunction for appearances:

> 'Allace!' quod scho, 'Quhat sall I do?
> And our doure hes na stekill!'[*latch*]
> And scho to ga as hir taill brynt,
> And all the cairlis to kekill
> At hir.
>
> (ll. 213-17)

Though ready to offer herself to the 'swain', to exchange herself in this sexualised marketplace, like both Meg and the earlier 'winklot', she is reluctant to reveal her sexuality openly.   Her hesitation to engage in sexual acts in the absence of privacy is but momentary: the absurdity of this careful self-presentation is pointed by Tisbe's obvious immoderation, going 'as hir taill brynt', the connotations of a burning 'taill' indicating an insistent sexual desire. This unbridled and distinctly lower-class feminine sexuality, despite class-conscious pretensions to pale skin and latched doors, is identifiable even to the least discerning of observers, the 'cackling' carls, her fellow-labourers.

In the same fashion, in 'Chrystis', misogynist discourse moves seamlessly from social pretension to sexual wilfulness. The freshly washed and kirtilled *kitties* of the first stanza become, in the alliterative epithet of the next, 'lassies licht of laitis' (l. 12), that is, *light of behaviour/manners*. Most often glossed as a sort of physical lightness, a lithe and dancing quality,[42] the metaphoric sense of 'light' as insubstantial morally, especially of women, is attested in Middle Scots since the late fourteenth century.[43] The next several lines return to detailing the 'damsellis' costly, affected dress, and conclude by again drawing attention to feminine sexuality: 'Thay wer so nyss quhen men thame nicht / Thay squeilit lyk ony gaitis' (ll. 17-18). Here modern editors have proffered rather innocent glosses, translating *nyss*, for example, as 'skittish' or 'giddy'.[44] Yet this reaction to male proximity, in collocation with the allusion of *squealing like goats*, animals long associated with lustfulness, is a sexualised sense, meaning something like *wanton, loose.*[45]

The motif of a socio-economically self-promoting feminine sexuality connects the two works. Here 'Gillie' is at first a parodic heroine sworn, in burlesque treatment of the motif of doomed ballad love-affairs, to love 'sweit Willie', despite strong familial opposition: 'thocht all hir kin had sworn hir deid' (l. 27). Her wooing by one 'Jok', then, is clearly doomed. Burlesque of this romance idiom is clear with her class-marked response in illicit speech, the flyting of the streets: 'Scho skornit Jok and skraipit at him / And murionit him with mokkis' (ll. 31-2). *Skorn*ing was a form of jeering explicitly associated with the rejection of proffers of love; possibly deriving from Fr. *escorner*, or a 'horned' state, this too suggests female sexual licence.[46] And *murjon*ing was not simply mockery, but a jeering through a grotesque physical contortion,[47] the romance heroine made monstrous through her physical wilfulness.

At this point the literary parody dissolves into a vision of distinctly venial feminine sexuality: it is apparently Jok's *economic* status, rather than any romantic faithfulness, which occasions Gillie's disdain: 'Scho *comptit* him nocht twa clokkis; / Sa schamefully his schort gown set him' (ll. 36-7; emphasis mine). Here is the language of the market: having accounted the value of a would-be suitor found lacking for his ill-fitting clothes, a sure sign of economic ill-health, a lower-class woman rejects him vigorously with her ungoverned tongue. Moreover, the measure of his worthlessness, 'twa clokkis',[48] suggests the mercantile nature of her disdain. He is not worth two *cloaks*; this points both his inadequate dress and alludes to the rural cloth industry, an important source of Scottish capital. In the succeeding lines, the shame of his short gown is revealed as legs 'lik twa rokkis [*distaffs*]' (l.38); this critique participates in the romance burlesque, yet also reminds us of Gillie's proper occupation and contribution to the economic commonweal, activity which she is patently neglecting in her mercantile bid to self-advancement.

'Chrystis Kirk on the Grene' and 'Peblis to the Ploy' thus offer a binary model of female sexuality as either will-less and indiscriminating, available to all for nothing, or self-willed and socially self-promoting, available at a price, an allusive prostitution in exchange for social climbing. The constellations of feminine pride, sexual wilfulness, whether restrictive or indiscriminate, and the consequent status violation which these two poems present invite historicised interrogation. Although 'continuing and long-standing medieval literary and philosophical traditions'[49] should temper any assertions of topicality, we nonetheless should not dismiss the nexus of class-containment and misogyny in 'Peblis' and 'Chrystis Kirk' as *merely* traditional. Not least as these texts insist upon their *locality*, their social and spatial specificity.

The two poems discursively mystify burghal networks of social transgression and discipline: the extramural constraint of the nonresident and the intramural constraint of the craftsmen. In 'Chrystis Kirk', it is specifically craftsmen who are satirised for their aristocratic pretensions, while merchants remain a revealingly absent presence within the poem. 'Peblis' figures the dangerous spatial and social permeability of the burgh: of necessity, a market invites the presence of the foreigner, the not-self, as the condition of its success. Such burghal non-residents as the 'wenches of the west' and their companions threaten the stability of the burgh both by class resistance and class-masquerade.

In both works, feminine misbehaviour represents these very groups most constrained by burghal merchant influence. The invitation of the goatish girls and the unbounded sexual plenitude of the *taill*-exposed 'winklot' are no less objects of satiric containment than the pretentious selectivity and prudery of their less accessible peers. The peasant/lower-class woman is thus an overdetermined site of misbehaviour, her sexuality insistently at issue. If indiscriminately, even passively, available to general masculine desire, rather than a sign of festival fertility, she evidences the riotous license of the lower orders. While if discriminatingly presented for appraisal only by the burghal elite, she embodies the threat of social indeterminacy, that a peasant woman may indeed be 'meit' for the only recently gentle merchant. Further, the masquerade of gentility and wealth that the finely-arrayed lower-class women enact offers to blur the distinction between burgess and non-burgess. In a setting of highly-regulated and deeply contentious burghal trade, the commodity offered without permission, without sale, is rendered devoid of value, while the merchandise mislabelled, dressed up as superior goods, signals the instability of class distinctions. In 'Peblis' and 'Chrystis', the necessary permeability of the burgh and its market is configured as the scandalous permeability and indeterminacy of the unruly female body.

Notes

[1] *Leges Burgorum* (*LB*) in *Ancient Laws and Customs of the Burghs of Scotland 1184-1424*, ed. by C[osmo] Innes, 2 vols (Edinburgh: Burgh Records Society, 1868), I, 9.

[2] *Curia Quatuor Burgorum*, in *Ancient Laws*, p.157.

[3] *LB*, p. 33.

[4] Ranald Nicholson, *Scotland: the Later Middle Ages* (Edinburgh: Oliver and Boyd, 1974), pp. 264-8; Jenny Wormald, *Court, Kirk, and Community* (London: Edward Arnold, 1981), pp. 10-13, 42-5.

[5] Wormald, pp. 48, 50.

[6] Attempted attribution of the poems rests inconclusively between two Scottish kings, James I and V; the weight of tradition supports the former, placing the works *ante* 1437.

[7] In addition to close formal similarity, 'Chrystis Kirk' refers to the other work in its opening lines:

> Was nevir in Scotland hard nor sene
> Sic dansing nor deray,
> Nowthir at Falkland on the grene
> Nor *Peblis at the Play* [...]

[8] R. Howard Bloch, *Medieval Misogyny and the Invention of Western Romantic Love* (Chicago: U Chicago P, 1991).

[9] Michel Foucault, *The History of Sexuality*, trans. by Robert Hurley, 2 vols (New York: Vintage, 1978), I, 103.

[10] The works' most recent editor argues a mid-fifteenth-century composition date. *The Christis Kirk Tradition: Scots Poem of Folk Festivity*, ed. by Allan MacLaine (Glasgow: ASLS, 1996), p. 150. Precise dating (cf. 6n. *supra*), is unnecessary for this analysis: through the fifteenth and into the sixteenth century, the Scottish burgh dominated national and local trade, exerting

strangling legislative hegemony over both non-burgess indwellers and the rural environs.

[11] At least one of the two settings, Peebles, was an historic royal burgh; G. S. Pryde, *The Burghs of Scotland: a Critical List* (Glasgow: OUP, 1965), p. 6.

[12] I. F. Grant, *Economic History of Scotland* (1934; Rpt. Edinburgh: John Donald, 1979), p. 72; T. C. Smout, *A History of the Scottish People: 1560-1830* (NY: Scribner's, 1969), p. 158; W. Croft Dickinson, *Scotland: from the Earliest Times to 1603*, 3rd edn (Oxford: Clarendon, 1977), p. 104; Theodora Keith, 'The Trading Privileges of the Royal Burghs of Scotland', *English Historical Review*, 28 (1913), 454, *passim.*

[13] This influence derived from twin strategies of loans to the chronically impoverished crown and marriage into the lower gentry. Dickinson, p. 111; Elizabeth Gemmill and Nicholas Mayhew, *Changing Values in Medieval Scotland* (Cambridge: CUP, 1995), p. 379.

[14] Cf. *Early Records of the Burgh of Aberdeen: 1317, 1398-1407*, ed. by W.C. Dickinson (Edinburgh: Scottish Burgh Record Society, 1957), p. xxv; *Extracts from the Records of the Burgh of Peebles: 1652-1714*, ed. by R. Renwick (Glasgow: Scottish Burgh Record Society, 1910), p. xvi.

[15] Dickinson, p. xxix; Elizabeth Ewan, *Townlife in Fourteenth-Century Scotland* (Edinburgh: EUP, 1990), p. 8.

[16] Grant, *Economic*, pp. 113-17.

[17] Dickinson, p. liii; Renwick, pp. 9, 28, 59; I. F.Grant, *The Social and Economic Development of Scotland Before 1603* (Edinburgh: Oliver and Boyd, 1930; rpt. Westport, CT: Greenwood, 1971), p. 562; 2.24, 2.30 in *The Lawes and Acts of Parliament Made by King James the First* [...] *of Scotland*, Part I. ed. by David Lindsay, (n.p.: [n. pub.], 1682.

[18] Renwick, p. 130.

[19] Dickinson, p. 279; Smout, pp. 159-60.

[20] *LB*, p. 46.

[21] For example, in Glasgow some hundred years later, varied municipal statutes attempted to constrain entry to burgesshood through restrictive fees, considering 'the greit inconvenient done to the towne, throw the multitude of strangers cumand to be burgesses'; the perception of the threat of the outsider can be seen in such observations of these strangers, 'throw the quilk the towneschip is abill [*likely*] to be opprest'. *Burgh Records of the City of Glasgow 1573-1581*, ed. by John Smith (Glasgow: Maitland Club, 1832-4), pp. 17, 73.

[22] Cf. *Extracts of the Records of the Burgh of Edinburgh: A.D. 1528-1557*, ed. by James D. Marwick and Marguerite Wood, 11 vols (Edinburgh: Scottish Burgh Record Society, 1871), II, 71, 94.

[23] All text citations from MacLaine.

[24] The rural folk are later identified as the youth of 'Hopcalye and Cardronow' (l. 41), villages within Peebles' burghal district. MacLaine, p. 151; *Poetic Remains of Some of the Scotish Kings*, ed. by George Chalmers (London: J. Murray, 1824), p. 108.

[25] Cf. a late-fifteenth-century noble fashion in headgear for stiffened kerchiefs spread over frames. Cited in *Early Travellers in Scotland*, ed. by P. Hume Brown (1891; rpt. NY: Burt Franklin, 1970), p. 47.

[26] Straights -- i.e. of Gibraltar, i.e. Morroccan leather.

[27] Cf. my extended discussion in '"Chrystis Kirk o' the Grene": Dialogic Satire in Fifteenth-Century Scotland', in *The European Sun*, ed. by Graham Caie, and others (East Linton: Tuckwell), pp. 300-8.

[28] Chalmers notes, 'from the Fr. *Catin* [...] for a mistress', p. 137.

[29] All connote visual carelessness and disarray -- allusively, sexual availability and indiscrimination: Towsy derives from *touse*, to dishevel, esp. hair, *Etymological Dictionary of the Scottish Language*, [*EDSL*], ed. by John Jamieson and others (Paisley: A. Gardner, 1879); Mald, possibly var. of *Maud*, echoes with both *malt* n. and *maldy* n., e.g. *medley*, a cheap particoloured cloth, a usage current from the mid-fifteenth century (*EDSL*); Dowie, var. of *Dolly*, means dismal, exhausted in apppearance or demeanor (*DOST* a., 1).

[30] *Statuta Gilda*, in *LB*, I, 77.

[31] MacLaine, p. 151; *DOST*, n.[1] 1, 3.

[32] A. J. Aitken, 'How to Pronounce Older Scots', in *Bards and Makars*, ed. by A. J. Aitken, M. P. McDiarmid, and Derick S. Thompson (Glasgow: UGP, 1977), p. 3.

[33] Usage recorded in Middle Scots from the fourteenth century, *DOST*, a.[1] 2.

[34] For example, *regrating*, the practice of retailing by purchasing goods for subsequent retail at or near the original purchase site, was a signal abuse, blurring the boundaries between the merchant and customer. Cf. Edinburgh proscriptions, Marwick and Wood, II, *passim*.

[35] Marwick, pp. 13-14.

[36] Ewan, p. 117.

[37] Cf. William Dunbar's 'Tretis of the Tua Mariit Wemen and the Wedo', in *Poems of William Dunbar*, ed. by Priscilla Bawcutt, 2 vols (Glasgow: UGP, 1998), I, 41-55 (l. 274).

[38] This MacLaine glosses, misleadingly, as 'You wait behind' (p. 4).

[39] *Peblis to the Play*, ed. by A.M. Kinghorn (London: Quarto, 1974); MacLaine p. 4. The term is solely attested by 'Peblis'.

[40] MacLaine, p. 8.

[41] *LB*, p. 50.

[42] Cf. Chalmers: 'light of limbs, nimble', p. 138; MacLaine: 'lively of manners', p. 11.

[43] *OED*, a.14b (c. 1375).

[44] Chalmers, p. 140; MacLaine, p. 11.

[45] Attested in Middle Scots in James I's 'Kingis Quhair', *OED*.

[46] *EDSL*; Jamieson confusingly observes of this etymology, 'to deprive of horns, hence to disgrace', but disgrace is the state of *possessing* horns, of being a cuckold: 'skorn' may derive from *ascorner*.

[47] *DOST*, n. a, b.

[48] Consistently and uncritically glossed as 'two beetles'.

[49] R. J. Lyall, 'Politics and Poetry in Fifteenth and Sixteenth Century Scotland', *SLJ*, 3.2 (1976), 5.

4

Women Fictional and Historic in Sir David Lyndsay's Poetry

Janet Hadley Williams

In *The Dreme* (c.1526) and *The Testament and Complaynt of our Soverane Lordis Papyngo* (1530), Sir David Lyndsay gives women salient roles, and in the *The Deploratioun of the Deith of Quene Magdalene* (c. 1537), produces a public statement of mourning for a woman. Yet overall Lyndsay's masculine focus is noticeable, especially in his earlier writing for his first intended audience and recipient, young James V of Scots. A shared male viewpoint, that of the king and his personal servant, is a literary strategy Lyndsay uses frequently to introduce or develop his case, as in *The Answer* [...] *to the Kingis Flyting* (c. 1535-36), or *Ane Supplication* [...] *in Contemptioun of Syde Taillis* (c. 1539-41). No corresponding female focus, however, appears in the poetry composed during the minority of James's daughter Mary, although Lyndsay, as Lyon King of Arms, retained a close link to the monarch and her deputies, James Hamilton, second Earl of Arran, and Marie de Guise-Lorraine, Mary's mother. Lyndsay shows some awareness of his bias when he laments his inability to address a child queen who presently 'dwellith in France' (*Ane Dialog betuix Experience and ane Courteour* (1553), 'Epistil', l. 13).[1] In her absence, he pointedly directs his work to the acting leaders of state and church resident in Scotland, James Hamilton and his brother John, archbishop of St Andrews (ll. 24-8). That both are male is not central to Lyndsay's point, but rather that they are adult leaders assumed to possess the knowledge to govern wisely and the responsibility to put that knowledge into practice, while Mary as yet cannot.

Granted that Lyndsay most often has a masculine focus or outlook, he nonetheless represents a rich assortment of women. They include stereotypic figures either allegorised as virtues and vices or non-allegorised, and one-dimensional female 'chorus' voices; these figures perhaps fuelled the long debate about Lyndsay's 'contempt of women'.[2] Yet Lyndsay also presents images of women as moral and ethical advisers of authority, contemporary figures named or unnamed, noble and not. Astute judges of character or situation and thus trustworthy witnesses, these advisors possess plain good sense or so deftly handle life's everyday complexities that, in thought and action, they compare favourably with the idealised fictional or legendary women invoked as the standard of perfection. A more balanced study of Lyndsay's portrayals of and attitudes towards women is thus necessary for an accurate and just evaluation of his work.

Analyses of three 'snapshots' of Lyndsay's women provide a cautionary preface to this study. In one, the poet catches 'cruikit carlingis [*lame old women*]' just as they 'get speche' after medical treatment by, purportedly, the king's 'nobill Leche', John Barbour (*Iusting*, ll. 15-16); in another, 'wyffis of the village' as they cry at the sight of the thieving magpie in their meadows (*Papyngo*, l. 712); and in a third, 'Uirginis, and [...] lustie burges wyiffis' as they line Edinburgh's streets to welcome the new Queen, their appearance 'celestiall' and their song a 'Harmonious sound Angelicall' (*Deploratioun*, ll. 155-8). In each image the women differ in social level, age, role, and mood, but all are energetic and opinionated. Such pictures are easily misunderstood without regard for genre and contemporary context; they must inform perceptions of the poet's responses to women.

The first example is from *The Iusting betuix [...] Watsoun and [...] Barbour* (c.1538-40), a poem of the mock-tournament genre. This generic context hints that the allusion to the old women's apparent 'cure' may not be straightforward in sense or tone; contemporary accounts provide support for this since John Barbour was not fictional but a real servant, whose office as groom of the wardrobe at James V's court[3] made him humorously unsuitable for both his roles in Lyndsay's poem as 'leche' [*physician*] and knightly jouster. Moreover, the old women Barbour is said to have treated are described as lame, not dumb, and their reported flow of words is thus less likely a joyful confirmation of a miraculous cure than curses exposing a medical charlatan. In keeping with his mock-heroic genre, Lyndsay is ridiculing the unskilled Barbour, not these unlucky women. Similarly, the 'snapshot' of the irate village wives does not illustrate the stereotype that women are scolds but is an opportunity for ironic comment on the magpie (*Papyngo*, ll. 656-60) who, on the basis of his black and white plumage, has declared himself an Augustinian canon. Through the eyes of these aggrieved women, the bird-cleric is revealed as an unprincipled plunderer who will seize domestic ducks and drakes as of right. In this satiric context, the women's cries add fuel to Lyndsay's exposure of the acquisitive and uncaring Church. Generic awareness also transforms the final image, from the *Deploratioun*. Without that awareness, the abundant superlatives describing the rejoicing women appear as evidence of Lyndsay's misogynistic outlook, either as his self-betraying wry comment on earthly women's inability to be divinely harmonious, or as an allusion to the popular 'impossibility' poem, which often expressed in terms of opposites an uncomplimentary attitude towards women.[4] Impressions of antifeminism dissolve, however, when these lines are considered generically, for such idealising terms were expected in the formal funeral lamentation.[5] Yet, in mourning the newly-married young queen's premature death, Lyndsay also modifies that convention. Using superlatives to 'recall' the unrealised joyousness of the Scotswomen's reception of the queen, Lyndsay emphasises the fervour of present sorrow. The necessity for generic and sometimes historical sensitivity when assessing these briefest of Lyndsay's female images is salutary preparation for the study of his longer portrayals of women both fictional and historical: two fictional women, the guide to the central vision of *The Dreme* and the articulate parrot-courtier of the *Testament of the Papyngo,* and two historical women, Madeleine de Valois and Marjorie Lawson.

First impressions of the *Dreme*'s female guide link her with courtly love. Describing her in traditional terms as 'of portratour perfyte', the melancholy dreamer notes his own reverential response to her beauty: 'I [...] of hir presens had delyte' and 'Tyl hir [...I] maid humyl reuerence' (ll. 150-1).[6] The lady herself undermines the expectation of courtliness, signaling the vision's didactic emphasis, by identifying herself as 'Dame Remembrance' (l. 154). Through this personified female counselor, Lyndsay adds his poem to others ultimately deriving from Boethius' *de Consolatione Philosophiae.* Boethius' authority figure, Lady Philosophy, had become by Lyndsay's day the model for the sympathetic and wise guide of many fictional philosophic examinations of real-life problems. Yet, by using the name Remembrance, Lyndsay also connects the *Dreme* fruitfully to *speculum principis* literature, wherein the mental faculty of memory was often important.[7] Memory was known from the classical era as an aspect of Prudence, one of the four virtues afterwards called the Cardinals. Prudence was traditionally depicted as a triple-eyed woman[8] for her three parts, memory, intelligence and foresight.[9] On this basis, Lyndsay's Dame Remembrance is a personification especially appropriate for dream interaction with the troubled narrator, who is so closely allied with the listening figure of the youthful king: she is clear-sighted in her comments on those imprudent in their past conduct, and wise in her instructions for the dreamer's future behaviour. Against this context and background, the lady's stylised courtly beauty does not distract from the poem's advisory matter.

Dame Remembrance is not a solitary allegorical figure but is supported, and her role extended, by a small network of other positively-presented female personifications, each helping to animate the *Dreme*'s advisory messages. Dame Nature and Dame Fortune, for instance, are cited in the narrator's concluding admonitions to the king as the sources of his physical gifts and material wealth (ll. 1046-51). References to these two, familiar in many literary works of the period and earlier, had many common details; thus Lyndsay's presentation of Fortune as beneficent, rather than as the more usual 'ay in variance' (as in, for example, *The Kingis Quair*, ll. 1111-55),[10] is a choice inviting notice. The portrayal of Justice as a woman had also become traditional;[11] its use in the dream's final section, 'The Complaynt of the Comoun Weill of Scotland', would seem unremarkable. Yet, as the only female figure among the many other personified qualities John the Commoun Weill mentions, including 'Plane wrang', 'Laute', 'Couatyce', and 'Deuotioun', Lyndsay's Justice also attracts attention (ll. 950-1, 980-2). Moreover, the poet signals her importance through kinship: she is sister to John, a figure of the kingdom's health and wealth (l. 948). A Cardinal Virtue like Prudence, Justice had been given prominence by other late medieval writers in the *speculum principis* tradition: Gilbert Hay, for example, called the quality 'the fairest vertu that is in a prince'.[12] Lyndsay endorses this attitude, his semi-dramatising allegory adding to the Virtue a sense of immediacy.

These allegorical women also further the poem's thematic and structural unity. Most significantly, these women link Remembrance, the counsellor within the dream vision, to the Virtue with which she is closely associated, Prudence, who is prominent in the poem after the dream has ended. Within the concluding 'Exhortatioun to the Kyngis Grace', in a list of the Cardinal Virtues set out for the king (ll. 1064-7), only Prudence is portrayed as a woman. Thus, as female personification, Prudence provides a bridge between the non-visionary, active world of James V and that larger philosophical dream cosmology of the personified Remembrance, with all that the connection implies for James's education as ruler.

Guiding their descent into Hell, Remembrance mentions or shows to the dreamer several non-allegorical images of women, among them sufferers who are self-condemning in their cries for former 'lustis delectabyll' (l. 291). Because of their vicious lives, these stereotypic 'Emprices, Quenis, and ladyis of honoris' are 'plungit in paine' in a 'den full dolorous' (l. 267, 271, 239). Their lechery, concludes the rapidly-instructed dreamer, has 'Brocht mony ane man to infelicitie' (ll. 280). Lyndsay's blame-apportioning phrase, alluding to the late medieval debate called the *querelle des femmes*, is a marker by which he groups these suffering women with those, in the image of Eve, who were thought to deserve admonition and denigration as the lures to men's destruction.[13] Again, however, Lyndsay is not thereby necessarily misogynistic since in this hell men, particularly spiritual and secular leaders, heavily outnumber women.[14] Instead, Lyndsay uses rhetorical conventions associated with the idea of women's evil nature to support his point that noble lineage, power, or sex, cannot exempt any human from divine punishment for immoral behaviour, sexual or other, public or personal.[15] This point is important to Lyndsay; he returns to it later in portraying the partly-legendary Semiramis (*Ane Dialog*, ll. 2811-3264; 2945-76). In similar fashion he does not simply condemn the queen for being sexually licentious and wicked,[16] but praises her courage repeatedly (ll. 3119-62, 3223), thus indicating that he was not adopting but adapting the familiar anti-feminist stance for his own discussion of the nature of good rule by either sex. Since Scotland then had a female monarch, his heedful analysis of the reasons for an earlier queen's downfall was an activity appropriate, if contentious.

During the following ascent through the spheres, Remembrance again shows the dreamer less positive female portraits, but their purposes are advisory, not misogynistic. The poet conventionally designates as female both the Moon and Venus, selecting carefully from their traditional attributes. In other portraits he echoes planetary descriptions in Henryson's *Testament*,[17] but here he departs from the portrayal of the Moon as a sibling-borrower of light 'at hir brother, / Titan' (ll. 258-9) so as to present both Moon and Phebus as monarchs.[18] These sovereigns have unequal power, Lyndsay explains, since the Moon obtains her light from 'the reflex of Phebus bemes brycht' (l. 390). While their relative status reflects the then-current idea of man's 'rightful' dominance over woman, Lyndsay is also illustrating a point of princely counsel, that a monarch who relies solely on, or is in an unequal relationship with, another monarch lacks real power and is a defective model of kingship. Similarly, Lyndsay portrays Venus, whose beauty '[s]wagis [*assuages*] the wraith of Mars, that god of Yre' (l. 413), as a promoter of peace, not as the more usual inconstant wanton who can be identified with Fortune. Nonetheless, that she offers another monarchical model with limitations is underlined in other details Lyndsay uses from Henryson: Venus is also '[p]rouocatiue with blenkis [*looks*] amorous' (*Test. Cresseid*, l. 226, *Dreme*, ll. 407, 416) and unstable ('full of variance', *Test. Cresseid*, ll. 224-35; *Dreme*, 'variabyll', l. 411).

At the climax of the dreamer's ascent, the view of the 'hevin Impyre', the dreamer sees the Virgin Mary seated beside Christ in his 'Sege

Royall' (ll. 514, 548). Lyndsay does not refer to Mary by her personal name, but as the 'Quene of Quenis' (l. 554), his indirectness not anti-Marian but according with other titles commonly used, such as 'quene of angellis' and 'qwene of hevyn'.[19] These titles define Mary through her relationship to her son, and exalt her above other women because her virgin impregnation excluded her from sexual sin. Lyndsay's collocation, by contrast, emphasises that the many male and female earthly monarchs mentioned within the vision are all subordinate to their divine equivalents. This was familiar advice, but Lyndsay's inclusiveness was less common, as evident in, for instance, John Ireland's similar but male-focussed 'quotation' of Daniel on Nebuchadnezzar's dream: 'the stane that come fra the hill [...] signifyis that all king and prince suld [...] submyt him to god that is king of kingis'.[20]

The female parrot of Lyndsay's *Testament of the Papyngo* is more deftly drawn and more complex than the poet's earlier figures of Remembrance and others, her female sex a teasing, sometimes crucial, part of this complexity. Her role is underpinned and her connotations as female enlarged by a witty literary allusiveness to classical and contemporary works.[21] The mortally-wounded bird has, for instance, serio-comic affinities with Henryson's Cresseid; the papyngo's four-stanza complaint to Fortune echoes wording in Cresseid's lament.[22] Both could be described as 'fallen women', although for the bird that might be seen as a literal as well as figural reference to her prideful fall from a tree-top onto a broken-off twig. Further, the papyngo is both a beautiful female among her avian kind and a courtier with a sex less well defined, who in her second epistle addresses her 'brether' at court as a bird ('Syne wantit wyngis', l. 366), but not distinctively as woman or man. And while she is an imaginary creature, the bird, at the same time, is not necessarily a complete fiction: a parrot is not listed in surviving records until 1538, but exotic birds had long been part of the royal Scottish household.[23]

As woman and bird, the papyngo's relationships with her royal audience and with the poet-narrator are complex. Although the king is silent, both he and the poet-narrator seem involved in, even pivotal to, her story, and the parrot's testament intimates as well a sexual aspect in the relationship.[24] Between them, the poet and the bird recount how the parrot was '[p]resentit' to James V who, having 'had delyte' in her 'lang tyme', gave her 'in gouernyng' to the poet-narrator (ll. 81-4) who so enjoyed the bird's company that he carried her everywhere on his hand. Recalling the sport of hawking, this image offers insight into the nature of the bird's relationship with the narrator and, it is hinted, with her royal owner. In the sport, the falconer bears on his hand the hunting bird, curbed from independent action by leashed jesses until the falconer frees the bird to do his bidding. Within Lyndsay's poem, the image implies that the parrot is, similarly, an agent for her trainer and perhaps for the king who appointed him. The form of her agency, however, is fitting for a speaking parrot: she is his mouthpiece.

Yet, once introduced, this suggestion of the bird as agent is undermined with a playful calculation in which sexual differencing sometimes is an element. In his catalogue of the parrot's many talents, for instance, the narrator takes care to separate skills he has taught her, 'language artificall' or imitative speech, and the dance tunes *Platfute* and *Fute Before* which she performs and whistles, from those abilities he ascribes to her 'Inclynatioun naturall' (ll. 86-91). These latter include mimicry of the voices of other birds and animals, acrobatic skills that enable her to '[c]lym on ane corde', and the ability to 'laugh and play the fule' (l. 97). The tongue-in-cheek aside with which the latter talents are qualified, that 'Scho mycht haue bene ane menstrall agane ȝule' (l. 98), fleetingly re-establishes her equivocal human status as it ridicules the parrot-like antics of the court entertainer in hopes of reward. Once the poet-narrator has set the bird on a branch, however, she asserts her independence and with it her feminine and avian differences from her male 'gouernor'. Her subsequent actions are among those presented earlier as 'naturall' and to a small extent are also those of a vain, pretty, and provocative woman: she begins to climb to the topmost twist of the tree and there, with 'wyng displayit' she sits 'full wantounlie' (ll. 162-3). Disregarding the narrator's warnings that she is plump, unused to flying, and could not cope with predators, the bird states that it is her 'kynd to clym, aye, to the hycht: / Off fedther and bone, I watt weill, I am wycht' (ll. 162-3). Her display of defiance does not denote the poet's sexual antagonism but rather foreshadows the result applicable to man, woman, or bird, of pridefully ignoring good counsel. Yet, significantly, the parrot is 'at liberty' when she answers the narrator and when a gust of wind causes her fatal fall: this freedom allows the tearful poet-narrator to assert his own male independence from her. In the tradition of the *chanson d'aventure*, the narrator describes how he drew under a hawthorne 'to heir [her lament] and se, and be vnsene' (l. 189), as the bird first swoons and then begins the complaint to Fortune that echoes Cresseid's.[25]

The fictions of her kind and of her independence from the trickily separate narrator are most fully developed in the poem's final and longest section, 'The Commonyng' between the papingo and her bird-executors. In this wholly avian world, which has affinities with Henryson's world in the *Fables* and his use of moral satire and delicate comedy, the parrot's distinctive voice and viewpoint expose and oppose those of the clerical-predatory birds. Yet the parrot's sex also takes a part, for Lyndsay uses it to emphasise her vulnerability as, alone and injured, she faces not the succour of the Church but exploitation by its corrupt and acquisitive male representatives. When at their request she lists the steps by which the Church has degenerated, her viewpoint as a woman strengthens the satire. Although such observations as 'The Prelatis spowsit wer with pouertie / [...] And with hir generit Lady Chaistitie' (ll. 794-6) are allegorically conventional, that she is female reinforces her assertion that the 'Systeris of the schenis [*Sciennes*]' [26] and their convent are 'ʒit vnthrall / To dame Sensuall' (ll. 919-25). Further, as female the parrot seems possessed of gender-privileged information when she accuses her male spiritual advisers of their sexual misuse of power: 'ʒe haif maid a hundreth thousand huris, / Quhilkis neuir hade bene, war not ʒour lychorus luris' (ll. 1063-4).

Matters involving male and female attitudes and identities have an essential role, moreover, in the savagely comic satire of the moments before the parrot's death. Promising to fulfil 'hir [testamentary] intent', the bird's raptor-executors try to emphasise their sincerity in terms of maternal bonds: 'We salbe to ʒow trew, as tyll our Mother' (ll. 1078-9). As birds, however, all three were known traditionally for thievery, greed, guile, garrulity, and unfaithfulness, not for their respect for such kinship ties;[27] also, as clerics their relationship to the Mother Church they purport to love and represent has been revealed as similarly deceitful. In her testament, the papyngo responds to these ironies with her own. Rather than leaving her 'naturall guddis' to the Church, she bestows them on other female birds who need her various attributes, whether those pertaining to her female beauty, such as her 'bricht depurit Ene [*eyes*]', or to her nature as one of God's creatures, especially her 'voce Angelycall' (ll. 1090-1103). Additionally, in a courtly gesture recalling the earlier reference to an intimate relationship with the king, which also indicates her distrust of the church and jestingly alludes to the literary gift-of-the-heart motif, the bird asks that her own heart be sent to the secular leader, her 'Souerane Kyng' who she knows will enclose her heart-gift 'in to one ryng' (ll. 1119-20).[28] The more serious underlying meaning is that the king will cherish and act upon her words. His responsibility to act, especially upon Scotland's corrupt clerics, is underscored when the bird's 'holye' executors tear her body apart '[q]uhill scho is hote' (l. 1151) and the friar-kite, after a noisy altercation, flies away with her heart.

Lyndsay again emphasises the poet-narrator's detachment, first in a Henrysonian comment that the other birds 'flew, all, out of my sycht' (l. 1171)[29] and secondly by the accomplished internal rhymes of the final two stanzas of traditional modest apology. There the poet suggests, self-disparagingly, that he has been mere craftsman-presenter and observer, not originator, of 'the sore complent, the testament, & myschance' (l. 1173) of the papyngo. As a result, Lyndsay's bird becomes a mere device to entertain, to tease with echoes of literary predecessors, and to admonish the court audience. Also, through her sex she has a distinctive and effective voice for the poet-narrator's advice to the king, epecially its sharply anti-curial satire. Given the veiled hints of her past intimacy with the king, the parrot may also be expressing views or policy intentions that, without directly attaching his name to them, James V himself might have wished to publicise.

As with these fictional representations, Lyndsay's choice of historical women is inclusive, and among his portraits are virtuous and reprehensible figures, some of whom Lyndsay must have known personally. Of five who bear witness to his faithful royal service, he chooses those closest to James V in his early years, his mother, nurse, and governess' (*Complaynt*, c.1530),[30] putting them forward unconditionally and implying they are as reliable as 'My lord Chanclare' (ll. 81-3). Another contemporary woman, an important abbess with undesirable notoriety, remains ostensibly anonymous in the *Tragedie of the Cardinal* (1547) where she is labeled a 'commoun hure' (l. 409) by the poem's speaker, the purported spectre of the assassinated Beaton. In damning the abbess via a speaker whose words are often self-condemning, the poet is not revealing his own hostility towards women; indeed Beaton's spectre, now repentant, appeals to the king on behalf of 'Uirginis profest in to Religioun' (l. 408), pointing out that the abbess's corrupting leadership puts them in peril.

Madeleine de Valois is also unnamed in the *Answer* [...] *to the Kingis Flyting*, written before the princess became James V's queen.[31] Lyndsay's metonymic description of her as 'ane bukler furth of France, / Quhilk wyll indure ʒour dintis' (ll. 68-9) is on one level innuendo; at another, it calls attention to behaviour proper to a prince, the patient seeking of a spouse with appropriate status. Lyndsay portrays the French princess as such, using the terms of a jousting opponent of sufficient prowess and courtliness to be the equal of a chivalrous Scottish king. Madeleine thus forms telling contrasts to the two other unnamed but identifiable women mentioned, the 'quene [*young female*]' whom the king is said to have thrown 'ouerthort ane stinking troch' during energetic lovemaking in a brewery, and the absent 'Lady that luffit [him] best', whose implied response to this sexual encounter, had she witnessed it, is disapproval and anxiety (ll. 53-7). Like the 'buklar', these women are also symbols rather than three-dimensional representations: the first, of the king's indiscriminate and time-wasting relationships, and the second, by supposed reassessment of what had been told as a high-spirited incident, of the attitude of those who truly care for the wellbeing of king and realm, especially for securing the succession.

A much more detailed picture of Madeleine appears in the *Deploratioun*, written just after her marriage and untimely death. However, although distinguished by epithets such as 'the first Dochter of France', she is recognised iconically, rather than by her personal qualities. For instance, Madeleine's behaviour is not favourably compared with that of contemporary women, but with that of the classical Hero and Penelope, known for their constancy (ll. 44, 50-2). Such elevating comparisons were the expected rhetorical dress of public mourning, but for the seventeen-year-old Madeleine, the allusion to her virtuous patience was a diplomatic reminder of the 'auld alliance', the military agreement long maintained between Scotland and France despite provocation from would-be alternative partners. More particularly, the comparison of Madeleine with others famed for constancy signified the length of time (twenty years) between the initial negotiations of the Treaty of Rouen and the marriage. Other epithets, too, like the concluding metaphor of Madeleine as a 'heuinly flour' with an indestructible perfume (l. 197), idealised her while quietly promoting the idea that constancy, the continuation of the alliance, was desirable. James V was to marry a second French woman, Marie de Guise-Lorraine, within the year.

In another example of his complex treatment of women, *The Historie of Squyer Meldrum* (c.1550), Lyndsay compares the contemporary Marjorie Lawson, widow of the Sir John Haldane killed at Flodden,[32] with the well-known figures Dido and Guinevere (ll. 876, 1080). Lawson was alive when Lyndsay wrote, but by omitting her name from the poem he lessens her distance from these fictional women. Paradoxically, the effect on this thought-provoking portrayal is to emphasise Lawson's distinctive character, as illustrated near the beginning where the young Meldrum is compared favourably with the heroic Lancelot not only in fighting skills but in his 'Lufe', specifically in the better footing of the relationship: 'His Ladie luifit him and no mo' (l.58). This comparison is germane to Lyndsay's main purpose, the depiction and commemoration of a modern-day man who upheld the old ideals of honour, but the comparison also has significant implications for Lawson as his partner. Like Madeleine, she is elevated by the implied comparison with a famous woman, but Lawson's 'just querrell' and widowed state also define her superiority to Lancelot's Guinevere, labelled an 'Adulterair' (ll. 49-59). While this moralistic attitude might seem misogynistic, Guinevere is not at the epicentre of the narrator's disapproval but her lover Lancelot; unlike Meldrum, Lancelot has 'jaip[ed] his Maisteris wyfe' (l. 62) and is condemned.[33]

In that first mention of her and when she welcomes Meldrum to her castle, Lawson is portrayed as having an independent mind and a practical outlook. Her forwardness in going to the squire's room results from that independent and practical nature, making her both like and unlike the women in early romances who take the initiative in love.[34] As Lyndsay presents her, Lawson is as eager to embrace as Meldrum, and though she plays as he does with the language and gestures of courtly love (for example, ll. 955-69), both show a gently mocking awareness of the courtly code's limited relevance, an awareness lacking in similar scenes from earlier literary examples or, if present, confined to a narrator's ironic aside. As she begins to fall in love with Meldrum, Lawson is compared with 'Quene Dido' (l. 876), with the implications for Meldrum as Aeneas hovering, but unlike Dido in other presentations, she is not depicted as a victim. Instead, realising from the beginning both the match's advantages and the temporary obstacle to their marriage, their kinship within the forbidden degrees, she behaves pragmatically by seeking proper dispensation and trusting her partner in the interim, so that her property might be protected and they might enjoy the consequences of their love. Later, in a similar fashion, Lawson acknowledges with courageous clear-sight her continuing vulnerability as an unmarried woman with goods and land (ll. 1245-6). When Meldrum clashes finally with Lawson's jealous and land-hungry neighbour, she becomes, by her initial attempt to save her partner by permitting her own capture, a woman who deserves the heroic defence Meldrum in turn attempts. In keeping with Lyndsay's focus on Meldrum, her behaviour adds to his stature, yet her portrayal in this situation as his equal also elevates her status. Moreover, her subsequent actions, like Meldrum's, are seen to be without blame: the pair's separation is beyond their control, and her documented marriage to another an action 'aganis her will' (ll. 1460-5). And once more Lawson's subsequent position is favourably compared with, and thus redefined in the light of, well-known women from classical and medieval literature: Penelope, Cresseid, and Helen of Troy (ll. 1471-9). Aptly, however, it is as herself, the 'Sterne [*star*] of Stratherne' (l. 230), that Lawson is bidden farewell in the *Testament of Meldrum*.

This study of selected representations of women in Lyndsay's verse reveals a poet who used his female images thoughtfully, not only those of historic women but those that were stereotypic, iconic, or idealised, as he attended to his generic aims and his audience's interests and expectations. The evidence suggests that Lyndsay was conservative in his attitudes but also aware that female agency and perspectives were valid in a variety of contexts and would well serve his themes. Lyndsay thus differs significantly from those writers who showed women stereotypically as either beautiful goddesses, as in Henryson's *Garmont of Gud Ladeis*, or their opposite, as in the Asloan Manuscript's *The Spectakle of Luf*.

Discernible, too, from some of Lyndsay's portraits, is that his most pronounced condemnation of women is reserved for those who, according to the mores of the day, have been sexually immoral, sometimes also deceitful towards that end, and who have abused positions of power. Above all, it is Lyndsay's constant awareness of how his portrayals of women of all types can be shaped to further his poetic and ideological concerns that emerges from this study. In other words, Lyndsay's verse is not characterised by a single attitude, misogynistic or other, towards women.

Notes

[1] All quotations from *The Works of Sir David Lindsay of the Mount*, ed. by Douglas Hamer, STS, 4 vols (Edinburgh and London: Blackwood, 1931-36). Abbreviations have been normalised.

[2] Cf. *The Poetical Works of Sir David Lyndsay of the Mount*, ed. by George Chalmers, 3 vols (London and Edinburgh: Longman, Hurst, Rees, and Orme, Constable, 1806), I, 45; Thomas Innes of Learney, 'Sir David Lindsay of the Mount, Lord Lyon King of Arms, 1538-1555', *Scottish Notes and Queries*, 13 (1935), 145-8, 170-3, 180-3 (p.171); James Bruce, *Lives of Eminent Men of Fife* (Edinburgh and London: Myles MacPhail and John Gibson, 1846), p. 202; Patrick Fraser Tytler, *Lives of the Scottish Worthies*, 3 vols (London: John Murray, 1833), III, 235.

[3] See *Exchequer Rolls of Scotland* [*ER*], ed. by J. Stuart, and others. (Edinburgh: [n. pub.], 1878-1908), XVII, 166, 281; *Accounts of the Lord High Treasurer of Scotland* [*TA*], ed. by T. Dickson and J. Balfour Paul (Edinburgh: [n. pub.], 1877-1916), VII, 116, 126, 158, 264, 276, 281, 314-15, 324, 333, 424, 476.

[4] See Francis Lee Utley, *The Crooked Rib: An Analytical Index to the Argument About Women in English and Scots Literature to the End of the Year 1568* (Columbus: Ohio State UP, 1944), pp. 133-4.

[5] Cf. Dunbar, 'Illuster Lodouick, of France most cristin king' (B 23), especially ll. 19-24. All quotations from *The Poems of William Dunbar*, ed. by Priscilla Bawcutt, 2 vols (Glasgow: ASLS, 1998), I, 100.

[6] Cf. Guillaume de Lorris and Jean de Meun, *The Romance of the Rose*, trans. by Harry W. Robbins; ed. by Charles W. Dunn (New York: Dutton, 1962), ch. 20 (ll. 4059-220 in the original Old French).

[7] Cf. *The Asloan Manuscript* [...] *written by John Asloan in the Reign of James the Fifth*, ed. by W. A. Craigie, STS, 2 vols (Edinburgh and London: Blackwood, 1923-25), II, 186; *The Bannatyne Manuscript Writtin in Tyme of Pest, 1568*, ed. by W. Tod Ritchie, STS, 4 vols (Edinburgh and London: Blackwood, 1928-34); Stewart, 'Schir sen of men', II, 256-7, and such counselling fictions-within-fictions as the 'buke of remembrans', *Thre Prestis of Peblis*, ed. by T. D. Robb, STS (Edinburgh and London: Blackwood, 1920), p. 350.

[8] Cf. *The Comedy of Dante Alighieri the Florentine*, trans. by Dorothy L. Sayers, 3 vols (Harmondsworth: Penguin, 1949-62), II, *Purgatorio*, 29.130-2; *The*

Riverside Chaucer, ed. by Larry D. Benson (Oxford: OUP, 1988), *Tr*, V. 744-9; all title abbreviations of Chaucer's works follow those of this edition.

[9] See Jean Seznec, *The Survival of the Pagan Gods* (New York: Bollingen Foundation, 1953), pp. 120-1; Frances A. Yates, *The Art of Memory* (London and Henley: Routledge and Kegan Paul, 1966), pp. 20-1.

[10] *James I of Scotland: The Kingis Quair*, ed. by John Norton-Smith (Oxford: Clarendon, 1971).

[11] A possible derivation is Psalm 84:11.

[12] See *The Prose Works of Gilbert Hay*, ed. by Jonathan A. Glenn, STS (Aberdeen: AUP, 1993), III, 'Buke of the Gouernaunce of Princis', fol. 124, ch. xxxiiij (orthography normalised).

[13] See also Utley, *Crooked Rib*, pp. 53-90; Joan Kelly, *Women, History, and Theory* (Chicago: U Chicago P, 1984), pp. 65-109; Constance Jordan, *Renaissance Feminism: Literary Texts and Political Models* (Ithaca and London: Cornell UP, 1990), pp. 86-94.

[14] Among them are Simon Magus, bishops Caiaphas and Annas, Judas, Pharaoh, Herod, Pontius Pilate, Choro, Dathan, and Abiron; and Emperor Nero.

[15] What was considered in the early 1500s to be immoral female behaviour, and by whom, is an important but separate issue not addressed here.

[16] See, for example, Chaucer, *MLT*, *CT* II (B^1) 359; *PF*, l. 288.

[17] All quotations are from *The Poems of Robert Henryson*, ed. by Denton Fox (Oxford: Clarendon, 1981); Fox, p. 362.

[18] Cf. also Lyndsay's 'Roye royall' (l. 426) with Henryson's Phebus as 'king royall' (l. 204).

[19] Cf. 'Hie empryss and quene celestiale', *Asloan MS*, ed. by Craigie, II, 245; and Dunbar, 'Hale, sterne superne' (B 16), ll. 6, 52.

[20] John Ireland, *The Meroure of Wyssdome*, ed. by Charles Macpherson, F. Quinn, and Craig MacDonald, STS, 3 vols (Edinburgh, London, and Aberdeen: Blackwood and Aberdeen UP, 1926-90), III, 159, ll. 31-5.

[21] Cf. Ovid, *Amores*, II, vi; Boccaccio, *De Genealogia Deorum*, IV, xlix; Jean Lemaire de Belges, *Les Epîtres de l'Amant Vert*, ed. by Jean Frappier (Lille et Genève: Librairie Giard et Librairie Droz, 1948), 'La Premiere Epistre'; 'Speke Parott', in *John Skelton: The Complete English Poems*, ed. by John Scattergood (Harmondsworth: Penguin, 1983), pp. 230-46.

[22] Cf. Anne M. McKim, '"Makand her mone": Masculine Constructions of the Feminine Voice in Middle Scots Complaints', *Scotlands*, 2 (1994), 32-46 (p. 38); also Elizabeth D. Harvey, *Ventriloquized Voices: Feminist Theory and English Renaissance Texts* (London and New York: Routledge, 1992), pp. 140-1.

[23] *TA*, VII, 390, 429; cf. Dunbar, 'Schir, ʒit remember as befoir' (B 68), pp. 21-3, designed to appeal to an earlier king interested in falconry.

[24] Cf. *DOST*, s.v. 'delyte' (*n*), 1b.

[25] Cf. Helen Phillips, 'Frames and Narrators in Chaucerian Poetry', in *The Long Fifteenth Century*, ed. by Helen Cooper and Sally Mapstone (Oxford: Clarendon, 1997), pp. 77-81.

[26] Sciennes was the Dominican nunnery founded in Edinburgh in 1517 and dedicated to St Catherine of Siena. The word 'Sciennes' is still used as a street name in modern Edinburgh.

[27] Cf. Beryl Rowland, *Birds with Human Souls: A Guide to Bird Symbolism* (Knoxville, TN: U Tennessee P, 1978), pp. 93-6, 102-5, 143-8.

[28] Cf. the bird's courtly associations in *Sir Gawain and the Green Knight*, ed. by J. R. R. Tolkien and E.V. Gordon; 2nd edn rev. Norman Davis (Oxford: Clarendon, 1967), pp. 607-12, and Chaucer, *Rom*, pp. 912-13; for the heart-ring association see Chaucer, *Tr*, III, 1368-72.

[29] Cf. Henryson, *The Preaching of the Swallow*, 1887.

[30] For Marion Douglas see *ER*, XIV, 350 and XVII, 289; for Elizabeth Douglas see *ER*, XIV, 287 and XV, 546; also *TA*, V, 146.

[31] The Frenchwoman could also be Mary of Bourbon, daughter of the Duke of Vendôme, who was from March to November 1536 James V's prospective bride; see Jamie Cameron, *James V: The Personal Rule 1528-1542*, ed. by Norman Macdougall (East Linton: Tuckwell, 1998), pp. 131, 133.

[32] Cf. *Works of Lindsay*, ed. by Hamer, III, 203-06.

[33] Contrast the narrator's cynical comment in Chaucer, *NPT, CT* (VII, 3212-13).

[34] See further, Judith Weiss, 'The Wooing Woman in Anglo-Norman Romance' in *Romance in Medieval England*, ed. by Maldwyn Mills, Jennifer Fellows and Carol M. Meale (Woodbridge: Brewer, 1991), pp. 149-61. Also *Medieval English Romances*, ed. by Diane Speed, 2 vols (Sydney: Department of English, University of Sydney, 1989), 'The Grene Knight', I, 235-57 (ll. 362-87).

5

Chastity in the Stocks: Women, Sex, and Marriage in *Ane Satyre of the Thrie Estaitis*

Garrett P. J. Epp

In an article entitled 'Normative Heterosexuality in History and Theory: The Case of Sir David Lindsay of the Mount', R. James Goldstein argues that, while modern scholars have usefully 'examined Lindsay's work in the context of the political and theological conflicts of his time, they have paid little attention to the relations among power, gender, and sexuality that pervade his work'. He notes further that, throughout this extraordinary body of work, 'Lindsay is conspicuously preoccupied by proper definitions of gender and the regulation of sexual desire'.[1] Those preoccupations are rendered especially conspicuous in his sprawling morality play, *The Satyre of the Thrie Estaitis*: exemplars of proper and improper sexual and gendered behaviour are given names, lines, and costumes, and placed onstage. Women, however, are rendered conspicuously absent in Lindsay's staging. This is especially notable given that, according to Henry Charteris, in 1554 the play was 'playit besyde Edinburgh, in presence of the Quene Regent', Mary of Guise.[2] The play presents the female body as abject and grotesque, as Goldstein amply demonstrates (pp. 359-61), while keeping that body resolutely offstage. There are female roles in the play, even very lively and interesting ones, but these roles are played by men, in ways that move beyond a conventionalised theatrical cross-dressing by male actors. The feminine is treated as a spectre that haunts and disrupts the proper realm of masculinity, even as it defines that realm.

Sex itself has been rendered relatively invisible in many modern treatments of the play, both theatrical and scholarly. In the introduction to his adaption of *The Thrie Estaitis*, based on the 'inspired selection of lines made by Robert Kemp for Tyrone Guthrie's celebrated Edinburgh Festival production of 1948', Matthew McDiarmid argues that '[c]onsiderable cuts' were made without damage to anything 'essential to the significance or effect intended by Lindsay'. His first example of such a cut is 'the unactable obscenity of the Pardoner's devil's ceremony of divorce between a cobbler and his wife'.[3] Other scenes with explicit sexual content remain, but have been notably abbreviated. Kemp and Guthrie had good cause to cut this material: had they not done so, as Guthrie has pointed out, the Lord Chamberlain's Office would have done so for them.[4] McDiarmid was under no such constraints: his version, ironically published just one year prior to the revocation of the Lord Chamberlain's power of censorship, was aimed at 'the student of literature' rather than at actors and producers (p. 10). And while McDiarmid does indicate the absence of the divorce scene, both here and in a marginal note where the scene should be, most of his cuts are unannotated. Much of the play's sexual content is thereby placed beyond the margins; it is 'unactable' precisely because it is no longer there. Contemporary criticism, too, tends to downplay the play's sexual content, stressing instead the more overtly political and courtly aspects of the play. Carol Edington, for instance, states that 'while it is the ethical drama which most forcibly hits the modern reader, it was surely the political message which struck home to a sixteenth-century audience'.[5] Yet what she rightly terms the play's 'profoundly political [...] concerns' (p. 69), and emphatically *not* its treatment of sexuality, is the stuff that most modern, scholarly criticism of the play addresses. As Goldstein notes, Edington shows little interest in the ways in which Lindsay's works 'place special emphasis on the regulation of heterosexual desire or the proper gendering of the royal body and the regime of power it enables' (p. 354). The play's infamous bawdy bits are not mere filler, aimed at 'delight[ing] an idling crowd between serious scenes',[6] but are central to the play's ethical and political concerns. The body politic is here explicitly a sexual body, and all the sexual play onstage has political and social implications.

This is hardly a novel assertion. Douglas Hamer wrote something similar more than sixty years ago, in response to David Laing's still earlier response to the aforementioned divorce scene. Hamer quotes Laing's 1879 edition of the *Poetical Works*, in which he states that 'this Interlude interrupts the progress of the play and [...w]as evidently intended to amuse the lower classes of the auditors'. Hamer responds: 'It was certainly a scene of comedy, but it is an integral part of the plot, and was likely to amuse more courtiers than craftsmen'.[7] Hamer apparently does not share this sense of humour, deeming it 'low' and 'coarse' (pp. 201-2). Still, he remains willing to explore its significance in his annotations, at least when he himself understands the joke.

The play's sexual subplots and jokes all turn on the usual question: who is doing it with whom, or rather, to whom? The answer is, as usual, the wrong people. What is less clear in this play is whether there is or can be such a thing as the right person where sex is concerned. Sex may be funny, but it is bad; the sexual foibles of others, both in and out of marriage, are to be laughed at, not emulated. For instance, near the end of the play, Folie addresses his unruly penis, which apparently rises at the sight of a particular audience member. Hamer thought this penis should be visible onstage, 'and perhaps detachable' (p. 155), but it was probably decently housed in an obvious codpiece. Folie may be aroused, but the audience should not be. Admittedly, not all audience members are likely to register the moment consciously as part of what Greg Walker rightly deems the play's 'final and most powerful blow to the credulity of the reformers';[8] in performance, less cerebral aspects of theatre tend to claim audience attention. Still, if we are distracted by the sight of that same 'fair las with the sating goun' (l. 4440) that Folie claims to see in the audience, or even by the body of Folie himself, his ostensible reaction to her should serve as a remedy against our arousal, causing us to laugh at ourselves as well as at him.

This is not to say that Lindsay tries to avoid titillating his audience entirely: Sensualitie in particular should probably look as attractive as everyone makes her out to be. Yet there is a joke here, too. Hamer asserts that she must be clad in a 'low-necked dress' that 'exposes her breasts' (pp. 152 and 174, n. 271-94); I think this highly unlikely, but not for reasons of propriety. The problem is that she is male, an actor whose prosthetic 'papis of portratour perfyte' (l. 282) were surely kept within his bodice. Folks could apparently do wonderful things in the centuries before Latex with 'white' or untanned leather, including 'naked suits' for Adam and Eve,[9] but visible, fake breasts would only be a distraction in this context; as with Danger's 'cunt lyke ane quaw-myre' (l. 835) later in the play, physical exposure of the named body part is not required by the situation or the script.

Moreover, the maleness of at least one female character is jokingly emphasised — one of the jokes that Hamer clearly did not appreciate. Fund-Jonet appears only briefly onstage; her lines could easily be reassigned to another of Sensualitie's female attendants with minimal disturbance to the script as a whole. Her chief functions as a character are, first, to be the woman who has taught those attendants 'baith to swyfe' (l. 318), and second, to sing with them. The song is not included in the script, but we do know that she sings bass (l. 316). Because of this, as Roderick Lyall notes, 'Fund-Jonet (literally 'foundling Janet') has proved something of a problem to editors' (p.180, n. 312). Hamer thought her 'a male assistant'(p. 175, n. 312), and so Kemp and Guthrie turned her into 'Fund-Jennet, a porter' (p. 6). However, as Lyall points out, 'Jonet is unmistakably a female name, and there really was a woman known by this nickname at the court of Mary of Guise in 1544-5'.[10] The first portion of that nickname might well mean 'foundling', but also suggests a pun on 'fundus', meaning base, or bottom. While it is conceivable that we are to think of her simply as having a voice that is, like Cordelia's, 'ever soft, / Gentle, and low, an excellent thing in a woman' (*King Lear*, V.3.246-7),[11] we are more likely expected to see her as an obviously cross-dressed male. As a character, she allows a dual reading: the old crone who teaches younger women how to gain sovereignty over men; and the over-sexualised, effeminate man, who hands his sovereignty over to women in his pursuit of sexual experience. In either case, a man is here playing — that is, either acting, or playing with, sexually — a woman's part, and thus compromising his fundamental masculinity.

Rex Humanitas himself is explicitly deemed by the Persone to be 'effeminate' (l. 1121), meaning that he is overly enamoured of, and therefore like, women.[12] While, as often argued, he resembles James V, whom Lindsay once described as 'Ay fukkand lyke a furious Fornicatour',[13] Rex Humanitas is also a stock dramatic character. In *The Arte of English Poesie* (1569), George Puttenham describes a very similar character and situation: 'In our Comedie intituled *Ginecocratia*: the king was supposed to be a person very amorous and effeminate, and therefore most ruled his ordinary affaires by the aduise of women'[14] — that is, like Lindsay's Rex Humanitas, the king is 'gydit be Dame Sensualitie' (l. 1122). And this, of course, is not a good thing. Lindsay amply demonstrates what Carol Edington terms his 'hostility to gynecocracy' (p. 76) in *The Monarche*, where he writes that 'all wemen [...] / Suld to thare men subiectit be' (ll. 1069-70). Lindsay's statement explicitly includes 'Quenis of moste hie degree', who are best kept 'like birds in tyll a cage' (ll. 1064, 1067). Edington protests, 'Surely Lindsay could not have countenanced the idea of his "Quene, of Scotland Heretour" finding herself in such a position', yet notes both that 'in the infant Mary Stewart Lindsay generally saw a queen rather than a sovereign' and that he considered 'Mary's reign [...] an unfortunate aberration to be endured in the expectation of future male rule'.[15] I doubt that Lindsay considered even Queen Mary an exception to the rule of subjection, nor the Queen Regent, before whom in Edinburgh, as already noted, *The Thrie Estaitis* was performed in 1554, while the Queen herself was still an unmarried child in France. Still, an effeminately overruled king is, for Lindsay, a greater evil than an unmanned Queen. Thus, as Edington points out, 'It is a highly charged moment when, at the height of his infatuation with Dame Sensualitie and at the nadir of his kingship, Rex Humanitas renders up to her his judicial authority' (p. 74).

Specifically, the king allows Sensualitie power over Chastitie, who is thrown into the stocks alongside Veritie in another highly charged moment. Yet the same negative charge would surely have affected any scene in which Rex Humanitas bowed to the feminine authority of Chastitie or Veritie, which is probably why none exists: he is merely told at the end of Part One to receive these two into his service along with the masculine figure of Gude Counsell, and to 'Use thair counsell' (l. 1759); only Gude Counsell is ever seen to give any. Chastitie and Veritie appear again only briefly, in the second part of the play, to 'mak thair plaint at the bar' (l. 3115) before a more masculine authority, Divyne Correctioun. Their own divine authority remains theoretical, not visible.

Lindsay thus manages to keep the 'good' female characters subordinate to men, if also, like the corrupting forces of Sensualitie, unmarried. Feminine power is denied any licit expression onstage, and even positive feminine expression remains subject to masculine correction. Lindsay's antifeminism, like his bawdy sense of humour, finds all too suitable a fit within what Carolyn Ives and David Parkinson deem 'a distinctively Scottish discourse "aganis evill wemen" [...] grounded in the authority of a transformed, Scottified Chaucer'.[16] As Ives and Parkinson argue, 'In Scotland, experience in sex and marriage often gets written about as if it were deathly, hellish, disorderly, and impoverishing' (p. 191). And women are, as usual, considered the root of the problem. In the prologue to *The Thrie Estaitis*, the herald Diligence — a character perhaps played in the 1552 performance at Cupar by Lindsay himself, as Edington has suggested[17] — makes the customary call for silence, saying 'Let everie man keip weill ane toung, / And everie woman tway' (ll. 76-7). But he has just told us that, later in the play,

> [...] the verteous ladie Veritie
> Will mak any pitious lamentatioun, [...]

> And Chastitie will mak narratioun
> How sho can get na ludging in this land...
>
> (ll. 62-3, 66-7)

Each of these two tongues is presumably singular; Truth herself, in particular, cannot be duplicitous. Then again, these are not actually women's tongues. While the ideal woman is ostensibly truthful and chaste, Lindsay presents truth and chastity as being purely abstract qualities, unavailable, or even antithetical, to actual women. Like the decidedly unvirtuous Fund-Jonet and everyone else onstage, both of these virtues are played by male actors.

An audience would have noticed and thought about this otherwise conventionalised and hence almost invisible crossdressing, even if modern critics have generally failed to do so, precisely because the play *as play* calls attention to it. Fund-Jonet's bass-line merely starts the process. Once her maleness has been consciously registered by the audience, it cannot easily become invisible again. That visibility has consequences. One further reason for Fund-Jonet's presence in the play is perhaps to allow all the king's men to be paired off onstage with Sensualitie's women: Wantonnes specifically couples with Hamelines; Placebo and Solace are later said to have both enjoyed Danger (ll. 830-3), but I suspect that Fund-Jonet makes her unnoted exit with one of those two. Her obvious masculinity would almost necessarily cast a homoerotic shadow over those couplings; in a culture that tended to call all illicit sex 'sodomy', such homoeroticism would simply add to the audience's sense that the king's coupling with Sensualitie is indeed illicit, and not a 'mariage' as Wantonnes ironically refers to it (l. 458). However, even if Fund-Jonet never joins the courtiers, their dialogue allows a similar effect. When Wantonnes asks Hamelines for her 'batye [*lusty*] tout', and suggests that they should 'junne [their] justing lummis' (l. 545), he keeps the audience aware that Hamelines, or rather the male actor that plays her, like himself, does indeed have a 'tout' — that is, 'tail', and not 'drink' as glossed by Lyall, following McDiarmid[18] — appropriate for homosexual 'jousting'. When he tells her, 'Fill in, for I am dry!' (l. 541), he may not be talking about a regular drink from a cup.

Audience awareness of the male bodies beneath female garb, and of the attendant homoerotic potential, is reflected in Lindsay's portrayal of married couples as well. The wives of the Sowtar (or cobbler) and the Taylour dominate not just their husbands but the stage. However, I sincerely doubt that Lindsay thought of them as role models. Like Chaucer's Wife of Bath they are women in search of sex and sovereignty;

they embody the danger posed by marriage. Yet again these are men playing women playing a supposedly masculine role, wrongly and unnaturally usurping the masculine privilege of domination. And I do mean men, not boys, *pace* Hamer, who at least notes that these roles are to be played by male actors.[19] Only the Taylour's daughter, Jennie, would likely have been played by a boy: for her brief appearance to have any purpose at all, she would need to appear younger than her mother; thus the maleness of the actor playing Jennie would also become relatively invisible, relative to that of the actors playing the older women. In any case, it is Jennie who innocently tells the women that her father, along with his friend the Sowtar, is drinking with 'ane lustie ladie' who intends 'to ludge with him all nicht' (ll. 1311, 1317). Phallic bedstaff and distaff in hand, the women confront the lady in question, Chastitie, and beat their beleagered husbands. Then they leave the playing area, crossing a stream. To accomplish this, the Sowtar's Wyfe explicitly 'lifts up hir clais above hir waist and enters in the water' (l. 1391), and the Taylour's Wyfe apparently follows suit. It is possible, but unlikely, that the actors would have worn undergarments; the point would seem to be the exposure of their masculine bottoms, in comic confirmation of the women's supposedly too-masculine behaviour in the scene as a whole.

This same scene exposes masculinity in another sense as well. The widow in William Dunbar's 'Tretis of the Tua Mariit Wemen and the Wedo' tells her two companions: 'Be amyable with humble face, as angellis apperand, / And with a terrebill taill be stangand as edderis'.[20] The image recalls the serpent in the garden of Eden, the devil as original cross-dresser, traditionally pictured as taking on the face of a woman, or of Eve herself. In the Cornish *Creacion of the World*, for example, Lucifer takes possession of 'A fyne serpent made with a virgyn face, and yolowe heare [*yellow hair*] upon her head', and then refers to himself (in Cornish) as being 'dressed up like a sweet angel'.[21] Yet the widow's advice, even more than the story of the temptation in Eden itself, also suggests that the most dangerous woman is always really male, or at least masculine, and that only a male can really disrupt the masculine order, in the guise of, or under the influence of, the feminine. Staging the wives of the Sowtar and the Taylour explicitly as cross-dressed men, exposing their stinging 'tails' to the audience, could arguably not only signify the excessive masculinisation of these monstrous women, and the relative feminisation of their husbands, but also allow Woman to vanish as effective threat. As the feminine is rendered spectral, a failed masculinity becomes the central spectacle. Certainly, the target of Lindsay's satire here is less women of any description than it is men, less these wives than their husbands. However, his argument rests on the presumption that the failure of masculinity is always or only to play the part, literally or figuratively, of Woman: an ever-present absence, a hole into which masculinity too easily falls.

Sarah Carpenter has argued that '[t]he wives' conventionally expressed sexual jealousy is undercut when their rival is not an embodiment of sexuality, but of chastity itself'.[22] That the wives see Chastitie as a sexual threat is indeed the central joke here, but also a serious statement. The craftsmen love chastity, but in the sense of celibacy, rather than of properly controlled, procreative sexual activity within marriage — a crucial slippage in the play. The two wives just want sex. As the Taylour's Wyfe complains, just before the confrontation, 'it is half ane yeir almaist / Sen ever that loun [*rogue*] laborde my ledder' (ll. 1331-2). The Sowtar's Wyfe has had a shorter interval of abstinence, little more than forty days (and nights), but notes bitterly, 'last quhen I gat chalmer-glew [*sexual intercourse*], / That foull Sowter began till spew' (ll. 1336-7). The women threaten Chastitie with violence knowing full well who she is, and what she signifies, even before they attack their husbands. The men in turn express their jealousy of the clergy, who 'may fuck thair fill and be unmaryit' (l. 1370). The misogamist sentiment, later echoed by the Pauper (ll. 2760-71), is conventional if bluntly expressed; the oddity is that this particular formulation is put into the mouths of men who would appear to have no interest in sexual activity. As Hamer reminds us, cobblers and tailors — favoured objects of satire in the poetry of William Dunbar, as well — work at home in stereotypically feminine occupations, with needle and thread, to supply clothing, which is associated with fashion, vanity, hypocrisy, and effeminacy. In social terms, they are not real men, and so are used, here as elsewhere, to signify a 'lack of virility'[23] that easily embraces chastity but leaves a vacuum in the marital power structure that is swiftly filled by their wives. In contrast, the clergy and the king do have masculine power, which is represented as being both social and sexual. However, being unmarried, and thus lacking a proper channel for that power, these men abuse it, or rather lose it, in the pursuit of Sensualitie. In both cases, the lack of a proper marital arrangement corresponds with a lack of proper virility. The Priores will later state that 'Mariage [...] is better religioun / as to be freir or nuyn' (ll. 3702-4). Thus the play as a whole strongly and explicitly advocates marriage, even as it represents that institution, like women, as being both unpleasant and morally dangerous for men.

This misogamist advocacy of monogamy brings us back, at last, to the infamous Interlude, wherein the Sowtar and his wife return to the stage and posteriors again are bared, this time in the course of what Edington refers to as an 'unnatural, not to mention illegal, "divorce" ceremony' conducted by the Pardoner. I am not certain what a 'natural' divorce ceremony might look like, but this one certainly is perverse. Edington comments:

> Instructing the Sowtar and his soon-to-be-former wife to kiss one another on the arse may have provided the audience with much scatalogical amusement, but more sinisterly, it conjures up visions of the diabolical pact, worthy indeed of 'Baliel's braid blissing'.
>
> (p. 192)

Hamer writes, 'This incident is probably the most cynical thing known to me in literature', but adds, 'It is not pure obscenity. In mediaeval devil-lore the devil is depicted with a face on his posterior, and the rites of Sabbatism included the ritual of the kiss on the posterior, in parody of the sacred kiss'.[24] The incident may also owe much to Dunbar's poem about a tournament in hell between a sowtar and tailor: at the end of the joust and of the poem, the devil permanently deprives both men of the virile right to bear arms and makes them 'harlottis bayth for evir'; in the process, the sowtar is thoroughly 'beschitten / With Belliallis ers unblist'.[25]

Yet neither scatology nor diabolic ritual, nor for that matter pardoners, have any obvious connection with marriage or divorce. This Pardoner, like his apparent model in Chaucer's *Canterbury Tales*, is a figure of sexual as well as spiritual deviance. When Chaucer's Pardoner calls the other pilgrims to kneel before him, and thus before his infamously ambiguous crotch, to kiss his false relics, the Host angrily refuses. However, both parties are then called to a kiss of reconciliation which effectively forces the Host into 'doing exactly what he had so strenuously rejected doing earlier: kissing an impotent and worthless relic (or, worse, performing an act equivalent to the heretic's kissing of the Devil's anus)'.[26] Lindsay reverses the meaning of that kiss while displacing the Pardoner's sexual ambiguity and perversity onto the theatrical spectacle of two men, one playing an effeminate man and the other his virago wife, kissing each other's naked bottoms. The reciprocal kiss of divorce is a version of sodomitical sin, a parodic corruption of properly ordered and controlled sexuality; this kiss does not reconcile, but divides men.

While Lindsay's Pardoner, like Chaucer's, serves as an instrument of sexual perversity, Lindsay's description of the Pardoner's collection of relics is surprisingly free of sexual innuendo. The collection is also less notable for its falsity -- unlike Chaucer, Lindsay does not give us a group of pilgrims heading off to see any 'true' relics, such as those of Thomas Beckett at Canterbury -- than for its inclusion of entirely secular, political items such as the rope 'Quhilk hangit [Jonnye] Armistrang' (l. 2100).[27] Again, the satirical target here is less the false claims of Pardoners, specifically, or even false spirituality more generally, which is already well-represented in this play, than divorce itself. Divorce, it seems, is at best simply invalid, a political expediency that is, like the Pardoner's relics, without spiritual basis; at worst it is a diabolical sexual sin, yet another example of misplaced, ungoverned, or misgoverned sexuality. While Lindsay clearly disagrees with church teaching on the celibate priesthood, he is orthodox in his treatment of the indissolubility of marriage -- a burning issue not only in Henry VIII's recently Protestant England, but also in Scotland, where Lindsay's courtly audiences are likely to have remembered James V's refusal, less than two decades earlier, to grant his estranged and already once-divorced mother, Margaret Tudor, Henry VIII's sister, a divorce from her third husband, Henry Stuart Lord Methven.

Lindsay here treats marriage as a necessary evil: necessary as a means of controlling all that is not masculine, including the male sex drive itself; and evil because it both brings men into sexual contact with women and, through the marriage debt, forces men to hand over at least some power and authority to women, if only in the arena of sex. Inside or outside marriage, Woman remains a threat to masculinity. Sexual contact outside of marriage is deemed sinful, yet sexual contact is presented as inevitable, virtually irresistible, specifically for men. Lindsay implies that, given the slightest chance, any real man, a category that does not include cobblers and tailors, will happily put Chastity in the stocks, although by doing so they will inevitably unman themselves, all too much like those cobblers and tailors.

In Lindsay's earlier poem, the *Testament of the Papyngo* (1530), Chastity is said to have been born as a result of the Church's marriage to Poverty (ll. 794-6); Constantine divorces these two, and has the Church marry 'dame Propirtie' instead (l. 810), which results in the birth of two more daughters: Riches and Sensuality, who together 'Frome *t*hat tyme furth tuke hole the gouernance / Off the moste part of the stait spirituall' (ll. 851-52). When the clergy decide 'Thay wald no more to mariage be thrall, / Traistyng surely tyll obserue Chaistytie' (ll. 860-1), here as in *The Thrie Estaitis* meaning celibacy, these men soon find that 'wantyng of Wyffis bene cause of appetyte' (l. 870). In this poem, Chastity eventually finds a home with the nuns at Sciennes (l. 919). There she remains -- safely, chastely, invisibly and unavailably '[i]nclusit' (l. 926). In *The Thrie Estaitis*, Lindsay theatrically 'enact[s] the total dissolution of all nunneries',[28] and places Chastitie in the stocks, where she is theatrically, spectacularly visible, but physically unavailable. Like Woman in this play, Chastitie is all show: a purely theatrical, if highly ambiguous sign of disorder in a masculine world: a costume, necessary to cover man's postlapsarian nakedness, but dangerous to wear.[29]

Notes

[1] R. James Goldstein, 'Normative Heterosexuality in History and Theory: The Case of Sir David Lindsay of the Mount', in *Becoming Male in the Middle Ages*, ed. by Jeffrey Jerome Cohen and Bonnie Wheeler (New York: Garland, 1997), p. 349.

[2] Cf. *Ane Satire of the Thrie Estaitis*, ed. by Roderick Lyall (Edinburgh: Canongate, 1989), p. xii. All references in this paper to the play itself are to this edition, and are given parenthetically by line number.

[3] *A Satire of the Three Estates*, by Sir David Lindsay, ed. by Matthew McDiarmid (New York: Theatre Arts Books, 1967), p. 9.

[4] *The Satire of the Three Estates*, by Sir David Lindsay, trans. and ed. by Robert Kemp (London: Heinemann, 1951), p. viii.

[5] Carol Edington, *Court and Culture in Renaissance Scotland: Sir David Lindsay of the Mount* (Amherst, MA: U Massachusetts P, 1994), p. 72.

[6] McDiarmid, pp. 9-10.

[7] *The Works of Sir David Lindsay of the Mount, 1490-1555*, ed. by Douglas Hamer, 4 vols (Edinburgh & London: Blackwood, 1936), IV, 202, n. l. 1925.

[8] Greg Walker, *The Politics of Performance in Early Renaissance Drama* (Cambridge: CUP, 1998), p. 150.

[9] The English stage directions of the Cornish Creation play (dated 1611 in the manuscript), for instance, refer to 'Adam and Eva aparlet in whytt lether' (l. 343); see *The Creacion of the World: A Critical Edition and Translation*, ed. by Paula Neuss (New York & London: Garland, 1983), p. 28. On stage nakedness in this and other plays, see William Tydeman, 'Costumes and Actors', in *Medieval English Drama: A Casebook*, ed. by Peter Happé (London: MacMillan, 1984), pp. 183-4.

[10] Lyall, p. 6; see also McDiarmid, p. 32n, l. 245.

[11] All references to the works of Shakespeare are to *The Norton Shakespeare*, ed. by Stephen Greenblatt, and others (New York & London: Norton, 1997). The reference to Cordelia's low voice might well be part of an elaborate joke of sorts, playing on the doubling of Cordelia and the Fool by an adult male actor, likely Robert Armin; see John C. Meagher, *Shakespeare's Shakespeare: How the Plays Were Made* (New York: Continuum, 1997), pp. 97, 110-11.

[12] See *OED effeminate*, adj. 1a, 3. This is the standard sense of the term throughout the early modern period, as exemplified by Romeo's complaint after Mercutio's death: 'O sweet Juliet, / Thy love hath made me effeminate' (*Romeo and Juliet* III.1.108-9). However, like the early modern understanding of sexuality, the term is subject to slippage, and can carry a sodomitical charge; see Garrett P. J. Epp, 'The Vicious Guise: Effeminacy, Sodomy, and *Mankind*' in *Becoming Male in the Middle Ages*, ed. by Jeffrey Jerome Cohen and Bonnie Wheeler (New York: Garland, 1997), pp. 303-20.

[13] 'The Answer quhilk Schir Dauid Lindesay maid to the Kingis Flyting', l. 49. All references to the works of David Lindsay other than *The Thrie Estaitis* are to Hamer's edition, vol. 1 (1931); citations by title and line number are hereafter given parenthetically.

[14] George Puttenham, *The Arte of English Poesie*, ed. by Gladys Doidge Willcock and Alice Walker (Cambridge: CUP, 1936; rep. 1970), p. 134.

[15] Edington, p.76. Gynecocracy was, of course, a central issue in sixteenth-century England and Scotland alike. John Knox's infamous *First Blast of the Trumpet Against the Monstrous Regiment of Women* was published in 1558, only four years after the Edinburgh performance of *The Thrie Estaitis* and the publication of Lindsay's *The Monarche*. Cf. C. Marie Harker, 'John Knox and the Monstrous Regiment of Gender', in *Literature, Letters and the Canonical in Early Modern Scotland*, ed. by Theo van Heijnsbergen and Nicola Royan (East Linton: Tuckwell, 2002), pp. 35-51.

[16] Carolyn Ives and David Parkinson, 'Scottish Chaucer, Misogynist Chaucer' in *Rewriting Chaucer: Culture, Authority, and the Idea of the Authentic Text, 1400-1602*, ed. by Thomas A. Prendergast and Barbara Kline (Columbus OH: Ohio State UP, 1999), p. 190.

[17] Edington, p. 29.

[18] Lyall, p.182n, l. 540: 'Batye tout' has puzzled previous editors: McDiarmid suggests that 'batty' means 'plump' and 'towt' a drink, but these senses are not attested before the nineteenth and eighteenth centuries respectively. Nevertheless, this is a more probable meaning than Hamer's desperate '? a drinking cup'.

[19] Hamer, p. 193n, l. 1376. See Richard Rastall, 'Female Roles in All-Male Casts', *Medieval English Theatre* 7:1 (1985), 25-50. Rastall points out that prepubertal male actors could well have been in their late teens, due to a later onset of puberty, but also notes the likelihood that the roles of older women were most often played by postpubertal actors in medieval theatre. Cf. Meagher, *Shakespeare's Shakespeare*.

[20] Dunbar, *William Dunbar: Poems*, ed. by James Kinsley (Oxford: Clarendon, 1958), p. 33, ll. 122-3.

[21] Neuss, p. 34, l. 409, and p. 45, l. 538.

[22] Sarah Carpenter, 'Early Scottish Drama', in *The History of Scottish Literature, Vol. 1: Origins to 1660 (Mediaeval and Renaissance)* (Aberdeen: AUP, 1988), p. 206.

[23] Hamer, p. 191, n. l. 1280.

[24] Ibid., p. 207, n. ll. 2170-5.

[25] Dunbar, 'Nixt that a turnament wes tryid', p. 56, ll. 94, 98-9. This particular poem is followed in Kinsley's edition by '[a]n ironical "amendis maid be him to the telyouris and sowtaris"' (p. 123n, quoting the Bannatyne MS), in which Dunbar praises these craftsmen for their ability to cover up physical deformity, concluding 'Thocht ye be knavis in this cuntre: / Telyouris and sowtaris, blist be ye' (ll. 39-40).

[26] Glenn Burger, 'Kissing the Pardoner', *PMLA*, 107 (1992), pp. 1146-7. For Burger, the kiss between Chaucer's Pardoner and Host 'aligns the Pardoner and his audience in ways that envelop and fold together the very categories and boundaries with which that audience has been seeking to define and distance him' (p. 1146), precisely because the just-maligned perversity of the Pardoner is effectively and subversively embraced rather than rejected. Lindsay instead allows his audience to distance themselves not only from the Pardoner but also, more importantly, from the Sowtar and his (former) wife.

[27] See Lyall, p. 193n., l. 2100: 'Johnny Armstrong, a notable Border reiver, was hanged [...] in July 1530 as part of a general attempt to crack down on lawlessness in the region [...]'.

[28] Walker, p.138.

[29] I must in closing give thanks to a few persons who have in different ways escorted me through this dangerous territory: first and foremost, to C. Marie Harker, to whose authority I have happily subjected myself and this paper; to David Parkinson, who convinced me to go to Scotland, and to write what became this paper; to Glenn Burger, for more inspiration than he knows of; to James R. Goldstein, Greg Walker, and a host of utterly corrupt students whose thinking on this play has fed my own; and finally, of course, to my partner, André Giasson, who patiently escorted me to those places in which various versions of this play were played, in Linlithgow, Cupar, Edinburgh, and my head.

6

The 'Fenȝeit' and the Feminine: Robert Henryson's *Orpheus and Eurydice* and the Gendering of Poetry

Kevin J. McGinley

Orpheus and Eurydice[1] by the Dunfermline poet Robert Henryson (c.1425?-c.1500) presents a moralised version of the Orpheus myth. The narrative depicts how Eurydice, walking with a handmaiden in a field, is attacked by the would-be rapist Aristaeus, bitten by a serpent while fleeing, and carried off to the underworld. The narrative then recounts Orpheus' quest to locate Eurydice, involving journeys through the heavens and through Hell, and his final loss of her when he looks back before leaving Hell. The poem concludes with a formal *moralitas*, wherein Orpheus is figurally interpreted as reason, Eurydice as the affections or human appetite, Aristaeus as good virtue, and the serpent as deadly sin. Henryson thus allegorises the narrative into an account of how appetite, when not properly subjected to reason, flees good virtue and leads the soul to embrace sin and carnality.

Critical analyses of the poem have largely focused on its sources and traditions[2] and on the awkward relationship between narrative and *moralitas* but have not addressed the relation of gender to these issues.[3] This essay will argue that *Orpheus and Eurydice* draws on and subverts a traditional metaphorical application of medieval stereotypes of femininity and masculinity to medieval definitions of poetry. The poem associates attention to the fictional narrative with femininity while attention to the inner meaning, the *sententia* as outlined in the *moralitas*, is associated with masculinity. Henryson's manipulation of the disjunctive relation between narrative and *moralitas*, or text and *sententia*, along with the poem's self-reflexive comments on this, are the chief areas in which this traditional gendering of poetry is invoked. The tensions between narrative and *moralitas*, however, are configured in a way that questions the gender hierarchy implicit in this model of poetry. In this, the poem undermines the patriarchal bias of the traditions on which it draws and ascribes a new level of authority to those elements of poetry traditionally gendered as feminine.

The most blatant, though not the only, instance of the disjunction between narrative and *moralitas* is the poem's treatment of Aristaeus' pursuit of Eurydice. The narrative accentuates the simplicity and innocence of Eurydice's pastimes, 'To tak the dewe and se the flouris spring' (l. 95) and the lustfulness and cruelty of Aristaeus: 'Prikkit with lust, he thocht withoutin mar / Hir till oppres' (ll. 101-2). As Douglas Gray notes, '[t]his little lyrical Maying scene is in deliberate contrast to the terror of the event which is to come'.[4] Henryson's emphasis sets the narrative in conflict with the *moralitas*' figural interpretation of Eurydice as errant sensuality and Aristaeus as good virtue.

The tensions thus evoked between the narrative and its allegorisation are constructed in the *moralitas* in gendered terms. The *moralitas*' exegesis of Orpheus' looking back and losing Eurydice implicitly comments on the hermeneutic problems which the poem presents:

> Bot ilk man suld be war and wisely see
> That he bakwart cast noucht his myndis ee,
> Gevand consent and dilectation
> Off warldly lust for the affection;
> For than gois bakwart to the syn agayn
> Oure appetite, as it before was slayn
> In warldly lust and sensualitee,
> And makis reson wedow for to be.
>
> (ll. 620-7)

The image of reason looking backwards and giving consent to the affections' worldly desires is analogous to the effect which the discord between narrative and *moralitas* has on interpretation. The backward glances of Orpheus and of the mind's eye parallel the readerly glance back to the narrative when faced with the discomfort aroused by the *moralitas*' association of a cruel and lustful rapist with virtue. Moreover, the image of reason as a widower depicts the relation between reason and the affections in terms of marriage, with reason and the affections being husband and wife, respectively. The poem thus presents a system of analogies in which the relation between the narrative's and *moralitas*' claims to hermeneutic authority is depicted in terms of the relation between appetite and reason and between feminine and masculine.

In evoking this set of analogies, Henryson draws on a longstanding medieval tradition in which poetry's fictive and overtly artificial aspects lead to poets being condemned as liars whose work inflamed the passions.[5] Poetic discourse is thus associated with false representation, superficial artifice, and sensuality, closely paralleling the stereotypical characteristics repeatedly ascribed to women in misogynist discourses of the Middle Ages.[6] As R. Howard Bloch has demonstrated, misogynist writings from the Patristic era onward repeatedly express 'the association of woman with the cosmetic, the supervenient, or the decorative' and 'the association [...] of man with *mens* or *ratio* and of woman with the corporeal' (p. 9). Woman, like poetry and rhetoric, is placed squarely in the realm of corporeality and of superficial representations which distort underlying truth. The suspicion of woman and the suspicion of poetic language thus become conjoined:

> The seductiveness of the feminine is for the medieval Christian West virtually synonymous with delusiveness of language embodied in rhetoric, whose seduction, that of 'mere words, worse than that of empty noises' (Augustine), recapitulates the original sin -- that 'she' in the words of John Chrysostom, 'believed in the one who professed mere words, and nothing else'.
>
> (p. 49)

This gendered construction of poetry, then, operates by bringing three distinct hierarchies into metaphorical conjunction: masculine over feminine; intelligible truth over sensible appearance; and inward meaning over 'mere words'.

Henryson most clearly deploys this gendered structure in the disjunctions between text and moralitas. While the narrative arouses interpretive expectations that privilege the letter of the text as the arbiter of meaning, the *moralitas* overturns this approach with an allegorical mode of reading concerned with relating the narrative to ideal truth. The poem thus arouses the temptation to allow reading to be governed by empty fictive signs, but does so only in order to warn more forcefully of the dangers of that temptation.[7] The *moralitas* classifies such privileging of the narrative as a submission to feminine cupidity and contrasts it with the *moralitas*' own rational and masculine subjection of feminine signs to intelligible and extra-textual truth. The resulting gendered image of Henryson's text is one in which, in Carolyn Dinshaw's words, 'Woman

[...] is dangerous cupidity: she is what must be passed through, gone beyond, left, discarded, to get to the truth, the spirit of the text'.[8]

But the *moralitas* of *Orpheus and Eurydice* also justifies poetry's feminine aspects by assigning them a valid subordinate function. Pure reason's contemplation of intelligible truths, unmediated by representation and 'separate fra sensualitee' (l. 430), is shown to be ineffective in embedding those truths in the mind of fallen humanity:

> Than parfyte reson [...]
>
> [...] passis vp to the hevyn belyue,
> Schawand till vs the lif contemplatyve,
> The parfyte will, and als the feruent lufe
> We suld haue alway to the hevyn abufe.
> Bot seldyn thare oure appetite is found,
> It is so fast in to the body bound.
>
> (ll. 445; 447-52)

Ratiocination alone is here shown as insufficient to move the appetitive part of the soul to espouse such truth, and the *moralitas* consequently directs Orpheus back to the sublunary realm (ll. 459-60). Reason, according to the *moralitas*, needs to employ corporeal figures in conjunction with intelligible truths. Intelligible truths presented in a pleasing sensible form move the affections and direct the appetite to desire and embrace ideal values:

> Bot quhen our mynd is myngit with sapience,
> And plais apon the harp of eloquence;
> That is to say, makis persuasioun
> To draw oure will and oure affection,
> In ewiry elde, fra syn and foule delyte...
>
> (ll. 469-73)

The *moralitas* thus proposes an interpretive mode in which a text's sensuous surface is viewed as an affectively useful mediator of meanings whose basis is outside the realm of representation. Moreover, the need for these concrete textual forms is seen as a necessary concession to fallen humanity's imperfections — their affection being 'so fast into the body bound'. In this respect, while the *moralitas* here defines a legitimate role for the stereotypically feminine qualities of the letter of the poetic text, this role remains a merely secondary, communicative one. The carnal and feminine distractions of the poetic text's formal and fictional elements are subordinated to the service of intelligible truth in an interpretive exercise of masculine rationality: reason playing on the harp of eloquence.

The narrative's description of the Muses who are Orpheus' immediate female forebears (his mother and aunts) also expresses this image of poetry as a womanly form acted on by a masculine hermeneutic. These passages appear to assign considerable significance and authority to feminine aspects of poetry, describing its benefits and dangers in gendered terms which extend beyond the image of the poetic text as dangerous feminine sensuality. But, despite this, the description of the muses affirms the patriarchal gendering of poetry. Three of the Muses do indeed embody the sensuous, textual aspects of poetry and song: Euterpe, Melpomene, and Polymnia. Euterpe and Melpomene are, respectively, 'gude dilectacioun', or delight (l. 37), and 'as hony suete in modulacion' (l. 39), or musical harmony. Polymnia is described as she '[q]uhilk could a thousand sangis suetly syng' (l. 53), again stressing the sensual force of the songs' sweetness. These three Muses, then, represent the sensuous form and corporeal effects of music and poetry. Terpsichore, Cleo, and Erato, however, are depicted not in terms of poetry's sensible forms and corporeal effects but in terms of its relation to intelligible realities. Terpsichore 'is gude instruction / Of ewiry thing' (ll. 40-1), while Cleo is 'meditation / Of ewiry thing that has creacion' (ll. 48-9). Erato is described as she '[q]uhilk drawis lyke to lyke in ewiry thing' (l. 51), suggesting that she represents the power of metaphor and analogy. This power, however, is more than a merely linguistic trope since, as the phrase 'lyke to lyke' indicates, it is a power based on a perception of real resemblances between different things. *Orpheus and Eurydice* thus associates woman not only with the superficial letter of the poetic text but also with its underlying spirit.

In the description of the remaining three Muses, 'Thelya', 'Caliope', and 'Wranya', the poem combines the sensible and intelligible dimensions of poetry. Thelya is assigned a clearly rational, moral function: 'Thelya syne, quhilk can oure saulis bring / To profund wit and grete agilitee / To vnderstand and haue capacitee' (ll. 54-6). Yet Thelya is also connected to the sensual dimension. The stress on her power to bring the soul to knowledge recalls the Scholastic definition of literary discourse as an affective art which employs sensually pleasing forms in moving the soul to embrace truth.[9] Wranya represents not just harmony, but the music of the spheres, the 'armony celestiall' (l. 59). This *musica mundana* is produced by the harmony and order of creation and embodies in eternal form those rules which are the source of terrestrial music.[10] This connection between the celestial and the terrestrial is indicated by the fact that this harmony is 'Reiosing men with melody and sound' (l. 60): it is the ultimate source of the sensual pleasures of music, connecting sensuous outward form to an underlying ideal basis. Finally, Henryson's designation of Caliope as 'of all musik maistresse' (l. 44) suggests a quasi-divine command over all aspects of music, combining both sensual appearance and inner truth. [11]

The description of the Muses thus associates femininity both with the sensible and intelligible aspects of poetry. But despite this apparent valorisation of femininity, the poem still conceives of the inner meaning of poetry as a feminine form dressed in an alluring outward garb of fiction and poetic language, revealed through a masculine undressing of the text, to arrive at the concealed truth. [12] And indeed, all these feminine aspects of poetry are ultimately depicted as subject to masculine reason. Caliope, described as the mistress of all music, 'was crownd / And maid a quene be mychti god Phebus' (ll. 61-2). Phebus, of course, is a god very much associated with reason, and this suggests that poetry, in all its aspects, is here being presented as a passive feminine object (note the passive forms in 'was crownd' and 'maid a quene') subject to interpretive acts of masculine ratiocination. In this, *Orpheus and Eurydice* confirms Carolyn Dinshaw's argument that

> Literary activity has a gendered structure, a structure that associates acts of writing and related acts of signifying — allegorizing, interpreting, glossing, translating — with the masculine and that identifies the surfaces on which these acts are performed, or from which these acts depart, or which these acts reveal — the page, the text, the literal sense, or even the hidden meaning — with the feminine.
>
> (p. 9)

The description of the Muses reaffirms this gendered structure by subordinating the merely textual, concupiscently feminine aspects of literary language to the intelligible and ultimately extra-textual *sententiae* which are the proper and seemly feminine objects of reason's masculine gaze.

Yet there are aspects of the poem which question this resolutely patriarchal hermeneutic model. The construction of the narrative's textual surface as dangerous and meaningless cupidity useful only in the service of a masculine exegesis depends upon reading the *moralitas* as commenting on the narrative. It is, however, equally possible to read the narrative as commenting on the *moralitas* and to do so reveals that the narrative implicitly raises points which reflect critically on the *moralitas*' hermeneutic mode and which reconfigure and question the validity of the poem's patriarchal structuring of literary activity.

This critical reflection is evident in points of tension between narrative and *moralitas*, occuring not just in the account of Aristaeus' attempted rape of Eurydice but throughout the poem. For instance, one of the key tensions, observed elsewhere in Henryson's writings,[13] is between a harsh judgemental perspective associated with the *moralitas* and a sympathetic identification with human experience associated with the narrative. This is evident in the attitudes to worldly love expressed in *Orpheus and Eurydice*. The narrative depicts such love in positive terms influenced by courtly romance treatments of the story in which secular values are prized.[14] Henryson's account of the lovers' happiness in no way suggests any viciousness in their relationship but rather innocent and fruitful joy: 'The lowe of luf couth kendill and encres / With myrth, blythnes, gret plesans, and gret play' (ll. 87-8). The only overtly doubtful comment on earthly love in the narrative certainly mentions its shortcomings: 'Off wardlie ioye, allace, quahat sall we say? / Lyke till a flour that plesandly will spring, / Quhilk fadis sone, and endis with murnyng' (ll. 89-91). Yet this is not a moralising voice which condemns earthly pleasure. Rather, it is a lament which articulates a keen sense of the beauty of earthly pleasure. The pathos of Orpheus' sorrow at losing Eurydice, so forcefully evoked in the lamenting refrain to his complaint in ll. 134-73, '"Quhar art though gane, my luf Erudices?"' (l. 143), similarly depends on an appreciation of the worldly value of what he has lost: his love and his kingdom. This is in stark contrast to the *contemptus mundi* approach of the *moralitas* which describes earthly love as 'this warldis wayn plesance, / Myngit with care and full of variance' (ll. 439-40). Narrative and *moralitas* thus express directly conflicting attitudes towards earthly pleasure.

The narrative's treatment of earthly love as valuable and as a source of pathos invokes a response which, in terms of the late-medieval gendering of poetry, is dominated by the stereotypically feminine characteristics of worldliness and sensual appeal to the affections. Undoubtedly, this aspect of the narrative could be interpreted in the light of the *moralitas*. In the *moralitas*' terms, the narrative provides an instance of the feminine delusions of poetic fiction as it employs rhetorical effect to provide a false image of worldly love, an image which should be corrected by the *moralitas*' masculine subordination of the text's significations to intelligible truth. However, the narrative's positive image of carnal love equally reflects negatively on the *moralitas*' moralising perspective. Gros Louis suggests that Henryson, through his employment of romance convention, 'makes the characters and their tragedy so attractive that the *Moralitas*, by comparison, becomes dull and ineffectual' (p. 646). While underestimating the subtler complexities of the *moralitas*' role in the poem, this comment aptly suggests that the narrative's moving depiction of earthly pleasures can be read as showing the *moralitas* to be overly judgemental, unpitying and harshly insensitive to sublunary values and desires which do no evident harm.

The passages of the narrative which deal with Orpheus' journey through the heavens further underscore the inadequacy of the *moralitas*' approach to explaining human life. For the *moralitas*, Orpheus' journey to the heavens represents the intellect's rising to contemplate divine truth with the emphasis on the perfection of this heavenly realm, stressing 'The parfyte will, and als the feruent lufe / We suld haue alway to the hevyn abufe' (ll. 449-50). Eurydice's absence from this celestial realm is taken to show the weakness of the affections in desiring inferior sensual pleasures: 'Bot seldyn thare oure appetite is found, / It is so fast in to the body bound' (ll. 451-2). Yet the narrative's depiction of Orpheus' celestial journey creates an impression not of the perfection of the transcendent heavenly aspects of reality but of their limitations when it comes to dealing with corporeal matters. Jupiter and Phebus are described as pitying Orpheus' plight: Jupiter 'rewit sare his lamentation' (l. 193), while Phebus 'changit all his chere' (l. 201). Yet despite their best efforts neither can locate Eurydice. The other planetary gods are not much more helpful: in Mercury's sphere Orpheus 'of his wyf thare knaulage gat he none' (l. 214), while the inapplicability of Mars' mighty divine power to such a mundane affair as a lost wife is reinforced by a bathetic rhyme: '...than doun he can descend / To Mars, the god of bataill and of stryf, / And soucht his spere; yit gat he noucht his wyf' (ll. 195-7). Venus alone provides some guidance, unsurprisingly since she is a goddess strongly associated with sensual love. But even her directions are vague, merely instructing him to '"seke nethir mare"' (l. 210). The narrative creates the impression that, despite the gods' divine natures and exalted positions in the universe, their vision is limited in scope and unable to be effectively applied to sublunary affairs. In exposing the limitations of this realm of transcendent heavenly truth, Henryson suggests that intellection is unable to provide insights into matters that require close engagement with the supposedly deceptive and imperfect feminine realm of *sensibilia*.

The narrative's tendency to privilege such feminine perspectives over those available through masculine reference to ideal truths is further emphasised in a digression on musical proportions. In the course of his celestial journey, Orpheus learns of 'tonys proportionate' (l. 226) from hearing the music of the spheres. In transcending the material world, his knowledge progresses from a merely practical understanding of how to play to an insight into the eternal numerical principles on which musical harmonies are based.[15] Such privileging of universal mathematical proportions over sensible auditory form was a commonplace attitude in medieval musical treatises.[16] Yet the narratorial comment which concludes this musical digression overturns this gendered hierarchy of the intelligible over the sensible: 'Off sik musik for to wryte I do bot dote, / Thar-for at this mater a stra I lay, / For in my lyf I coud newir syng a note' (ll. 240-2). Far from privileging an idealising speculative approach to music, this comment proposes that it is practical musical ability, command over its sensible auditory form, that should be the prime qualification for discussion of music. Even more forcefully, the phrase 'I do bot dote' dismisses the discussion of abstract numerological proportions, in the absence of any practical ability, as idiocy. The concluding phrase 'at this mater a stra I lay' primarily means, as Fox notes, 'here I stop'.[17] But the secondary sense of 'I value this matter as much as a straw' is surely relevant, particularly given the dismissive tone of the lines immediately preceding and following. The narrative thus invokes an idealist perspective that seeks to assign privilege to abstract and intelligible dimensions of reality only to dismiss that perspective as irrelevant in its lack of connection to the music's sensuous materiality. Again, the stereotypically feminine forms of art are seen as having an irreducible value in themselves, while the rational masculine interpretive attempt to transcend them seems a retreat from the most fundamental elements of reality rather than an insight into its higher levels.

In these passages, then, the narrative of *Orpheus and Eurydice* invokes, as a means of critiquing the *moralitas'* perspective, what the traditional medieval gendering of poetry defines as feminine elements. The narrative stresses the positive value of earthly pleasures and appeals rhetorically to the passions in order to draw the reader into an imaginative identification with the joys and sufferings of its characters. This focus on corporeality and seductive rhetoric enables sensitive attention to the pleasures and problems of earthly life. Henryson thus effectively criticises the *moralitas'* masculinist privileging of abstract intelligible truths, showing such a focus to be severely limited in its capacity to address human concerns associated with worldly happiness and its loss. Thus, the only consolation that the *moralitas* can offer when faced with the pathos of Orpheus' suffering is that the pleasure whose loss he mourns is worthless and sinful. The narrative, of course, cannot provide a solution to these problems of suffering and loss. But its sensible form can provide a degree of consolation by displaying a concrete understanding of them and an imaginative appreciation of and sympathy with the pain they can produce. Such consolation suggests that those superficial, corporeal, and concupiscent aspects of poetry can in fact give a more effective account of contingent existence than the masculine exegetical mode which locates truth in eternal intelligible verities.[18]

In *Orpheus and Eurydice*, then, the concrete images and rhetorical emotive force of the feminised poetic text display a capacity to engage with aspects of human life and psychology which are beyond the limited vision of the traditionally masculine exegetical focus on intelligible truth. Admittedly, on one level, the relation between narrative and *moralitas* evokes the concupiscent temptation of the feminine letter in order to warn against it, thus reaffirming the traditional patriarchal gendering of poetry. But in those elements of the narrative which so forcefully critique the *moralitas'* allegorising focus on intelligible truth, *Orpheus and Eurydice* critically adapts the text's stereotypically feminine characteristics. The emphasis on worldliness, sensual power, and material surfaces counters the referential inadequacies of the *moralitas'* abstractive hermeneutic by more directly invoking contingent experience and relating meaning more closely to it. In contrast to the *moralitas'* attempt to reaffirm a patriarchal derogation of woman, the narrative posits a model of feminine writing in which, while the traditional definition of the poetic text as womanly is maintained, the text's stereotypically feminine features are no longer denigrated but are assigned a new referential authority.

Notes

[1] Robert Henryson, *Orpheus and Eurydice*, in *The Poems of Robert Henryson*, ed. by Denton Fox (Oxford: Clarendon, 1981), pp. 132-53. All subsequent references to Henryson's works are to this edition.

[2] Much of this debate has focused on the question of whether Henryson was influenced by continental humanism. Cf. John MacQueen, 'Neoplatonism and Orphism in Fifteenth-Century Scotland: The Evidence of Henryson's "New Orpheus"', *Scottish Studies*, 20 (1976), 69-89; Roderick J. Lyall, 'Did Poliziano Influence Henryson's *Orpheus and Eurydice*?', *Forum for Modern Language Studies*, 15 (1979), 209-21.

[3] For an analysis in which narrative and moral are seen to be in tension, cf. Kenneth R. R. Gros Louis, 'Robert Henryson's *Orpheus and Eurydice* and the Orpheus Tradition of the Middle Ages', *Speculum*, 41 (1966), 643-55. For an attempt to harmonise the two elements of the poem, see J. B. Friedman, *Orpheus in the Middle Ages* (Cambridge, MA: Harvard UP, 1970), pp. 194-210.

[4] Douglas Gray, *Robert Henryson* (Leiden: Brill, 1979), p. 221.

[5] For a brief general discussion of this concern, see James J. Murphy, *Rhetoric in the Middle Ages: A History of Rhetorical Theory from St Augustine to the Renaissance* (Berkeley and London: UCP, 1974), pp. 50-4. For further discussion of these issues, especially as they pertain to the early-medieval Christian responses to the Second Sophistic, a response which shaped attitudes to imaginative writing for centuries to come, see Murphy, pp. 35-8; Charles S. Baldwin, *Medieval Rhetoric and Poetic* (New York: Macmillan, 1924), pp. 2-50.

[6] For a wide-ranging sample of medieval misogynist stereotypes, see Alcuin Blamires, *Woman Defamed and Woman Defended: An Anthology of Medieval Texts* (Oxford: OUP, 1992). For a full discussion of the connections between gender and writing in medieval misogynist texts, see R. Howard Bloch, *Medieval Misogyny and the Invention of Western Romantic Love* (Chicago: U Chicago P, 1991), pp. 37-63.

[7] On Henryson' using the narrative to lead his reader into interpretive error which is corrected in the *moralitas*, see Evelyn S. Newlyn, 'Affective Style in Middle Scots: The Education of the Reader in Three Fables by Robert Henryson', *Nottingham Medieval Studies*, 26 (1982), 47-56.

[8] Carolyn Dinshaw, *Chaucer's Sexual Poetics* (Madison: U Wisconsin P, 1989), pp. 21-2.

[9] On the sensuous aspects of poetic imagery as having an affective function, see A.J. Minnis, *Medieval Theory of Authorship: Scholastic Literary Attitudes in the Later Middle Ages*, 2nd edn (Aldershot: Wildwood, 1988), pp. 49-52. For a discussion much more squarely focused on secular poetry, see also Judson Boyce Allen, *The Ethical Poetic of the Later Middle Ages: A Decorum of Convenient Distinction* (Toronto: U Toronto P, 1981), pp. 21-52.

[10] On the numerological connection between *musica mundana*, *musica humana* (the proportions governing the human body), and *musica instrumentalis* (instrumental music), see Boethius, *De Institutione Musica*, in *De Institutione Arithmetica; De Institutione Musica*, ed. by Godofredus Freidlein (Leipzig: [n. pub.], 1867; repr. Frankfurt: Minerva G.M.B.H., 1966), 1. ii. 187-9.

[11] On the sources of Henryson's description of the muses, see Dorena Allen Wright, 'Henryson's *Orpheus and Eurydice* and the Tradition of the Muses', *Medium Aevum*, 40 (1971), 41-7.

[12] See Dinshaw, p. 21.

[13] See George Clark, 'Henryson and Aesop: The Fable Transformed', *English Literary History*, 43 (1976), 1-18; Daniel M. Murtaugh, 'Henryson's Animals', *Texas Studies in Literature and Language*, 14 (1972), 405-21.

[14] On the prizing of secular values in courtly convention, along with more general discussion of Henryson's *Orpheus and Eurydice* in terms of courtly romance and of earlier romance versions of the story, see Gros Louis, pp. 645-6. See also Carol Mills, 'Romance Convention in Robert Henryson's *Orpheus and Eurydice*', in *Bards and Makars: Scottish Language and Literature Medieval and Renaissance*, ed. by A. J. Aitken, Matthew P. McDiarmid, and Derick S. Thompson (Glasgow: GUP, 1977), pp. 52-60.

[15] For discussion and analysis of Henryson's musical terminology in this passage, see Fox, *Poems*, pp. 401-2n.

[16] Boethius, for instance, asserts that the most valuable part of music is the mathematical relations underlying it. This leads him to claim that the true musician is he who is aware of these relations, not he who can best put them into practice, a view expressed in many medieval musical treatises. Boethius, *De Institutione Musica*, 1. 34. 223-5. See also Jacobus of Liege, *Speculum Musicale*, ed. by Roger Bragard, 7 vols (Rome: [n. pub.], 1955-73), I, 1. 3. 17-19).

[17] Fox, *Poems*, p. 403n.

[18] Henryson's privileging of concrete reality may be related to developments in late-medieval philosophy, such as the rise of nominalism and the Aristotelian problem of the One and the many. See Etienne Gilson, *History of Christian Philosophy in the Middle Ages* (London: Sheed and Ward, 1955), pp. 471-520; Etienne Gilson, *Being and Some Philosophers* (Toronto: Pontifical Institute of Medieval Studies, 1949), pp. 50-1. For discussion of these and related issues, see Jorge J. E. Gracia, 'The Legacy of the Early Middle Ages', in *Individuation in Scholasticism: The Later Middle Ages and the Counter-Reformation 1150-1650* (Albany, NY: SUNY P, 1994), pp. 21-38.

Part Two

'Writing Women'

7

A Methodology for Reading Against the Culture: Anonymous, Women Poets, and the Maitland Quarto Manuscript (c.1586)

Evelyn S. Newlyn

In disciplines ranging from art history to science, scholarship has found accomplishments by women in earlier periods often hidden under the attribution to 'anonymous'. That familiar concept that 'anonymous was a woman' has pointed to *possibility*, as it suggested places worth searching for previously unrecognised accomplishments by women. Although in recent decades recovered women's writing has expanded the literary histories of England and Europe, few scholars of the medieval and early modern literature of Scotland have been engaged in the search that elsewhere has had such beneficial effects.[1] Yet early Scottish literary manuscripts such as the Maitland Quarto, a collection of approximately 95 Scottish poems that is internally dated 1586 and named for the politically and socially important Maitland family of Lethington, contain many anonymous poems, some of which seem very plausibly to have been written by women.[2]

Critics claiming that women are unlikely to have written much early poetry have pointed to medieval and Renaissance conditions that inhibited women's writing. External and internal barriers ranged from a lack of such basic requirements as space, time, and materials, to restrictive cultural attitudes toward women, including women's attitudes toward themselves and their proper roles.[3] Moreover, because pervasive and institutionalised misogyny associated women with weaker abilities in and toward characteristics society considered 'good', and with stronger,

innate abilities for characteristics considered 'bad', women were thus
believed to be intrinsically an inferior and destabilising element in the
culture.[4] Since women could hardly avoid internalising such commonly-
held ideas, even when their own experience and knowledge seemed to
disprove them, such beliefs inevitably affected many women's ability to
write creatively, or confined their writing to religious or moral topics
considered appropriate to the feminine gender role. Alexandra Barratt
cites psychological obstacles hindering women as writers, including the
cultural beliefs that the 'written text both carried and created "authority"',
and that authorship was therefore 'incompatible with femininity'; she
notes further that between 1475-1640 women produced only 0.5% of
published writing.[5] Yet some women were able to maneuver around
external barriers and to manage their own internal obstacles so as to write
but may have felt compelled to do so anonymously.[6]

In consequence, a researcher must formulate a methodology for
approaching the literary artifact that employs analytical procedures and
criteria that may uncover evidence supporting an argument for a woman
creator. To do this requires, as Derek Pearsall has said of all new
approaches to manuscript studies, 'a degree of adventurousness', a
'certain readiness to try out ideas that have not been tried before and may
turn out to need reformulation', and the arrangement of information into
'perceivable or plausible patterns of order by the postulation of bold
hypotheses, or even theories'.[7] Demonstrating the adventurousness and
creativity that Pearsall recommends, some critics of anonymous medieval
and Renaissance literature have employed criteria such as the following
when searching particular manuscripts for women writers. Elizabeth
Hanson-Smith, for example, studying the Findern manuscript, suggested
the following criteria as indicating female authorship: 'references to men
as the object of love'; 'the unique occurrence of these poems in a single
manuscript'; 'errors that appear authorial rather than scribal in nature';
'the experimental quality of the verse'; and 'the originality of some
themes'.[8] Some of these criteria seem, however, less reliable than others:
positing that 'references to men as the object of love' attest a woman
author assumes a universal heterosexuality; and arguing convincingly that
an error is 'authorial' rather than 'scribal' is quite difficult in the absence
of another manuscript witness. Seeming equally problematic are other
suggestions that a female author may be indicated if the poem concerns
real life and feeling, or if the speaker's voice is 'without irony or
detachment and not overtly dramatised'.[9] However, the uniqueness of
poems to a manuscript, the 'experimental quality of the verse', and
thematic originality seem worth considering as possible criteria. To the

end of shaping a general methodology for searching early anonymous poetry, this essay proposes steps for the process by modifying or reconsidering criteria such as the above, and by offering additional criteria. The resulting methodology is then applied to the Maitland Quarto manuscript and a few of the Quarto's anonymous poems. The Quarto's historical connection to Mary Maitland, its structure, and its contents make it a particularly promising manuscript for such analysis.

A necessary first step in such a methodology for seeking 'anonymous' women writers is for the researcher to acquire a transgressive perspective so as to 'read against the culture' and thus to avoid unacknowledged assumptions, to become aware of ideologies governing both self and text, and to recognise the value of the subjective as well as the 'objective'. Traditional unacknowledged assumptions, not peculiar to Scottish poetry but still general in western culture, are that men were the authors of anonymous work and that women's authorship is improbable and must be proved by holographic or other incontrovertible evidence. Because women writers, especially through the sixteenth century, are thus not usually allowed even 'possibility', critics searching for women writers must transgress those culturally and societally ingrained assumptions and expectations.[10]   Since none of us brings to our reading a cultural *tabula rasa*, overcoming those well-instilled limitations so as to read against the culture is not a simple task, as Stallybrass has observed:

> To know the boundaries within which we move and dwell and have our being, we would have to stand outside ourselves, comparing the known and the unknown, our perspective and the perspective that transgresses what is ours [...] Those boundaries which are the very horizons of the obvious, of what is taken for granted, must first be revealed as precisely limited horizons.[11]

To avoid being critically imprisoned by the boundaries of our own limited horizons and assumptions and instead to transgress them, we must first recognise that just as an apolitical canon does not exist, neither does an apolitical and disinterested critical perspective.

Literature and criticism, products of human intellects, are inherently and inevitably ideological and political. Certainly, feminist criticism is ideological but, in acknowledging itself as such, differs significantly from traditional criticism, whose proponents not only believe but insist that their approach is 'not political', not ideological. Moreover, in addition to recognising our own ideological perspective as such, we must also recognise the text's ideological matrix. As Louis Renza urges, we must 'document, unmask, and challenge a text's socio-literary situation, particularly its conformity or resistance to the specific canonical criteria that underwrite [...] prevailing social values at the time of the text's production and later reception'.[12] Then, conscious of the ideological forces inherent in critic, text, and critical act, we can work toward the transgressive critical perspective that enables us to see meanings veiled, disguised, or shuttered from us when we employ only the critical lens crafted by the culture's dominant ideology.

With a transgressive perspective the critic will attempt to work outside conventional suppositions and would thus assume, for example, in the absence of overt designation in the text, that a poet or a poem's speaker could be of either sex and that a love poem should not *ipso facto* be understood as being spoken by a man to a woman but may instead voice a woman's love for a man, or any person's love for one of the same sex. That perspective is necessary to read accurately such poems as the Maitland Quarto's poem #49, which only within the last decade has been studied and acknowledged as an erotic love poem addressed by a woman to her female beloved.[13] That transgressive perspective also permits the judicious use of subjectivity; as Renza explains, 'In order to revise canonical thinking in the *right* way' [emphasis his] critics must 'go against the grain of canon-complicit methods of literary criticism such as "objective" interpretation'.[14] An inherently transgressive subjective sense that a poem may be woman-authored can help identify poems meriting further scrutiny. Moreover, subjectivity admitted is, of course, more critically honest than the usual implied claim of an objectivity that is impossible. That subjective sense has led me to undertake study and analysis of some of the poems discussed in this essay.

A second step in the methodology is to identify manuscripts with potential for including women's work because of provenance, history, or a known association with a woman or women or with a particular place or family. The Maitland Quarto, for example, has long been associated with Mary Maitland, member of a prominent and educated family; her father, Richard Maitland (1496-1586), held important positions under James V; Mary, Queen of Scots; and James VI.[15] The beginning of the Quarto contains, twice, Mary Maitland's name and the date of 1586, and she is the subject of at least two poems: poem MQ #69 embeds her name at the beginning of lines 41-2, and poem MQ #85 apostrophises Mary and links her to Sappho and to the sixteenth-century Italian poet Olympia Morata.[16] Yet, although poems MQ #69 and MQ #85 confirm Mary Maitland as a poet, no poems are explicitly attributed to her in the Quarto, which does attribute poems to Alexander Arbuthnot, Alexander Montgomerie,

Thomas Hudson (T.H.'), Robert Hudson ('R.H.'), and especially Richard Maitland, Mary's father, who is the author of 43 of the Quarto's 95 poems.[17] Perhaps Mary Maitland was inhibited by the long shadow of her eminent father, a poet of literary and cultural significance.[18] Mary Maitland may also have been hesitant, in the way Barratt has suggested, to claim poetic authority even though she was clearly a poet. Since women seem likely authors of those poems MQ #69 and MQ #85 which concern Mary Maitland, and given those poems' content, perhaps the authors with Mary formed a supportive poetic community of women who wrote verse to and about each other. In such ways women could circumvent the inhibiting socio-cultural traditions under which they lived, and the Maitland Quarto may be evidence of such circumvention.

The third step in the methodology is to consider whether the physical nature of a manuscript can shed any light on authorship: whether such matters as the compilation of gatherings, details of paleography, or arrangement of poems may be suggestive. For the Quarto, unfortunately, no definitive codicological and paleographical study has been done; the manuscript's binding makes assessing the compilation difficult, and determination of paleography is complicated by a scribe's custom of writing in different styles. The early editor, John Pinkerton, considered Mary Maitland the Quarto's scribe; William Craigie disagreed, stating that 'the whole appears to be by the same hand' but was probably 'written for her by some expert penman'.[19] However, nothing precludes proposing Mary Maitland as scribe rather than some man; in fact, Esther Inglis was the preeminent scribe then in Scotland.[20] Although I consider it likely that Mary Maitland herself was scribe for the Quarto or most of it, uncertainty about compilation and paleography obliges this study to focus on other aspects of the manuscript's structure, such as the arrangement of poems. Although some have thought the manuscript was put together at random, several features of the Quarto's content suggest instead a deliberate structure that, moreover, may provide clues to the location of poetry by women.

The Quarto's contents, by virtue of authorship and by some poems' functions, seem to fall into six sections to which I have assigned Roman numerals; the manuscript's four core sections II-V are framed by sections I and VI. Section I, which forms an opening frame in the Quarto, consists of a single dedicatory poem thought to concern Mary's father, Richard Maitland; perhaps this anonymous poem is an example of Mary Maitland's own verse. This initial poem is set off from the rest of the manuscript by its location on an unfoliated leaf. The manuscript's foliation begins on the subsequent leaf which commences section II and the manuscript's four core parts. Those four core sections, II-V, contain a total of 88 poems (MQ #2-89): 43 by Richard Maitland, 12 poems by other male writers, and 33 anonymous poems. Section VI, a series of epitaphs on Richard Maitland's death, is distinguished from the core sections not only by content but by characteristics of style and placement, and by the consistent use in that section of only the rectos of the leaves. Balancing the dedicatory poem of section I, this concluding section VI stands as end frame to the manuscript.

A reasonable possibility is that after Richard Maitland's death the Quarto's four core sections (II-V) were supplemented by the epitaphs in section VI (MQ #90-95) and perhaps by the unfoliated dedicatory poem of section I (MQ #1). In fact, the four core sections II-V may have been envisioned originally as constituting a whole, since some of the content toward the end of section V seems to signal an ending. In the fourth poem (MQ #86) from the end of section V, for example, which consists of eight lines in the top third of a verso otherwise blank, the poem's speaker calls upon the gods and particularly on Diana and her nymphs 'to end this worthelie' (l. 8). Not only does this poem thereby signal an approaching conclusion to the four core sections but the specific petition to Diana and her 'nymphes of chastetie' (l. 6) suggests a female rather than a male author of this poem, and perhaps a female compiler/scribe. Pinkerton believed this poem was written by Mary Maitland, and Sarah Dunnigan has recently suggested this as well.[21]   The content of such a poem and its placement in the manuscript's structure can thus be significant indicators in a search for women writers.

The Quarto's four core sections are delineated by authorship, with sections II (MQ #2-34) and IV (MQ #50-9) devoted entirely to poems by Richard Maitland. Of these 43 poems by Richard Maitland in sections II and IV, all except three in section II are also found in a second important Maitland family literary manuscript, the Maitland Folio, which contains 182 poems and is an important source for verse by William Dunbar as well as Richard Maitland. The undated Maitland Folio is thought to have preceded the Quarto, but the Quarto does not always follow the Folio's order, especially when one would expect it might, as in presenting Richard Maitland's poems that are also in the Folio. The Quarto's different ordering for many of Richard's poems may, then, be evidence that the Quarto's compiler was not simply copying from the Folio but was working toward a particular structure. Section III contains fifteen poems (MQ #35-49), six attributed to Arbuthnot (MQ #35-7, 41-2, 45), and nine unattributed; however, since two of those nine unattributed poems (MQ #43, 45) are in the Folio assigned to John Maitland, section III of the

Quarto then contains only seven anonymous poems. If the Quarto scribe used the Folio as exemplar, the omission of attribution for these two poems is odd. Section V, the last of the 'core' sections with 30 poems (MQ #60-89), contains only four poems attributed and 26 that are anonymous.[22] In addition to thus broadly organising the manuscript by function and authorship, the Quarto's compiler also attended to structure on a smaller scale, demonstrated by the clustering of poems with similar content or purpose, as in a group primarily on friendship (MQ #75-6, 78-80) or a group offering laments and consolation for afflicted dear ones (MQ #41-7). Such attention to structure at both larger and smaller levels also supports the assertion of an intentional and meaningful design for the Quarto, which gives further signification to MQ #86 as it insinuates a woman author, compiler, and scribe.

Given the control thus exercised over the manuscript's structure, the placement of most of the anonymous poems at the end of the core sections has substantial import. The compiler obviously intended a structural organisation giving priority of place in sections II, III, and IV for work by Richard Maitland and Arbuthnot. Then, in section V, the compiler placed over three-quarters of the manuscript's anonymous poems because, I propose, several of these poems were written by women. Certainly this placement of so many of the anonymous poems in the last section of the Quarto, after three sections (II-IV) devoted primarily to known male authors, is provocative, and suggests the presence, in 'the back of the book', of women poets. Studying such aspects of a manuscript's structure as the arrangement of material can thus be a productive third step in a methodology, a step that focuses on the physical nature and qualities of the manuscript.

Manuscripts that include a number of anonymous poems may thus have potential for including women's work. Observing that 'to have a few songs or poems appear anonymously or under a pseudonym in a miscellany carried minimal risk to a woman's modest reputation', Elaine Hobby states further that 'many more women wrote and published in this fragmentary way than ever set their names to an entire book or pamphlet'.[23] Additionally, the presence of a fair number of anonymous poems that are also unique to the manuscript may be another feature indicating the potential for woman-authored poems. For example, over one-third of the Maitland Quarto's poems, or approximately 38 of the total 95, are anonymous, and many are unique to the Quarto.

The fourth and perhaps the most difficult step in the methodology may be choosing and applying a constellation of criteria to employ in analysing individual poems. The criteria must focus on several meaningful

and persuasive aspects of a poem, and the transgressive critic must again
be cautious in using some criteria that have been earlier suggested, even
as part of a constellation with other indicators. A pronoun, for example,
as in the anonymous poem MQ #78's title, 'Ane freindlye letter to his
friend', does not provide reliable evidence of author or persona. Despite
the title's masculine pronoun, the poem's content, rhetoric, and tone as
they are demonstrated in the poem's ambiguity, indication of
powerlessness, distress over injuries and 'uneis' inflicted by others (l.
26), fear of an error in judgment, and overall concern with 'securitie' (l.
9), seem to point instead to a female speaker and possibly a female poet.
Since male pronouns were commonly used indiscriminately, a male
pronoun should not, in the absence of other indicators, be assumed as
designative.

Similarly, while a single theme may not be adequate to argue for a
female author, the presence of several themes or subjects seeming more
likely of female than male production may be significant. Such themes as
a desire for virginity, fear of choosing wrongly, suffering from social
criticism, misery caused by oppression and malicious others, and a lack
of control over one's life, in conjunction with the speaker's attitude and
response, could be important elements in the fourth step's constellation of
criteria suggesting a female poet. Such themes are present in poem MQ
#38, which appears to be placed contiguous with MQ #39 for purposes of
contrast. Both poems concern the speaker's separation from a loved
woman, and both make no overt reference to the speaker's sex.
However, the speaker of MQ #39 seems obviously to be a man speaking
in a traditional manner of love for a woman and using courtly
conventions to do so; the speaker of MQ #38, in contrast, subtly employs
rhetoric and conventions in a veiled discourse that suggests not only that
a woman is speaking of love for a woman but also that poem MQ #38
may have been written by a female poet.

The speaker of MQ #39, relying upon effusive and conventional courtly
platitudes of praise and devotion, employs the themes and coercive
techniques common in courtly poems wherein a male speaks of a resistant
female: he blames the woman for his suffering since his life and death are
at 'her plesour' (l. 45) and 'onlie scho [his] meladie may mend' (l. 69), he
asserts that submission to his desire will benefit her since 'Sum better
thing sall follow' (l. 77), he implicitly charges her with cruelty in making
of his 'miserie' her 'mirth' (l. 95), and he includes the customary threat
that her refusal of him endangers her womanliness, whereas her
acceptance of him will indicate that she has the 'wisdome' to choose
'womanheid' (l. 99). The contiguous love poem MQ #38, however,

provides sharp contrasts of theme, tone, and originality. The speaker in poem MQ #38 never suggests the woman loved is resistant but instead, referring to the beloved as 'my luif absent' (l. 25), indicates that the cause of suffering is not the beloved's unresponsiveness but their separation. Moreover, the speaker makes clear that at some time they had been together but were parted, seemingly by some external force, since the speaker states that 'from hir I sinderit wes away' (l. 12). The choices of diction in that statement attest the speaker's overall powerlessness to have prevented the parting. Unlike the courtly male lover, this speaker makes no suggestion that their separation could be ended by some courtly acquiescence by the beloved and therefore has no hope at all for the future. Further contrasting the courtly lover, the speaker in MQ #38 does not threaten and at no time blames the woman loved but rather laments the unhappy situation. Finally, after despondently expressing a hatred for life, the speaker makes a decision that reveals an attitude much approved for women in western culture: 'I me foirsaik / for otheris saik' (ll. 104-5).

This self-abnegation constitutes a bridge to the last stanza wherein the speaker articulates a resignation, an acceptance of imposed circumstances without complaining, that seems much more likely from a woman at that time than a man. This pair of poems, then, sharply divergent in focus and attitude, demonstrates some of the polarities in female and male perspectives, the poems' contiguous placement calling attention to the dichotomous themes, approach, tone, and rhetoric given two speakers who both lack the women they desire. The dichotomies and dissimilarities thus emphasised argue for opposite sexes in the two speaking lovers and may, perhaps, further imply for MQ #38 a female poet.

Other themes or ideas that may support a proposal for a woman writer, such as resistance to the requirements of the feminine gender role, may also be in part conveyed by tone and attitude. In poem MQ #69, for example, the narrator relates a vision wherein Mary Maitland appears carrying a sign pronouncing that 'trew Virginitie' is what she has 'socht and luiffit best of all', and that in the future she will 'with cair most diligentlie / sustein the same that it ressaue no fall' (ll. 45-8). Such a dedication to virginity might arise out of religious conviction but, in light of evidence here and in MQ #85 confirming Mary Maitland as a poet, her dedication in this vision may also suggest a preference, known to her intimates, for a life wherein she might develop herself and her talents.[24] The poem may then be a friend's gentle parody of a firmly-held position, since for a woman considered by herself and others as a poet, virginity could symbolise and constitute a desired manner of living. Poem MQ #69's supportive tone and attitude toward such a choice and the jocularity that is common between close friends also seem to suggest composition by a female poet, perhaps one of Mary Maitland's friends.

In addition to combinations of themes and tone, the nature and form of a poem are criteria to examine as part of the methodology's fourth step. Poetic structures and strategies with disruption, incompleteness, discontinuity, redirection, and similar complexities may, with other criteria, signal the unexpected woman writer or persona. Additionally, the unconventional employment of rhetoric and language, the use of unusual metaphors and patterns of imagery, and the manipulation of traditional conventions and topoi, all of which can allow meanings to be layered in a poem, are devices a woman poet might use so as to be true to her art and her ideas but to present them in socially acceptable ways. In poem MQ #38, for instance, the poet manipulates two epic similes so that the poem, at its surface, appears to equate the speaker with men while actually avoiding a definitive identification with that sex. To do this the poet relies on the traditional reader's assumptions about an epic simile's conventions and rhetorical patterns, assumptions which influence the reader to 'see' what is generally expected. However, the poet twists and redirects the similes so that the comparison actually but subtly does not do that which it appears at the surface to do; instead, the rhetorical redirection helps veil the covert indications that a woman is speaking of love for a woman. Such a tactic permits an unconventional topic to be layered beneath one conventional, thus creating for the poem social and moral acceptability. Also worth noting here is the location, in this same section, of poem MQ #49 that treats erotic love between women; the presence of both these poems attests that the Quarto's compiler/scribe was not adverse to including poems about love relationships between women.

The author of MQ #38 employs rhetorical disruption and redirection in one epic simile that begins with the vehicle 'As he that suimmis' (l. 36), and explains that the more this swimmer strives for shore, the more 'he is forced backward by the 'windis blast' (l. 38). This vehicle establishes as antecedent the male subject, preparing the reader to anticipate in the tenor that the speaker will complete the simile by saying 'So I [like that male swimmer] strive'. Instead, in an inexact comparison which may, in its subtlety, escape notice by the non-transgressive reader, the tenor actually has as its subject not the speaker who would be comparable to the male swimmer, but instead an emotion, the speaker's grief: 'So wors be day / my greif growis ay' (ll. 40-1). The tenor's subject, then, is not equivalent in kind to the vehicle's subject, the male swimmer. The poet's use of redirection, and of the reader's rhetorical expectation, allows the suggestion at the poem's surface of a common meaning while actually resisting it and advancing a meaning less common.

The traditional reader's automatic assumption that a love poem to a woman is spoken by a male lover thus permits the poem to 'pass' at the surface as concerned with heterosexual love. If that reader noticed the lack of comparability in vehicle and tenor, that lack might be assigned to the poet's incompetent construction of the simile. A transgressive reader, in contrast, would not assume rhetorical incompetence but would consider whether the redirection was possibly deliberate and purposeful, and what that redirection accomplishes: in this poem, the socially-acceptable intimation at the surface of a male speaker, even as the transgressive reader is invited to understand the speaker is female. In such ways, as Ann Rosalind Jones has asserted, women 'do more than modify poetic style' and instead 'rewrite the rules of the game'.[25] The creator of these ambiguous and redirected epic similes in MQ #38 is clearly 'rewriting' rhetorical rules.

In another of this poem's epic similes the poet again twists rhetorical form to allow the unconventional subject of female lovers to exist beneath, and be disguised by, the conventional heterosexual subject. The poet follows the same strategy of redirecting the rhetorical device; positioning the male as the vehicle's subject in the phrase 'as men may the turtill trew persaif' (l. 18), the simile encourages the reader to expect in the tenor the construction 'So I [like those men] perceive' a creature or person. Again, however, the tenor's subject is not the speaker but the speaker's emotion of desire which, like grief, is not comparable to 'men'. Thus, while appearing in this instance as well to make a comparison indicating a male speaker, the poet again redirects the simile to elude a sex-determining comparison. These uses of elision and rhetorical manipulations to disguise and layer meaning suggest that the author of poem MQ #38 is a woman, a poet treating a love relationship generally unrecognised and therefore invisible in the culture.[26] This level of meaning is discernible from the transgressive critical perspective that, assuming neither male personae and poets nor a heterosexual meaning, is therefore open to meanings that required masking. In contrast, a traditional perspective, hindered by conventional assumptions that automatically heterosexualise a text, does not perceive such possible clues toward authorship.

In addition to varied and unconventional structures of form and rhetoric, the kinds of imagery used may be another element in a constellation of criteria supporting female authorship. In MQ #38 the speaker, because of hopeless love, races painfully towards death faster than the hare, terrified out of its wits, races to escape from the greyhound. That a male lover, even if unsuccessful and lamenting, would be cast as prey in a rhetorical construction designed to convey powerlessness, inevitability, and victimisation of this sort seems implausible. If the lover is female, however, the metaphor is not incongruous but apt. A female poet voicing a despairing female speaker could well see the powerlessness of the hare as entirely analogous to the powerlessness of the woman who is not only unwillingly separated from the beloved but generally without agency in the culture. The figures and themes of this metaphor, then, may further support a case for female authorship. Other metaphors and imagery of this type in MQ #38 also seem more likely the product of female rather than male authorship. For example, when enumerating the troubles and sorrows caused by other people's deliberate efforts to make the lover's life miserable, the speaker compares the number of those troubles and sorrows not just conventionally to the stars in the sky but also to imagery not traditionally associated with men, such as 'drawing colouris' and 'scipping froggis' (ll. 81-2), metaphors which seem more probably to betoken the imagination and perspective of a female poet rather than a male. In a constellation of indicators such metaphors can help suggest the sex of personae and poets and thus assist in a methodology for seeking women writers.

Because reading against the culture so as to find possible women writers in anonymous work requires the critic to acknowledge the ideological function of literature and criticism, the methodology proposed here has as its essential first step the acquisition of a transgressive critical perspective that is aware of its assumptions, open to possibility, and willing to pursue other than just objective approaches. A second step is to identify, by provenance, history, and association with women, potential manuscripts such as the Maitland Quarto, long associated with Mary Maitland. The methodology's third step is to examine aspects of the manuscript's physical construction, organisation, and overall content, particularly its anonymous verse; the last three of these aspects of the Quarto seem clearly to reveal women's influence and women's writing, and also substantiate Mary Maitland's reputation for poetry. A fourth methodological step is to select a plausible constellation of criteria for use in analysing individual poems, criteria such as a preponderance of certain themes, unconventional approaches and tones, unorthodox use of rhetorical devices, and employment of atypical metaphors and patterns of imagery. Application of this methodology reveals that the Quarto contains poetry by women and seems structurally designed to that end;

more important, though, are the indications that Mary Maitland is present in the manuscript not only by virtue of her name's inclusion in the manuscript but as anonymous poet and as likely compiler and scribe as well. Reading against the culture, then, can help create for Scotland a more complete, and accurate, literary history.

Notes

[1] Cf. Sarah Dunnigan, 'Scottish Women Writers c.1560-c.1650', in *A History of Scottish Women's Writing*, ed. by Douglas Gifford and Dorothy Macmillan (Edinburgh: EUP, 1997), pp. 15-43; and 'Reclaiming the Language of Love and Desire in the Scottish Renaissance: Mary, Queen of Scots and the Late Sixteenth Century Female-voiced Love Lyric c. 1567-86', in *Older Scots Literature*, ed. by Sally Mapstone, 3 vols (East Linton: Tuckwell, forthcoming 2004). Also R. J. Lyall, ' "A New Maid Channoun"? Redefining the Canonical in Medieval and Renaissance Scottish Literature', *SSL*, 26 (1991), 1-19.

[2] The Maitland Quarto Manuscript, PL 1408, Pepys Library; cf. W.A. Craigie, ed., *The Maitland Quarto Manuscript*, STS (Edinburgh and London: Blackwood, 1920); John Pinkerton, ed., *Ancient Scotish Poems* (London: Charles Dilly, and Edinburgh: Wm. Creech, 1786). Quotations are from Craigie's edition, designated 'MQ', and cite the poems' numbers there; line numbers are parenthetical in the text. I have modernised thorn. See also W.A. Craigie, ed., *The Maitland Folio Manuscript*, STS, 2 vols (Edinburgh and London: Blackwood, 1919), 1927. I wish to thank the librarians of the Pepys Library for their very kind and helpful assistance.

[3] See Sara Mendelson and Patricia Crawford, *Women in Early Modern England: 1550-1720* (Oxford: Clarendon, 1998), p. 65. Betty Travitsky observes that some women 'wrote "feminist" tracts to protest the writings or behavior of particular men, but they did not suggest that women not continue to be submissive to men, their heads'; cf. *The Paradise of Women: Writings by Englishwomen of the Renaissance* (Westport, CT, and London: Greenwood, 1981), p. 12.

[4] See, for example, *Representations of the Feminine in the Middle Ages*, ed. by Bonnie Wheeler and Stephen Stallcup (Dallas: Academia, 1993). Also Dyan Elliott, *Fallen Bodies: Pollution, Sexuality, and Demonology in the Middle Ages* (Philadelphia: UPP, 1999).

[5] Alexandra Barratt, ed., *Women's Writing in Middle English* (London and New York: Longman, 1992), pp. 1, 5. Also Margaret King, *Women of the Renaissance* (Chicago: UCP, 1991), pp. 157-239.

[6] Laurie Finke remarks that 'the mere fact of oppression alone is not enough to silence women as a group', in *Women's Writing in English: Medieval England* (London and New York: Longman, 1999), p. 3.

[7] Derek Pearsall, 'The Value/s of Manuscript Study', *Journal of the Early Book Society*, 3 (2000), 167-81 (p. 176).

[8] Elizabeth Hanson-Smith, 'A Woman's View of Courtly Love: The Findern Anthology', *Journal of Women's Studies in Literature*, 1 (1979), 179-94 (p. 179). Also Sarah McNamer, 'Female Authors, Provincial Setting: the Re-versing of Courtly Love in the Findern Manuscript', *Viator*, 22 (1991), 279-310 (p. 282); and Rosemary Appleton, 'Gender and Manuscripts: Cambridge University Library MS Ff.1.6', *Medieval Feminist Newsletter*, 26 (Fall 1998), pp. 12-17. Opposing is Julia Boffey, 'Women Authors and Women's Literacy in Fourteenth- and Fifteenth-century England', in *Women and Literature in Britain, 1150-1500*, 2nd edn, ed. by Carol Meale (Cambridge: CUP, 1996), pp. 159-82. Additionally, Dunnigan's 'Reclaiming'; and Elizabeth Heale, 'Women and the Courtly Love Lyric: The Devonshire Manuscript (BL Additional MS 17492)', *Modern Language Review*, 90.2 (1995), 296-313.

[9] Barratt, p. 262; McNamer, p. 289.

[10] Similarly, Elizabeth Ewan observes the considerable amount of research on women in Scottish history that has yet not made 'an impact on mainstream Scottish historical writing'; 'A Realm of One's Own? The Place of Medieval and Early Modern Women in Scottish History', in *Gendering Scottish History: An International Approach*, ed. by Terry Brotherstone, Deborah Simonton, and Oonagh Walsh (Glasgow: Cruithne, 1999), pp. 19-36 (p. 20). Also see Ewan and Maureen Meikle's collection, *Women in Scotland c.1100-c.1750* (East Linton: Tuckwell, 1999).

[11] Peter Stallybrass, 'Boundary and Transgression: Body, Text, Language,' *Stanford French Review*, 14, (1989), 9-23 (pp. 10-11).

[12] Louis A. Renza, 'Exploding Canons,' *Contemporary Literature*, 28.2 (1987), 257-70 (p. 258).

[13] Jane Farnsworth, 'Voicing Female Desire in 'Poem XLIX',' *Studies in English Literature 1500-1900*, 36.1 (1996), 57-72; and Dunnigan, 'Scottish Women Writers', p. 49.

[14] Renza, p. 258.

[15] Richard Maitland held the positions of Keeper of the Great Seal, Keeper of the Privy Seal, and Lord of Session.

[16] Dunnigan discusses these poems and connected the 'Olimpia' in MQ #85 to Olympia Morata; 'Scottish Women Writers', p. 29.

[17] The person designated 'G.H.' in MQ #66, 'Ane Elagie translatit out of frenche,' is not known; MQ #67's attribution to 'Iacobus Rex' is usually not accepted.

[18] Alasdair A. MacDonald renewed attention to Richard Maitland's literary importance in 'The Poetry of Sir Richard Maitland of Lethington', *Transactions of the East Lothian Antiquarian and Field Naturalists' Society* 13 (1972), 7-19.

[19] Pinkerton, p. 467; Craigie, *MQ* pp. v-vi. Priscilla Bawcutt describes the Quarto as 'a woman's book' possibly written by Mary Maitland; '"My Bright Buke": Women and their Books in Medieval and Renaissance Scotland', in *Medieval Women: Texts and Contexts in Late Medieval Britain*, ed. by Jocelyn Wogan-Browne and others (Turnhout: Brepols, 2000), pp. 17-34 (p. 28).

[20] Priscilla Bawcutt, 'The Earliest Texts of Dunbar', in *Regionalism in Late Medieval Manuscripts and Texts*, ed. by. Felicity Riddy (Cambridge: Brewer, 1991), pp. 183-98 (p. 191).

[21] Pinkerton, quoted by Craigie, MQ #2; and Dunnigan, 'Scottish Women Writers', pp. 29-30.

[22] MQ #63 and 64 are attributed to Montgomerie; MQ #66 to 'G.H.'; and MQ #67 to 'Iacobus Rex'.

[23] Elaine Hobby, *Virtue of Necessity: English Women's Writing 1649-98* (Ann Arbor: UMP, 1988), p. 207.

[24] Thanks to Sarah Dunnigan for suggesting the connection of chastity and the intellect.

[25] Ann Rosalind Jones, 'Assimilation with a Difference: Renaissance Women Poets and Literary Influence', *Yale French Studies*, 62 (1981), 135-53 (p. 153).

[26] On lesbian invisibility in the culture see, among many, Marilyn Frye, *The Politics of Reality: Essays in Feminist Theory* (Freedom CA: Crossing, 1983), pp. 152-73. Also Valerie Traub, 'The [In]Significance of 'Lesbian' Desire in Early Modern England,' in *Queering the Renaissance*, ed. by Jonathan Goldberg (Durham and London: Duke UP, 1994), pp. 62-83.

8

An Unequal Correspondence: Epistolary and Poetic Exchanges between Mary Queen of Scots and Elizabeth of England

Morna R .Fleming

At a time when there was considerable pamphlet debate illustrating stereotypically negative attitudes towards women, it is ironic, as well as an accident of fate, that two queens should be found in the one small island. This serendipitous event did not lead to friendship and mutual support between Mary Stewart, Queen of Scots, and Elizabeth I of England. Their relationship was founded on antagonism and mistrust, the Scottish queen eventually being imprisoned and then beheaded at the behest of the English. The two monarchs never met.

Despite Mary's hopes from the time of her arrival in Scotland as a widow in 1561, Elizabeth never acceded to the face-to-face meeting that Mary was convinced would allow them to reconcile their differences. Their relationship became a rhetorical construct, composed of letters, reports, and the occasional poem. The first letters from Scotland, addressed to 'Richt excellent, richt heich and michty Princesse, oure richt deir and weil belovit suster and cousing', hope for 'gude nychtborheid' and 'peax and amytie with hir realme'.[1] Mary's rhetorical advances to Elizabeth foreground their parallel situations, queens regnant in a kings' world. Addressing her sister queen by exactly that phrase, 'Madame, ma bonne soeur', Mary emphasised their kinship, the equality in their positions, and their feminine alliance. Her letters communicate an intimate speaking voice, unmoderated by concerns of political or rhetorical propriety.[2] Mary's poetry to Elizabeth, in contrast, employs contemporary stylistics derived from her reading of the Pléiade poets while at the French court, the deployment of internal antitheses mirroring the disjunction between the queens. In the context of physical absence, Mary's verbal and rhetorical presence is the means by which her relationship with Elizabeth is articulated. This essay explores the way Mary employed different kinds of written texts to give expression to the vicissitudes of her political situation.

Political attitudes to female rule in the mid-sixteenth century were polarised.[3] The detractors were epitomised by John Knox, in *The First Blast of the Trumpet Against the Monstrous Regiment of Women* (1558) who held the very concept of the accession of a female ruler 'repugnant to Nature, contumlie to God, the [...] subversion of good Order, and all equitie and justice'.[4] It was this attitude that apologists for Elizabeth had to contend with on her accession to the throne in 1558. John Aylmer, perhaps the best-known of the defenders of women's rights, directly confronts Knox's argument by pointing out that Elizabeth's birth was 'a plain argument, that for some secret purpose [God] myndeth the female should reigne and governe'.[5] Aylmer also cites linguistic examples to show that 'king' and 'queen' are, in languages other than English, cognate, thus revealing that the gender is merely an attribute rather than a defining feature.[6]

Both queens faced similar difficulties in their own countries confronted by continual dispute and plotting by factions led by powerful magnates. The Protestant Elizabeth Tudor had inherited the throne from her Catholic half-sister, Mary, and, having restored her father's Protestant church, faced Catholic plotting against her rule throughout her reign. The Catholic Mary Stewart, late consort of the French King Francis II and absent to her own nation since the age of five, had been for many of her subjects an irrelevance. Two important Scottish agreements, the Treaty of Edinburgh of July 1560 and the parliamentary reform of August of that year, were concluded by the Lords of the Congregation in Mary's absence.[7] On her return, the queen's refusal to accede politically and personally to these reforms set her on a collision course with the majority of her subjects and with Elizabeth.

In political terms, Mary was a threat to Elizabeth's stability, as she had at least as strong a claim to the English throne as did Elizabeth herself (more, in fact, given Elizabeth's proclaimed illegitimacy).[8] Had the English nation refused to acknowledge Elizabeth as queen on the death of Mary Tudor in 1558, Mary Stewart had the potential in her person to unite the thrones of Scotland, England, and France (and thus to fulfil the prediction repeated by the poet-courtier Alexander Scott in his New Year's poem).[9] Henri II of France did in fact proclaim Mary so, following her signing away of her Scots inheritance to France in April of that year.[10] The situation in England in the 1560s, with Mary pressing to be acknowledged as Elizabeth's heir (even more urgently after her marriage to her cousin Darnley, as a child of that marriage would be doubly descended from Margaret Tudor), mirrors the situation in England in the 1550s when the Protestant government of Edward was destabilised by the expected succession of the Catholic Mary, and Mary's government was itself destablised by the plotting to ensure the succession of the Protestant Elizabeth. Elizabeth would now find herself in exactly the same situation if she declared the Catholic Mary Stewart her heir.[11] It is this complex political background against which the correspondence between Mary and Elizabeth in the 1560s takes place.

Elizabeth seems to have maintained a powerful silence in the face of Mary's persistent garrulity, as her responses to many of Mary's letters can only be inferred from the occasional references to receipts, and to answering points raised by earlier correspondence. Elizabeth's relative taciturnity to Mary, the result of her posture as the socio-political enunciatee regally silent but still an object of adoration, is conceivably mirrored by Mary's articulation of calculated, silent threats in embroidery.[12] A common motif Mary used in numerous small panels was an interlaced framework of lilies (France), roses (England) and thistles (Scotland), illustrating the persistence of her claim to these thrones.[13] As Elizabeth had also used embroidery in the early uncertain period of her life to ingratiate herself with her father, Henry VIII, Mary stitched to construct her imaged identity of queenship.[14]

The mood of 1561-2, although friendly and apparently open on Mary's side, is cool and reserved on Elizabeth's, as the latter's letter of 23 November 1561 shows in its insistence on Mary's ratification of the Treaty of Edinburgh before there can be true amity between the two queens.[15] Elizabeth's concern was for a more formal alliance, which would, from her viewpoint, secure England's northern borders by confirming Scotland's position as a satellite state, independent of French influence and domination.[16] Mary's reluctance to put her seal to it, while causing annoyance, is taken by Elizabeth as the opportunity for some personal negotiation:

> [...] we think it better that ye shuld communicate [...] by yo[r] awne lettres to us, what be the very iust cawses that mooue yow thus to stay in the ratificacion [...] [Y]ow shall well perceyue we will require nothing but that which honour, iustice, and reason shall allow us to aske and that which in lyke honour, iustice and reason yow ought to grawnt.   (p. 68)

Elizabeth's tone is adamant but invitational, illustrating her confidence in her persuasive power. There is an implicit sense of indignation that her motives could be suspected, highlighted by the repeated 'honour, iustice and reason'. It is unclear whether Mary had received this letter when she wrote from Edinburgh on 7 December 1561 that she hoped that she and Elizabeth would become

> [...] fast friends of which each day furnishes fresh proofs, wherewith I feel myself wondrously content because of my desire that our friendship should follow the commencement already so happily made [...which] makes me write to you thus freely [...] and communicate to you my affairs, in order to receive your good advice about them. This I will follow as gladly as [I would the counsel of any] lady there is in the world.
>
> (p. 62)

A letter of the following month from Seton repeats the sentiments:

> You see, my good sister, how, in accordance with the assurance that you have given me that you would take it in good part, I am speaking frankly with you, trusting myself to you in all that concerns me, which makes me sure that you will take my familiarity in good part, as I should do if an occasion offered itself in which I might give you a like proof of my good will.
>
> (p. 67)

Mary's characteristic style is here illustrated plainly. She writes as if to a family member, treating Elizabeth as her equal, although she allows her cousin the wisdom of age in submitting herself to her advice and counsel.[17] Although this tone would vary in the course of the years to come, there is no reason at this point to doubt Mary's sincerity. Aware as she was of the troubles she would confront from her own magnates, she needed to know that she had Elizabeth on her side, but she appears cheerfully to ignore the lurking threat of the unratified Treaty.

A more formally structured greeting appears in the poem 'Adamas loquitur', sent by Mary to Elizabeth with the gift of a diamond ring.[18] Such a gift was very popular in sixteenth-century Scotland, usually as a love token where the accompanying verses express the giver's hopes for acceptance. Mary's heart poem, a courtship gift in the political sense, is rather different, as it purports to be the voice of the diamond. The original French version is lost, and all that remains are two Latin versions, one published by Sir Thomas Chaloner in 1579 and the other by George Conn in 1624. P. Mackenzie-Stewart Arbuthnot, in her edition *Queen Mary's Book* (1907), contends that this poem must date from 1562 rather than any later because of the rhetorical expression, which appears confident and sincere in its desire for rapprochement. This contention is supported by Mary's reported conversation with Randolph:

> Above everything, I desire to see my good sister; and next, that we may love like good sisters together, as your mistress hath written unto me that we shall. I have here a ring with a diamond fashioned like a heart; I know nothing that can resemble my goodwill unto my sister better than that. My meaning shall be expressed by writing, in a few verses, which you shall see before you depart, etc.' [19]

Arbuthnot produced a five stanza English version of the lost French poem from Sir Thomas Chaloner's Latin in which each stanza has five iambic pentameter lines rhyming *ababc*. Robin Bell, in his edition,[20] reconstructed the English version from the Latin in alexandrines, assuming that Mary wrote in rhyming couplets as in the later 'Meditation'. Despite the rhetorical differences in structure, syntax and style, the essential import of the translated versions in comparison to the original texts is similar.[21]

The Latin poem opens with a catalogue of negatives then a qualifying 'but' (*non / nec / nec / sed*): it is not the hardness of the stone, the cutting of the gem, its setting, its purity, all of which could have been used by Mary to praise her own (or Elizabeth's) attributes, but the writer chooses to focus on the shape of the jewel, which is used as the correlative to her desire for friendship: 'But rather because my form is a heart, like unto / My Mistress' heart (but for hardness) that I'm sent to you' (ll. 5-6). In conventional sixteenth-century terms, as found in the many 'heart' poems written by Alexander Scott, Mary's court poet,[22] the hardness of the mistress' heart would normally be the focus of the writer's pleas, but Mary turns the trope neatly on its head.

Where a heart poem or a heart gift would conventionally be sent by a lover to an intended mistress, in the hope of grace returned, these verses have a more political intent, expressed for a mutually-supportive alliance, a point which is brought out clearly in Bell's translation:

> O would I could join them with an iron band alone
> (Though all prefer gold) and unite their hearts as one...
>
> Then they'd say among treasures I was most renowned,
> For I'd have two great jewels in one setting bound.

Then with my glitt'ring rays I should confound the sight
Of all who saw me, dazzling enemies with my light.

(ll. 13-14, 17-20)

Arbuthnot's version employs a more conventional love rhetoric which underplays the desire for political alliance in favour of a more simple praise poem which could have been addressed to a lover rather than a fellow queen. Mary's rewriting of the conventional rhetoric reveals the Scottish queen's sensitivity to poetic self-representation and self-presentation as an equal with her English cousin.

Mary's tone changes markedly when she replies plainly to Elizabeth's letter of 23 November 1561 in a long letter of 5 January 1562. Using no circumlocution or decoration she makes clear that she sees through the terms of the treaty to its intention to bar her from the succession and warns Elizabeth plainly that it will not do:

We know how neir we ar discendit of the blude of Ingland, and quhat devisis hes bene attemptit to make us as it wer strangear from it. We traist, being so neir 30ur cousine, 3e wald be laith [*loath*] we suld ressave so manifest any injurie, as aunterlie to be debarrit from that title, quhilk in possibilitie may fall unto us. We wil deale franklie with 30u, and wiss that 3e deale frendlie with us [...] For that treatie, insafer as conceernis us, we can be content to do all that of reasoun may be requirit of us, or rather to entre into a new of sic [*such*] substance as may stand without oure awin preiudice, in favouris of you and the lawchfull ishe [*issue*] of 30ur body; providit alwayes that oure interest to that crown, fail3eing of 30ur self and the lawchfull ishe of 30ur body, may thairwithall be put in gude suretie, with all circumstances necessar and in forme requisit.[23]

After an indignant rejection of Elizabeth's apparent duplicity, this letter indicates clearly Mary's frankness in delivery and confidence in the rightness of her cause, and the plainness of her dealing with her sister queen. Whereas formerly she had addressed her cousin in familiar terms, using the first person singular pronoun, here she stands firmly on ceremony, using the royal 'we'. The use of Scots reinforces at once the difference between the two queens and Mary's consciousness of her Scottish kingdom. The extract cited above does not read like Mary's familiar discourse, but rather evokes the legal advice she has undoubtedly taken from her counsellors. This could be the actual wording of the new treaty she would be willing to sign, as what she was concerned with was her acknowledgement as Elizabeth's heir, which would of course lapse were Elizabeth to produce issue.

Once she has made her political point, the letter continues in a much more conversational vein, reiterating the writer's desire for sororial rapprochement:

> Quilk [*which*] mater being anys in this sort knyt up betwix us, and be the meanes thairof the haill sede [*seed*] of dissentioun taken up by the rute, we doubt nocht bot herefter oure behavour togidder in all respectis sall represent to the warld als grite and firm amytie, as be storyis is expressit to have bene at any tyme, betwix quhatsamever cupple of dearest frendis mentionat in tham.[24]

Mary's letters tend not to use metaphorical comparison, although this was a trait that Elizabeth favoured, and it could be that by deliberately using the homely image of rooting out dissent, and referring (but without being able to find an appropriate parallel) to the kind of friendships cited in literature and in homilies as patterns of perfection, Mary is attempting to meet Elizabeth rhetorically, if not personally. Her desire to meet Elizabeth face to face is expressed in this same letter, in order that Elizabeth 'sall mair clerelie persave the sinceritie of oure gude meaning, than we can express be writing'.

But this meeting was never to take place. Although there were preparations for a meeting at York or nearby between 20 August and 20 September 1562, and then again for the following year, the outbreak of religious war in France conspired to ensure that it never happened. In fact the only surviving *lettre intime* from Elizabeth to Mary during the period is dated 15 October 1562, following Elizabeth's alliance with the Huguenots, and could be said to mark the close of the potential intimacy between the two queens at this time.[25] This letter, addressed 'Tres chere Sœur', is superficially apologetic in tone, but shows a mastery of the barbed understatement and the veiled accusation. The letter is in French, which further underscores the irony of much of the content, relating as it does to Mary's Guise relatives. Elizabeth begins by lamenting the current events in France and the necessity of action on her part if she were not to prove 'unworthy to govern a kingdom', and if she were not 'also skilled in my own affairs: a Prometheus, as well as acquainted with Epimetheus'.[26] The religious source of the war is the crux, in addition to the inflammatory actions of the Guises:

> And when it came to my mind how it touched your [kinsfolk], Mon Dieu, how I gnawed my heart! [...] Notwithstanding, when I saw

that necessity had no law, and that it behoves us carefully to guard our houses from spoil, when those of our neighbours are ablaze so close at hand, I have not even so much as a suspicion that you would refuse to draw away nature's veil and gaze on the naked cause of reason.

(pp. 76-7)

The invitation to support Elizabeth's stand even against her own relatives or be accused of unreasonable behaviour continues in masterly vein throughout the letter. Elizabeth deplores the lack of action on the part of the French king, contrasting his impotence to her determined and principled opposition to the forces of revolt:

[...] having received letters from the king and the queen-mother that they could do nothing, I well perceived that though king by title, in fact he was ruled by others. Seeing this I devote myself entirely to prevent those evils which would come to pass if that realm became a prey within their talons.

(p. 77)

Elizabeth's seizing of the initiative, her overt contrasting of her own actions against the apparent impotence of the French king, and her open revulsion at the Guise actions shows clearly the difference between the two queens: Elizabeth assertive in her rule; Mary, like the French king, deferential to stronger powers.

The next stage in the campaign, the proposed marriage to Henry Darnley, was certainly seen by Elizabeth as a direct challenge to her authority. Despite the opposition of the Knox-led Calvinists, the Scottish mood at the time of the marriage was optimistic. Mary's choice was anathema to Elizabeth, who had hoped to influence if not dictate Mary's choice of husband, to the extent that she had suggested her own favourite, Robert Dudley, Earl of Leicester, as a possible consort. Mary's instructions for Sir John Hay, Master of Requests, expresses the writer's astonishment that Elizabeth should object to Darnley:

[...] we hard [...] of hir greit discontentioun and mislyking of oure choyse of the erle of Ross to be oure husband; ane mater quhilk [which] at the first apperit to ws maist strange and uncouth, thinkand rather to haif ressavit gude will and approbatioun of oure intentit purpois [...] and be the contrar, undirstude hir said mislyking and discontentment, we culd not winder aneuch [*be more astonished*], finding oure sincere meaning swa mistaking [*mistaken*].[27]

The language of the instruction is, as usual in the letters, plain and undecorated, but shows a more conscious rhetorical structuring in that the unreasonableness of Elizabeth's stated position is fully explained and reiterated with verbal echoes. The fact was that the marriage to Darnley, although a love-match, was overtly political, designed to oust from executive power Mary's half-brother Moray and secretary Maitland.[28]

The letter of the following day, 15 June 1565, rather hypocritically, however, protests love and friendship. This letter is addressed to Elizabeth as 'Madame ma bonne sœur', and its tenor is entirely self-sufficient and calculatedly opaque. Sir John Hay is being sent to 'inform you further of my good wish to embrace all reasonable means to ensure that you do not change your opinion of me'. Mary confides herself to 'the competence of the bearer', and offers to 'kiss your hands', the first time such an expression had been used.[29] She could not know that Hay's arrival at court would coincide with Elizabeth's sending the countess of Lennox, Darnley's mother, to the Tower, and that Moray, Châtelherault, Argyll, and Rothes, with Elizabeth's backing, were even then plotting her capture and imprisonment in the farcical escapade which would come to be known as the Chaseabout Raid.

The similarity in the situations of the two queens, both regnant against opposition, both threatened by periodic rebellion of subjects, both subject to religious differences, each dependent to some extent on the other for the maintenance of the integrity of their borders, developed into major differences after Mary's marriage to Darnley. Elizabeth's continuing unmarried and childless state eight years into her reign caused unease, only increased by Mary's marriage and early pregnancy. There may perhaps be a dig at Elizabeth's state in the afterthought of the letter of 2 February 1566: 'I beg you to excuse my bad handwriting, for my state [in the fifth month of her pregnancy] does not easily permit this work'.[30] This letter twice mentions 'le Roy mon mary', which could be seen as calculated to annoy under cover of sororial courtesy.

There is a plethora of letters written in February and March 1566, in French and in Scots,[31] all complaining of the 'coolness' of Elizabeth and the threats heard in Scotland about English support for Scottish rebels, including a complaint that the English ambassador Randolph had furnished the Scottish rebels with 3000 crowns. Elizabeth countered with a request that Mary receive the earl of Moray and his supporters back into Scotland. Elizabeth's support of Moray -- she openly offered him succour if Mary would not -- infuriated Mary to the extent that she could no longer maintain a diplomatic tone:

How ȝe can be so inclynit rather to believe and crecdit the fals speikingis of sic [*such*] wnworthy to be callit subjetis than ws, quha [*who*] ar of ȝour awin bluid and quha alsua never thocht nor maid ȝow occasioun to use sic rigour and menassing of us as ȝe do, throw the persuasioun of thame quhilkis [*which*] eftirwart ȝe will knaw assuritlie never to have deservit ȝour favour nor assistance to *th*air wikkit and mischeifvous interprisis [...].[32]

The indignation is plain, and again there is the reversion to the royal pronoun, with the reiteration of the blood relationship, the hint of the inheritance to come. The letter continues to describe the murder of Riccio, and the attempted imprisonment of the queen, and develops into an open threat to seek help and support elsewhere in the event of rebellion. Elizabeth should not wish to count herself amongst those who support rebels to a rightful queen:

Praying ȝow *th*airfoir to remember ȝour awin honour and how neir of bluid we ar to ȝow; thinking upoun the work of God quhilk [*which*] commandis that all princes sould favour and defend the just actiouns of uther princes alswele as their awin; quhilk we doubt nocht bot ȝe will do onto us, knowing ouris to be so just as all the world may testifye.[33]

Once again, the pregnancy is nodded at, this time to excuse the letter's being dictated to a secretary. Elizabeth will not be allowed to forget that Mary is effectively her heir, however she may mislike the idea, and that Mary is about to produce her own heir.

The two events, the birth of the Scottish heir and the possible acceptance of Mary as Elizabeth's heir, coincided in July 1566, by which time the relationship between the two queens had improved through the offices of Melville and Cecil to the extent that Elizabeth had consented to be godmother to the infant James VI. Mary refers in a letter to Robert Melville, the ambassador in London to 'the grat joy she hath taken at our happy delivery and also by the gentil grant she has maid to be gossope'.[34] The matter appears to be resolved in the letter of 3 January 1567, the *rapprochement* all but achieved:

[...Q]uhair [*where*] as ȝe require that by a reciprocq contract to pas betuix ȝou and ws, it may be manifested to the warld that we meane not to pretend ony thing may be derogatory eyther in honour or utherwayes to ȝour self during ȝour lyff, or ȝit efter the same, to the

lauchfull yssue of ȝour body; and on the uther part that ȝe will nevir
do nor suffer any thing to be done to the prejudice of our titill and
interest quhilk we have as ȝour nixt cousing, bot at ȝour utermaist
will represse and subdue all maner of attemptis that sall directlie or
indirectlie tend to the owerthrawe or hinderance thairof. [35]

This is a very formal undertaking, rather than a friendly letter, echoing
the legal terminology seen in the earlier letters in references to Mary's
title to the English throne.   Again the royal pronoun reiterates the
queenly position, but this time, Mary was finally ready to ratify the
Treaty of Edinburgh and sent her envoy to England to that purpose.

   This, as in so many other instances, proved a false dawn of amity, as
there was never to be a final reconciliation. Elizabeth was horrified to
hear of the murder of Darnley, and left Mary in no doubt of her feelings:

My ears have been so astounded, and my heart so frightened to hear
of the horrible and abominable murder of your husband and my own
cousin [...] but yet I cannot conceal that I grieve more for you than
for him.[36]

The lexis and tone, reminiscent of the letter of 15 October 1562 (see
above) reveal genuine emotion, and none of the pedantry and austerity of
style which tends to characterise Elizabeth's writing.   Perhaps such a
deed so close to the queen's person reminded her of the dangers of her
own early reign, and she could genuinely sympathise with her cousin.
However, the letter's tone changes markedly hereafter:

As for the three matters communicated by Melville, I understand
your wish to please me and that you will grant the request by Lord
Bedford in my name to ratify the treaty made six or seven years
past.[37]

The coldness of this in contrast to the warmth of the opening of the letter
is astonishing.   As Mary had continually reiterated her desire to be
named Elizabeth's heir, so Elizabeth had consistently descanted on the
requirement for the ratification of the Treaty of Edinburgh.   Even in a
time of extreme danger, the political necessities came first.

   After Mary's flight from Scotland following the disaster of Carberry
Hill in 1567, England found itself in the unprecedented situation of
housing both a legitimate female monarch (with all the semiotic
difficulties that phrase itself subsumed) who had possibly murdered her
second husband, and had been forced to abdicate her neighbouring

throne by her own rebellious subjects, and an illegitimate, excommunicated, unmarried female monarch who apparently willingly took on the role of jailer to the first and eventually consented to her execution.[38] Mary's sonnet, written to Elizabeth in both French and Italian, pleads yet again for a face-to-face meeting.[39] This sonnet in Petrarchan form is tightly structured on oppositions, playing hope against doubt, sweetness against bitterness in the first quatrain:

> Un seul penser qui me profite et nuit,
> Amer et doux, change en mon coeur sans cesse;
> Entre le doute et l'espoir il m'oppresse
> Tant que la paix et le repos me fuient.
>
> (ll. 1-4)

> *One thought, that is my torment and delight*
> *Ebbs and flows bittersweet within my heart*
> *And between doubt and hope rends me apart*
> *While peace and all tranquillity take flight.*

The structure and the tenor show the influence of Pierre de Ronsard, who was the court poet while Mary was Queen Consort in France. The internal rhyme in French is skilfully handled, highlighting the contrary meanings: 'profite', 'nuit' and 'fuient', 'doux' and 'doute' and 'l'espoir' and 'repos'. The queen then proceeds to compare her state to that of a ship stricken while it waits to enter harbour, or the sudden appearance of clouds in a clear sky, to clear Elizabeth of blame for the delay and to blame the fortune of the times:

> Ainsi je suis en souci et en crainte,
> Non pas de vous mais quant aux fois [où] à tort
> Fortune rompe voile et cordage double.
>
> (ll. 12-14)

> *Likewise fear and distress fill all my hopes,*
> *Not because of you, but for the times there are*
> *When Fortune doubly strikes on sail and shroud.*

The imagery, although not the rhetorical style and structure, is of the same mould that Elizabeth used in her own occasional poetry, drawn from the elementary forces of nature. Elizabeth, in her private reply to this, not sent to Mary, employed the characteristic rough-hewn moralistic style of the mid sixteenth-century, in traditional English poulter's measure employing alliteration and assonance to express similar antithetical sentiments:

> The doubt of future foes exiles my present joy,
> And wit me warns to shun such snares as threaten mine annoy;
> For falsehood now doth flow, and subjects' faith doth ebb,
> Which should not be if reason ruled or wisdom weaved the web
>
> No foreign banished wight shall anchor in this port;
> Our realm brooks not seditious sects, let them elsewhere resort.
> My rusty sword through rest shall first his edge employ
> To poll their tops that seek such change or gape for future joy.
>
> (ll. 1-4, 13-16)[40]

Whereas Mary's stance is conciliatory and pleading, Elizabeth's is rational and antagonistic, the final lines foreshadowing the future fate of the 'banished wight'. In fact, this poem, in its simple analysis of the situation and how it should be resolved, anticipates the earliest poems of James VI.[41] The Protestant government in Scotland under Mary's illegitimate half-brother, Lord James Stewart, was conducive to Elizabeth, hence she had no desire to assist Mary in her attempts to regain the throne. As Elizabeth herself had been the focus for Protestant intrigue during the reign of Mary Tudor, Mary Stewart either restored to her throne in Scotland with English support or at liberty in England was a focus for Catholic plotting, clearly evidenced by the revolt of the Catholic earls of Westmoreland and Northumberland and their attempt to free Mary from captivity. Mary's letters and poetry were read by some of the magnates, like the Catholic northern earls,[42] as a sociolinguistic corollary to the Catholic shadow queen lurking behind Elizabeth and as pleas for the revival of Catholicism in England. Mary in captivity in England exploited her epistolary and poetic presence to maintain her claim to the throne to the outside world, as is evidenced by the steady stream of letters to and from Catholic sympathisers. Through these writings, the narrative of the future martyr queen was plotted and developed to the inevitable dénouement of 1587.

Notes

[1] Prince Alexandre Labanoff, *Receuil des Lettres de Marie Stewart, Reine d'Écosse*, 7 vols (London: Charles Dolman, 1844), I, 105. Although I would have preferred to use the original MS sources of Mary's letters, Labanoff's exhaustive collection is generally regarded as the standard, and establishes a coherence in the corespondence.

[2] Melville in his *Memoirs* (Edinburgh: Bannatyne Club, 1827) avers that there was a 'sisterly frendschip between the twa Quenis and ther contrees [...] sa that letters and intelligence past oukly be post between them, and nothing mair desired for the first then that they mycht sea vther, be a meating at a convenient place, wherby they mycht also declair ther hartly and loving mynds till vther' (p. 91).

[3] Amanda Shepherd, in *Gender and Authority in Sixteenth-Century England: The Knox Debate* (Keele: Ryburn, 1994), has explored the pamphlets and tracts which were published at various times of crisis throughout the century.

[4] *The Works of John Knox*, ed. by David Laing, 6 vols (Edinburgh: Bannatyne Club, 18), VI, 349-420.

[5] John Aylmer, *AN HARBOROVVE / FOR FAITH/FVULL AND TREVVE / SVBIECTES, / agaynst the late blowne Blaste, concerning the Go / uernmet of VVemen, wherein be confuted all such / reasons as a straunger of late made in that / behalfe, with a briefe exhortation to / OBEDIENCE.* (Strasborowe, (London): [n. pub.], 1559), sig. B3.

[6] Aylmer, sig. K3^v.

[7] The most important clause of the Treaty of Edinburgh required Mary to renounce her claim to the English throne, which she had maintained throughout her life, quartering the English arms with those of France and Scotland on her own standard; while the parliamentary reform banned the Latin mass and papal authority within Scotland.

[8] As Mary was directly descended from Margaret Tudor, Henry VIII's elder sister, who married James IV of Scotland, and Elizabeth was the issue of Henry's second marriage to Anne Boleyn, a marriage not recognised by the Catholic church, Mary was the legitimate heir of Queen Mary Tudor, who died in 1558.

[9] 'Ane New 3eir Gift to the Quene Mary, quhen scho come first Hame, 1562' in *The Poems of Alexander Scott*, ed. by James Cranstoun, STS (Edinburgh and London: Blackwood, 1895-6), pp. 1-8, repeats the prophecy:

> The Frensch wyfe of *the* Brucis blude suld be:
> Thou art be lyne fra him *the* nynte degree,
> And wes King Frances pairty maik and peir;
> So be discence *the* same sowld spring of *the*.
> (ll. 196-9)

[10] Jenny Wormald, *Mary Queen of Scots: Politics, Passion and a Kingdom Lost* (London: Taurus Parke Paperbacks, 2001), p. 21.

[11] David Starkey, *Elizabeth* (London: Vintage, 2001), p. 321.

[12] Joanne Knowles, 'Intertextuality in Elizabethan England: Mary Stewart's Writings and Embroidery', Pacific Northwest Renaissance Conference, Tacoma, Washington, 10 April 1992; qtd in *Tudor and Stewart Women Writers*, ed. by Louise Schleiner (Bloomington and Indianapolis: Indiana UP, 1994), p. 83.

[13] Margaret Swain, *The Needlework of Mary Queen of Scots* (New York and London: Van Nostrand Reinhold, 1973), p. 84.

[14] Susan Frye, 'Sewing Connections: Elizabeth Tudor, Mary Stuart, Elizabeth Talbot, and Seventeenth-Century Anonymous Needleworkers', in *Maids and Mistresses, Cousins and Queens: Women's Alliances in Early Modern England*, ed. by Susan Frye and Karen Robertson (New York and Oxford: OUP, 1999), p. 171.

[15] *A Letter from Mary Queen of Scots to the Duke of Guise*, ed. by John Hungerford Pollen, S. J. (Edinburgh: Scottish Historical Society, 1904), p. 68; unless otherwise indicated, all quotations of this and other letters are from this edition, English translations by Pollen from the original French.

[16] Gordon Donaldson, *All the Queen's Men* (London: Batsford Academic and Educational, 1983), p. 30.

[17] These letters can be contrasted with the correspondence between Elizabeth and Mary's son, James VI, in which the elder monarch overtly appropriates the letter as a form of advice manual to the King of Scots, and wherein James refers to Elizabeth as both 'sister' and 'mother', acknowledging the lesson. *Elizabeth I: Collected Works*, ed. by Leah S. Marcus, Janel Mueller and Mary Beth Rose (Chicago and London: UCP, 2000), pp. 261-9, 274-7, 281-2, 286-7, 289-97.

[18] There is considerable dispute over the date of this poem, but critics appear to agree that it is more in tune with the mood of 1562 than of later, after the disastrous marriage to Darnley: *Queen Mary's Book*, ed. by P. Stewart-Mackenzie Arbuthnot (London: G. Bell and Sons, 1907) pp. 173-5. There is a reference in a letter sent from Dundrenan, after the disaster of Langside, to the return of a heart-shaped diamond formerly sent to Mary by Elizabeth as a pledge of her amity and goodwill.

[19] Randolph to Cecil, 17 June 1562, in Arbuthnot, pp. 173-4.

[20] *Bittersweet Within My Heart*, ed. by Robin Bell (San Francisco: Chronicle Books, 1992).

[21] I could have given Sir Thomas Chaloner's Latin version plus a prose translation, but have preferred to use Robin Bell's own verse translation, as he has constructed it in a deliberate echoing of Mary's other poetic utterances.

[22] Alexander Scott produced a number of poems addressed to his heart, such as 'Hence, Hairt, with hir that most departe', 'Haif Hairt in Hairt, ȝe Hairt of Hairtis haill', 'The Anschir to Hairtis', 'Vp, helsum hairt', 'Oppressit Hairt, indure', 'Returne the[e], Hairt', all found in Cranstoun *op. cit.*, but these are all on the subject of the bodily organ. The production of heart-shaped jewels and keepsakes was a concretising of the conventional metaphor.

[23] Labanoff, *Receuil*, I, 125.

[24] Ibid.

[25] Pollen , *A Letter*, pp. 74-6.

[26]The comparisons of Prometheus and Epimetheus (forethought and afterthought) were among Elizabeth's favourites in her writings.

[27] Labanoff, *Receuil*, I, 267-8.

[28] Wormald, p. 143.

[29] Labanoff, *Receuil*, I, 273.

[30] Ibid, p. 314.

[31] Series of letters in *Calendar of State Papers, Foreign Series, Elizabeth I*, vol. 8 1566-1568, ([London]: [n. pub., n.d.]; Kraus Rpt., 1966), pp. 21-33.

[32] Labanoff, *Receuil*, I, 335-6.

[33] Ibid, p. 336.

[34] Ibid, p. 361.

[35] Ibid, pp. 389-90.

[36] *The Letters of Queen Elizabeth*, ed. by G.B. Harrison (London: Cassell, 1968), p. 49.

[37] Ibid.

[38] Schleiner, pp. 82-3.

[39] Bell, pp. 62-4. Bell gives the poem in Mary's French and Italian, and his own English translation.

[40] Leicester Bradner, *The Poems of Queen Elizabeth I* (Providence, Rhode Island: Brown UP, 1964). Although there is a contention that this is a poem of the 1580s, Bradner contends that it was written before 1570, as it appears in Bodleian MS Rawlinson poetical 108, fol. 44[v], compiled, according to the *Summary Catalogue*, about 1570. This contention is supported by Marcus, Mueller, and Rose in their edition, taking the version in the Folger Library MS V.b. 317, fol. 20[v], 'doubtless written in response to the threat posed by Mary's flight to England in 1568'. After Mary's execution, it was thought to refer to that event.

[41] I am thinking here of 'Sen thocht is frie', in the Maitland Quarto MS, and Englished and subtitled in Add. MS. 24195 as 'the first verses that euer the King made'; *The Poems of King James VI of Scotland*, ed. by James Craigie, STS, 2 vols (Edinburgh: Blackwood, 1955-8), II, 132-3.

[42] *Women Poets of the Renaissance*, ed. by Marion Wynne-Davis (London: J. M. Dent, 1998), p. 84.

9

Daughterly Desires: Representing and Reimagining the Feminine in Anna Hume's *Triumphs*

Sarah M. Dunnigan

Daughterly desires, both dutiful and dissenting, haunt the extant published writing of the Lowland Borders writer Anna Hume (*fl.* 1644). Her only known incarnation is as a loyal daughter, faithful to the memory of her father, Sir David Hume of Godscroft (c.1560-c.1632), pre-eminent 'Scoto-Latinist' poet and humanist historiographer.[1] Amidst political controversy, she ensured the posthumous publication of his work, *The History of the Houses of Douglas and Angus,* a seemingly arduous duty but one which she honoured in the apparent fulfilment of her father's desire.[2] In 1644, the *History* was published by the Edinburgh printer, Ewan Tyler; the daughter's translation of Petrarch's first three *Trionfi*, entitled *The Triumphs of Love: Chastity: Death: Translated out of Petrarch,* was issued by the same press and in the same year, conceivably the textual incarnation of her desire to be 'other' than the dutiful daughter. This essay suggests that Hume constructs a new 'daughterly' identity for herself in the realm of the symbolic: the *auctoritas* of the literary father, Petrarch, is transferred to a new female *auctoritas*, the Princess Palatinate, daughter of Queen Elizabeth of Bohemia, to whom the work is dedicated and to whom Hume presents herself as 'the humblest of your Highnesse servants'. While Hume does not renounce Petrarch, she reimagines the Petrarchan feminine in the image of the Princess.

The balance between conformity and dissent, humility and hubris, which is a marked feature of Hume's writerly practice, is implicit within the art of translation *per se.* Loyalty or duty owed to the text which is the subject or source of translation is delicately balanced by the subtle processes of *reinterpretatio* which inevitably compel the creation of a new text, reimagined not only at linguistic and semantic levels but aesthetically and intellectually too. In a Renaissance context, the relationship between the original and translated text could be conceived by the metaphor of the originary, fatherly or 'patriarchal' source text. The implicit notion of a gendered, hierarchical creativity can be witnessed in the professed self-conception of French essayist and *philosophe*, Marie le Jars de Gournay (1565/6-1645), as the 'fille d'alliance' of Michel de Montaigne;[3] but this is a gendered model which has only partial and subtle application to Hume's *Triumphs*. This essay contends that Hume's marginalised work depends on allegiance or loyalty to the 'fatherly' text, the Petrarchan *Trionfi*; but argues that other, more complex relations of dependence and independence, 'filial' fidelity and disobedience, arise out of Hume's desire both to amplify Petrarch's portrayal of the feminine and to justify her sensitivity to Woman's representation. Such desire is located in the dedication of the work to the Princess Elizabeth where Hume begins her endeavour to breach the boundaries of Petrarch's presentation of the beloved Laura. Structurally, this is enabled by the division of Hume's *Triumphs* into two contrasting discourses: the translated Petrarchan text (the first three *Trionfi:* 'd'amore', 'della castità', and 'della morte'), and a secondary text composed of the commentaries or 'annotations' which Hume appends to each *trionfo*.[4] These permit Hume to explore the symbolic iconography of Woman in the *Trionfi*'s weave of classical, mythographic, and historiographical traditions.

The consequent 'metacommentary' emerges as a compound of 'daughterly' loyalty to, and rebellion from, the early Renaissance Italian tradition of Petrarchan commentary.[5] Though Hume's translation avowedly rests in the shadow of 'great PETRARCH's name',[6] nominally endorsing the suggestion that translation for Renaissance women entailed adoption of 'a relatively passive role',[7] her commentaries are frequently rebarbative, audacious, and arguably 'proto-feminist' in the tradition of the seventeenth-century European female *philosophe* or *prècieuse*, and claim the sanction or patronage of the Princess Palatinate.[8] Accordingly, the dual discourses of Hume's work acquire gendered associations. The translation, in its direct relationship with the 'fatherly' source-text, may be conceived as 'masculine', putatively authoritative and, of necessity, limited (partly because Hume can only 'ventriloquise' Petrarch's love for Laura). The commentary, marginal in both literal and symbolic senses, may accordingly be conceived as 'feminine' in its pre-eminent concerns with the representation of Laura and the figure of Woman, and by its dedicatory framework to the Princess Elizabeth.

Hume's desire to translate *I Trionfi* in the first half of the seventeenth-century may have been fostered by the intellectual and cultural conditions of contemporary women's writing. Given the partial ideological strictures which still remained at that time against women's publication of original, and even translated, secular works, Petrarch's theological and philosophical allegory conceivably offered 'protection' against any charge of moral or intellectual impropriety; perhaps this may be why, despite her fascination with Laura, she did not choose the *Rime sparse* or *Canzionere*. Hume's *Triumphs* can justly claim to be the first printed example of women's secular writing in Lowland Scotland.[9] Several notable precedents of *Trionfi* translation existed in Tudor and Elizabethan England: notably Henry Parker, Lord Morley's, version of all six *trionfi*; the Countess of Pembroke, Mary Sidney's, translation of the *trionfo della morte* in 1593; and, in Jacobean Scotland, the complete translation by William Fowler (1560-1612).[10] In the *Triumphs'* preliminary matter, Hume professes that she has not consulted any text but Petrarch's own: '[...] I never saw them [*I Trionfi*], nor any part of them, in any other language but Italian, except the poore-words in which I have cloathed them' (p. 96). One can speculate about the degree to which Hume is indebted to earlier versions of *I Trionfi* (whether mediated through earlier French translations), to Fowler's which, as a Scottish exemplar, may have retained some cultural currency in Hume's circle, and to Sidney's which offers interesting, often similar, variants in the depiction of Laura. Hume's preludic 'confession' should still be recognised as a conscious rhetorical ploy, a version of the *excusatio* which, as deployed by other Renaissance women writers, and in the courtly, petitionary text *per se*, was a persistent, frequently obligatory, and often intellectually useful device.

Nevertheless, it is probable that Hume shared the aesthetic and intellectual sympathies of earlier translators such as the popularity of its Christian and Senecan consolations to fifteenth and sixteenth-century readers. Fowler's preface to his translation eulogises the *Trionfi*'s 'morall sentences, godlye sayings, brawe discourses,' apparently 'ma[n]gled' by both French and English versions until redeemed by his own (I, 17). Other factors may have compelled Hume's decision. Reception of the Petrarchan canon in Renaissance Europe was inevitably shaped by changing artistic and literary sensibilities but religious or doctrinal proclivities were also influential. A prolific number of Petrarchan printed texts and commentaries appeared in the late fifteenth and early sixteenth centuries, each promoting a different paradigm, or an ideologically different Petrarch.[11] A considerable metamorphosis in Petrarchan reception occurred in England by the late sixteenth-century, suggesting that the *Trionfi* had been appropriated as a Protestant or 'protestantised' text; as Francis A. Yates claims, safely 'reformed and anti-papal' for its dedicatee, Elizabeth I.[12] The *Trionfi*'s Elizabethan version may have influenced, or justified, Hume's dedication to the Princess Palatinate. Its association with royal panegyric would have gratified the seemingly conservative, royalist sympathies of Hume's family. Yet, even without this particular vein of ideological royalism, the *Trionfi* contains a peculiarly apposite reflection or model of female sovereignty, polity, and power. In the second *trionfo della castità*, for example, the allegorical and iconographical procession of the virtue of chastity, incarnated in the beloved Laura, and therefore rendered feminine, symbolises the overt 'triumph' of feminine virtue, while iconographically Laura is regally depicted by her crown; she speaks with moral and philosophical authority in her instruction and consolation of the bereaved, sorrowing Petrarch; and she remains imperial when confronting the personification of death in the third *trionfo*.[13] These conceits of sovereignty intrinsic to *I Trionfi* may have convinced Hume that the text was ideal as a monarchical 'gift.' Her dedication to the Princess Palatinate endorses the interesting choice *per se* of a female patron or dedicatee by an early modern female writer. The importance of appropriate female models, however rare, to legitimise the endeavours of Renaissance women writers, and to provide the potential for endorsement and affirmation, has been observed.[14] Though Hume's dedication is unusual among early seventeenth-century Scottish writers, Lilias Skene, the Aberdonian Quaker writer, composed evangelising letters to the Princess.[15]

Within Hume's series of prefatory poems the symbolic 'meaning' of the Princess becomes apparent. Hume's panegyrics mirror Gérard Genette's definition of the dedication (*dédicace*) or 'paratext' as both a material and a symbolic act (the dedicatee embodies the 'ideal reality'[16] of the work), which is ultimately public and performative. Hume's 'paratexts' assemble a rhetoric of majesty which blends the Princess's imperial and literary powers into one judgement which, in Genette's phrase, the reader is called upon 'to witness' (p. 134):

> That my rude lines durst meet the dazeling rayes
> Of Majesty, which from your Princely eyes
> Would beat the owner back, blame them not, they
> Want sense, nor had they wit to bid me say
> Thus much in their behalfe: else having heard
> Y'are mercifull, they could not be affeard:
> Or doubting some arrest of sudden death
> Made haste to be reprived by your breath![17]

Other writing by Hume is also imagined to await Elizabeth's life-sustaining 'breath'. The Princess's salvific power is imaged by an act of literal and symbolic intimacy: the suspiration which renews and resurrects the literary text from imagined death and which binds the Princess in a gesture of intimate proximity with the book. Hume's projection of Elizabeth's ability to procure 'salvation' is an almost hubristic act in its deliberate denial of 'boldnesse' (l. 12) and yet its irrevocable certainty of royal dispensation. In the second preface or dedication, Hume declares her 'ende', by implication, the overarching desire, motivation, and purpose of the work, to be the realisation of her role as 'a reall friend' (l. 18) to

> [...] chaste *Lauretta,* whom since I have tane
> From the dark Cloyster, where she did remain
> Unmarkt, because unknown.
>
> (ll. 19-21)

The diminutive appears to suggest an increasingly revealed structure or hierarchy of feminine authorities within Hume's text. Such exemplary self-revelation seeks to vindicate Hume morally, as the second creator and 'redeemer' of the beloved Laura. She achieves the humanisation of Laura at the same time as her exaltation. The expressed desire, 'To make her [Laura] happy, by attending you [the Princess]' (l. 22), is the verbal embodiment of Hume's offering to Laura: recompense for what Hume figuratively portrays as her Petrarchan obscurity and suffering. The 'gift' of the prefatory poems is therefore dually layered, the promise of belated symbolic resurrection and contemporary glorification bequeathed respectively to Petrarchan icon and to historical sovereign. The simultaneous address of both Laura and the Princess, made with almost naive representational intimacy, makes the dedication a weave of historical reality and fictive conjecture. Its imaginative *jouissance* ensures that the supreme paragon of female virtue is no longer the iconic Laura but the Princess: from her alone, the Laura 'reborn' or resurrected in the early seventeenth century may 'learn more vertue than she yet hath knowne' (l. 24).

Though Hume subtly qualifies Laura's perfection in the newly imagined meritocracy of the dedications, they still present the most compelling reason for her desire to 'translate' Laura anew. The trope of aesthetic resurrection and death is discovered again in the second prefatory poem through Hume's aspiration to lead Petrarch's beloved out of her 'dark Cloyster' ('Second Dedication,' l. 5). Her desire to lead Laura into the light, as it were, is *already* achieved ('whom since I have tane', l. 19), an accomplishment presented for the Princess's approbation. The cloister metaphor, with its evocations of the claustral, of sepulchral seclusion, even of the virgin enclosed within the convent, suggests that Laura's emergence is an emancipation from 'unmarkt' anonymity to symbolic recognition. The funerary connotations of 'unmarkt' imply that, given Laura's death in the third *trionfo*, the shadowy cloister may well function as her grave, though any such entombment is only at the level of the bodily since spiritually she endures. Similarly, Hume's resurrection of Laura can only be attained at the symbolic, interpretive level of the commentary text since she is confined, in the body of the translation, to the literal rendering of Petrarch's creation of Laura. Conformity at the level of *litera* is preceded by, and prefigures, the strategies of daughterly dissent in the prefatory material and the commentaries. Indeed, in her preface, Hume has a custodial role over her inherited protagonist. Her tender fascination for Laura is not simply allusion towards the symbolic and spiritual importance of the *Trionfi*'s feminine icon but reflects her emotional and intellectual response to the Princess herself. Laura, held up as a mirror of commended 'wise wordes' (II.2.136), to Elizabeth, is ultimately subsumed into the figure of Hume's patron so that praise of one becomes reflected praise of the other.

Hume's approbation of Elizabeth as the 'true glory' of her 'sex' ('First Dedication,' l. 9) is rooted in a contemporary tradition of praise for the 'star' or 'wonder of the north', whose intellectual gifts earned her the *sobriquet* of 'la Grecque'.[18] Her philosophical reputation is grounded in her epistolary correspondence with the philosopher Descartes, which began in 1643.[19] He assumed in part the roles of intellectual confidante and spiritual director, despite the Princess's avowedly Protestant faith. By the time that Hume dedicated the *Trionfi* to her, Elizabeth was in residence at the Hague. Having rejected three opportunities of marriage (the last, Ladislas IV of Poland, on religious grounds), her dedication to the single state seemed to coincide with the consolidation of her scholastic pursuits: an act of apparent renunciation commemorated a new kind of devotion. In 1644, the year in which Hume published her *Trionfi*, Descartes dedicated his *Principia philosophiae* to the Princess, praising, as Hume does, her 'true wisdom'. Hume's apparent failure to translate the remaining three of Petrarch's *Trionfi*, despite her pledge at the *Triumph*'s end to do so, may reflect the increasing difficulties of the Princess's life after 1644 (the Catholic conversion of her brother, Edward, which disquieted her; estrangement from her mother in 1646; in 1649, the execution of her uncle Charles I) which may have convinced Hume that such an endeavour would be neither appropriate nor wise.

Given the received symbolic status of the Princess in the early 1640s as a young, gifted, and reclusive intellectual, Hume's creation of an intimate alliance between Elizabeth and Laura can be seen as part of a new procedure of filial loyalty: she can remain a loyal Petrarchan daughter but intensify the significance of Laura's redemptive agency through the contemporary historical framework. Laura's presence in *I Trionfi* arguably represents the philosophical 'authentication' of the feminine by which Petrarch renounces the guilt expressed in the *Rime sparse* for loving the created thing and not the creator. In the second *trionfo della castità*, the angelic Laura returns to the earth-enchained Petrarch to offer him consolation after her death: 'Wise conceits, healing cordials' (III.2.155). The third *trionfo della morte*, composed of two parts, constitutes an elegy, the act of mourning and memorializing for a female paragon: 'A pillar of true vallour' who 'gain'd / Much honour by her victory' (III.1.4-5), glorified for her 'chaste mind' (III.1.6) and the gift of her wisdom. Laura's ethereal return permits the spiritual validation of Petrarch's desire.

Where in the *Rime sparse* Laura remains the passive object of Petrarch's adoration, later subsumed into the figure of the Virgin Mary, the *Trionfi* permits the iconically silent beloved to speak. In the *Rime*, her direct speech is recorded only once; her words are otherwise imagined, embodied in the silent language of her eyes, gestures, tears.[20] Laura's 'song', to which the *Rime* refers, is alluded to in the extended speech which she delivers in the second *trionfo della morte*. Hume is drawn to this climactic point at which Laura's desire is rendered unspeakable.

> But say, Was not my Love then cleere
> When I receiv'd the lines you sent before
> Your face and song? My Love dares say no more[21]
> My heart was stil with thee, though I restrain'd
> My lookes...
>
> (III. 2. 128-132)

This statement, typographically emphasised in the printed text with italics, finds brief exegesis in Hume's annotation: 'She sung a song, beginning thus, for an indirect excuse of her reservation'.[22] Earlier she translated 'mi taccio' by the simplicity of 'I held me quiet' (III. 2. 107); Fowler, for example, offers the less emotive 'I held my toung, yit in my hart I had on the remorse' (p. 94, l. 218). These passages signify the apogee of feminine desire, as Hume perceives its significance in *I Trionfi*: Laura's desire is neither a chaste, idealised absence nor negated by her 'reservation'. 'Indirectly,' as Hume's gloss implies, the pure intensity of Laura's desire precludes its verbal articulation.

Such 'reservation' is not just verbal but given physical, or bodily, realisation. Even within the translated text, Hume explores Laura's desire to remain enclosed within her love, and implicitly alludes to the encloistered image of the prefatory dedication:

> I studied to conceale my Love, such care
> And providence dwell not with hope and feare;
> My countenance you saw but not my heart,
> I turn'd and staid thy course with heedfull Art
>
> (III. 2. 79-82)

Hume's point here is the justification of Laura's physical and spiritual virtue. In translating Petrarch's 'E se fu passion troppo possente / e la fronte e la voce a salutarti / mossi, ed or timorosa ed or dolente' (III. 2. 106-8), Hume resonantly offers: 'when I observ'd thy passion grow too strong, / I then reserv'd my selfe, as if with griefe or feare opprest' (III. 2. 90-1). Laura's singular act of self-withdrawal, her retreat into physical and spiritual intactness, is again foregrounded.

This notion of withdrawal, first embodied in Hume's opening claustration metaphor, is reflected in other motivated linguistic choices: 'But mine I hid [...] / Griefe is of no lese weight, because conceal'd' (III. 2. 121, 125). For Petrarch's recognition of Laura's unique consolation, embodied in the litany 'grave e saggia, allor honesta e bella' (III. 2. 66), Hume offers 'her divine / Wise councels, healing cordials [...] honest mirth and chearful gravitie' (III. 2. 253-4, 259). In Hume's text, Laura will be mourned not only for the 'Angelicall Sweet musick of her voyce' (III. 1. 136-7, for 'chi udira il parlar di saver pieno / e 'l canto pien d'angelico diletto') but for her 'wise words'. In contrast, Fowler's translation diminishes the separate sense of her wisdom: 'who evir hard so sweit a speache so full of wit alwayes?' (p. 84, l. 184); the divine *sweetness* of the voice comes first. Hume therefore gives greater importance not only to Laura's literal and symbolic purity but to her intellectual gifts. Hume's adoration of Laura, witnessed in both her panegyric and her 'affective' bond with Petrarch's beloved, achieves her quasi-canonisation: the rendering of Petrarch's 'o vera mortal Dea!' (III. i. 124) as 'True Saint on earth' (III. i. 111) is less faithful than both Mary Sidney's and Fowler's 'mortall goddesse'. Hume may here be mirroring the Marian / Laura cult in this beatification of Petrarch's beloved and her 'blessed life' (III. i. 110), despite the probability that the appropriated 'Protestantism' of the *Triumphs* made it apposite for the Princess.

Hume's refiguring of Laura, the deliberate foregrounding of certain attributes, purposefully solicits the Princess's interest. The discourse of female containment in Hume's translation of III. 2, where Laura keeps herself '[f]or pittie [...] silent, shame, and [in] feare', eulogises the silence which does not entail renunciation or negation of love's intensity. 'Reservation', that conventionally desirable virtue of female conduct, is reconceived as an intellectually and emotionally superior gesture. The portrayal of Laura as a model of quiet cloistered wisdom may be construed as a reflection of the 'cloistered' Elizabeth. A kind of superior female morality or 'protectorate' is constructed which endorses the *Trionfi*'s identification of the feminine, as incarnate in Laura, with reason, and the masculine with the impulse of non-rational desire. Specifically, the *trionfo della castità* is important for considering the ways in which the Princess may be 'immanent' within the *Trionfi;* the 'glorious troup' which surrounds the allegorical protagonist, Chastity, for example, may symbolically depict the Princess and her court. In describing the triumphal procession of Chastity's female attendants, Hume observes their 'Honours and blushes' (II. 63), as well as 'Prudence and Modesty [...] Glory and Perseverance' (66-7). The existence of 'True Chastitie' within 'brave souls' which 'doth modest thoughts beget' intensifies the Petrarchan phrase, 'in cor gentil oneste voglie' (II. 182). Perhaps the *trionfi della castità* rather than the second *capitolo* of the *trionfo della morte*, in which Laura returns to offer the consolation of spiritual eternity against earthly and corporeal suffering, suggests exactly how Hume perceives Laura's transcendent power. The ideal of *virginitas*, which Hume appears to stress opportunely (offering the phrase 'chaste mind' for 'cor pudico' at III. i. 7), may seem a conservative gesture, reproducing the ideology of Renaissance conduct-books. Yet, as attested by the medieval female *vita sancti*, it is important to realise the degree to which intactness signifies physical and spiritual power. Purity of body is to be equated with purity of spirit and intellect; concomitantly, the virtue of *silenzio* is conceived as being neither resignatory nor renunciatory. Hume's apparent criticism of Laura's claustration in the prefatory poem is not really denunciation of Petrarch's portrayal of Laura; rather, Hume seeks to persuade her new readership that the iconicity of Petrarch's beloved is decisively rooted in her intellectual and spiritual agency, and not the apparent orthodoxy of her passive beauty.

Hume's authorial role in the *Triumphs* can ultimately be considered as a kind of ventriloquism. She ensures the articulation or visibility of Laura and the Princess who are themselves constructed as philosophical authorities. Such a device is itself the reflection of a characteristically precarious balance between hubris and humility in Hume's own writerly persona. The nexus of female authorities on which this tripartite relationship is based produces a kind of hierarchy: Laura awaits the poetic revelations of Hume who herself awaits the literary 'sentence' or judgement of Elizabeth. The superior *auctoritas* is ultimately not the memoralised Petrarch but Elizabeth to whom Hume symbolically presents herself as a loyal and deserving daughter. Although both this self-representation and the intensification of Laura's spiritual and intellectual 'virginity' in the translation imply 'daughterly' conformity, there is a significant vein of 'daughterly' dissent in Hume's work. Such nonconformity is enabled by the emotive or affective regard in which Hume holds her protagonist, the almost ingenuous tenderness claimed by the female writer for her female subject. In the text of the 'Annotations' which Hume appends to each *capitolo*, the figure of Laura seems to license Hume's intellectual confidence as challenge is made to the authority of previous Italian commentaries, unidentified by Hume but probably those by Velutello, Gesualdo, and Daniello, specifically in their expositions of Petrarch's *innamorata*.[23] Hume is concerned, for example, to exonerate Laura from the apparent charge of discontent with her birthplace, 'Cabriers, an obscure village', and to clarify the precise day on which Petrarch first saw Laura. In what forms the longest annotation, she questions the interpretation by the 'Commentar', unidentified but made singular, of III. ii. 164-71:

> The sense here seemed cleare to mee, that *Lauretta* being well descended, but borne in Cabriers, an obscure village, shee was onely displeased with that particular; yet the honour of his love was recompence enough for that misfortune [...]; and if hee had not seen her, it is like hee might have loved another, so should shee have missed that honour [...]: but when I looke on the *Italian Commentary*, I finde hee takes the meaning quite other wayes. [...] As if shee had said her greatest misfortune was feare or jealousie, that hee disliking the place in which shee lived (though shee thought it sweete enough) might change his affection, and bee drawne to love some other: Let him that reads or compares, take the sence hee approveth most.
>
> (pp. 96-7)

Successfully asserting the virtue of *both* Laura and Petrarch, Hume refutes their seemingly inappropriate concern with social propriety, and qualifies the image of a Laura proudly preoccupied with renown. The transparent emotional significance with which Hume invests the *Trionfi's* portrayal of Laura and Petrarch lends an affective simplicity to such an exegesis such as 'Other crowned Saints that came along with her, because like hee thought they must dote on her, as hee did' (p. 96). Hume's Laura is not just a philosophically weighted emblem. Affective intimacy is broached in an intellectual sense. The opening assertion within the above passage of interpretation ('to mee') might seem either as supremely confident self-vindication, or naively acknowledged tendentiousness. Hume freely concedes the ambiguity of interpretation: neither condemning the authority of the commentaries nor sanctioning her own, she refuses to portray *I Trionfi* as a static text, transfixed by the cultural and literary readings of previous centuries. New readerly approbation becomes a category of the aesthetic for Hume.

The commentary text comprised of Hume's 'Annotations' (in length usually three or four octavo pages for each *capitolo*) implies that she consciously emulates an earlier humanist tradition of learned exposition. Although not an exclusively male province in the early modern European context, the commentary tradition's self-evident display of learning implies that a female commentator could audaciously assume the intellectual authority prohibited by Renaissance educational and instructional treatises for women. In that sense, the annotations are intrinsically transgressive. The delicate oscillation between daughterly dissent and conformity is found once again. While Hume has no desire to contradict or challenge Petrarch's words, she manages to produce a defense of women, the creation of a miniature *querelle des femmes* text within the overall exegetical text. Recognition of this 'embodied' text clarifies certain impulses in the translation itself. In translating 'schiera che del suo nome empie ogni libro', Hume asserts 'with her [Hersilia's] valorous train / Who prove all slanders on that sexe are vaine...' (II. 132); Fowler offers only 'whose worthines dois euerie booke and storye furth proclame' (p. 74, l. 202). Significantly, Hume's glosses which 'defend women' make no allusion, as do those which are more conventional, to the commentary source which she never explicitly identifies. Naturally, the *trionfo della castità* contains the most extensive catalogue of female *exempla*; here, Hume can only echo, or rather amplify, the honorific status of these virtuous women in Petrarch's text. Yet what emerges as a topos in Hume's commentary is recurrent praise for female self-sacrifice, suffering, and a 'heroism' which is usually unrewarded. Hume's approbation of female martyrdom in a secular literary context has partial root in the Ovidian tradition of abandoned women who have recourse to death; for example, Hume commends Phyllis who 'very wisely, hanged herself' (p. 11). But where wisdom in the body of the translated text possesses a spiritual and philosophical currency, Hume's acerbic and elegant wit here transforms it into a virtue which, quite facetiously, ensures female equality, if not superiority. The nymph Aegeria, differing from her character in the mythological narrative found in Livy, is proclaimed 'as wise as her husband' (p. 26). While closely using Livy as the source for Sophonisba, whose 'affliction added lustre' (pp. 22-3),[24] Hume elaborates the latter's speech to make an exemplar of virtuous and willing female self-sacrifice: the phrase, 'she said no more', prefaces Sophonisba's resolution to die. Interestingly, Hume does not translate Livy's term 'blanditias' which defines Sophonisba's language by connotations of persuasive flattery; instead, Hume's adjective 'eloquent' (p. 22) constitutes a less pejorative, and more dignified, testament to the power of female speech.

Just as affective bonds imaginatively exist between Hume, her dedicatee, and her protagonist, so she cultivates in a way foreign to the traditional esoteric commentary tradition an idiosyncratic personal and affective voice; she thanks Petrarch for his 'sympathy' towards the much-maligned Dido (p. 70), although her actual gloss of Dido's identity echoes those of Velutello, Daniello, and Gesualdo, which cite the pernicious characterisation of Virgil. This example crystallises in miniature the oscillation between daughterly conformity and dissent in Hume's writing. Dissent, in the context of the commentary text, may be conceived as a combination of the *querelle des femmes* debate which Hume extrapolates from the Petrarchan text and the frequent deployment of a subversive wit. This quality suggests that here Hume ironically solicits a female readership, whether a larger community of women readers or the Princess herself, by the rhetorical expressiveness of such wit, and by the celebration of both Laura and *I Trionfi*'s panoply of female protagonists. Only in her dedicatory preface does Hume make rhetorical concession to that *desideratum* of the early woman writer which is humility; but even that virtue is fostered by the need for honorific subservience to Elizabeth.

Hume sustains her dialogue with the *querelle des femmes* tradition until the question of chastity appears. Though she refuses to condemn apparently sinful women, Semiramis, Biblis, and Mirrha,[25] she condemns those who have 'sinned' against chastity: Hypsiphile through 'too much kindnesse' (p. 11); and Sappho (p. 53).[26] The exaltation of female virginity, however, brings full circle Hume's preoccupation with Laura's physical and spiritual state of grace. Hume's reclamation of the encloistered Laura, and the 'hidden' feminine, constitutes the most unusual and radical of dissenting desires.

Hume's *Triumphs* addresses the rhetorical and intellectual dilemmas of early modern female *eloquentia*: to what degree, and with what authority, can the early woman writer comment upon a work, such as Petrarch's *Trionfi*, itself in possession of cultural *auctoritas*? The ultimate 'revelation' of Hume's work is how the act of interpretation is a complex and delicate. negotiation of aesthetic, intellectual, and cultural sensitivities. That act is also gendered, for Hume reads and recreates Petrarch as a literary daughter who is loyal but seeks to illuminate further the philosophical and spiritual significance of the Petrarchan feminine. Hume can be placed in a tradition of dissenting and imaginative female readers which begins with Christine de Pisan and the debates of the *querelle de rose* and *querelle des femmes*. Hume's translation of the feminine, however, is ultimately sanctioned by the further cultural and historical 'translations' which she obtains for her book by gifting it to the Princess Palatinate. The significance of Hume's dedicatee ensures that the final *auctoritas* of the text is ultimately not Petrarch but a contemporary royal model of female intellect. Laura is read by Hume in the symbolic image of the Princess, although her text works also to reinstate the cult of Laura, not least in her quasi-beatification of the implicit Marian figure. Hume is loyal to Petrarch, but she is most faithful to her female subject and patron, both 'milde soule[s]' (III.1.118), with whom she unites in the ways suggested above to create an overarching feminised wisdom. It is neither a relationship of abjection, nor of explicit female-female erotics; rather, perhaps, the tender projection of an idealised female imaginary. The Princess ended her life as Abbess of a Lutheran nunnery, historically returned to 'the cloister', to use the sepulchral conceit of Hume's text. Yet the *Triumphs* succeed in imagining her spirit, as well as Laura's, by means of the aesthetic and intellectual trinity which is Elizabeth reading Hume reading Laura.

Notes

[1] In the absence of substantial archival material, a detailed biography of Hume is not yet possible. For a provisional account, see Sarah M. Dunnigan, 'Scottish Women Writers c. 1560 - c. 1650,' in *A History of Scottish Women's Writing*, ed. by Douglas Gifford and Dorothy McMillan (Edinburgh: EUP, 1997), pp. 15-43 (pp. 34-8). She belonged to an erudite family who lived in Berwickshire, near Jedburgh. Hume's brother, James (*fl.* 1639), published several mathematical treatises from Parisian presses.

[2] See Dunnigan, pp. 34-5; for an authoritative account of her father's career and an account of the *History*'s publication controversy, see David Reid's

introduction to his edition of Hume's *History of the Houses of Douglas and Angus*, STS, 2 vols (Edinburgh, 1996). I would like to thank Dr. Reid for kindly discussing the Hume family with me.

[3] On the notion of de Gournay's 'adoptive father', see Patricia Francis Cholakian, 'The Identity of the Reader in Marie de Gournay's *Le Proumenoir de Monsieur de Montaigne* (1594)', in *Seeking the Woman in Late Medieval and Renaissance Writings. Essays in Feminist Contextual Criticism*, ed. by Sheila Fisher and Janet Halley (Knoxville: University of Tennessee Press, 1989), pp. 207-32.

[4] A third discourse exists within the commentary text: the prefatory couplets placed at the beginning of each *trionfo*, summarising 'The Argument'.

[5] The most influential annotated edition was Bernardo da Pietro Lapini da Montalcino (1475), echoed in later expositions by Alessandro Velutello, Giovanni Andrea Gesualdo, and Jacopp Pollio. See Gian Carlo Alessio, 'The *lectura* of the *Triumphi* in the fifteenth century', in *Petrarch's Triumphs: Allegory and Spectacle*, ed. by Konrad Eisenbichler and Amilcare A. Iannucci (Ottawa: Dovehouse, 1990), pp. 269-90.

[6] 'To the most excellent Princesse, her Highnesse, the Princesse ELISABETH, Eldest daughter to the King of Bohemia', l. 14 (for convenience, the two prefatory poems, Sigs. A2-3, are abbreviated in the text as 'First' and 'Second Dedication'). Quotations from the translation are identified by the relevant *trionfo*, *capitolo*, and line reference (eg. I. ii. 3); those from the 'Annotations' are cited by page reference only. All quotations are based on the 1644 edition.

[7] Tina Krontiris, *Oppositional Voices: Women as Writers and Translators of Literature in the English Renaissance* (London: Routledge, 1992), p. 20.

[8] I have not yet discovered documentation of Elizabeth's apparent patronage of Hume, or evidence that Hume visited the Princess's court; their relationship may only be imagined within Hume's text. The exiled Elector and Electress created a considerable intellectual and artistic society at the Hague, reflecting the nascent prosperity of the Dutch Republic.

[9] See the 'Introduction' to this volume for further discussion of this point.

[10] *The Tryumphes of Fraunces Petrarche tr. H. Parker, Lorde Morley* (1555); *Lord Morley's Tryumphes of Fraunces Petrarcke. The First English Translation of the Trionfi*, ed. by D.D. Carnicelli (Harvard: HUP, 1971). For Mary Sidney, see *The Collected Works of Mary Sidney Herbert Countess of Pembroke*, ed. by Margaret P. Hannay, Noel J. Kinnamon, and Michael G. Brennan, 3 vols (Oxford: Clarendon, 1998), *Poems, Translations, and Correspondence*, I, 255-318. For William Fowler, see *The Works of William Fowler*, ed. by Henry W. Meikle, James Craigie, and John Purves, STS, 3 vols (Edinburgh: Blackwood, 1912-39), I, 13-134.

[11] See William J. Kennedy, *Authorizing Petrarch* (Ithaca: Cornell UP, 1994).

[12] Francis A. Yates, *Astraea: the Imperial Theme in the Sixteenth Century* (London: Routledge and Kegan Paul, 1975), p. 113.

[13] *Works of Mary Sidney*, I, 263-4.

[14] Cf. Joan Kelly's essay, 'Early Feminist Theory and the *Querelle des Femmes* 1400-1789', *Signs*, 8 (1982), 4-28 (p. 26), on the inspiration of female 'power figures' for women writers. Aemilia Lanyer has no less than nine female

dedicatees for *Salve Deus, Rex Judaeorum* (1611); Marie de Gournay dedicated the *Egalité des hommes et des femmes* (1622) to Anne of Austria (1601-66). *Eliza's Babes: or, the Virgins-Offering. Being Divine Poems and Meditations* (London, 1652), signed 'By a Lady' and dedicated 'To my sisters' is an anthology of mostly religious material, some of which is dedicated to specific women; interestingly, it may have been produced at the court of Queen Elizabeth of Bohemia.

[15] Hume's dedication has broad precedent in seventeenth-century Scottish royalist traditions: the Ovidian epistles of the Scottish NeoLatinist, Arthur Johnston (1577-1641), were inspired by the dangers facing Frederick and Elizabeth at the beginning of the Thirty Years War; in his *Poemata Omnia*, Hume's father included an elegy on the death of Prince Henry and a poem on James VI's return to Scotland in 1617. On Skene, see Gordon DesBrisay's essay in this volume.

[16] Gérard Genette, *Paratexts: Thresholds of Interpretation*, trans. by Jane E. Lewin (Cambridge: CUP, 1997), p. 117.

[17] 'First Dedication', ll. 1-8.

[18] For diverse accounts of the Stuart Queen, see C. Benger, *Memoirs of Elizabeth Stuart, Queen of Bohemia*, 2 vols (London, 1825); Carola Oman, *Elizabeth of Bohemia* (London: Hodder & Stoughton, 1938); Rosalind K. Marshall, *The Winter Queen. The Life of Elizabeth of Bohemia 1596-1662* (Edinburgh: Scottish National Portrait Gallery, 1998). For a general account of seventeenth-century Bohemian politics, see James Van Horn Melton, 'The Nobility in the Bohemian and Austrian Lands, 1620-1780', in H.M. Scott ed., *The European Nobilities in the Seventeenth and Eighteenth Centuries*, 2 vols (Essex: Longman, 1995), II, 110-43.

[19] See Andrea Nye, *The Princess and the Philosopher. Letters of Elisabeth of the Palatine to René Descartes* (Rowman & Littlefield, 1999); *Women Philosophers of the Early Modern Period*, ed. by Margaret Atherton (Indianapolis: Hackett, 1994), pp. 1-21.

[20] Sara Sturm-Maddox, *Petrarch's Laurels* (Philadelphia: Pennsylvania State UP, 1992), p. 119.

[21] Mary Sidney's gloss is almost identical to Hume's, 'my love dares speake no more', though it is almost impossible that Hume had read Sidney's manuscript version.

[22] This partly accords with the commentary tradition such as Giovanni Andrea Gesualdo's *Il Petrarcha con l'espositione* (Venice, 1581): 'in lingua Provenzale [...] nostra amor cantando' [*in the Provençal language [...] singing of our love*] (p. 84).

[23] On the Italian commentaries which Hume may have used, see Dunnigan, p. 37.

[24] This evokes a classical tradition of female glorification through suffering or renunciation. Hume's citation of 'Titius Livius' alludes to Livy's *Ab urbe condita libri*, XXX.

[25] 'Biblis loved her brother: Semiramis loved her sonne, yet some Authours thinke it a calumnie. Mirrha loved her father' (p. 42).

---

[26] Unexpectedly, Hume is critical of Sappho (p. 53), adding a caustic gendered judgement to the favourable assessments of the Italian commentary tradition.

10

'Neither Out nor In': Scottish Gaelic Women Poets 1650-1750

Colm Ó Baoill

Sin far am biodh i na seasamh, is cha robh i muigh is cha robh i staigh.
That was where she would stand, and she was neither out nor in.

South Uist tradition

Gaelic society in the Scottish Highlands has been remarkable in the number of women poets it has produced over the centuries and in the degree of suspicion and mistrust it seems to have accorded them. While their poems and songs testify to their prominent place in the maintenance of the social fabric, women poets of the period 1650-1750 were distrusted and, on the evidence of surviving stories and traditions, widely believed to be involved in witchcraft and sexual profligacy. Modern oral tradition suggests that though they might compose certain types of song (lullabies, waulking or 'wool-felting' songs, and light songs generally), women were not supposed to compose large-scale panegyrics to clan heroes.[1] Ambition or 'excess' could be condemned on moral grounds. The phrase from South Uist tradition found in the epigraph, 'neither out nor in',[2] is a metaphor which evocatively expresses the status ascribed to the female poet within the Gaelic oral tradition: as a poet she was 'in', but as a woman who composed she was not entirely so.[3] This essay explores in turn the work of four seventeenth and early eighteenth-century women poets — Màiri nighean Alasdair Ruaidh, Sìleas na Ceapaich, Mairghread nighean Lachlainn, and 'An Aigeannach' — and their paradoxical 'threshold' status. To understand the literary, cultural, and political contexts in which these women poets composed, it is first

136

necessary to consider the historical conditions which shaped the emergence of new kinds of Gaelic verse in the seventeenth century.

In Gaelic Scotland women poets have been prominent from the period in which vernacular Gaelic can first be identified. The sixteenth-century manuscript collection known as *The Book of the Dean of Lismore* presents the earliest substantial evidence for the distinctively Scottish form of Gaelic, and contains three poems composed in the medieval *amour courtois* tradition ascribed to aristocratic Campbell women of the fifteenth century; alternatively, all three may be the work of Iseabail Ní Mheic Cailéin.[4] Scotland far exceeds Ireland in the number of Gaelic women well known as poets. One reason for this may be the fact that, to a large extent, Highland Scotland remained an heroic society until the defeat at Culloden in 1746; the parallel Gaelic heroic society in Ireland had been effectively destroyed in a series of English victories in the seventeenth century. Another reason for their relative prominence may be the popularity of the Waulking Song tradition in the Scottish Highlands, comprising songs which were primarily composed as an aid to the waulking, or fulling, of cloth according to a distinctive Highland method. The new cloth was soaked and beaten in a traditional process involving a number of women, generally round a table, who sang as they worked, drawing on a store of songs which are clearly women's songs and which provided accompaniment for the beating of the cloth.[5] This song type belonged mainly to women of lower social status, but it might be argued that the clan-centred society of the Highlands had long been familiar, and at ease, with the idea that women could be poets. However, the better known women poets after 1600 were not mere makers of work-songs: they can be considered 'public' poets in that their work is more concerned with political rather than personal or lyrical subjects.

This mirrors the nature of poetry produced by the traditions of Gaelic male poets. In the pre-1600 social polity of Gaelic Scotland, political leaders and professional poets depended on one another. The poet served as the political sophisticate who could advise the warrior chief and provide him with highly learned praise poetry on demand. Important and powerful literary families constituted a learned middle class. However, by the seventeenth century, traditional Gaelic learning had sharply declined and, other than the appearance of a small number of religious texts, new written material in Gaelic is almost entirely absent. James VI believed that the Gaelic Highlands must be 'civilised' by the spread of the gospel and the extirpation of the Gaelic language. Education was directed forcefully towards literacy in English. Nevertheless, an entirely new genre of Gaelic poetry emerges c. 1600: a song tradition composed in the Scottish Gaelic language of the common people, less learned and less metrically complex than the creations of professional poets; the new poets are non-literate and apparently not paid for their verse. Still, the subjects of this new tradition echo those of the earlier songs: namely, endorsement of the social and political *status quo* through praise of clan, chief, and political achievement or ambition. The liminal cultural status of the four poets here examined, and the distinctive nature of their poetry, must be understood in the context of the changing political and social conditions of late medieval and early modern Gaelic Scotland.

Màiri nighean Alasdair Ruaidh (c. 1615 - c. 1705) was a MacLeod, 'the daughter of Alasdair Ruadh', and a highly respected poet of her clan. It is reported from oral tradition that Màiri directed that she herself should be placed face down in her grave in St Clement's church in Rodel, Harris, that 'the lying mouth should be underneath her'.[6] A similar tradition exists in relation to another poet, Mairghread nighean Lachlainn (discussed later), sometimes with the addition that Mairghread was to be buried, face down, under a pile of stones. It has been noted that such burials are similar to instances derived from Norse tradition for witches, and in Tacitus' *Germania* for assorted male malefactors.[7] While the tradition of witchcraft is probably a relatively recent import into Gaeldom, it may be that these two women poets were viewed by the tradition-bearers as wielders of sinister supernatural powers. Màiri's songs, of which there are about twelve, first written down after 1746 (her songs survived for at least forty years, and some for a century, in oral tradition), do not betray such implications. Most are concerned with MacLeod chiefs, either with those of the principal family, the MacLeods of Dunvegan (to whom she herself was distantly related), or with their cadet Sir Norman MacLeod of Berneray (c. 1614 - 1705). Màiri adheres to the panegyric code as faithfully as any male poet: the subject's ancestry is portrayed as impeccable, his allies the noblest and most courageous. He himself is handsome, loving, and kind to the weak and the young and to his friends, but fearsome to his enemies; he is a master of warfare, hunting, and seafaring. Much attention is given to the excellence of his weapons, from shield and helmet to bow and arrow and gun. He is the perfection of generosity and hospitality, and in this context his *talla*, his stately home, becomes a theme in itself: both its lavish accommodations and the glorious evenings of liberal entertainment, with wine, whisky, gambling, music of various kinds, and the skilled contentions of the poets. Màiri's panegyric is aptly exemplified by three verses from a lament on the death by drowning of Mac Gille Chaluim, MacLeod of Raasay in 1671:

Bu tù sealgair a' gheoidh,
Làmh gun dearmad gun leòn
Air am bu shuarach an t-òr
Thoirt a bhuannachd a' cheoil;
Is gun d'fhuair thu na's leòir is na chaitheadh tu.
(ll. 296-300)

Thou wert a hunter of the wild-goose, thine a hand unerring and unblemished, to which it were a light thing to bestow gold for the maintenance of music; for thou hast gotten plenty, and all that thou wouldst spend.

Spealp nach dìobradh
An cath no an strì thu,
Casan dìreach
Fada fìnealt;
Mo chreach dhìobhail
Chaidh thu a dhìth oirnn
Le neart sìne,
Làmh nach dìobradh caitheadh oirre.
(ll. 308-15)

A gay gallant wert thou that shrank not in strife or battle; thy limbs straight, long, and shapely; alas, I am sadly reft, thou art lost to us by strength of tempest, thou whose hand would cease not to make thy vessel speed.

Is math thig gunna nach diùlt
Air curaidh mo rùin
Ann am mullach a' chùirn
Is air uilinn nan stùc:
Gum biodh fuil ann air tùs an spreadhaidh sin.
(ll. 322-26)

A gun that readily answereth, well would it become my dear warrior in the cairn's summit or or on the elbow of the peaks; blood would flow in front of its discharge.[8]

In another of her songs, addressed to MacLeod of Berneray, a single verse summarises the 'panegyric code':

> Lean-sa 's na tréig
> Cleachdamh is beus
> T'aiteim gu léir,
> Macanta sèimh,
> Pailt ri luchd theud,
> Gaisgeil am feum,
> Neartmhor an déidh tòrachd.
>
> (ll. 784-90)

Follow thou and forsake not the use and practice of thy kindred all: mild and gentle, liberal to harpers, valorous at need, mighty in pursuit. [9]

It may be significant that in two of her songs Màiri, when praising her male MacLeod hero, devotes a stanza or more in the poem's conclusion to praising his wife (ll. 568-82, 1167-71), though this practice was not uncommon among the professional male poets of the pre-1600 era.

The panegyric conventions of Scottish Gaelic song poetry were therefore observed as closely by women as by male poets in the popular poetry of clan and politics.[10] Donald MacAulay's suggestion that 'skill in versification and verbal wit culminating in the well-wrought, memorable phrase' was the 'basic requirement' for the songs[11] is exemplified by Màiri's verse,

> Tigh mór macnasach meadhrach
> Nam macaomh 's nam maighdean,
> Far am bu tartarach gleadhraich nan còrn.
>
> (ll. 240-2)

That was a mansion blithe and festive, thronged with young men and with maidens, where the clangour of the drinking-horns was loud.[12]

Part of a song to a MacLeod chief, it is well-wrought in its complex of rhymes and alliterations, rhythm and melody, a perfect comment on the heroic *talla*, the ideal home of any aristocratic Gael. This song, and many others of this kind by women in the period, reflects the fundamentally pagan heroic values of society. It suggests that Màiri occupied a secure position within the culture.

Yet, at some point after 1675, on the internal evidence of one of her songs, Màiri appears to have been in exile from Skye (or Berneray?). Various suggestions have been made as to why she was exiled but one tradition simply states that she had offended MacLeod of Dunvegan with one of her songs; another that she was accused of transgressing convention by composing a major song of heroic praise. When she was at length allowed to return home, we are told that it was on condition that she compose no more songs. Another tradition (not directly linked to the exile) is that she was given to composing satirical or even obscene songs.[13] She was first forbidden to sing her songs outdoors, and later they were forbidden indoors too. Consequently, Màiri was to be found singing while standing in doorways: in short, across thresholds. The formulation of Uist tradition, 'sin far am biodh i na seasamh, is cha robh i muigh is cha robh i staigh' (that was where she would stand, and she was neither out nor in), appositely summarises Màiri's liminal predicament. Her apparently faithful adherence to the panegyric code, and therefore by implication to social and political orthodoxy, appears not to have endured, or at least to have been tolerated. Màiri is remembered as something of a witch, a woman given to obscenity (though her extant songs give no hint of this) and to flouting the rules of society. The question remains open whether such traditional 'memories' do not arise essentially from a fear of women poets and their powers of transgression, whether potentially imagined or actually realised.

Sìleas na Ceapaich ('of Keppoch'; c. 1665 - c. 1729) was a daughter of Gilleasbaig, chief of the MacDonalds of Keppoch. Twenty-three songs more or less reliably ascribed to her are extant;[14] few are concerned with Keppoch or its ruling family since she married Alexander Gordon, a north-easterner acting as chamberlain for the Duke of Gordon, around 1685. They settled down in upper Banffshire and in 1700 acquired Beldorney Castle, near Dufftown, where Sìleas probably lived for the rest of her life. She is perhaps best-known as the poet of the 1715 Rising and of the battle of Sheriffmuir; the Gordons and the MacDonalds of Keppoch were allied together in support of the Stewarts, and Sìleas proves to be no impartial observer of events. While the four female poets considered here are all political poets, to the extent that their productions seek to bolster the *status quo* of clan society, Sìleas is the only one whose songs show serious involvement with national, as well as clan, politics. This may be partly due to her kinship with the MacDonald aristocracy and partly to the involvement of one or more of her sons in the armies of 1715.

Sìleas' song addressed 'To the Army of the Earl of Mar' is effectively a list of clan leaders whom she solicits to enlist in military support of James Stewart in 1715. Such a list, if sung widely among the people, would undoubtedly have imposed great pressure on the clan concerned. This kind of 'Song of the Clans' became popular again during the 1745 Jacobite Rising, and it is believed to be a poetic development of the part of the panegyric code which calls for a listing of the heroic subject's allies. One might argue that Sìleas innovatively devised the use of such a clan roll as a form of political 'blackmail' but there is another song composed by a male poet extant from 1715 which deploys a similar device; the question of origin is therefore uncertain. Two verses from Sìleas' song are extracted below: the first expresses confidence in her own Keppoch family, whose land was the Brae of Lochaber:

> Beir soraidh an deaghaidh nan laoch,
> Gus a' bhuidhinn ga'n suaicheantas fraoch,
> Gu ceannard a' Bhràghad
> S a' chuid eile de m' chàirdibh:
> Buaidh shìthne 's buaidh làrach leibh chaoidh.
>
> (ll. 253-7)

Convey a greeting after the heroes, to the band whose badge is the heather, to the leader of the Brae and the rest of my friends: may you have victory in hunt and in battle forever.

> Tha ùrachadh buidheann tighinn oirnn:
> Mac Coinnich, Mac Shimidh 's Mac Leòid,
> Mac Fhionghain Srath Chuailte
> 'S an Siosalach suairce;
> 'S se mo bharail gum buailear leo stròic.
>
> (ll. 258-62)

Fresh troops are coming to us: Mac Coinnich (the MacKenzie chief), Fraser of Lovat and MacLeod, Mackinnon of Srath Chuailte and the affable Chisholm; I am confident that they will strike rending blows.[15]

This song, sung to a rousing tune, contains an early instance of the metrical unit which later evolved into the 'limerick'; the use of this form, and others, by Sìleas may suggest a close link between the aristocratic Highland songmaker and her consumers among the Gaelic commonalty. Yet her poetic tradition remains the traditional heroic kind in which the poet praises the chief as the ideal, thereby reinforcing the social system. History shows that Alasdair Dubh, the chief of the MacDonalds of Glengarry who died in 1721, was in fact an admirable heroic warrior; Sìleas' great lament for him is an extreme example of heroic hyperbole:

> Bu tu 'n lasair dhearg 'gan losgadh,
> Bu tu sgoltadh iad gu'n sàiltibh,

Bu tu curaidh cur a' chatha,
Bu tu 'n laoch gun athadh làimhe;
Bu tu 'm bradan anns an fhìor-uisg,
Fìreun air an eunlaith 's àirde,
Bu tu 'n leómhann thar gach beathach,
. Bu tu damh leathan na cràice.

(ll. 831-8)

You were the red torch to burn them, you would cleave them to the heels, you were a hero in the battle, a champion who never flinched; a fresh-run salmon in the water, an eagle in the highest flock, lion excelling every creature, broad-chested, strong-antlered stag.

Bu tu 'n loch nach fhaoidte thaomadh,
Bu tu tobar faoilidh na slàinte,
Bu tu Beinn Nibheis thar gach aonach,
Bu tu chreag nach fhaoidte theàrnadh;
Bu tu clach uachdair a' chaisteil,
Bu tu leac leathan na sràide,
Bu tu leug lòghmhor nam buadhan,
Bu tu clach uasal an fhàinne.

(ll. 839-46)

A loch that could not be emptied, a well liberal in health, Ben Nevis towering over mountains, a rock that could not be scaled; topmost stone of the castle, broad paving-stone of the street, precious jewel of virtues, noble stone of the ring.[16]

Other poems by Sìleas demonstrate clearly her devout Roman Catholic faith. In her poem *An Eaglais* ('The Church'), the Catholic church is presented allegorically as a castle (a traditional idea in religious literature); one verse in particular alludes to its builders:

Rinn iad sgliata de chrùn draigheann
Agus staidhir de chrois cheusaidh;
Rinn iad le traisg is le ùrnaigh
A teannachadh gu dlùth ri chéile;
'S i Moire Bhain-tighearn a h-ùrlar;
Dh'fhùirneisich dà ostal deug i —
'S mór a fhuair iad rithe shaothair
Feadh an saoghail gus an d'eug iad.

(ll. 1205-12)

They made slates from His crown of thorns and stairs from His Passion cross: they welded it tightly together with fasting and prayer. Lady Mary is its floor. Twelve apostles furnished it; they devoted much labour to it all their lives until they died.[17]

Other religious poems by Sìleas contain more personal reflections, which is unusual in Gaelic literature of the period. In the two verses below, she laments the deaths of her husband, Alexander, and daughter Anna in 1720 (the first addresses Alexander directly):

> 'S tric mo shùilean ri dòrtadh
> Ona thug iad thu Mhòr-chlaich a suas,
> 'S nach faic mise 'n t-àite
> 'S an do chuir iad mo ghràdh-sa 's an uaigh;
> Dh'fhàg sibh Anna aig a' bhaile
> 's bidh mise 'ga ghearan gu cruaidh,
> A' sìor-amharc a' bhalla
> Aig na chuir iad i 'm falach gu buan.

(ll. 683-90)

My eyes frequently shed tears since they took you up to Mortlach, for I shall not see the place where they laid my love in the grave. You left Anna at home, and I shall lament that bitterly ever looking at the wall where they have hidden her forever.

> 'S beag mo ghnothach ri féilltibh
> No dh' amharc na réise ri m' bheò,
> No m'aighear ri daoine:
> Chaidh mo chuid-sa dhiùbh cuide fo 'n fhòd;
> Ona dh'fhalbh iad le chéile,
> An dithis nach tréigeadh mi beò,
> Rìgh thoir dhomh-sa bhith leughadh
> Air an aithreachas gheur a bh' aig Iòb.

(ll. 707-14)

I shall have little to do with fairs or with watching the races for the rest of my life,[18] *and I shall have little joy with people: those who belonged to me have been buried as one. Since the two who would never have left me in life have gone away together, O Lord let me read of the grievous repentance of Job.*[19]

Sìleas' range appears much wider than that of most other Gaelic poets of the time. It is not unfair to suggest that this may be due, at least partly, to the fact that she had left Keppoch, which is near the centre of the Gaelic Highlands, for the Gordon country of the North-east. Living there, still within the upper layer of society into which she was born, she may have been exposed to the transmission of ideas and influences from Lowland and English literary traditions. These may have included the poetic freedom to speak openly about personal anxieties and to reflect intimately on such topics as her youthful excesses and her weaknesses; these are entirely absent from traditions of earlier Gaelic verse, perhaps because they are of no literary interest within heroic society. Such openness on Sìleas' part has inevitably been used for ammunition by those who wished to damage her reputation. Her poems contains a strikingly candid song, instructing girls on how to deal with sexual advances. Her own experience is cited as an authority:

Nach fhaic sibh òig-fhear nam meall-shùil bòidheach,
    Le theangaidh leòmaich 's e labhairt rium [...]
Saoilidh gòrag le bhriathraibh mòrach
    Ga cur an dòchas le glòr a chinn:
'A ghaoil, gabh truas rium 's na leig gu h-uaigh mi;
    Do ghaol a bhuair mi bho ghluais mi fhìn [...]'

Mar shamhladh dhà sud gaoth a' Mhàirt ud
    Thig bho na h-àirdibh 's nach taobh i seòl:
'Nuair gheobh e mhiann dith gun toir e bhriathra
    Nach fhac e riamh i, 's car fiar 'n a shròin.

[...] A nis is léir dhomh na rinn mi dh'eucoir
    'S a' mheud 's a dh'éisd mi d' am breugan bàth.
                                        (ll.52-3, 56-9, 64-7, 82-3)

See the youth with the winsome attractive eyes and the affected speech speaking to me; [...] at his pompous words a foolish girl will think that his voice gives her hope: 'My love, have pity on me and do not let me die; love for you has afflicted me since I took my first step.'

He is just like the March wind which blows from on high and favours no sail: when he fulfils his desire with her he will swear, with a twist in his nose, that he never saw her.

It is clear to me now the wrong I did by the number of those foolish lies of theirs I listened to. [20]

The subject of sexuality is differently embraced in an orthodox verse response to a song by George MacKenzie of Gruinneard in praise of *An Obair Nodha*: this term has been translated as 'The New Wark', clearly denoting the promotion of simple sexual licence which is depicted as a new 'movement' or 'trend'. In urging her audience to reject such ideas, she again draws knowingly, or playfully perhaps, on her own experience:

> Mo nianagan bòidheach
> Nam b' eòlach sibh mar mise,
> Mun a' bhrosgul bhréige
> Seal mun éirich air a' chriosan!
>
> (ll. 919-22)

My lovely girls, if only you were knowledgeable, as I am, about the false flattery that precedes the rising of the girdle![21]

The apparent admission of sexual misdemeanour here has ensured that Sìleas' own early sexual conduct has been viewed negatively by editors and commentators, probably drawing on popular oral tradition. An important song of hers mourns the death in the 1720s of Lachlann Dall, a harper she had clearly known well for many years and who had visited her home in Banffshire; inevitably, early commentators report a clandestine love affair between the poet and the harper, for which there is no real evidence at all.[22] Ironically, her song against the New Wark has even been considered scandalous and unprintable, despite the fact that it is an entirely orthodox reaction, firmly opposed to sexual immorality. It could be argued that Sìleas had crossed the moral threshold of acceptability in merely composing on the subject of sexuality, even though its moral excesses were condemned. Sìleas' Highland relatives in the late nineteenth century were evidently uncomfortable with the reputation she had acquired. Keith Norman Macdonald writes in 1900 that: 'The Keppoch family believe that some songs were attributed to her that she never composed. They hold that her tone was a high one from the beginning'.[23]

Sìleas suffered severe illness and a near-encounter with death. Some authorities elaborate on this, possibly on the basis of oral tradition, and describe this illness as, in fact, a 'trance' in which she was (according to an eighteenth-century manuscript which is the only source for one of the religious poems)[24] without food, drink or the power of speech for no less than three years. Imbued with suggestions of witchcraft, this legend is starkly punitive. Despite, or perhaps because of, Sìleas' poetic gifts, she remained 'outside' conventional boundaries; both oral and popular printed traditions have placed Sìleas within the framework of a conventional narrative: that of the fallen and transgressive woman.

Little is known presently about Mairghread nighean Lachlainn ('daughter of Lachlann'; her surname is yet unknown) to whom eleven songs are ascribed, all of which are in praise of Maclean leaders and are centred on the island of Mull and the surrounding area. It might be assumed that she was herself a Maclean but one nineteenth-century source for some of her songs states that she was a MacDonald. Her birth and death dates are unknown though two songs, lamenting the deaths of chiefs in 1716 and 1750, suggest a life-span c. 1660-1751. Her poetry mirrors the conventional codes of panegyric as did the poetry of Màiri nighean Alasdair Ruaidh. Similarly, while her subjects remain the male chiefs, in the 1716 lament for Sir Iain Maclean of Duart, a verse towards the end expresses praise for a woman named Catrìona; not, apparently, his wife, but so far unidentified. In another lament, the grief of the subject's wife is observed.[25]

In her lifetime, Mairghread's beloved Macleans lost their prestige and power and, consequently, she emerges as the chronicler of *dol sìos Chlann Ghilleathain* (the decline of the Maclean clan). The Earls of Argyll increasingly acquired Maclean lands and titles, and in the early 1690s the Maclean chief, Sir Iain, was effectively forced out. He lived in France and London where he supported James Stewart, returning to participate in the unsuccessful battle of Sheriffmuir; he died shortly after in 1716, never having regained his lands. His son Eachann, also a Jacobite, lived most of his life abroad; the Macleans fought on the losing Stewart side at Culloden in 1746, but Eachann was in prison in London at the time and died in Rome in 1750. In the face of such disaster, Mairghread's songs preach the glory of the Macleans' past and, with diminishing confidence, the imminence of their restoration to that glory.

In another tradition (from a manuscript account written perhaps in the 1930s)[26], Mairghread is said to have been a *bean tuiridh*, a professional mourner of a kind better known in Ireland: a woman who might be employed on the occasion of a death or a funeral to chant or sing (or 'keen', Gaelic *caoin*) in public mourning for the deceased. Such women are documented mainly because they earned the disapproval of the Church for their commercial *caoineadh* or mourning.[27] It was perfectly normal for poets, such as Mairghread, as earlier illustrated, to compose laments on the deaths of chiefs or other leaders, and terms like *caoineadh*, 'weeping', frequently occur in their songs. Aptly, grief is seen as one of the principal markers of Mairghread's verse by the poet Sorley Maclean (Somhairle MacGill-Eain, 1911-96).[28] Yet importantly these songs which follow the panegyric code differ in nature from the *caoineadh* of the professional mourners. In Mairghread's case it may be that her 'title' was diminished to that of *bean tuiridh* because society was uneasy about considering her a 'proper' poet. The same manuscript account relates how Mairghread, in furtherance of her duties as *bean tuiridh*, once waited at a quay in Mull for the boat taking the body of a deceased Maclean leader (for whom she, in fact, formally mourned) to the island of Iona for burial, but the boat failed to pick her up. She then crossed Mull on foot and was waiting on Iona when the boat arrived. No detail is given to explain how she got across to Iona, but we are left with the strong implication that it was enabled by magic. The association of magical, supernatural or, indeed, devilish powers with Gaelic women poets remains persistent. Mairghread, too, acquired the reputation of being a witch; it was her fate, earlier described, to be buried face downwards under a pile of stones.

The disparity observed between the nature of these women's songs and the personal and sexual mythologies which surround them is seen starkly in the fourth and final poet considered here, known only as 'An Aigeannach': only this 'nickname' survives which has been taken to impute sexual immorality.[29] Only two songs are extant, one of them in praise of the Maclean of Coll chief, Dòmhnall mac Eachainn Ruaidh (1656-1729), perhaps composed about 1718. The subject's home, Breacachadh Castle in Coll, is praised according to the panegyric code. Yet she moves beyond convention, as this excerpt illustrates which includes a reference to the chief's wife, a daughter of Sir Norman MacLeod of Berneray:

> Gheibhte do phannal a' fuaigheal
> De ghruagaichean àraid
> Aig nighin Thormaid mhic Ruaidhri
> Dh'am bu dualchas àrdan,
> Bhiodh cuide rith' dèanamh lèintean,
> Tarraing grèis le snàthaid,
> Iomairt air chodaichean trice:
> Is mise bha anns an làthair.

Your bevy of excellent maidens were to be found sewing in the company of the daughter of Norman son of Ruairidh, an inheritor of pride, helping her make tunics, drawing embroidery with the needle and stitching pieces together: I was there among them!

Gum biodh na cùirteinean daite
Air na leapanan clàraidh
Agus cluasagan dha-rèir sin
'S gach nì dh'fheumte làmh riu;
Blacha lìn agus bratan,
Culaidh chadail shàmhaich
Far am biodh blàths aig na h-uaislean --
Cha tig fuachd nan dàil ann.

Brightly-coloured quilts on the box-sided beds, pillows to match, and every convenience; sheets and bedspreads, all that was needed for restful sleep where the gentlefolk could have warmth -- no cold comes near them there.[30]

These verses extend elements of the *talla* episode in the panegyric code farther than any male poet has of the period. As far as I know, no other contemporary song expresses such clear devotion to the chief's castle; as she is proud to reveal, she herself was present among all the women.

Her other song revises panegyric convention even more explicitly since it 'inverts' panegyric conventions. It is addressed (c. 1730?) to 'The Lady of Cladh na Macraidh',[31] whose name was Anna and whose husband, Dùghall Campbell (1701-69) of Cladh na Macraidh in Argyllshire, a minor landowner, was also one of the Duke of Argyll's sub-tacksmen in Tiree and Coll. Subjects such as warfare, hunting, and seafaring are obviously not used as points of praise for Anna, but she is praised for her physical beauty in significant detail, her noble ancestry and kin, and her generosity. The last verse is devoted to dutiful praise of Dùghall.[32]

Yet, in being identifiable only by her nickname, 'a self-willed boisterous female' or even 'une fille de joie',[33] An Aigeannach is already condemned before her songs are seen or heard. The absence of even a Christian name for this woman poet is part of a strategy of deliberate denigration; elsewhere another *Aigeannach* is abused in a well-known poem of the mid-eighteenth century for being a prostitute. While printing the only surviving text of Aigeannach's song to Anna of Cladh na Macraidh, her 1821 editor regrets that 'she prostituted her genius at the shrine of immorality'.[34] No evidence corroborates this, and the familiar alliance between female poetic creation and sexual depravity is again enforced.

Màiri nighean Alasdair Ruaidh, Sìleas na Ceapaich, Mairghread nighean Lachlainn, and An Aigeannach practised the literary conventions and codes of their male counterparts, upholding the heroic clan-based society through formal praise of its leaders. Their songs survived because they reflect enduring feelings and ideas. Yet the legendary oral traditions which each of these women accrued, during their lives and after, speak of profound anxieties within the culture regarding women poets; perhaps, specifically, concerning the legitimacy of women composing serious songs about politics and the clan. All four are charged with unacceptable sexual and 'unnatural', or magical, powers. Refused full acceptance as poets, they remained 'neither out nor in'. It is to be hoped that the rediscovery of the full importance of their work may enable that threshold finally to be crossed.[35]

Notes

[1] *Transactions of the Gaelic Society of Inverness* [hereafter *TGSI*], 41 (1953), 15-16; *Scottish Gaelic Studies* [hereafter *SGS*], 11 (1966), 9-10.

[2] *Tocher*, 27 (1977), 150-1; *SGS*, 11, p. 7; Allan McDonald, *Gaelic Words and Expressions from South Uist and Eriskay* (Oxford: OUP, 1972), p. 46, s.v. *bonn*.

[3] For other Gaelic traditions about women in doorways and about liminality see Séamas Ó Catháin, *The Festival of Brigit* (Blackrock, Co. Dublin: DBA Publications, 1995), pp. 146-7, 156. For a different view of a (male) poet composing in a doorway, see Dáithí Ó hÓgáin, *An File: Staidéar ar Osnádúrthacht na Filíochta sa Traidisiún Gaelach* (Baile Átha Cliath: Oifig An tSoláthair, 1982), p. 11.

[4] William J. Watson, ed., *Scottish Verse from the Book of the Dean of Lismore*, Scottish Gaelic Texts Society [SGTS] (Edinburgh: Oliver & Boyd, 1937), pp. 234, 307-8. For John Bannerman's view of the authorship of these poems, see *The Renaissance and Reformation in Scotland: Essays in Honour of Gordon Donaldson*, ed. by Ian B. Cowan and Duncan Shaw (Edinburgh: Scottish Academic, 1983), p. 230.

[5] J.L. Campbell and Francis Collinson, eds., *Hebridean Folksongs: a Collection of Waulking Songs by Donald MacCormick* (Oxford: Clarendon, 1969), pp. 3-30.

[6] J. Carmichael Watson, ed., *Gaelic Songs of Mary Macleod* (1934; Edinburgh: Oliver & Boyd, 1965), pp. xiv, xix. All Màiri poems and translations cited from this edition.

[7] *TGSI*, 41, 15-16; *Ildánach Ildírech: a Festschrift for Proinsias Mac Cana*, ed. by John Carey and others (Andover, MA: Celtic Studies, 1999), p. 12; cf. P.V. Glob, *The Bog People: Iron-age Man Preserved* (London: Paladin, 1971), pp. 79, 114.

[8] Watson, ed., pp. 26-9.

[9] Watson, ed., pp. 64-5.

[10] See John MacInnes, 'The Panegyric Code in Gaelic Poetry and its Historical Background', *TGSI*, 50 (1978), 435-98.

[11] Donald MacAulay, ed., *Nua-Bhàrdachd Ghàidhlig: Modern Scottish Gaelic Poems* (Edinburgh: Southside, 1976), p. 46.

[12] Watson ed., pp. 20-1.

[13] *SGS*, 11, p. 7. For another assessment of the significance of Màiri's exile see Roxanne L. Reddington-Wilde's interesting essay, 'Violent Death and Damning Words', in *Celtic Connections: Proceedings of the Tenth International Congress of Celtic Studies*, vol. I, ed. by Ronald Black and others. (East Linton: Tuckwell, 1999), pp. 265-86 (pp. 272-3).

[14] Colm Ó Baoill, ed., *Bàrdachd Shìlis na Ceapaich*, SGTS (Edinburgh: Scottish Academic, 1972). All Sìleas poems and translations, unless specified, are predominantly based on this edition.

[15] Ó Baoill, ed., pp. 22-3.

[16] Ó Baoill, ed., p. 72; English translation from Derick Thomson, ed., *An Introduction to Gaelic Poetry* (Edinburgh: EUP, 1990), pp. 137-8.

[17] Ó Baoill, ed., p. 102.

[18] Sìleas' mention of fairs and watching the races might be taken as a formulaic reference to aristocratic life but I have found no other such allusion in the songs of this period. It is more likely that this refers specifically to events in her own life and to a well documented tradition of an annual race meeting at Huntly, Aberdeenshire, some 12 km from Sìleas' home at Beldorney Castle, between 1695 and 1734. See Jane How, 'The Huntly Race and its Trophies', in *From the Stone Age to the 'Forty-five: Studies Presented to R.B.K. Stevenson*, ed. by Anne O'Connor and D.V. Clarke (Edinburgh: Donald, 1983), pp. 108-113.

[19] Ó Baoill, ed., pp. 58-61.

[20] Ó Baoill, ed., pp. 6-9.

[21] Ibid., pp. 78-9.

[22] Ibid., no. XXI; see pp. lxiii, 252.

[23] Keith Norman Macdonald, *Macdonald Bards from Mediaeval Times* (Edinburgh: Norman McLeod, 1900), p. 92.

[24] GUL MacLagan MS 165; see further Ó Baoill, ed., pp. xxviii, 207.

[25] Paruig Mac-an-Tuairneir, ed., *Comhchruinneacha do dh' Orain Taghta, Ghaidhealach* (Duneidionn : T. Stiùbhard, 1813), p. 8, ll. 4-11; p. 12, ll. 13-14.

[26] This is Morison MS A, as described in Colm Ó Baoill, ed., *Eachann Bacach and Other Maclean Poets*, SGTS (Edinburgh: Scottish Academic, 1979), p. xxvi; the manuscript is in Gaelic.

[27] On the professional mourner or wailer, or *bean chaointe*, in Ireland, see Seán Ó Súilleabháin, *Irish Wake Amusements* (Cork: Mercier, 1967), ch. IX. The confusion between heroic laments and the singing or chanting of professional mourners has largely been clarified (in Irish) in Breandán Ó Buachalla, *An Caoine agus an Chaointeoireacht* (Baile Átha Cliath: Cois Life, 1998), Cuid II. For some accounts of the *bean tuiream* in Gaelic Scotland, see Alexander Carmichael, *Carmina Gadelica*, 2 vols (Edinburgh: T. & A. Constable, 1900), II, 292; V (1954), 344-5.

[28] Somhairle Mac Gill-eain, *Ris a' Bhruthaich*, ed. by William Gillies (Stornoway: Acair, 1985), p. 188.

[29] The meaning of the adjective *aigeannach*, particularly when used (in nominal form) as a nickname for a woman, was to some extent discussed by John Lorne Campbell in *SGS*, 12 (1971), 65, and by Colm Ò Baoill in *SGS*, 13 (1978), 103, citing nineteenth-century dictionary meanings of the term as 'une fille de joye' and 'a self-willed boisterous female'. The adjective itself occurs in verse, and in William J. Watson, *Bàrdachd Ghàidhlig* (1918, Glasgow and Stirling: An Comunn Gaidhealach; A. Learmonth, 1959); his vocabulary translates it as 'spirited, mettlesome'.

[30] Colm Ò Baoill, ed., *Duanaire Colach 1537-1757* (Obar-Dheathain: An Clo Gaidhealach, 1997), p. 32, ll. 842-57.

[31] [Duncan MacCallum], ed., *Co-chruinneacha Dhan, Orain, &c* (Inverness, 1821), pp. 123-7; *SGS*, 13, 106-8.

[32] This inversion, with the main text praising the woman and the 'duty' verse(s) at the end given to the husband, does not occur elsewhere in the Gaelic song verse of our period, as far as I know. But there are instances in professional classical verse.

[33] *SGS*, 13, 103.

[34] MacCallum, *Co-chruinneacha*, p. 127n.

[35] I am indebted to Dr John MacInnes and the late Reverend William Matheson for their thoughts on this material expressed in their numerous writings and in conversations I have been privileged to enjoy with them. The paper is a revised version of one read at the seminar 'Women, Manuscript and the Four Nations' as part of the Trinity/Trent Colloquium at Nottingham Trent University on 5 February 2000. I would like to express my gratitude for helpful comments made by participants in the seminar, and for the help and efficiency of the organiser, Dr Jill Seal.

11

Holy Terror and Love Divine: The Passionate Voice in Elizabeth Melville's *Ane Godlie Dreame*

Deanna Delmar Evans

Alexander Hume, Scottish clergyman and poet, dedicated his 1599 volume of verse to the 'faithfvll and vertvovs Ladie, Elizabeth Mal-vill, Ladie Cumrie'.[1] This 'Ladie' almost certainly was Elizabeth Melville, daughter of Sir James Melville of Halhill,[2] and wife to John Colville of Culross. Little is known about her life except that she wrote some poetry, was respected as a pious woman,[3] and went out of her way to encourage ministers of her religious persuasion who suffered for their faith. She wrote a sonnet of encouragement for the imprisoned pastor John Welsh[4] and several letters to the exiled pastor John Livingstone.[5] But even with such a sincere desire to minister to others, Elizabeth Melville had no opportunity to provide religious comfort or exhortation from a Scottish pulpit. The 'Scots Confession' of 1560, an important document of the Scottish Reformation, expressly barred women from preaching or engaging in other pastoral roles.[6] To circumvent such restrictions, Melville drew upon the well-established literary tradition of the dream vision to illustrate the Reformist doctrine of 'justification' while yet a woman writer and also implicitly to lay claim to her own justified state.

In this allegorical dream vision, Melville adheres to many of the conventions of medieval dream vision poetry. The tripartite structure of the *Godlie Dreame* begins with a pre-dream narrative written as first-person autobiography. That narrative depicts the dreamer as being in a troubled state, which is common in dream vision poetry.[7] However, in this instance, Melville's dreamer appears to be 'under conviction', a spiritual state in which the Holy Spirit has enabled her to realise her 'fallen' human nature; the dreamer comments that 'this wretchit warld did sa molest my mynde' (l. 9) and desperately begs Jesus to 'cum and saif thy awin Elect' (l. 41),[8] and the ensuing dream *visio* provides an answer to that prayer. Such dream vision poetry customarily presents a guide for the dreamer, who is often depicted as naïve. Reflecting this tradition, Melville's naïve dreamer first mistakes her guide as 'Ane angell bricht with visage schyning cleir' (l. 92), but the guide identifies himself as the spiritual bridegroom in a rich anaphoric series of biblical allusions:

> I am the way, I am the treuth and lyfe,
> I am thy spous that brings thee store of grace:
> I am thy luif, quhom thou wald faine imbrace,
> I am thy joy, I am thy rest and peace.

> (ll. 129-32)

The guide is, of course, the Holy Spirit coming to the dreamer in the guise of the resurrected Christ to whom the narrator had prayed. As a result of what she learns from her dream experience, the narrator is in the post-dream stanzas a transformed person. No longer depressed and frightened, she is a bold female preacher who delivers a Jeremiad in which she exhorts her peers to keep the faith in the midst of religious persecution. Indeed, the vehicle of the dream vision form allowed Melville, through identification with her dreamer protagonist, to do what she could not do in real life. Hume's 'vertvovs Ladie' had found an effective means to circumvent the restrictions barring women from preaching.

Apparently Melville's peers did not recognise the subversive elements in *Ane Godlie Dreame*. The poem was published in Edinburgh in both Scots and English versions circa 1603.[9] To be sure, the poem was worthy of publication, for it has literary merit. Written in sixty *ottava rima* stanzas, *Ane Godlie Dreame* contains some striking imagery and a sustained, coherent narrative. Following the practice of the day, Melville also carefully blends biblical verse and allusion into the fabric of her poem with remarkable effectiveness, a technique Sarah M. Dunnigan perceptively describes as 'a seamless allusive weave' in which 'direct Scriptural quotation [...] is combined with broader metaphors entrenched within the Christian imagination'.[10] Functioning as Melville's 'sermon', the poem also conveys its dominant theological message within the *visio* by means of a spirited dialogue between the dreamer and her guide. By putting her theological message into a fabricated 'voice of God', Melville gives it credibility and at the same time distinguishes it from genuine revelation. Then by having 'God's voice' directly address her first-person narrator, the poet's fictional persona, Melville artfully validates her own voice and convictions.

The dominant theological message of *Ane Godlie Dreame* reiterates a fundamental component of Reformation dogma, the doctrine of Justification by Faith.[11] Justification has been briefly defined as 'the means whereby a man passes from a state of damnation due to sin to a state of grace'.[12] The concept was endorsed by Scotland's best known reformer, John Knox:

> None may or can honour God except the justified man [...] yet they alone, in whome the Holy Spirit worketh true Faith (which never wanteth good workes) are just before God [....] The substance of Justification is, to cleave fast unto God, by Jesus Christ, and not by our selfe, not yet by our workes'.[13]

Melville seems to have read Knox's treatise on this topic since, in the last third of the *Dreame*, the female narrator-turned-preacher passionately repeats and restates some of Knox's words as she suggests that one 'cleave to', 'call on', or 'cry on' Christ (ll. 342, 367, 391), and 'clim fast' to him (l. 419) who is 'your convoy' (ll. 419, 430). Considering Knox's treatment of Queen Mary and his attitude toward women in leadership roles, it is not without irony that Melville usurps some of his words and ideas to put them into the mouth of her fictional woman preacher, perhaps thereby indicating, in a most subtle manner, that the words and the ideas they convey are valid and effective, no matter the sex of the person voicing them.

Melville most completely illustrates the theological concept of justification and also demonstrates her ability as an effective preacher in the allegorical *visio*. In this section of the poem she analytically dissects the notion of 'Justification' and translates that concept into allegory as the dreamer first 'hears' of the concept from the mouth of her divine teacher and then discovers it experientially. In addition, the dreamer is taught that the doctrine of Justification corrects a 'false teaching' of Roman Catholicism: the concept of Purgatory.

As this section of the poem begins, the female protagonist describes her life before the dream when she was 'Ane pilgrime puir / consuit [*consumed*] with siching sair' [*sorrowful sighs*] (ll. 107-8). Her guide offering her his hand, she sets out with him on an instructive journey. Seeing a 'Castell fair', a symbol of heaven, the dreamer naively attempts to climb its stately steps, but because she is a creature living in a fallen world, she is unsuccessful. Her divine guide then directs her vision downward, where she 'saw ane pit most black, / Most full of smuke and flaming fyre most fell' (ll. 257-8). Horrified, she questions her guide about what she sees, begging him to tell her the truth and demanding to know whether this horrible pit is 'the Papists purging place' (l. 262), or Purgatory. The guide figure's response articulates clearly one of the signal positions of the Reformers, one insistently hostile to the Catholic doctrine of Purgatory, for he states: 'The braine of man maist warlie [*vainly*] did invent / That Purging place,' (ll. 263-4). Moreover, the guide indicates that the concept of Purgatory was motivated by demons who sowed the seeds of greed among fallen humans: 'spytfull spreits [*spirits*]' promulgated the lie that 'saulles in torment mon [*must*] remaine, / Till gold and gudes releif them of thair paine', (ll. 269-70). Thus, this 'voice of God' condemns the sale of 'Indulgences', a practice detested by all the reformers; those who participate in the practice, he says, are 'blindit beists' (l. 271). This brief lesson on Purgatory is concluded by the spiritual guide's decree that 'My blude alone did saif thy saull from sin' (l. 272), thus restating the concept of Justification.

But 'hearing the word' apparently is not sufficient. The dreamer must be given experiential knowledge as well; this 'object lesson' will reinforce Melville's teaching of the doctrine of Justification. The visual impact of the episode also reveals that Melville, via her female narrator, proves herself as able as any Calvinist preacher of the day to create images that will strike fear into the hearts of listeners. In this most dramatic episode of the poem, Melville reveals her talent as an allegorist: she vividly illustrates that even those who attempt to 'walk with the Lord', as the dreamer is doing during the *visio*, are standing on the brink of damnation unless 'justified' through Christ. Consequently, in this scene the dreamer is depicted as being paralysed by fear as she stares into the pit of hell; because she is in that fearful paralysis, she is unaware of the presence of an evil spirit who snatches her away from the dream guide. Then, as she explains, the evil spirit 'held mee heich [*high*] above ane flaming fyre' (l. 312). With this terrifying visual image of the Christian soul being snatched out of God's hand and suspended above the pit of hell, Melville allegorically illustrates that evil is ever ready to destroy the unwary, including members of the 'elect' who permit fear to distract them from their Christian 'walk'.

In terms of the theological message of the poem, this dramatic allegory reveals that no one is perfect enough to escape damnation except through the blood of Christ, i.e., Justification. Also noteworthy, in this episode Melville shows that the dreamer's 'sin' is not a heinous crime but merely a product of human nature, the desire for self-preservation. At the moment that her fear overcomes her faith, the dreamer releases her

Lord's hand (ll. 315-17). However, to complete her 'lesson', Melville allegorically demonstrates that 'the Lord is near to those who call upon Him' (Ps. 91:15), for as soon as the dreamer cries out to the Lord, He immediately comes to save her. Nevertheless, the momentary lapse of faith followed by the dreamer's horror serves as an effective 'reawakening device' for the literary dream vision; as such, it 'serves nicely to remind readers that the narrative […] they have read is and has always been a dream'.[14] The conclusion of the *visio* brings the poem back to where it had begun, with the Lord answering the narrator's anguished prayer and bringing her to a new level of awareness.

In the post-dream stanzas, as noted earlier, the narrator has been transformed by her dream experience into a 'doer' of 'the word'; her voice is then that of a preacher with a fervent desire to help others. In these stanzas the narrator shows great compassion for her readers, whom she believes live in the same kind of fear she had experienced, referring to them as 'sillie saullis [*innocent souls*] with paines sa sair opprest [*sorely oppressed by pain*], / That love the Lord and lang for Heaven sa hie [*high*]' (ll. 345-6). Her desire now is to share her experience and thereby encourage others. She exhorts her readers to live '[l]yke pilgrims puir and strangers in exile' because 'The Devill, the warld and all that they can mak / Will send thair force to stop 30u in 30ur way' (ll. 355, 357-8). The narrator perceives her mission as a matter of some urgency because she apparently believes that she and her intended readers are living in a pre-millennial age.

Melville had foreshadowed the concept of 'pre-millennialism' in the pre-dream stanzas of the poem. There the narrator calls her complaint a 'lamentatioun', the word implying a correspondence between the evils Melville and her peers are experiencing with the afflictions of 'God's chosen people' in the days of Jeremiah. The narrator indicates in a prayer that Scotland needs deliverance: 'how lang is it thy will, / That thy puir Sancts sall be afflictit still?' (ll. 27-8). In her prayer for the 'elect',[15] Melville is opening up the significance of her message, moving from the allegorised 'self' to Christians in general, the 'puir Sancts', and finally to Scotland itself, where those 'Sancts' are suffering. The narrator urges the Lord to 'Mak haist' to fulfill His promise and 'to end our painefull pilgraumage' (l. 31). As her lamentation continues, her pre-millennial belief becomes more evident:

> Thir ar the dayes that thou sa lang foretold,
> Sould cum befoir this wretchit warld sould end:

> Now vice abounds and charitie growes cald,
> And evin thine owine most stronglie dois offend.
>
> (ll. 49-52)

Melville's reference to 'thine owine' in this passage may subtly allude to the ongoing divisive struggle for leadership within the Scottish Reformation church. The central issue was how the church should be governed and by whom. Some, including the 'crown' and the majority of titled landowners, desired to maintain a hierarchical church with a system of bishops, an episcopacy. Others, especially Andrew Melville and his 'radical colleagues', wanted the church less under the control of the rich and powerful: they supported the 'second' *Book of Discipline* (1578) which demanded the removal of bishops from the reformed church, 'their duties to be undertaken by committees of ministers soon to become known as presbyteries' and insisted that attendance at the General Assembly, the reformed church's governing body, 'be restricted to ministers and elders'.[16] Elizabeth Melville does not take sides in her poem, most probably because it was a fight among men, one from which she was excluded. But with this allusion, she suggests that controversy among the leaders of the reformed 'kirk', those men who considered themselves the Lord's 'owine', was contrary to the will of God. Her response to the controversy is to offer her own 'Jeremiad' in the post-dream stanzas. By transforming the voice of her narrator into the voice of a prophet, Melville's speaker, in the penultimate stanza of the poem, reminds them that 'the tyme is neare', and so they must all 'be sober watch and pray' (l. 469).

By writing this poem, Melville exhibited a certain amount of bravery as she exposed herself to possible criticism and censure by moving herself and her protagonist out of the feminine gender role: her protagonist dares to preach to men and, by writing the poem, Melville herself usurps masculine 'writing space' in a religious culture that suppressed the female voice. If she were identified too closely with her female protagonist, she could be accused of spiritual pride; after all, the poem claims in the *visio* that the Lord spoke to her. At worst, the 'Dreame' could have been construed as evidence of some kind of demonic visitation and used to prove Melville was a witch. Such an accusation was highly unlikely, of course, for by adopting the dream vision form, Melville made no claims to divine revelation except within the self-effacing medium of the dream vision genre. Yet it is noteworthy that when Melville wrote her poem, most probably in the 1590s, Scotland was experiencing its first decade of serious witch hysteria: the notorious North Berwick witch trials began in 1590, and King James VI wrote his short book on witchcraft, *Daemonologie*, in 1597.[17]   The history of the time provides ample evidence that the feminine voice was subject to containment of the harshest sort. However, the orthodoxy of Melville's theological message, with its emphasis on Justification, her position on Purgatory, and her choice to write within the dream vision genre all worked to her advantage.

In a late stanza of the poem, Melville's female persona indicates her authorial intention. She says that she had written about her 'dreame' because she knew that she lived in difficult times and wanted to encourage other 'godly' people, also living under such conditions, to keep the faith:

> This is ane dreame, and ʒit I touch [*consider*] it best,
> To wryte the same, and keip it still in mynde:
> Becaus I knew, thair was na earthlie rest,
> Preparit for us, that hes our hearts inclynde
> To seik the Lord, we mon [*must*] be purgde and fynde,
> Our dros [*error*] is greit, the fyre mon [*must*] try us sair:
> But ʒit our God is mercifull and kynde,
> Hee sall remaine and help us ever mair.
>
> (ll. 329-6)

The first line of this stanza refers explicitly to the 'dreame' described in the *visio*; thus Melville self-consciously, even with a degree of solipsism, calls attention to her own written product while she claims that her purpose was to help others in their spiritual journeys. As the preceding explication of the *visio* indicates, Melville, by having her female persona receive instruction from a fabricated Holy Spirit, illustrates her belief that what is being taught in the *visio* is life-saving, biblically-based religious truth fully in accord with orthodox Reformation theology.

It is doubtful that Melville ever intended to subvert the social order of her society when she wrote her poem; her theology strictly conforms to Reformation teaching. Yet the creative way in which she circumvented societal restrictions imposed on the female voice by adapting the medieval dream vision form is much to be admired. This poetic form enabled Melville to overcome the restrictions of being female in a Calvinist society that suppressed women's voices in the pulpit, thereby allowing her to voice her most deeply held religious convictions. Melville was able to overcome her feelings of helplessness and powerlessness in such a patriarchal religious climate by making the poem her pulpit.

Notes

[1] *The Poems of Alexander Hume*, ed. by Alexander Lawson, STS (Edinburgh: William Blackwood and Sons, 1902), pp. 3-5.

[2] Her father had authored the *Memoirs of His Own Life*; cf. edition by Gordon Donaldson (London: Folio Society, 1969).

[3] Hume's dedication is dated 16 February 1598; in that dedication he remarks: 'It is a rare thing to see a Ladie, a tender youth, sad, solitare, and sanctified, oft sighing & weeping thorugh the conscience of sinne' (Lawson, pp. 3-4).

[4] For Melville's sonnet (c.1605) written for Welsh, see Germaine Greer's edition, *Kissing the Rod: An Anthology of Seventeenth-Century Women's Verse* (London: Virago, 1988), pp. 33-4; *An Anthology of Scottish Women Poets*, ed. by Catherine Kerrigan (Edinburgh: EUP, 1991; rpt. 1993), p. 156.

[5] Several letters from Melville to the exiled pastor John Livingstone were published as a supplement to Livingstone's 'Life' in *Select Biographies*, ed. by W. K. Tweedie (Edinburgh: Wodrow, 1845-7), pp. 351-70. In *A Brief Historical Relation of the life of Mr. John Livingstone, minister of the Gospel, containing several observations of the divine goodness manifested in Him, in the several occurrences thereof. Written by himself during his banishment in Holland* [...], ed. by Thomas Houston of Knockbracken (Edinburgh: John Johnstone, 1848), Livingstone indicates that Melville remained an 'icon' of spirituality in her mature years: 'Of all that ever I saw, she was most unwearied in religious exercises; and the more she attained in access to God therein, she hungered the more' (p. 346).

[6] *The Constitution of the Presbyterian Church (U.S.A.)* Part I: Book of Confessions (Louisville, KY: Office of the General Assembly, 1966), contains the full text of the 'Scots Confession' of 1560, pp. 11-25; within the 'Confession' is an attack on the Roman Catholic hierarchy: 'they even allow women, whom the Holy Ghost will not permit to preach in the congregation, to baptise' (XXII, 3.22), p. 23.

[7] J. Stephen Russell, *The English Dream Vision: Anatomy of a Form*, (Columbus: Ohio State UP, 1988), p. 116.

[8] Hume, *Poems*, ed. by Lawson; Appendix D, pp. 185-97, provides a complete text of Melville's poem as it was printed by Robert Charteris in 1603; this and all subsequent citations of *Ane Godlie Dreame* are from Lawson's edition and will be referred to by line number.

[9] The earliest two prints of the poem are at the National Library of Scotland, but Elizabeth Melville is listed as author in only one. The cover page of the dated print bearing the Scots title, *Ane Godlie Dreame*, is said to be 'Compylit in Scottish Meter be M. M. Gentelwoman in Culros, at the requiest of her freindes' and was printed by Robert Charteris in 1603. The other, also printed by Charteris (c.1603), is a more ornate edition lacking a date; the print bears the anglicised title, *A Godly Dreame*, on its cover page and is said to be 'Compyled by Eliz. Melvil, Lady Culros Yonger at the request of a friend'. I assume 'Eliz. Melvil' of the anglicised version to be the same as 'M. M. Gentelwoman in Culros'.

[10] Sarah M. Dunnigan, 'Scottish Women Writers c.1560-c.1650', in *A History of Scottish Women's Writing*, ed. by Douglas Gifford and Dorothy McMillan (Edinburgh: EUP, 1997), p. 33.

[11] Within the Augsburg Confession, written by Philip Melanchthon in 1530 and approved by Martin Luther, is a detailed definition of Justification, beginning with a brief definition: 'Men cannot be justified before God by their own powers, merits, or works, but are justified freely for Christ's sake through faith [...] who by His death hath satisfied for our sins [...]'. *Protestantism*, ed. by J. Leslie Dunstan (New York: Washington Square Press, 1962), p. 63

[12] Maurice Taylor, 'The Conflicting Doctrines of the Scottish Reformation', in *Essays on the Scottish Reformation 15-14-1625*, ed. by David McRoberts (Glasgow: Burns, 1962), p. 45.

[13] *The Works of John Knox*, ed. by David Laing, 6 vols (Edinburgh: J. Thin, 1854; rpt. New York: AMS Press, 1966), III, 15.

[14] Russell, p. 127.

[15] There can be little doubt that Melville considered herself a member of the 'elect', for Livingstone in *Brief Historical Relation* indicates that Melville's father 'professed he had got assurance from the Lord, that himself, wife, and all his children should meet in heaven' (p. 346).

[16] Ian Donnachie and George Hewitt, *A Companion to Scottish History: From the Reformation to the Present* (New York: Facts on File, 1989), p. 24.

[17] Ibid., pp. 108, 207-8.

12

Lilias Skene: A Quaker Poet and her 'Cursed Self'

Gordon DesBrisay

Lilias Skene was a model of female Presbyterian piety who in 1666, shortly after the birth of the last of her ten children, turned Quaker and became a preacher, a prophet, and a poet. Thirty-three of her lyric poems, 1,472 lines in all copied from an original manuscript now lost, survive in the private papers of the literary historian William Walker, who published selections in 1887.[1] One tract, a letter of pious rebuke addressed to a Presbyterian minister in 1678, was published in her lifetime.[2] A prophetic sermon of 1677 circulated in manuscript until it was published in 1753.[3] She also wrote a series of warmly-received evangelising letters to the Princess Elizabeth of the Rhine, cousin to the Stewart kings, but these have not survived or remain to be found.[4] Though her surviving works of poetry and prose are few and currently exist only in archives and rare editions, they constitute one of the largest bodies of literary work by a non-aristocratic Scottish woman of her era.

Lilias Skene was reasonably well known in her day. Her Quaker activism made her notorious in Aberdeen, and attracted unfavourable attention in Edinburgh: when the Scottish Privy Council levied heavy fines on Quaker men in 1676, her husband's penalty was increased by half to account for Lilias' 'transgressions'.[5] The Quaker patriarch George Fox asked to be remembered to her, and Friends in England wrote to request copies of her writing.[6] Since her death in 1697, however, she has been almost completely forgotten. As a woman and a Quaker, she has been doubly marginalised from the main currents of Scottish literary and historical scholarship; as a Scot, she has been little noticed by historians of English and American Quakerism.[7]

When Lilias joined the Society of Friends in 1666, they were a tiny and persecuted minority in Aberdeen, but they offered her spiritual solace and a unique degree of female empowerment.[8]   Quakers believed that God's light was in every person, and so allowed women, especially educated and spiritually 'gifted' women like Lilias, to serve as preachers, prophets, missionaries, and writers; female Friends accounted for a hugely disproportionate share of publications by seventeenth-century English-speaking women.[9]   Lilias found in Quakerism a liberating discourse to shape her thoughts and words, and a community of fellow writers to encourage and critique her work.   In Quakerism she also encountered a crisis that compelled her to step forward.   Her searing prophetic sermon of 1677, 'A Word of Warning to the Magistrats and Inhabitants of Aberdene', was provoked by the wholesale arrest of Quaker men there:

> As at severall seasons and in diverse maners I have witnessed against the will-worship & blind obedience of the inhabitants of this city since the Lord opened myne eyes & drew me out of that fearfull pitt, So at this season I ame moved in this same Zeal for truth and compassion upon your Soules, Magistrats preachers and people, to bear ane open testimony against the spirit of persecution [...]. Wherefor in the fear of the Lord & in tender love towards [ye] I warne you to consider what ye have done or are doing, that ye draw not upon your selves & this city innocent blood for assuredly the Lord will not hold you guiltless...[10]

Formal declarations of this sort were rare: when women spoke out in public, they tended to do so in allegedly spontaneous bursts of anger or outrage such as those recorded in court records, rather than in carefully scripted jeremiads like this.[11]

To justify her speaking, Lilias insisted, like other Quaker women and, indeed, all mystics and religious radicals, that she spoke not as herself but as 'moved' by the spirit of God.   More conventional Christians had to accept that this was possible in theory, but they argued that in practice Quakers were self-regarding egoists whose pronouncements were, at best, delusional: 'our giddy people', sniffed Henry Scougal, the young professor of divinity at King's College, Aberdeen, 'go over to that sect and party, where all ranks, and both sexes, are allowed the satisfaction to hear themselves talk in publick'.[12]   Skene's writing suggests that any 'satisfaction' she derived from speaking out was tempered by lingering fears that her self-abnegation might be incomplete or illusory. Extinguishing the self was required of any preacher, but for women like

Lilias Skene it was especially fraught: in a culture where women's public interventions were by definition transgressive, the self-erasure demanded of women who would speak for the Lord had to be preceded by an act of self-assertion.[13] The paradox was not lost on Lilias, whose struggles may have been more than merely formulaic or rhetorical. 'How shal I yet delyvered be', she asked in one of her final poems, 'Whil cursed self remains with me'.[14]

She was born Lilias Gillespie in Kirkcaldy, in 1626 or 1627.[15] Her father and both her grandfathers were ministers of the Kirk, and she grew up in a time of religious radicalism and change. Her older brothers, Patrick and George Gillespie, were famous Covenanting divines: the former became principal of Glasgow University, the latter a member of the Westminster Assembly. Reflecting as a Quaker on the first, Presbyterian, half of her life, Lilias explained that she 'was one, who according to my education and information and inclination from my child-hood was a true lover of that called the Glorious Gospell, and a constant attender upon the declarations thereof'.[16] In 1646, she married Alexander Skene, son of a wealthy Aberdeen merchant and an ardent Covenanter like herself.[17] The first of her ten children was born and died amidst a plague epidemic in 1647, and two others died in infancy before the last was born in 1665.[18] By then, the Restoration of monarchy and episcopacy begun in 1660 was making life difficult for radical Presbyterians: Lilias' brother Patrick, for example, was tried for treason. It was, she wrote, 'a very serious season'.[19] Her earliest known writing, a poem of 116 lines, is a product of these dispiriting years. The lost manuscript of Lilias' verse that William Walker transcribed was begun on 12 February 1676 when poems from the previous eleven years were copied down and dated, preparatory to new poems being added.[20] 'On Growing Tryalls', dated 1665, is the only poem that seems to predate her conversion to Quakerism, albeit by a matter of months. Drawing a familiar analogy between covenanting Presbyterians and God's first chosen people, it begins 'When Israel in Egypt land / Did grone for libertie', and offers what Walker called 'a godly ballad on how, when people are struggling for spiritual freedom, they cannot but expect (as illustrated in Scripture history) greater griefs and tyrannies than usual'.[21]

Having urged the Presbyterian faithful to stay the course, Lilias Gillespie suffered a midlife crisis of faith that prompted her defection to Quakerism in 1666 and propelled her into the public eye. It was the pivotal event in a life subsequently understood in terms of a 'before' and an 'after', the transition neatly marked by her adoption of her husband's surname twenty-odd years into their marriage and contrary to Scottish custom, but in keeping with the English style favoured by Scottish Quakers. Lilias' distinguished family and reputation for godliness made her apostasy all the more sensational: years later, Friends still boasted of having attracted a woman once held in such high esteem by the Aberdeen ministers, especially the Quaker-baiting George Meldrum.[22] Her conversion was doubly schismatic because, as for many first-generation Quaker women, it also entailed a break from her husband — in this case just as he was reconciling with the political and religious establishment. Alexander converted six years later, however, and as a couple the Skenes moved to the centre of Quaker affairs in Aberdeen.[23] By 1672 there were still only two dozen adult Friends in the town, but Aberdeen had become an important Quaker outpost thanks to the presence nearby of Robert Barclay of Ury, whose influential writings made him a leader in the international Quaker movement.[24] The Skenes opened their house to meetings for worship, hosted English Friends (including visiting female preachers), and shared a subscription to every Quaker publication licensed by the Quaker authorities in London.[25] Lilias took part in disciplinary proceedings and helped establish the first school for Scottish Friends.[26]

Speaking and writing, however, were at the heart of her activism. Lilias was rare among seventeenth-century Quakers in writing verse as well as prose. Yet she was typical in making copious reference to scripture and in drawing upon her own experiences for didactic, polemical, and evangelical purposes. The experience she made the most telling use of was her own conversion, which she recounted in both a poem and a published letter. The difference between her two versions of her conversion story and the one told by the Aberdeen Quakers illustrates the tension, evident in much Quaker writing of the time, between individual and collective identity.[27]

The title of Lilias' second poem, 'A Song of praise when, the Lord first revealed to me His mynd, that I should not joyne in this Communion at Aberdeen 1666', allows us to date her conversion with some precision: the Lord's Supper was announced on 4 July 1666 and scheduled for 1 August.[28] A celebration of religious and social unity, communion was the most divisive issue separating Presbyterians and Episcopalians. After much struggle, Lilias became convinced that God required that she reject not just the tainted Episcopalian version of the sacrament, but the sacrament itself and the Church of Scotland with it.

'A Song of praise' describes her conversion as a definitive break from the Kirk and a shattering moment of revelation:

His power I called to mynd but could not feell it

> Yett fearing waited yt Hee would reveall it
> From silent grones to utter teares and cryes
>
> ...
>
> Then from his face He puld away the vail
> And from my understandinges eye the scale
> And by a strong hand he did me instruct,
> What through this desert must my soule conduct
> Hee said thy light is in the Living God
> Goe not elsewhere to seeke it from abroad.[29]

These lines evoke characteristic Quaker themes of silent waiting, direct revelation, and the 'light within all men'. God ignores her pleas until fear overcomes her and she learns to wait for Him, subordinating her conscious mind and opening herself to a fuller sensual experience. Lilias draws on erotic imagery to convey the profundity and physicality of the moment of revelation when His 'precious lyffe begin to ryse' within her, evoking her 'silent grones' and 'utter tears and cryes'. Finally, she tells us that God spoke directly to her, personally endorsing the doctrine of the light within and warning her not to seek it 'abroad' in external forms and institutions. In a published 1678 letter to Robert McWard, an exiled Covenanting minister who had attacked Robert Barclay in print, Lilias reiterated her assertion that revelation was an event rather than a process — 'it was the thing ye school-men call Immediat Objective Revelation, (which my desire is ye were more particularly and feelingly acquainted with)' — but she also emphasised that it was an individual experience by stressing that the Quakers had not recruited her:

> It is very well known to all that lived in the place where I sojourned, I was none who conversed with them, I was never at one of their meetings, I never read one of their books, unless accidentally I had found them where I came, and lookt to them, and laid them by again.[30]

By insisting upon her direct connection to God, Lilias was defending her right to speak by invoking the only condition under which it was allowed. As another Aberdeen Quaker, George Keith, explained, unlettered men might speak in meetings for worship, but even a 'godly and spiritually learned woman' could preach only 'if the spirit of the Lord command', a circumstance that trumped even her husband's natural authority over her, for 'in that case she is the Lord's more than her husband's'.[31]

Quakers believed that individual inspiration could only occur within the context of a community of believers, and in the Aberdeen Quakers' account of Lilias' conversion, written in the 1680s, she is drawn to the Lord through an indirect encounter with female Friends.[32] Their version differs from Lilias' in part because it was designed to make different points: in her own tellings, Lilias aimed to establish the authenticity of her religious experience and the authority she drew from it; as Friends told it, Lilias' story revealed the falsehoods of a Church of Scotland minister, the scriptural truth of Quakerism, the magnetic power of female preaching, and the centrality of communal fellowship. 'Providentially' homesick when the family was at church and the house quiet, from next door she heard

> [...] two English women friends declaring Truth and Praying. To which she Listening very attentively, [...] was abundantly convinced of the dreadful Lyes and Impudence of the allegations of her admired Preacher [George Meldrum] in so callumnating them. She having taken great notice That the whole substance of their Testimonies was in the very Scripture words, and was affected with the Life of Jesus in their prayers In whose name Life and power they were.[33]

Although her colleagues agree with Lilias that she was a passive recipient of enlightenment, their version is otherwise difficult to reconcile with hers. Where Lilias deems it unnecessary to recount the external circumstances of her conversion, the Quakers describe the circumstances but stop short of the decisive moment itself.

The tension here is not simply between the individual and the collective because in some sense the parties collaborated. Lilias' letter to McWard was published by Robert Barclay and almost certainly written and possibly revised in consultation with him and other Quaker writers. At the same time, the Aberdeen Quaker version comes from a collective history compiled by Alexander Skene and, presumably, approved of by Lilias Skene. This apparent blurring of authorship mirrored the blurring of individual and collective identities with which Lilias seems to have struggled even as she engaged in this process herself.[34] In the extract quoted from her letter to McWard, she strips the story of some of its specificity by referring to Aberdeen not by name but as 'the place where I sojourned', a deft touch of preacherly vagueness signalling that there are wider issues at play. This willingness to rework her life stories for effect also suggests that the stories were not entirely her own, that she saw them as a kind of communal property: her contribution to a collective Quaker identity within which individual identities were meant to be subsumed. As she wrote in a 1672 poem to imprisoned Friends in Montrose, 'One lyffe, one love, one peace, on[e] joy, one way / One is our principle, our strenth, our stay'.[35]

Deliberately rendering her own life story generic was part of Lilias' wider effort toward self-abnegation. Another aspect of this process involved the rhetorical crossing of gender boundaries. Authoritative speech was by definition masculine speech, so when Quaker women preached and prophesied they often adopted the language, symbols, and rhetorical posture of biblical patriarchs.[36] In 1677, for example, at the height of the persecution of Quakers in Aberdeen, Lilias addressed three prophetic poems to imprisoned Friends, consoling them with visions of the Lord smiting their enemies.[37]

> For everie souldier he hath weapons there
> For some a battle ax, a sword a bow
> As hee hath service, weapons he'll bestow
> With some hee'll bend the bow with others fill it
> By some Hee'll wound the beast by others kill it
>
> . . .
>
> The words gone forth the sound hath reached me
> A sacrifice in Bozrah is to be
> The Lord will bath his sword in Edoms blood
> And vengeance recompense on all her brood
> Who have engadged in this holy warre
> And followers of the Lamb accounted are.[38]

In these lines from an untitled poem, Lilias, like other Quaker women, constructs herself ('the sound hath reached me') as a prophet and couches her bellicose pronouncements in biblical stories and imagery that justify the sentiments and language used but further distance what she says from who she personally is.

Masculine speech was authoritative yet had the privilege of being considered generic. The point of a woman adopting a masculine voice was not to speak as a man but to shed her specific identity altogether, and sexual difference with it.[39] At the same time, utilising a masculine voice paradoxically called attention to her feminine identity, emphasising rather than mitigating the provocative nature of women's public speech acts. In Lilias' first clear evocation of a masculine persona, a sixteen-line poem dated 1668, the combative tone is set by the unwieldy title: 'Ane answer to a nameless authour of a letter wrot full of mistakes & groundless challenges with reflexiones upon truth'.[40] A marginal note in the original manuscript identified her target as 'G. M.', George Meldrum. The incendiary nature of this poem lies not so much in the language as in the context of a woman addressing a minister of the kirk in these terms.

> Thy queries all I answere come & sie
> Then shall thou know the doctrin if it be
> Of God or not when thou hath done his will
> Iff whats already knowne thou doe fullfill
> Then with me come bow downe thy neck & take
> The cross of Christ & beare shame for his sake.[41]

Like several male Friends in Aberdeen, Lilias challenges her former minister to debate Quaker principles with her: 'Thy queries all I answere come & sie'.[42] A debate presupposes two evenly matched or at least comparable parties, and Lilias' challenge and assured rhetorical stance, positioning herself as her people's champion, presumes parity with, if not superiority to, the minister. Conventional Christians thought it the height of presumption for a male Quaker to address a university-trained and church-sanctioned clergyman on an equal footing; for a woman to do so was even more outrageous.[43] A woman who assumed a generic masculine persona in public disputation risked diverting attention from the message to the messenger; a gesture offered as self-effacement could seem to sceptics like self-aggrandisement.

Yet Lilias had adopted a masculine persona for calculated effect (to gain access to public discourse and lose her self in God), and she was just as capable of writing in a 'feminine' persona as the situation demanded. In 'Sion Now Unite', a poem in the form of a prayer dated March 1670, the bold confidence of 'Ane answer to ane nameless author' is replaced by a chastened tone:

> SION NOW UNITE o Lord
> Work a perfect full concord
> The chyld shall not parted be
> Nor's seamles coat rent by me
> My Conserne I doe resigne
> In thy handes my God & King
> Lett me have no more repute
> Then may truely contribute.[44]

The biblical imagery here is resonant of familial and domestic concerns traditionally associated with women, as are the themes of obeisance and reconciliation invoked when the speaker declares her desire to subordinate her individual ego ('Let me have no more repute') to the collective cause of unity in God. The poem is addressed to God but may also be intended, in a more literal way, as a plea for unity within Lilias' own family (her husband had yet to convert) and on behalf of other Quaker women and their divided families.

Lilias' most complex deployment of gendered rhetorical positions is found in her 1677 prophetic sermon, 'A Word of Warning to the Magistrats and Inhabitants of Aberdene', quoted above. Assuming the mantle of a biblical patriarch, she interprets current events in light of scriptural precedents as she demands that the authorities let her people go. 'Like Egypts taskmasters', she chides, 'ye have increased the tale of Brick, and instead of setting them at more liberty ye have added to their bonds'.[45] 'The Lord having sent me as from the dead to warn you', she tells her audience, justifying her speaking by offering her conversion as a return from spiritual death that purged her worldly self and equipped her to deliver God's message; she sustains a prophet's commanding masculine tone throughout — 'for my part your severityes and crueltyes are a confirmation unto me, that truth is not on your side' — but she does not sustain a generic masculine persona.[46] Most Quaker women prophets strove, as Phyllis Mack puts it, to achieve 'their essential absence from a scene that they outwardly appeared to dominate', but Lilias places herself, or a version of herself, at the rhetorical heart of her sermon.[47] Drawing on personal circumstances well known to her audience, she accuses the persecuting authorities of betraying the very traditions of 'good neighbourhood' which they accused Quakers of undermining:

> Neither would ye unnecessarily throng in honest men that have families wives and children deeply suffering with them & in them in those cold nasty stinking holes, where ye have shutt them up; who have been as neatly handled and tenderly educated & as usefull in their generation as any amongst you.[48]

Lilias' language here is powerfully direct, shorn of biblical analogies and other distancing devices embraced by women keen to banish themselves in the act of speaking out. She asserts her personal authority as a neighbour, a witness to suffering, and a woman known to every Aberdonian as the wife, mother, and mother-in-law of prisoners.

After the cessation of persecution in 1679, Lilias issued no further prose, but in her poetry she continued to explore the thorny issues of identity and self-abnegation. Although she no longer engaged in public disputes with the authorities, she was sometimes embroiled in conflicts within the Quaker community. As the solidarity that saw Friends through the persecution gave way to bickering and recrimination, internecine conflict propelled her into further rounds of troubling self-assertion followed by remorse and self-doubt. In a poem dated 1682, she reflected upon a particularly vitriolic dispute with Isabell Keilo, a founding Aberdeen Quaker turned schismatic.[49] Lilias considered herself the aggrieved party ('Come cure my many bruises Lord'), but the poem expresses regret at her apparent inability to resist responding in kind, and a longing for self-cancellation and reassurance that God is with her:

> And when I meet with unjust accusations
> Lett me obtaine that inward approbation
> O lett the sence of it with me remaine
> In feeling the selfe Justifier slaine.[50]

Reassurance was not always forthcoming. Lilias was unusual among Quaker writers in admitting to spiritual struggles after her conversion: Friends routinely wrote of their despair prior to 'convincement', but rarely committed subsequent doubts to paper.[51] In a harrowing poem from 1681, she describes her continuing struggle:

> The paines of hell tooke hold on me
> My hopes have me disceaved
> The harvests past, summer I see
> And yett I am not saved
> Afflic't and toss'd with tempests I
> Yet not conforted am
> Discourag'd yea despondencie
> Is my habittuall frame.

Despondency, doubting God's good will, is a sin born of clinging to the self:

> My freindes & fathers trust in thee
> And have delyvered been
> But I'm a worme & worse I see
> And doe myselfe esteeme

The poem concludes bleakly: 'My soule & flesh longs in parcht land / Wherein no watters be'.[52] Only its title, 'In ane houre of weaknes & deepe Discouragement', carries a seed of hope, a reminder that an hour (even a metaphorical hour) is bounded and finite.

Lilias' next dated poem of September 1683 restores hope. It offers her most consistent metaphor, that of a tree sustained through the seasons by '[t]he living substance in the root': '…each retirement of this sap/A fresh spring issues in/Which is of spirituall thinges a map/Throw death lyffe doth begin'.[53] This reminder that spiritual life issues from the death of the worldly self offers conventional reassurance. In its hopeful resolution, this untitled poem, the last that can be securely dated to the 1680s, points toward the more spiritually confident verse of the poet's final years.[54] Lilias completed ten poems, nearly one-third of her total output, in the last six years of her life, starting in 1691. Alexander Skene died in January 1694: 'But oh my suett is gon' she lamented in a poem dated that month.[55] By then, Lilias was about 67 years old, living simply with her daughter Anna and two female servants, preparing for her own death.[56] The poems composed in these years have a valedictory tone as salvation seems secure and imminent.

> If to the end I doe indoor
> Throw faith & patience I am sur
> My sufferings long will end at last
> As all my former pleasours past.[57]

As a writer, Lilias depended on communicating her spiritual and physical torment. Quaker male prophets endured their share of bodily infirmities, but it was usually only women's health that was commented on: Robert Barclay introduced Lilias to the Princess Elizabeth as 'a woman of great experience and tenderness of heart who through great tribulations both of body and mind hath attained the earnest of the Kingdom [of God]'.[58] By the end of her long hard life, she was in a position to assure her audience that sorrow and suffering were not only part of God's plan, but signs of special favour, as she explained bluntly in this verse from an untitled poem dated 18 January 1695:

> Gods deerest children in this life
> Hav suffrings for ther lott
> Surly they wold prov bastars iff
> He excersees'd them not.[59]

In her earlier preaching and prophetic modes, Lilias had tried to follow the convention of adopting masculine forms for the sake of an undistorted transmission of God's message. Yet in these late poems, she emphasises her identity as a woman. An untitled poem of April 1696, for example, retells the story of Mary Magdalene who maintained her vigil at Christ's tomb despite being told not to.

> To Marie at the Sepulcher
> An Angell did apeer
> Altho he knew she sought the Lord
> And did rebook her fear
> She took no notes of himself
> Nor yet of what he said
> But stil she sought to find the Lord
> Or kno wher he was Laid.[60]

Mary Magdalene's steadfastness in the face of the angel's opposition was duly rewarded when Christ revealed himself to her. For Lilias (as for Margaret Fell and other Quaker women) Mary Magdalene's adherence to her own inner spiritual compass helped justify women's speaking, for it proved that God worked his mysterious ways through women as well as men.[61] In what may deliberately evoke the theological defenses of the medieval *querelle des femmes* debates, Lilias reminds her readers that women played critical roles at the two great turning points in human history: damnation and salvation:

> A women was the instroment
> Of mankinds los and fall
> A woman broght the ferst report
> Christ had restored all.

Though Eve and Mary Magdalene are not unproblematic role-models, Lilias could identify with them to the extent that she understood her own life as being enmeshed in paradox. Although turning Quaker freed her from many of the restrictions by which seventeenth-century women were bound, enabling her to act and speak and write in ways unimaginable in her former life, she could experience her liberation as a kind of enslavement: God and the Quakers gave her a voice, but they also gave her a script and pushed her onstage. In an untitled poem dated April 1694, Lilias invoked an especially dark and violent simile to express her terror when testifying in public. When she first described her encounter with God as a new convert in 1666, she had used the language of physical love. Nearly thirty years later, in describing the feeling of being assailed by sin, her language evokes rape:

> Bot as the vergen when deflurd

> If heard aloud for help to cry
> By Law, was cleared from gilt, thereby
> My lamentations to the Lord
> Doeth manefest sin I abhord.[62]

Just as by law a rape victim's only hope of justice depended on witnesses hearing her spontaneous and authentic cries, Lilias' salvation required that her lamentations to the Lord be heard by others. The dread she felt when He compelled her to speak out was compounded by the necessity that she somehow deny her own identity as an individual and a woman in the very act of self-assertion. The price of saving her soul was losing her self. Whether called upon to disappear periodically beneath God's words or to dissolve into the collective identity of the Quakers, Lilias Skene had always to contend with her 'cursed self'.[63]

Notes

[1] Aberdeen University Library [AUL] Historic Collections, William Walker Papers, MS 2774; William Walker, *The Bards of Bon-Accord, 1375-1860* [*Bards*] (Aberdeen: Edmund and Spark, 1887), pp. 85-102. On Walker, see Alexander M. Kinghorn, 'William Walker and the Bards of Bon-Accord', in *Selected Essays on Scottish Language and Literature: A Festschrift in Honor of Allan H. MacLaine* ed. by Steven R. McKenna (Lewiston: Edwin Mellon, 1992), pp. 211-39.

[2] Lilias Skene, 'An Expostulatory Epistle, Directed to Robert Macquare', in Robert Barclay, *Robert Barclay's Apology* [...] *Vindicated from John Brown's Examination and Pretended Confutation thereof* (London, 1679). Last reprinted, in slightly bowdlerised form, in *Diary of Alexander Jaffray* [...] *With Memoirs of the Rise, Progress, and Persecutions of the People Called Quakers in the North of Scotland* ed. by John Barclay, 3rd edn (Aberdeen: George and Robert King, 1856), pp. 438-44.

[3] NAS, CH 10/3/35: Lilias Skene, 'A Word of Warning to the Magistrats and Inhabitants of Aberdene [...]', in Alexander Skene, and others, 'A Breiffe Account of the Most Materiall Passages and Occurances [...] During That Great and Long Tryall of Sufferings and Persecution at Aberdene' (c.1681), fols 37^r-39^r; Joseph Besse, *A Collection of the Sufferings of the People Called Quakers*, 2 vols (London: [n.pub.], 1753), II, 522-3. See also *Diary of Alexander Jaffray*, pp. 294-7.

[4] The correspondence is referred to in letters between Robert Barclay and the Princess. *Reliquiae Barclaianae: Correspondence of Colonel David Barclay and Robert Barclay of Urie and His Son Robert* (London: privately published, 1870), pp. 7, 8, 14, 20-3. The only known extant letter by Lilias was to Viscountess Anne Conway, the bedridden philosopher and Quaker convert whom she visited

in England. *The Conway Letters: The Correspondence of Anne, Viscountess Conway, Henry More, and their Friends, 1642-1684*, ed. by Marjorie Hope Nicols, rev. ed. (Oxford: Clarendon, 1992), p. 438.

[5] NAS, CH 10/3/35, fol. 23^r.

[6] *Reliquiae Barclaianae*, p. 44. Isabel Yeamans, daughter of Quaker matriarch Margaret Fell and an eminent preacher in her own right, wrote to Robert Barclay for a copy of a paper by Lilias (p. 45).

[7] An exception is Phyllis Mack's magisterial *Visionary Women: Ecstatic Prophecy in Seventeenth-Century England* (Berkeley: U California P, 1992), pp. 267, 379.

[8] On the Aberdeen Quakers, see most recently Michael Lynch and Gordon DesBrisay with M. G. H. Pittock, 'The Faith of the People', in *Aberdeen Before 1800: A New History*, ed. by E. Patricia Dennison, David Ditchburn, and Michael Lynch (East Linton: Tuckwell, 2002), pp. 303-8; DesBrisay, 'Catholics, Quakers, and Religious Persecution in Restoration Aberdeen', *IR*, 47 (1996), pp. 136-68.

[9] In addition to Mack, see Bonnelyn Young Kunze, *Margaret Fell and the Rise of Quakerism* (Stanford: SUP, 1994); H. Larry Ingle, 'A Quaker Woman on Women's Roles: Mary Penington to Friends, 1678', *Signs*, 16 (1991), 587-96. On publications, see Michael Mascuch, *Origins of the Individualist Self: Autobiography and Self-Identity in England, 1591-1791* (Stanford: Stanford UP, 1997), p. 121.

[10] NAS, CH 10/3/35, fol. 37^r.

[11] See for example Elizabeth Ewan, '"Divers Injurious Words": Defamation and Gender in Late Medieval Scotland', in *History, Literature, and Music in Scotland, 900-1560*, ed. by R. Andrew Mcdonald (Toronto: U Toronto P, 2002), pp. 163-86; and Laura Gowing, *Domestic Dangers: Women, Words, and Sex in Early Modern London* (Oxford: Clarendon, 1996).

[12] Henry Scougal, 'Of the Importance and Difficulty of the Ministerial Function', in his *The Life of God in the Soul of Man* (London: [n. pub.], 1726), p. 370.

[13] Mack, pp. 172-8.

[14] Untitled, April 1694. AUL, MS 2774, p.51. In quoting Lilias Skene's poetry, I have followed the spelling, punctuation, stanza breaks, dates, and titles given in William Walker's manuscript transcript in preference to Walker's printed extracts, where applicable, on the grounds that his manuscript is a step closer to the lost original. Quakers calculated the year from 1 March, however, and I have silently converted all dates to standard form

[15] See 'Lilias Skene', *NDNB*, for further biographic details and references.

[16] 'An Expostulatory Epistle', p. 202.

[17] Alexander Skene of Newtyle was a magistrate and ruling elder of Aberdeen in the 1650s and in 1671. He converted to Quakerism in 1672 and published a number of works; see further *NDNB*.

[18] *Memorials of the Family of Skene of Skene*, ed by William Forbes Skene (Aberdeen: New Spalding Club, 1887), p. 77; for the correct birthday of the last child, however, see 'Diary of John Row, Principal of King's College', *Scottish Notes and Queries*, 7 (1893), 85.

[19] 'An Expostulatory Epistle', p. 196.

[20] AUL, MS 2774, p. 1. The original was labelled 'This pertains to Lilias Skein & is for containing some verses upon severall subjects made by her severall yeares ago this 12th of [February 1676]'. Though mainly in Lilias' hand, Walker noted that some of the later poems were copied by her husband or daughter Anna. There is no suggestion that anyone other than Lilias composed them. *Bards*, p. 89.

[21] AUL, MS 2774, p. 1; *Bards*, pp. 88-9.

[22] NAS, CH 10/3/36: Alexander Skene, and others, 'A Brieff Historicall Account and Record of the First Rise and Progress of the Blessed Truth, Called in Derision Quakerism, In and About Aberdeen', ([n. d.: n. pub.]c.1687), p. 30.

[23] NAS, CH 10/3/36, p. 30.

[24] 'Robert Barclay', *NDNB;* D. Elton Trueblood, *Robert Barclay* (New York: Harper and Row, 1968).

[25] W. F. Miller, 'Gleanings from the Records of the Yearly Meeting of Aberdeen, 1672 to 1786', *Journal of the Friends' Historical Society* [JFHS], 8 (1911), 43, 45. Quakers published about sixty-five titles a year in the 1670s. Mascuch, p. 121.

[26] Miller, 'Gleanings', p. 45; W. F. Miller, 'Notes on Early Friends' Schools in Scotland', JFHS, 7 (1910), 105-10.

[27] Luella M. Wright, *The Literary Life of the Early Friends, 1650-1725* (New York: Columbia University Studies in English and Comparative Literature, 1932), pp. 10-11; Mack, pp. 8, 160-1; Elspeth Graham, 'Women's Writing and the Self', in *Women and Literature in Britain 1500-1700*, ed. by Helen Wilcox (Cambridge: CUP, 1996), pp. 214-15.

[28] AUL, MS 2774, p. 7; *Extracts From the Council Register of the Burgh of Aberdeen: 1643-1747*, ed. by John Stuart (Edinburgh: SBRS, 1872), p. 231.

[29] AUL, MS 2774, p. 7.

[30] 'An Expostulatory Epistle', p. 203.

[31] George Keith, *The Woman Preacher of Samaria* (London: [n. pub.], 1674), p. 11, cf. Mack, p. 177.

[32] Elaine Hobby, '"Come to Live a Preaching Life": Female Community in Seventeenth-Century Radical Sects', in *Female Communities 1600-1800: Literary Vision and Cultural Realities*, ed. by Rebecca D'Monté and Nicole Pohl (New York: St. Martin's, 2000), pp. 79-81; NAS, CH 10/3/36, p. 29.

[33] NAS, CH 10/3/36, p. 29.

[34] Graham writes of a Quaker's 'capacity for collective selfhood', pp. 214-15.

[35] AUL, MS 2774, pp. 29-30. Printed in full in *Bards*, p. 91.

[36] Mack, p. 174.

[37] AUL, MS 2774, pp. 23-8.

[38] Untitled, dated 15 December 1677. AUL, MS 2774, pp. 25-6. Walker published additional lines from this poem, and a similar poem (in its entirety) dated ten days later, 'Some thinges concerning freindes in Prison [...]', with spelling changes and punctuation added. *Bards*, pp. 94-5.

[39] Mack, pp. 133, 136; Suzanne Trill, 'Religion and the Construction of Femininity', in Wilcox, ed., pp. 46-7.

[40] Dated 21 September 1668, AUL, MS 2774, p. 43.

[41]Walker published the entire poem, changing some spelling and adding punctuation (*Bards*, p. 90).

[42] NAS, CH 10/3/36, p. 29; Gordon DesBrisay, 'Quakers and the University: The Aberdeen Debate of 1675', *History of Universities*, 13 (1994), 91-2.

[43] Meldrum, in keeping with Kirk policy, did not deign to respond directly to Lilias' or any other Quaker challenges.

[44] AUL, MS 2774, pp. 15-16.

[45] NAS, CH 10/3/35, fol. 37^r.

[46] Ibid., fol. 38^r.

[47] Mack, pp. 177-8.

[48] NAS, CH 10/3/35, fol. 38^r.

[49] *Bards*, pp. 97-8.

[50] AUL, MS 2774, pp. 30-2. Reprinted in its entirety (punctuation added) in *Bards*, pp. 98-9.

[51] Mack, p. 160.

[52] AUL, MS 2774, pp. 33-5.

[53] Ibid., pp. 40-1. Walker added punctuation and a title, 'True Lyffe', not in his original transcription (*Bards*, p. 99).

[54] All but six of the poems (three of them anagrams of the names Lilias Gillespie, Alexander Skene, and their son Patrick Skene) are dated in Walker's manuscript.

[55] AUL, MS 2774, p. 50; *Bards*, p. 101.

[56] John Stuart, ed., *List of Pollable Persons Within the Shire of Aberdeen, 1696*, 2 vols (Aberdeen: [n. pub.], 1844), II, 614.

[57] Untitled, April 1694. AUL, MS 2774, p. 52.

[58] *Reliquiae Barclaianae*, 7-8 (28 October 1676). On representations of women's health and frailty, see Mack, pp. 385-6.

[59] Untitled, 18 May 1695. AUL, MS 2774, p. 54. Similarly: 'Hee shew me that my loathing self / And sence of missorie / War evedences sur that he / Was passified with me'. Untitled, 3 October 1691. AUL, MS 2774, p. 46.

[60] This reworking of the story accords most closely with John 20:1-18.

[61]Rebecca Larson, *Daughters of Light: Quaker Women Preaching and Prophesying in the Colonies and Abroad, 1700-1775* (New York: Knopf, 1999), p. 23; Margaret Fell, *Women's Speaking Justified Proved and Allowed of by the Scriptures* (Amherst, Mass.: Mosher Book and Tract Committee, 1980).

[62] Untitled. Dated April 1694. AUL, MS 2774, pp. 51-2.

[63] I wish to thank Pamela Giles for sharing her transcription of William Walker's manuscript, and Susan Blake, Warren Johnston, David Parkinson, Frank Klaassen, Walter Klaassen, Sharon Wright, and members of the University of Saskatchewan History Faculty Research Workshop for commenting on drafts. Many thanks also to the helpful staff of the National Archives of Scotland, Aberdeen University Library Historic Collections, and Haverford College Quaker Collection.

13

Scottish Women's Religious Narrative, 1660-1720: Constructing the Evangelical Self

David George Mullan

From the period c.1600-c.1725 at least 50 Scottish religious narratives have survived. About twenty of these were written by ministers, while of the approximately thirty written by lay people, the proportions are nearly equal, with sixteen by women; others are known to have been written.[1] Indeed, one woman learned to write at the age of 58 for no other purpose than to tell her own story.[2] The prose presented here explores female religious subjectivity in explicitly autobiographical form or in the context of journals which are largely autobiographical in nature. This essay briefly describes eleven of the female narratives and discusses the materials from which their expressions of religious and 'writerly' selfhood are composed.

The earliest female autobiography to be written, or at least to survive, during this period was that by Mistress Rutherford[3] who wrote 14,500 words about her life in Midlothian (Edinburgh and environs) and Ireland from childhood through to child-bearing, beginning early in the century and continuing into the 1630s. The time of authorship is uncertain but external factors would suggest a date after 1660, if only because evangelical autobiographical writing, even by men, was rare before then in Scotland and England.

Katharine Collace (Mistress Ross) was born in Edinburgh c.1635, one of five daughters born to Francis Collace, minister of Gordon in the Borders. In 1650 she contracted a disastrous marriage with John Ross. This was only a year or two after an adolescent conversion experience, and she reproached herself for not being observant enough 'in waiting for his [God's] counsel, the omission whereof, in a weighty case, bred me twenty-four years grievous afflictions; and the root of it was my woeful natural disposition, unwilling to displease others; for I did not please myself in that particular'.[4] Her husband is otherwise invisible in the story, aside from the fact of twelve children born to the couple, none of whom survived their mother. Collace moved to the north of Scotland and fell in with leading figures amongst the radical Covenanters, notably Thomas Hog, whom Robert Wodrow (1679-1734), the great chronicler of the period of persecution, described as 'this great and truly extraordinary man of God'.[5] She later moved to Fife and then again to the north, dying in Edinburgh in 1697. She was a teacher of sewing and was well read in Presbyterian divinity, including the letters of Samuel Rutherford.[6] These were also read by some of the other life writers, perhaps drawn by Rutherford's intense Puritan piety couched in the language of erotic mysticism from the Song of Solomon. Katharine's autobiography, much focused on her inner state, extends to 29,000 words.

Her sister, Jean Collace, worked as a domestic in Moray and as a teacher in Falkland, Fife, and wrote 'Some short remembrances of the Lord's kindness to me, and his work on my soul, for my own use', almost 25,000 words in length. Her memoir exists in at least three manuscript recensions,[7] and is based upon a diary. The content is similar to that of her sister's narrative: introspective evangelical religion; a deep antipathy to episcopacy and the imposed curates whom she denounces as 'the enemies of God' (p. 121); her relationship with admired and persecuted ministers; and preoccupation with her own, her sisters', and mother's sicknesses.

Mrs Goodale wrote about herself but then noted the regret her husband (whom she married in 1657) expressed on his deathbed in 1700 about not having written his own life, which she proceeded to do for him, thus transforming the autobiography into a biography.[8] Her narrative (c.4700 words) takes her from Edinburgh to the Netherlands because of her Presbyterian commitment, and then to Ireland where religious conflicts with episcopalian structures engaged her.

Lady Henrietta Campbell[9] was a daughter of Alexander Lindsay, first earl of Balcarres, who died in 1659; her mother Anna MacKenzie's second marriage to Archibald, ninth earl of Argyll, made her the earl's stepdaughter. Henrietta married Sir Duncan Campbell of Auchinbreck before 28 February 1680, and died c.1721.[10] She went to numerous communions, and she was diligent in recording her indebtedness to various ministers, whether Patrick Campbell at Inverary or Robert Fleming at Rotterdam. The document (c.65,000 words) begins with a considerable interest in the external world, but later retreats almost entirely into a private world of piety, with notices of the services she attends in Holland (1686-9), and particularly those conducted by her favourite minister, the exiled Scot, Robert Fleming.

Marion Veitch was married to a Covenanting minister, William, who himself wrote an autobiography. Her story (c.21,500 words) reveals little about contemporary events, though their shadow hangs ominously over her narrative, which discloses that she spent many years in England, sometimes separated from her husband, who found refuge in the Netherlands. Her tortured concern for her sons and husband in danger is powerfully conveyed, dealt with in the context of an intense evangelical understanding of God.[11]

Elizabeth Blackadder (1659/60-1732) wrote 'A short account of the Lord's way of providence towards me in my pilgrimage journeys' (c. 12,000 words).[12] She was the daughter of a famous Covenanting preacher who died in 1686 while imprisoned on the Bass Rock. She discusses some of her early religious experiences, writes out her personal covenant, attends celebrations of the Lord's Supper, marries, and copes with childbirth and the deaths of her husband and some of her children.

Elizabeth West wrote 85,000 words about her life from the period c. 1692 until 1709. The personal context surrounding this date would suggest that she was born c. 1680. She was the daughter of an Edinburgh couple, and she continued to live in and around the city, doing service in the homes of various well-to-do families with whom she might have gone to England near the time of the Union of 1707. However, her sympathy for Presbyterianism led to a deep antipathy toward the English ('a deceitful and cunning people, who would, if it lay in their power, ruin all their neighbour nations, to advance their own interest')[13] and their church, perverted by episcopacy. Her literary style and sensitivity make this the most accomplished among the documents noted here.

Several of the authors lived well beyond the end of the period considered here (c.1720) but they grew up within it. Elizabeth Cairns lived from 1685 to 1741, writing about 60,000 words on her life until c. 1736. She was born in the parish of Blackford, north-east of Stirling, the larger town where she spent some of her adult years as a teacher. Her parents paid for their Covenanting commitments, and she was born under the conditions of dispossession and flight.[14]

Mary Somervel lived out her days in Ayrshire.[15] Like many of her contemporaries she was left an orphan but, like Rutherford, was looked after by religious folk: 'Tho' me my parents both should leave, the Lord will me uptake'.[16] Though she suffered ill-health, she lived until 1762 (being at least 84). Her memoir of c.14,000 words is pronouncedly inward-looking.

Marion Shaw (1700-64) included in her narrative (c.33,000 words) all but the final two years of her life, which were supplied by an unknown hand. She lived in East Monkland in Lanarkshire, and Slammanan, near Falkirk. Her parents were 'respectable' and taught her reading and religion. She survived a childhood peril, a typical memory in this kind of devotional 'life-writing' by both women and men, and when she minded the sheep in summer, she read the Bible and a catechism. Later, like many others, she spent many weekends 'gadding', as the English put it, attending communion services in various localities.

Elspeth Graham recognises that the practice of self-writing is 'tied up quite directly with issues of social class or rank, with groups and group cultures as well as individual motivations and personalities'.[17] If the poetic women of the early modern period 'were socially privileged, belonging to the educated aristocratic and upper classes',[18] that is rarely true of these religious autobiographers, although Mistress Rutherford was connected to the landed classes and one of her protectors was Robert Foulis, a prominent legal figure, while Henrietta Campbell was well-born and also married well. The other writers noted here came from the middle ranks which could generally provide at least some education for girls, a notion emphasised by Sir George Mackenzie of Rosehaugh in his romance, *Aretina* (1660), where a rescued lady claims: 'Thus he [her father] lived, educating his children, me especially, in ordinary learning, scorning alwayes those who thought knowledge rather a burden, than a qualification to those of our sex, and that it was enough to a woman to know how to bring forth children'.[19] Many of these women were capable of reading serious works of divinity; some at least would have been exposed to such publications in their home, given that three were daughters of ministers (the Collaces and Blackadder) and one a minister's wife (Veitch).

The publication of English Puritan women's self-writing began in the middle of the seventeenth century, but that by Scottish women was delayed at least in part by the unfavourable conditions surrounding the press. A number of these lives derived from the furnace of persecution in which many Covenanters were fined, dispossessed, driven into hiding, exiled, and executed; during that period up to the Glorious Revolution, circulation *had* to be in manuscript rather than printed pamphlets. English women's religious literature, however, was published in Scotland during this time: Elizabeth White's *The Experience of God's Gracious Dealing* was published in Glasgow in 1696 and 1698, and some works of Anne Murray, Lady Halkett, were published in 1701 in Edinburgh.[20] The earliest[21] Scottish woman's religious prose to be published was *An Account of the Particular Soliloquies and Covenant Engagements of Mrs Janet Hamilton*. The first edition was in 1707, or possibly earlier, if an undated edition preceded it (as early as 1695, by internal dating of the contents). The next item was West's autobiography in 1724 (then Jean Adam's *Miscellany Poems* in 1734, containing some personal religious items), followed by Katharine Collace's journal in 1735. The publication history of Scottish men's self-writing was similar. The printing of these religious lives was undoubtedly tied up with adverse political conditions but many had a long history of manuscript circulation, perhaps making publication less urgent. We should also acknowledge Kate Chedgzoy's caution about 'fetishizing women's access to a public print culture as the sole indicator of their participation in the literary domain'.[22] Graham writes that English women's self-writing has survived in print and also, though to an unknown and limited extent due to the greater likelihood of loss, in manuscript. The history of both types of lives, whether in manuscript only or subsequently published, is unclear. None of these Scottish manuscripts are autographs, and it is only fair to ask whether there might have been a process of (masculine) editorial intervention in their coming to the press. There is, however, no evidence of this, and in the 1724 edition of West's *Memoirs* the preface claims that 'this book is exactly copied from the original manuscript'. Somervel's title page claims that the piece is being 'printed from her own manuscript', which was given to her nephew 'with strict instructions to publish them [spiritual experiences] after her death'. The prefatory letter to the reader states that 'the following sheets contain *part* of the religious exercises and experiences of Mary Somervel' [emphasis added], and also professes the following: 'There has [*sic*] no liberties been taken in correcting of it but what are entirely circumstantial, and her own phraseology has been carefully retained, excepting in flat repetitions, or where it marred the construction'. Elizabeth Cairns's title page states that the work is indeed her own composition, 'and now taken from her own original copy with great care and diligence'.

West's editor commented that her writing 'hath been desired by many pious and judicious Christians who have perused the same, and hath often been transcribed, which also made hope that the publishing of it would not be unacceptable'. In the case of Cairns, however, that circulation was in the first instance without the author's permission and quite horrified her. During her forty-sixth and forty-seventh years, she was troubled to find that twelve years earlier her private scribblings, 'from my young days', left with a friend, had gone abroad in unauthorised copies. This threw her into confusion because 'what was recorded there, I never told mortal of, and was fully of the mind to have kept these secrets between God and my own soul'. She wrote her thoughts without considering how others might react to them. Also, her handwriting was easily misconstrued, and then there was the matter of her shyness, perhaps related to issues of gender: 'all along, I never had freedom to discover the secrets of religion to the world: the Lord knows I never loved to make appearance this way' (p. 165). The effect of this accident on her as author was that she 'would write no more'. The result was entirely negative: she forgot what happened to her, and she became spiritually lazy. Writing had become such an essential part of her life that she was compelled to take up her pen again, despite the loss from memory of events during the years 1731-6.

Others may also have written for themselves, like Elizabeth Nimmo: 'Having had many convictions for not recording more exactly the wonderful doings of the Lord about me in my pilgrimage condition I therefore here resolve to take notice of some particulars thereof, briefly, as the Lord shall be pleased to help me' (p. vi). Others clearly wrote for the public: Campbell, so 'as to commend the way of God to others in whose hand this may come' (p. 201), Somervel for her 'dear nephews and nieces' to excite them to performance of Christian duties. Shaw aimed 'to tell posterity such a covenant-keeping God I have had'. Toward the end of her book Veitch wrote that 'I thought fit to leave this on record, to encourage all mine, and all his friends and followers; for I can say, He will be found of them that seek Him, and that He hath made His word sweeter to me than thousands of gold and silver. That which I have experienced of God's hearing me, may condemn all atheists' (p. 57).

Scottish women undertook, without apology, to share their inner selves with a wider public, and found no resistance from a religion which encouraged feminine piety no less than masculine.[23] To trace this literary impulse one might start around 1600 with divines such as Alexander Hume of Logie, James Melville, Archibald Simson, Robert Blair, and John Forbes of Corse, who either advocated the recording of providences or actually engaged in the practice of life-writing themselves.[24] Among lay people of the first half of the century, Christian Hamilton, Lady Boyd, the Ayrshire farmer James Mitchell, and the legal figures Sir Archibald Johnston of Wariston, John Spreul, and Sir Thomas Hope absorbed this influence and produced spiritual diaries or other memoirs partly religious in content. The famous Hog kept a diary, apparently lost,[25] but which once might have induced the Collace sisters to write. John Willison, minister at Dundee, wrote a book entitled *The Afflicted Man's Companion* (1727). A couple of years before she began her autobiography, Shaw discovered this book 'wherein are contained many useful instructions to old and dying people, to leave good advices to their children and relations'.[26]

The increasingly popular pious practice of writing out personal covenants also exercised an important influence. Several female autobiographies include covenants; others, including Janet Hamilton's, exist outside the autobiographical context. West stated that at a communion service the minister preached on Jeremiah 50:5,[27] and 'prest Covenanting on all of us, which accordingly I did at the table' (p. 90). Blackadder also wrote her covenant after being encouraged by various ministers:

> Remember, O my soul, that upon the 29th day of March 1684 on Saturday morning, thou dost deliberately enter into a solemn engagement to be the Lord's; and did humbly dare to avouch, the Lord, the living God, Father, Son and Holy Ghost, to be thy God; and was most willing to accept him upon any Termes that he could offer; And did most heartily renounce all thine own righteousness, intirely laying hold upon the imputed righteousness of Jesus Christ; utterly dispairing of all other ways for salvation. [...] And in witness and testimony of my intire willingness to stand to all this, I do in the presence of the great and dreadfull God (whom from henceforth I will humbly dare to call *my God*). Subscribed this with my hand the 31 of March 1684. Elizabeth Blakader.
>
> (p.389)

If these women had few anxieties about the practice of life-writing, what were the constraints on their style and content, and what were the materials for constructing these literary lives? None of the authors benefited from patronage, so in this respect they were free,[28] but there were other sources of inspiration which directed them. They wrote as representatives of a clearly defined community and, almost unexceptionally, within its permissible range of discourse. Cairns's narrative is marked more than any other by a visual element which caused some to express concern about the nature of her piety. Following 'a sight of his [God's] glory', she shared her mind with 'an experienced Christian' who told her that 'sensible manifestations were reserved for eternity' (p. 47), that is, she was in danger of transgressing the boundary between earth and heaven. In a similar vein, Wodrow turned apologist for Campbell who was in Holland at the time of the Revolution. On the occasion of her husband's voyage to England with William of Orange, she had a dream involving Bibles, and took it 'as some emblem of that clear knowledge and the settlement of the gospell, and the use making of the scripture in opposition to Popery that followed the happy Revolution. This person is a lady of great piety and good sense, and no visionary', Wodrow protested (I, 281). At no point do any of these women authors express anything which might smack of new revelations, as in the instance of the French mystic, Madame Antoinette Bourignon (1616-80),[29] whose behaviour and words led to her departure from the Roman Catholic Church but also gained her a following both in Europe and the north-east of Scotland.

The fast bond between these Scottish women and the 'orthodox', or uncompromising, evangelical Presbyterian clergy is demonstrated by Jean Collace. She wrote of Hog: 'if ever I attained to the hope of an interest in Christ on any sure foundation, he was the instrument made use of by God for my direction and establishment' (p. 99). Clearly, the religion which these women practiced and which supplied both form and content for their self-invention was absorbed from masculine sources: men preached the sermons and wrote the divinity books. Yet the responsiveness of these women to ministers and their messages and devotional techniques could not have failed to shape contemporary piety. Religion in the home was not the sole preserve of the husband/father; given the frequent absences of the man, the woman's function in family piety might be paramount. It is important to emphasise that women were not, and could not be, subservient to all male figures. In fact, West criticised her father and was merciless toward ministers who, in her judgement, were not up to the mark. Similarly, Shaw was at odds with her parents for discouraging her gadding to Kilsyth on a day other than the Sabbath. She believed that God had called her to attend, 'and although it was my duty to obey my parents, yet only in the Lord, and to obey God rather than man' (p. 22). Presbyterian women were compelled to choose between persecuted, nonconforming ministers and episcopal curates intruded by authority, while Cairns much disliked her parish minister, and this unhappy relationship was part of her motivation for moving away. She and the other women who wrote their lives laboured under a number of gender-based constraints but could act on their own convictions. Religion may have served to constrain them; it worked also to embolden them.

The role of the Bible in shaping the form which these lives were constructed cannot be overstated. Women's self-writing is replete with biblical references, many of them taken from the book of Psalms which lends itself readily to the autobiographer and diarist seeking the means of literary self-invention. These authors read the Bible in a way which personalised both the selection and the content. Autobiographers and others wrote that 'that word was born in',[30] 'that word being set home', or 'this word came in my minde'.[31] Blackadder wrote about the Moses story: 'This scripture, though it seems not so very applicable, yet the Lord my God was pleased to bless it as a mean to quiet my troubled heart at that time' (p. 398). Upon a minister's advice Goodale began to read, and then came 15 June 1677, 'a day never to be forgotten. I was reading in Isaiah the fiftie-fourth chapter; when I did begin my heart did warm [anticipating John Wesley's 1738 reaction to Luther's preface to Romans, 'I felt my heart strangely warmed'], and when I read the 4th verse, I found it was to me' (p. 482). Furthermore, they had no trouble finding references to blessed women in the Bible,[32] and in one instance Lady Campbell, quoting Song of Solomon 2:3, altered 'sons' to 'daughters', borrowing from a nearby verse (p. 321).

If ministers offered motivation, and the Bible provided a rich and diverse source of language, these women then actively sought regular opportunities to develop their religious lives. Mistress Rutherford frequently retreated from social intercourse to find space and time alone; West also spent much time alone in closet and field. Cairns had time for reflection between the ages of five and thirteen when she minded her father's sheep and cattle. She marvelled that her mother had not taught her to read earlier than eight but thereafter would read the Bible and the *Shorter Catechism* while in the fields. In adolescence she began to work in the home with the effect that she had less time alone, and her work put more demands on her mind: 'this put me into a great strait, how to keep my mind with God, and not to slight my business' (p. 23) and, indeed, her parents chastised her for her lack of attentiveness. During her mother's lengthy sickness Cairns's writing was much hindered. At this time she was a teacher in Stirling: 'After this, for the space of four years, I got none written; for I had but one room, and having both my mother and school, I could get neither time nor place for that purpose; but now, it hath pleased the Lord to take away my mother by death; so I desire to look back on these melancholy years and record somewhat of the Lord's way with me, as it shall please him to bring it to my mind' (p. 142). Somervel regretted the lack of a 'place of retirement at home, on account of another woman that resided with me' (p. 37).

Some of these writers, while deeply committed to writing about their religious interpretations of worldly experiences, remarked upon the limitations of narrative as a means of embodying the transcendent, mystical substance of their lives. On several occasions Cairns begins a description of a religious experience, only to conclude that 'what I met with, in my being brought thus near [to God], *I can neither word nor write*, but it is such as my soul knows right well' (p. 151; emphasis added). The evangelical had to be able to decipher another mode of communication, as West noted. She developed a fever and declared that this 'providence had a loud language to me' (p. 145), but it was not easily understood. Such instances point to the ineffable, mystical heart of evangelical religious experience, and the Lord's supper[33] in this same religious ethos is to be construed, significantly, as the (periodic) triumph of *mythos* over *logos*.[34]

None of these women attempted to appropriate the public voice of religion. At the end of Katharine Collace's autobiography there is 'A Speech of the foresaid person, being under a pardoned condition'. It begins 'Come, my friends, I'll tell you what the Lord hath done for me' (p. 91). The heading and the appeal to the second person are probably a rhetorical position so that the intended mode of delivery was writing and not speech. Cairns wrote dutifully: 'Was there ever any of the female sex, that obtained the Lord's mind concerning his church?'[35] But this did not keep her from writing about the negative alterations in the Church of Scotland as a result of the Union, the Act of Toleration, patronage, and the Oath of Abjuration. Veitch was equally opposed to episcopacy, but perhaps she was not quite so reserved in her discourse:

> One day I was speaking of the Church of Scotland to some; I told them that I hoped He would yet appear in his glory there, and that I should see it; and they told me, I might never see that, for Mr Livingstoun and Mr Wellwood, two famous ministers, had as great hopes to see that sight, and were disappointed; which took deep impression on my spirit, and I went to God and poured out my spirit before him [...] that I might not expect that from him, that was but a woman, and so little a plant in his garden, when he had denied it to his faithful ministers...
>
> (p. 27)

However, she found solace in the scripture passage 'out of the mouths of babes and sucklings' (Psalm 8:2; Matthew 21:16), then alluded to Samson's mother (Judges 13): 'And Manoah's wife saw more than the man' (p. 27).

Scholars have noted the tension within the isolated and lonely pilgrim who is simultaneously drawn into the relational concerns of a religious community.[36] Katharine Collace learned 'to prize the people of God more, and their fellowship, as pleasant and profitable in the time of straits; yet to dote upon them less...' (p. 64). Somervel regretted that sickness kept her from church meetings, and noted that 'I have been often refreshed in Christian conference and fellowship-meetings' (p.63). West suffered alone but moved in a circle of praying people, and like

Rutherford, also had a special friend, a woman, in whom she confided.

Watson and Smith emphasise the androcentric qualities of the autobiographical *genre* itself, for it gives existence to the masculine while functioning 'as an exclusionary genre against which the utterances of other subjects are measured and misread'.[37] Yet Mary G. Mason provides a different perspective on the question of generic androcentricity, claiming that masculine writers 'never take up the archetypal models of Julian, Margery Kempe, Margaret Cavendish, and Anne Bradstreet'.[38] She argues that there is a fundamental difference between autobiographies by the two sexes. Stauffer states that 'as a class they [autobiographies by women] are far more interesting and important than the autobiographies by men; more personal, informal, and lifelike'.[39] One might suggest that male examples of life-writing in this period are more preoccupied with the external world than female examples, which remain more focused on the interior life though this interiorisation must be interpreted carefully. Perhaps some men benefited psychologically from their roles in wider social entities; perhaps some women had too few social contacts, thus imposing a psychological distinction upon the life-writings of the two sexes. In any event, the rather obsessive resort to spiritual self-analysis led to despair from which escape was too often temporary. Ministers were not immune to this condition, and it was sometimes severe. The Collaces were deeply attached to a shadowy wandering preacher, John Wellwood. In one of his letters to Thomas Hog, dated 5 October 1675, he wrote: 'There is another thing in your letter about not giving way to damps. I have indeed been ruined with melancholy [...] if ever I be rid of them [damps], I know not'.[40] Webber writes that 'the more Calvinist the doctrine, the more stress seems to be laid on the incompatibility of election with despair',[41] but the redeemed life of these elect would only be known in the midst of spiritual anguish.

Ultimately, these spiritual life-narratives tell a story of women sharing in a common humanity with men, for their writing was neither coerced nor ghost-written by domineering men, and they may also have influenced the lives of men, as further research will undoubtedly sustain. These devotional writers located constructive roles for themselves in the evangelical Presbyterian community where they were esteemed for their contributions to the common life of faith. Katharine Collace wrote of 'sickness of body, death of children, outward difficulties, and many crosses from my nearest relations', all of which helped to make her 'a stranger on the Earth' (p. 46). But she and the others found in their faith intimacy, grace, and love. Religion taught them to take themselves seriously, even to assert themselves, finding voices that others might know the experiences they had undergone, indeed the selves which they had constructed from Bible and pulpit discourse. Their stories deepen our understanding of early modern Scottish religion and society and of an early stage of women's writerly self-expression.[42]

Notes

[1] *Narrative of Mr James Nimmo, 1654-1709*, ed. by W. G. Scott-Moncrieff (Edinburgh: Scottish History Society, 1889), p. v.

[2] *Elijah's Mantle: or, the Memoirs and Spiritual Exercises of Marion Shaw* (Glasgow: [n. pub.], 1765), p. vi.

[3] EUL, Laing MSS, La.III.263: Wodrow MSS, Octavo 33, no. 6; to be published as *Mistress Rutherford: A 17th Century Scottish Woman's Religious Autobiography*, ed. by David G. Mullan, forthcoming in *Scottish History Society, Miscellany xiii*; and see also David G. Mullan, 'Mistress Rutherford's Narrative: A Scottish Puritan Autobiography', *Bunyan Studies*, 7 (1997), 13-37.

[4] David George Mullan, ed., *Women's Life Writing in Early Modern Scotland: Writing the Evangelical Self c.1670-c.1730* (Aldershot and Burlington, VT: Ashgate, 2003), p. 44. I am grateful to Dr. Louise Yeoman for permission to make use of the article on K. Collace/Ross she has written for the *NDNB*. See also Andrew Stevenson, *Memoirs of the Life of Mr Thomas Hog* (Edinburgh: [n. pub.], 1756), p. 28.

[5] Robert Wodrow, *Analecta*, 4 vols (Edinburgh: [n.pub.], 1842-3), II, 162.

[6] Rutherford wrote a great deal of divinity, and after his death some of his letters appeared as *Joshua Redivivus* ([Rotterdam], 1664; many subsequent eds). See John Coffey, *Politics, Religion and the British Revolutions: The Mind of Samuel Rutherford* (Cambridge: CUP, 1997), esp. ch. 4; and David George Mullan, *Scottish Puritanism, 1590-1638* (Oxford: OUP, 2000), pp. 38-41, 161-3, 169.

[7] Mullan, *Women's Life Writing*, p. 26; all quotations from Collace appear in this edition.

[8] *Select Biographies*, ed. by W. K. Tweedie, 2 vols (Edinburgh: Wodrow Society, 1845-7), II, 481-93.

[9] Mullan, *Women's Life Writing*, pp. 26-7; all quotations from Campbell appear in this edition.

[10] James B. Paul, *The Scots Peerage*, 9 vols (Edinburgh: David Douglas, 1904-14), I, 520.

[11] *Memoirs of the Life of Mrs Veitch*, in *Memoirs of Mrs William Veitch, Mr Thomas Hog of Kiltearn, Mr Henry Erskine, and Mr John Carstairs* (Edinburgh, 1846); see Kenneth W. H. Howard, *Marion Veitch: The Memoirs, Life & Times of a Scots Covenanting Family (1639-1732)* in *Scotland, England and the Americas* (Osset, W. Yorks.: Gospel Tidings Trust Christian Bookshop, 1992).

[12] Mullan, *Women's Life Writing*, pp. 384-409; all quotations from Blackadder appear in this edition.

[13] Elizabeth West, *Memoirs, or Spiritual Exercises* (Edinburgh: [n. pub.], 1724),

p. 218.

[14] *Memoirs of the Life of Elizabeth Cairns* (Glasgow: John Greig, 1762), p. 58.

[15] *A Clear and Remarkable Display of the Condescension, Love and Faithfulness of God, in the Spiritual Experiences of Mary Somervel* (Glasgow: Archibald McLean, Jr., 1766).

[16] Psalm 27:10, quoted from *The Psalms of David in Metre. Newly translated* [...] *Allowed by the Authority of the General Assembly of the Kirk of Scotland, and appointed to be sung in Congregations and Families* (Edinburgh: [n. pub.], 1699), p. 15.

[17] Elspeth Graham, 'Women's Writing and the Self', in *Women and Literature in Britain, 1500-1700*, ed. by Helen Wilcox (Cambridge: CUP, 1996), pp. 211-12.

[18] Sarah M. Dunnigan, 'Scottish Women Writers c.1560-c.1650', in *A History of Scottish Women's Writing*, ed. by Douglas Gifford and Dorothy McMillan (Edinburgh: EUP, 1997), p. 39.

[19] [Sir George Mackenzie of Rosehaugh], *Aretina: or, the Serious Romance* (Edinburgh: [n. pub.], 1660), p. 7.

[20] Myra Reynolds, *The Learned Lady in England, 1650-1760* (Boston: Houghton Mifflin, 1920; rpt. Gloucester, Mass.: Peter Smith, 1964), p. 94.

[21] The publication history of these documents is not yet clear, and both other writings and earlier editions may yet turn up.

[22] Kate Chedgzoy, 'Introduction: "Voice that is Mine"', in *Voicing Women: Gender and Sexuality in Early Modern Writing*, ed. by Kate Chedgzoy, Melanie Hansen, and Suzanne Trill (Keele, Staffs: Keele UP, 1996), p. 2.

[23] Mullan, *Scottish Puritanism*, ch. 5.

[24] Ibid., p. 137.

[25] In NLS, Wodrow MSS, Octavo 31, no. 2, there is an item entitled, 'Arguments or considerations wherby in all probability the Lord is departing from the land. By Mr Thomas Hog. Kiltairn. Sept. 15, 1659'. At the end of this short piece, Wodrow, in whose hand it is transcribed, wrote the following: 'Thir hints of Mr Thomas Hog, minister at Kiltairn, are copyed from his own copy, almost illegible, with 2 vols of his diary in my Lord G. hands, in which diary ther is not very much save some pleasant remarks upon the chapters of the Bible as they occurred in daily reading' (fol. 39ʳ).

[26] Shaw, p. vii; see John Willison, *The Afflicted Man's Companion* (Edinburgh: Samuel Willison, 1755), p. 79. On dating, see my 'The Royal Law of Liberty: A Reassessment of the Early Career of John Glass', *Journal of the United Reformed Church History Society*, 6 (1999), p. 243, n. 52.

[27] '[...] let us join ourselves to the Lord in a perpetual covenant that shall not be forgotten'.

[28] A. A. MacDonald, 'Early Modern Scottish Literature and the Parameters of Culture', in *The Rose and the Thistle: Essays on the Culture of Late Medieval and Renaissance Scotland*, ed. by Sally Mapstone and Juliette Wood (East Linton: Tuckwell Press, 1998), p. 86.

[29] See Leszek Kolakowski, *Chrétiens sans Église: La Conscience Religieuse et le Lien Confessionnel au xviiᵉ Siècle*, trans. by Anna Posner (1965; Paris: Gallimard, 1987), pp. 640-84.

[30] Mullan, *Women's Life Writing*, p. 224.

[31] Barbara Peebles, 'Ane Exercise of a Privat Christian in the 20 of July 1660', in NLS, Wodrow MSS, Quarto 26, fol. 283^v.

[32] West, pp. 211-15.

[33] Leigh Eric Schmidt, *Holy Fairs: Scotland and the Making of American Revivalism*, 2nd ed. (Grand Rapids, Michigan: William B. Eerdmans, 2001), pp. 47-8, refers in the context of communion revivals to the narratives of Mary Somervel, Elizabeth West, and Elizabeth Blackadder.

[34] Goodale, p. 484.

[35] Cairns, p. 92. Certainly Grizell Love of Paisley sought it, and wrote about it in a lengthy piece of evangelical devotional literature which consistently embraces the visionary. 'Exercise of Grizall Love in Paislay', NLS, Wodrow MSS, Quarto 72, fols 193^v-194^r.

[36] Graham, p. 214; Margo Todd, 'Puritan Self-fashioning', in *Puritanism: Transatlantic Perspectives on a Seventeenth-Century Anglo-American Faith*, ed. by Francis J. Bremer (Boston: Massachusetts Historical Society, 1993), p. 62, 73, 75-6; Mullan, 'Mistress Rutherford's Narrative', p. 28.

[37] Julia Watson and Sidonie Smith, 'De/Colonization and the Politics of Discourse in Women's Autobiographical Practices', in *De/Colonizing the Subject: The Politics of Gender in Women's Autobiography*, ed. by Sidonie Smith and Julia Watson (Minneapolis: U Minnesota P, 1992), p. xviii.

[38] Mary G. Mason, 'The Other Voice: Autobiographies of Women Writers', in *Autobiography: Essays Theoretical and Critical*, ed. by James Olney (Princeton: PUP, 1980), p. 210. This essay was republished in *Life/Lines: Theorizing Women's Autobiography*, ed. by Bella Brodzki and Celeste Schenk (Ithaca: Cornell UP, 1988).

[39] Donald A. Stauffer, *English Biography before 1700* (New York: Russell & Russell, 1964), p. 209.

[40] NLS, Advocates MSS, 32.4.4, fol. 2^r.

[41] Joan Webber, *The Eloquent 'I': Style and Self in Seventeenth-Century Prose* (Madison, WI: U Wisconsin P, 1968), p. 9.

[42] I am grateful to Professor David Wright and Dr Jane Dawson for giving me the opportunity to read a similar paper to the Ecclesiastical History Seminar at New College, Edinburgh, on 10 May 2001. The ensuing discussion was of great benefit to me. My research in Edinburgh was underwritten by a grant from the Social Sciences and Humanities Research Council of Canada. I am also grateful to Dr Sarah Dunnigan for her careful reading and constructive criticism of the essay. I have generally modernised spelling and capitalisation.

Part Three

'Archival Women'

14

Elizabeth Melville, Lady Culross: 3500 New Lines of Verse

Jamie Reid-Baxter

My discovery in September 2002 that Elizabeth Melville, Lady Culross, wrote the verses which appear in a MS volume of sermons by Robert Bruce[1] suddenly turned her into one of the most prolific of Scottish early modern women writers. Here were twenty-nine separate, unknown examples of Melville's work. The manuscript itself contains no dates or scribal colophons, but the sheer number of correspondences with Melville's *Godlie Dreame* — subject matter, countless phrases, rhyme schemes, and even an entire half stanza — made authorship self-evident. Independent proof is written in capitals above the opening sonnet: '*Ane Anagram*: SOB SILLE COR', i.e. ISBEL (or ELISB) COLROS. 'Cor' is Latin for 'heart', and the sonnet is an impressive statement of Lady Culross's heartfelt, life-long creed, summed up in its opening and closing lines:

> *Sob sille cor*, since lyke ane pilgrime pure
> Thou lives below and can not sie thy love [...]
> Here is thy hell, and sin assaillis thee sore
> *Sob sille cor*, and grone to sie that glore.
> (ll. 1-2, 13-14)

Placed at the outset as a kind of signature, the anagram is never used again. The tone of voice, however, will be sustained over some 3000 lines (and indeed, it characterises all of Lady Culross's writings).

When did she write these poems? On 16 February 1599, Alexander Hume had spoken of Melville as 'a ladie, a tender youth, sad, solitare and sanctified, oft sighing & weeping through the conscience of sinne',[2] and sighing and weeping, along with sobbing, much occupy the exceedingly sin-conscious speaker in the new verses, who twice addresses herself as being 'young in yeiris' (poems VI, l. 9, and XI, l. 17).[3] The verses range from a fine *dixain* through three short sonnet sequences to lengthy meditations in various complex stanza forms including *sixain, dixain, rime couée*, rhyme royal, 'Solsequium stanza',[4] and, repeatedly, the eight-line ballat royal used for the *Godlie Dreame*. All are confidently handled, as is the use of alliteration. The meditations, mostly titled and prefaced by short Biblical quotations, are long: the shortest has 12 stanzas, most have a minimum of 20, and the longest 54. There is less paraphrase of Scripture than one might expect; but poem X, 'Ane Lamentatioun for sin with ane consolatioun to the afflicted saull', contains many instances, as here:

> O dolent death quhair is thy deadly sting
> devoring hell quhair is thy victorie
> the sting of death is sin, but Chryst our king
> hes it ov'rcum triumphing on the trie
> though we appeir befoir the world to die
> we pas from death to evirlesting lyfe
> from baill to bliss to rest from all our stryfe.
>
> (ll. 120-6)

The sequence in which the 29 poems are copied is not sheer happenstance: the atmosphere of spiritual bereftness definitely lightens, with poem X marking a real turning point. But there is so much repetition of the same points, in very much the same words and images, that progress is made by taking two steps forward and one back, with periodic slides right back into near-despair. The undoubted high points are the fourteen sonnets, particularly the concluding seven-sonnet sequence. Sonnet IV, unusually, deploys a sustained metaphor:

> In brittil bark of fraill fant feble flesch
> my sillie saul with contrair windis is tost
> calms me corrupt, in stormis I frett and fasch
> in rest I roust, in trubell all seimis lost...
>
> (ll. 1-4)

and sonnet VI, the climax before the serene 'coda', builds on material from its predecessors, and effortlessly deploys internal rhyme:

> Though sence of sin do more and more incress

yit not the les it sall be weill at last
hold Jesus fast and he sall send redres
in deip distres your cair upoun him cast
and thoucht a blast do ding yow from the mast
be not agast bot quicklie ryse agane
pauss not for paine anone it sall be past
if grace be [*sic* for ?ye] ask ye cannot cry in vane
if ye complaine he constant sall remaine
can he disdaine the hevie hairt to heir
thocht he reteir he can not long refraine
his dew sall raine youre wofull saull to cheir
    then grace and peace then love with lyfe and lycht
    ye weill sall feill quhen Chryst sall cleir your sicht.

The closing couplet's typically Scottish double internal rhyme also appears in that of the preceding sonnet: 'Then grace and peace sall fill my hairt with joy / thy licht and micht sall still be my convoy' (ll. 13-14), thus confirming Laing's disputed reading of the final couplet of the 1605-6 sonnet to John Welsh: 'A sight most bright thy soul sall schortlie see / Quhen store of glore thy rich reward sall be'.

The metrical fireworks of the 12 'Solsequium' stanzas of poem XII, 'Ane Thankisgiving', are matched by those of the untitled poem XVII, whose opening stanza refers to Ps.42:[5]

As hairtis full fant
doth braith and pant
    for rinning riveris cleir
opprest with wo
I sigh also
    for thee my god most deir
My hairt doth brist
my saull doth thrist
    for thee the well of lyfe
quhen sall I sie thy majestie
and leave this vaill of stryfe?
        (ll. 1-11)

This is clearly written to a song melody. The lengthy dirge, 'The Winter Night', is to the same tune as the Rev. James Anderson's earlier diatribe;[6] while the song 'Give me thy hairt', from *The Gude and Godlie Ballatis*, is reworked in four stanzas, followed by sixteen of exegesis.

There is every reason to think these 29 poems are (some of) the 'compositiones so copious, so pregnant, so spiritual' which led Alexander Hume to tell Melville in 1599 that for poetry she 'excelles any of youre sexe in that art, that ever I hard within this nation [...] I doubt not but it is the gift of God in you'.[7] Until David Laing's 1826 publication of Melville's sonnet to John Welsh, found among the Wodrow Manuscripts, the only poem known apart from the *Dreame* was its printed companion piece, a sacred parody of a secular love-song, 'Away vaine world', erroneously claimed for Alexander Montgomerie in 1821.[8] More recently, Priscilla Bawcutt discovered an eighteenth-century manuscript copy of 'A Call to come to Christ wrote by my lady Culross' in Yale University, a parody of Marlowe's *Passionate Shepherd to his Love*.

The Bruce manuscript's sacred parodies corroborate Melville's authorship not only of 'Away vain world' and 'A Call to come to Christ', but also of 'Loves Lament for Christs Absence', preserved in a bad late seventeenth-century copy of a copy, engrossed in Wodrow Quarto XVIII in the National Library of Scotland. Wodrow's contents list attributes the pages to Thomas Melville; a minister of that name was related to Lady Culross.[9] A prefatory stanza, 'The transcriber to the reader his friend', indicates that Thomas circulated Elizabeth's splendid poem, whose tone is exemplified by the third stanza:

> Oh for a fountaine in my head, my head
>   In streams of love then bath should I
> Then should I mourne without remeed, remeed
>   My eyes should dreip and never dry
> Untill his presence made me glade
> Whose absence makes my saull so sad
>   Alace, alace how long
> My martyrd mynd doth turne and tosse
> Oh if I could lament my losse
>   And sing a lovers song
> The night is come all joy's away
> Vntill I see my wished day.

(ll. 36-47)

In January 2003, Pamela Giles discovered another sacred parody, at the end of the 1644 Aberdeen print of the *Dreame*, 'Come sweet LORD, let sorrow ceass'. This skilfully juxtaposes Adam and Christ, as in stanza 4:

> GOD for ADAM did prepare,
> A Garden, for his Habitation.
> CHRIST was in a Garden fayr,
> Troubled in Mynd, for my Salvation.
> The cruell Death HIM so affears:
> In that, Cumbat, HEE grat, and swat.
> In the Garden Bloodie Tears.
>
> (ll. 22-8)

Strongly Scots in vocabulary and rhyme, it is a theological tract, where -- most unusually for Melville -- the first person singular appears only once. Yet here almost certainly another of Melville's poems which circulated in manuscript, the solsequium tune 'Thankisgiving', is equally impersonal and theological. Her oeuvre, therefore, now amounts to an impressive 4042 lines.

Elizabeth Melville's poems are spiritual exercises, prayers and sermons. Each individual poem is a genuinely impressive statement of doctrinaire Scottish Calvinism, but Melville eschews creative exploration of the resources of language (metaphors are very few and far between, and vocabulary restricted). The resultant oeuvre is quite remarkably homogeneous. In purely linguistic terms, she vividly illustrates the impact of the Geneva Bible on the Scottish mind, fixing it in set patterns of English expression and thinning down the native Scots tongue. This is a real potential pitfall for Melville's non-Scotophone readers. Despite the southern orthography so often used, her language is *not* English but broad Fife Scots, and her poems declaim most effectively -- if *ch* (even when spelled *gh*) is aspirated, final -*is* pronounced 's', initial *k* sounded, intervocalic *v* generally elided, *prayer* often dissyllabic, like *-ioun,* and *twelve* and *self* rhyme with *tell*, etc.

Elizabeth Melville's Scots identity needs stressing. To refer to her as 'Elizabeth Colville' is to trample underfoot her own self-perception, let alone her Scottishness. Scotswomen of her and earlier ages *never* referred to themselves by their husbands' names. Nor was she ever 'Lady Colville'; her ill-starred husband was (far) below the rank of earl. It is simply wrong to describe her as other than Elizabeth Melville, Lady Culross. Detailed knowledge of her Scottish context is essential for interpreting her writings. She was an integral part of that peculiar Scottish religious world which political developments would transform into the National Covenant of 1638. Elizabeth unquestionably read English publications, Puritan and otherwise, but her work is also bound to reflect what she knew as a child and adolescent in her own country. Alexander Hume's *Breife Treatis of*

Conscience (1594) and James Melville's *Fruitfull and Comfortable Treatise anent Death* (1597) reveal a striking number of verbal parallels with Melville's verse. So, too, do the sermons of Robert Bruce, including those on Hebrews XI which the 29 new poems accompany. But then, even Scots literary scholars have not so far taken any interest in Robert Bruce; had they done so, Elizabeth's voluminous output would long have been available to the wider world.

Notes

[1] See G. D. McNicol, *Master Robert Bruce, Minister in the Kirk of Edinburgh* (Edinburgh: Oliphant, Anderson & Ferrier, 1907; repr. London: [n. pub.] 1961), pp. 193-212, (p. 194). The sermons were preached in April and May 1591; the poems written some years later. See the Introduction to my *Elizabeth Melville: Poems and Letters* (Ontario: North Waterloo Academic, forthcoming 2004). The manuscript is now in New College Library, Edinburgh University.

[2] Alexander Hume, *Hymnes and Sacred Songs*, ed. by Alexander Lawson, STS (Edinburgh and London: Blackwood, 1902), dedication 'To the faithful and vertuous ladie, Elizabeth Melville', p. 3.

[3] Poems numbered as in *Poems and Letters*.

[4] Used by Alexander Montgomerie in his 'Lyk as the dum solsequium' (sung on CD GAU 249, *The Songs of Alexander Montgomerie*) and his paraphrase of Ps.1; cf. *The Poems of Alexander Montgomerie*, ed. by David J. Parkinson, STS 2 vols (Edinburgh: Blackwood, 2001), I, 33-6, (pp. 3-4). Also used by James Melville in a whole series of Scriptural paraphrases, mainly psalms, the first appearing in his *Fruitfull and Comfortable Exhortatioun anent Death* (1597) (STC 17815.5).

[5] Opening lines also quoted in poem VI:

> Lyke as the hairt that for the riveris cleir
> Doth braith and bray, so thristis my saull also
> For thee my god, Och quhen sall I appeir
> Befoir thy face, and leave this vaill of wo.
>
> (ll. 51-4)

[6] *Ane godly treatis, callit the first and second cumming of Christ, sung to the tune of the Winters Night* (95 *rime couée* stanzas written sometime betweeen 1574 and 1582), surviving editions Edinburgh 1614 (STC 572.5) and Glasgow 1713.

[7] Hume, 'Epistle Dedicatorie', p. 4.

[8] Montgomerie died in 1598; the original parodied by Melville was published only in 1600. See *The Poems of Alexander Montgomerie*, II, 5.

[9] See Introduction to *Poems and Letters*.

15

Early Modern Women's Writing in the Edinburgh Archives, c. 1550-1740: a Preliminary Checklist

Suzanne Trill

This checklist is the result of work undertaken during a year long research fellowship generously provided by the Leverhulme Trust, 2001-2. My primary aim for that year was to establish how many manuscripts by early modern women are currently deposited at the National Library of Scotland. While I focused my attentions there, I also made preliminary searches of the catalogues for the Edinburgh University Library Special Collections and the National Archives of Scotland. Although I consulted pre-existing reference sources, the majority of the entries are derived from a painstaking search of the libraries' catalogues, most of which are not currently online. The holdings proved to be rich and varied. Over 200 different women's names appear on this list, some familiar, but many previously unknown. It includes writing by women of different social status, including servants, a postmistress and a lodging-house keeper, as well as women of the gentry and aristocracy. While the majority of writers are identifiably Scottish, sex rather than nationality is the primary criteria for inclusion. Consequently, I have also recorded texts by women from England, Europe, and beyond. It references, for example, two letters by the English diarist Lady Anne Clifford to King James VI and I and at least two letters by lesser known women who had moved to the 'new world'. Collectively, these texts span a wide range of genres, from recipe books to music books, through devotional texts to 'auto/biographies'. For ease of reference, the checklist is divided into generic categories, each of which is organised alphabetically. Each entry provides the shelf-reference, the author's name and the date of writing (where known), and the title of the text (where known), and where appropriate. Where genealogical information is provided, it has been derived from existing catalogues. When dates or names are doubtful, they are indicated by a question mark. One genre predominates, however; that is, letters. The main reason for this emphasis was a desire not to overlap with the work of those involved in the Perdita Project, which specifically excludes letters from its catalogue.[1] However, it also reflects the fact that this genre witnesses the largest growth -- and the widest participation -- in the period. These factors are indicative of both increasing female literacy and the development of the postal service.[2] The letters cover a variety of subjects, from letters of suit to familiar letters and beyond. Although some women are represented by a single letter, significant numbers produced, literally, volumes of letters: see, for example, Elizabeth Campbell, née Tollemache, Duchess of Argyll. Consequently, this genre is subdivided into two sections, single letters and correspondence; the latter ranges from 2 to 215 letters by the same writer.

By anyone's estimation, 215 letters is a considerable accomplishment. However, the most prolific individual woman writer included in this list is undoubtedly Lady Anne Halkett. Of the 21 manuscript volumes that Halkett is known to have produced, 14 are deposited at the NLS.[3] While Halkett is currently most famous for her *Memoirs*, the volumes of 'select' and 'occasional' meditations dwarf that achievement. While the volume of her writing is in itself quite remarkable, its quality and content make it all the more so. Although primarily a religious exercise, Halkett's writing is both a fascinating example of the development of an autobiographical consciousness and a mine of information about contemporary events, whether local (relating mostly to Dunfermline) or national (for example, the Dutch Wars, the accession of William and Mary). The only other woman to be granted an individual entry is Esther Inglis/Kello. Thirteen of her texts can now be located in the EUL special collection and at the NLS. Deservedly, Inglis has recently become the focus of much critical attention because of her beautifully crafted, calligraphic texts. The items listed here provide some indication of her range of writing and the extent of her skill.[4] Both Halkett and Inglis embody the main criteria upon which a writer is included in this listing; namely, that the text should be demonstrably written by a woman. Signature alone is not a sufficient basis for inclusion. Consequently, there are numerous legal texts, particularly in the NLS Advocates' Collection, that are attributed to women but are excluded from this list. Many of these documents will, however, undoubtedly be of interest to social and economic historians: for example, bonds, petitions, funeral and wedding invitations, and accounts. The only exception to this is the 'auto/biography' section of the listing. The majority of those texts are copies by later hands of original texts. While this does raise the question of doubtful authorship and the problematics of transmission, the texts are included here because they at least purport to represent a female 'voice'. I am continuing to explore the archives and am in the process of constructing a website devoted to this topic which will provide more detailed descriptions of both the manuscripts identified here and further discoveries. While the checklist for the NLS collections identified below is fairly comprehensive, the listings for the other two archives are far from complete. The following checklist is, therefore, merely preliminary and should not be assumed to be exhaustive.[5]

KEY TO SHELFMARKS & LOCATIONS

GD. (Gift Deposits)	National Archives of Scotland.
La. (Laing)	Edinburgh University Library Special Collection.
Acc. (Accessions)	
Adv. (Advocates)	
Ms. (Western manuscripts)	National Library of Scotland.
Wod.Oct. (Wodrow Octavo)	
Wod.Qu. (Wodrow Quarto)	

Entries marked with a * indicate that the entry has also been noted by those involved with the Perdita Project; further details of these texts and their writers will eventually be included in their online catalogue. Entries marked with a † are taken from 'Scottish Women Writers, c. 1560-c.1650' by Sarah M. Dunnigan in *A History of Scottish Women's Writing*, ed. by Douglas Gifford and Dorothy McMillan (Edinburgh UP: Edinburgh, 1997), pp. 15-43.

PRELIMINARY CHECKLIST

AUTO/BIOGRAPHY

Wod.Qu.XCIX, no. 38	**ALISON, Isabel.**	1680
fol. 244	(Account of Execution of.)	

Wod.Qu.XXVIII, fol. 116-19.	**ANON.** (*Ane account of the sad trouble of one sorely vexed with the Devil, for a long time: as it was easily told by her self, & easily observed by those who were witnesses thereof.*)	1701
La.III.274.	**ANON.** (Diary.)	c17th
La.II.27-30.	**ANON.** (Dying speeches.)	n.d.
La.II.614.	**ANON.** (Fragment of religious diary.)	n.d.
Wod.Qu.LXXXII (I).	**BEIR,** Agnes. (Testimonial.)	1687
Ms. 1037.	**BLAKADER,** Elizabeth. (*A Short Account of the Lords Way of Prouidence towards me.*)	1724
Wod.Oct.XXXI (viii), fols 181-210.	**CAMPBELL,** Lady Henrietta. (Copy of her Diary.)	1660-89
Acc. 9769 84/1/3.	**CAMPBELL,** Lady Henrietta. (Diary.)	1689
Wod.Oct.XXXI (vii), fols 163-80.	**COLLACE,** Jean. (*Some short remembrances of the Lords kindness to me.*)	n.d.
*Adv. 34.5.19, fols 238ᵛ-84ʳ.	**COLLACE,** Jean. (Another copy.)	n.d.
Adv.32.4.4, fols 78ᵛ-126ᵛ.	**COLLACE,** Jean. (Another copy.)	n.d.
Wod.Oct.XXXI (vii), fols 142-62.	**COLLACE,** Katherine, d. 1704. (K.C, Mistress Ross, her Diary. Copy of.)	n.d.
*MS 874, fols 363-84.	**CUNNINGHAM,** Margaret. (Copy of autobiographical writing, plus a letter from her to her first husband, and a letter to her sister.)	c.1622
*MS 906.	**CUNNINGHAM,** Margaret (Another copy.)	c.1622
Wod.Qu.XXVII, fols 171ʳ-3ᵛ.	**DOUGLAS,** Margaret. (Account of death of.)	1678
Ms. 1909.	**DUCHALL,** Margaret & Margaret Taylor. (Confessions of witchcraft.)	1689

Wod.Qu.XVIII, fols 166ʳ-68ᵛ.	**ELCHO,** Lady Ann. (Account of Death of.)	1700
La.III.261, no.1.	**ELIOT,** Margaret (Last words of.)	1675
Wod.Qu.XVIII, fols 159ʳ-62ʳ.	**ELLIOT,** Margarit, Lady Coltness, spouse of Thomas Stewart of Coltness. (Last words of.)	1675
Wod.Qu.LXXXIV (ix), fols 27ʳ-8ʳ.	**FENWICK,** Ann. *(AF's answer, before the Bishops, In High Commission Durham, Oct.10. 1622. On the Oath Ex Officio.)*	1622
Adv. 32.3.9, fols 79ʳ-85ᵛ.	**GOODALL,** Mrs. wife of John, Wheelwright, Edinburgh. (Covenant and Memoirs.)	Early c18ᵗʰ
MS. 2832, fols 58-63.	**HANNA,** Jannet *(The Dying Testimony of Good and godly Jannet Hanna who had lived sometime at Glasgow.)*	n.d.
Wod.Qu.XXXVI, no. 30 fols 104ʳ-11ᵛ.	**HARVEY,** Marion. *(Testimony Ian. 24. at her examination and conuersation with Mr Riddoll.)*	1681
Wod.Oct.XV, fols 22ʳ⁻ᵛ.	**JAMESON,** Mrs. *(An Observable Exercise of a Dying Christian.)*	1652
Wod.Qu.XXXVII, fol. 276.	**KENNEDY,** Jean, wife of John, Colmonel, née Mckie. (Account of Sufferings of.)	c. 1682
Wod.Qu.XXXVI, fol. 301.	**KER,** Agnes. (Account of Sufferings of.)	n.d.
Wod.Qu.XCIX, no. 35-6, fols 232-42.	**KING,** Mrs. (Account of M John King's Life, Tryall and Death.)	1679
Wod.Oct.XV, fols 1-16.	**LIVINGSTON,** Joan, Lady Wariston. *(A Memorial of Gods work upon JL, with an account of her carriage at her execution.)*	1600

Ms. 2832, fols 137-46.	**MCGINNIES** Janet. *(A short but True Relation of the Lord's way of dealing with Janet McGinnies who Lived in the Parish of Dalry in Cunningham in the Shire of Air.)*	c. 1716
Wod.Qu.XXXI (x), fols 213-4.	**PATON**, Agnas. *(The way of God with my Soul.)*	1697
Wod.Oct.XXXI, fols 142-62.	**ROSS**, Katherine. (Memoirs.)	n.d.
*MS Adv. 32.4.4, fols 27^r-78^v.	**ROSS**, Katherine. (Memoirs, another copy.)	n.d.
*Adv. 34.5.19, fols 184^r-238^r.	**ROSS**, Katherine. (Memoirs, another copy.)	n.d.
*Laing III. 263.	**RUTHERFORD**, Mrs. (Spiritual journal of.)	c. 1630
Ms. 2201, no. 39, fols 73-97.	**RUTHERFURD**, Marie *(Ane narrative of the blessed death of Ladie Dame Marie Rutherfurde Ladie Hundalie spous to Sir James Ker of Craillinghall and Marie McConnal Cousine to the said Ladie.)*	1638
Wod.Qu.XXXVI, fol. 320.	**SCOTT**, Janet, Craigthorn, Glasgow. (Account of Sufferings of.)	1666-84
Ms. 2832, fols 147-50.	**SHEL**, Jean. (Personal convenants of.)	n.d.
Ms. 874, fols 479-84.	**STEWART**, Lady Jane. (Anecdotes of the Family of Leven & Melville, copy of.)	n.d.
Wod.Qu.XXXI (ix), fols 211-12.	**STEWART**, Marion. *(Being the Seventeenth year of my Age.)*	1716
Adv.34.6.22 & Adv. 34.6.25.	**VEITCH**, Marion, Wife of William, Minister of Dumfries, née Fairlie. *(An Account of the Lord's Gracious Dealing with me and of his Remarkable Hearing and answering my Suplications.)*	c.1711

Adv. 34.6.25.	**VEITCH,** William	1727
	(Memoirs of, includes references to	
	his wife, Marion.)	
Wod.Qu.XXXVI, fol.	**WEIK,** Elizabeth.	1687
234.	(Personal Testimony.)	
Ms. 2832, fols 9-16.	**WRIGHT,** Isobell.	1697
	(The Dying Testimony of that so	
	tender Christian & faithfull	
	contender for Christs Truth, widow	
	cleghorn alias Isobell Wright who	
	lived & dyed in Ede.)	

COMMONPLACE BOOKS

Ms. 165.	**ANON.**	c17th
	(Commonplace book in different	
	hands, includes both extracts from	
	histories and recipes.)	
Ms. 3008.	**ANON.**	1712-81
	(Religious.)	
Ms. 2485.	**COCHRANE,** Lady.	1813
	(Includes comments on	
	Shakespeare.)	
Ms. 1882.	**ELEANORE.**	1680-90
	(In French.)	
Ms. 2205.	**WALKER,** Elizabeth.	1717-62
	(Memorandum Book.)	

OTHER BOOKS

Showcases Bk 91	**?ANON.**	c15th
(EUL).	(Meditations on the Passion.)	
Showcases Bk 45	**ANON.**	1596
(EUL).	(Hours of the Virgin, owned by a	
	woman.)	
* GD158/957	**BAILLIE,** Grisell.	Late c17th
	(Memorandum book.)	
*MS 10231.	**BEST,** Dorothy & Mary	1689 &
	Fothergill.	1692
	(Receipt book.)	

*Ms. 9449.	**CAMPBELL,** Lady Jean. (Music Book.)	c. 1640
*MS 3031.	**ELCHO,** Anne, Lady & Jean Wemyss. Inscription in fly leaf states: 'This Book was my mothers in wch are many Receits wch shee had from ye most famous Phisitians yt Liued in her tyme, shee Dyed in Novbr 1649, A. W. Southerland'. (Receipt book.)	c17th
*MS 5159.	**ERSKINE,** Mary. (Household book)	1648-54
*Laing III. 487.	**HAY,** Anna & Mary Hay. (Music book.)	n.d.
*Ms. 5786.	**HOLLANDINA,** Princess Louise (French maxims.)	1629
*Adv. 5.2.17.	**HUME,** Agnes. (Music book.)	1704
†Ms. 5448.	**KER,** Lady Ann. (Music book.)	Early c17th
*MS 1880.	**MEYRICK,** Jane. (Household account book.)	1650-60
*MS 2987.	**NICOLSON,** Magdalen. (Account book.)	1671-93
*Ms. 15937.	**ROBERTSON,** Margaret. (?Collection, c19th copy.)	1630
*[NAS]	**STEWART,** Marie, Countess of Mar. (Account book.)	n.d.
*Dep. 313/502.	**WEMYSS,** Jean, later Countess of Sutherland. (Account book.)	1650-4
*Dep. 314/23.	**WEMYSS,** Lady Margaret Wemyss (Songbook.)	c. 1643-4

CORRESPONDENCE

Adv. 29.3.5, fols 6-12.	**ALISON**, Margaret. (Mistress of the 1st Duke of Argyll) Letters by & to.	n.d.
Adv. 29.1.2 (ii), fols 1-10 & Adv. 29.3.4, fol. 95.	**ALLAN**, Jean, née Anderson wife of John, agent in Islay. Letters by & to.	1716-22
Adv. 29.1.2 (i), fols 179-225.	**ANDERSON**, Janet. (Daughter of James W. Anderson, genealogist.)	c. 1712-19
Adv. 29.1.2(i), fols 1-8, 11-14.	**ANDERSON**, Jean, née Ellis. (Wife of genealogist.)	1709-12
Ms. 1095.	**ANNE**, Queen of England.	1707-8
La.III. 350-1.	**ANON**. Godly woman.	n.d.
Ms. 6409, nos. 142-4.	**BAILLIE**, Lady Grisell. (To John McFarlane.)	1725
Ms. 1127.	**BARCLAY**, Margaret, née Malcolm. (To John & George Mackenzie.)	1716-23
Adv. 82.1.3, fols 67-77.	**BETHUNE**, Katharine.	1738
GD 26/13/596.	**?BOLTON**, Lady	c. 1725
GD 29/1948.	**BRUCE**, Lady, and other family members.	1698-1704
GD 26/13/359.	**BUCCLEUCH** and **MONMOUTH**, Anna. (To the Earl of Melville, and the Earl & Countess of Leven.)	1677-1701
Adv.33.1.1, nos, 74, 78, 82.	**BUCKINGHAM**, Kate. (To King James VI & I.)	n.d.
Adv. 81.1.12, fols 6-120.	**BURNET**, Lady Margaret, née Kennedy.	1661-9
Adv.29.1.1(iii), fols 187-93.	**CAMERON**, Isabel, of Dundallon, née Cameron.	1723-30
Adv.33.1.1, vol. 10, nos. 123, 125, 132.	**CAMPBELL**, Anne, Countess of Argyll, née Cornwallis.	?1617
Adv. 29.5.4. (Two volumes)	**CAMPBELL**, Elizabeth, Duchess of Argyll, née Tollemache. (150 by, 35 to.)	1691-1726

Adv. 29.1.2(v), fols 146-53.	CAMPBELL, Elizabeth, Lady of Calder, née Lort. (Letters by & to.)	c.1709-10
Adv. 29.5.4 (ii), fols 143-52.	CAMPBELL, Elizabeth, Lady of Calder, née Lort. (Letters by & to.)	1704-19
GD 26/8/26 [104-109].	CAMPBELL, I. (To her husband.)	1689
Adv.81.1.12, fols 126-36.	CARNEGIE, Anna, Countess of Southesk, née Hamilton.	1667, 1671
GD 26/13/522.	CARNEGIE, Christian. (To David, Earl of Leven.)	1716-22
Adv. 33.1.7 nos. 22, 24.	CLIFFORD, Lady Anne, Countess of Dorset, Pembroke & Westmoreland. (To King James VI & I.)	n.d.
La.II.639, 18.	CLINTON, Elizabeth.	1675-6
Adv. 32.4.4, fols 1-25ᵛ.	COLLACE, Elizabeth & Katherine. (Letters to and from Mr John Walwood.)	1675-7
Adv. 29.1.1 (iii), fol. 181; 29.1.1 (v), fols 210-13.	COUTTS, Anna.	1728; n.d.
Adv.31.1.8, fols 17, 29, 64.	CRAWFURD, Margaret, of Kilbirine, née Crawfurd.	1664, 1669-70
Adv. 29.1.2, Vol. I, fols 165-77.	CRAWFURD, Margaret, née Anderson. Wife of George Crawford, historian. (To her father & her brother.)	1711-12, 1718, 1723
Wod.Qu.XCIX, (xxxvi), fol. 240.	CRICHTON, Janet.	1628-80
GD 29/1999.	DE WET, Helena. (2 letters, the second in Dutch.)	1688
Ms. 1260.	DENUNE, Isabella, née Hepburn.	1704-17
Ms. 6409, nos. 64-5.	DOUGLAS, Lady Anne, Lady Anne Keith, Countess of Marischal.	?1670s
Ms. 1262.	DUNBAR, Christian, née Mackenzie.	1683-1720

Adv. 80.1.1, fols 50-1, 53-5.	**DUNDAS**, Anne, Lady of, née Menteith. (To 'dauid mitchall marchant & burgis in Ed{r}'.)	1609
Ms. 1031.	**HAMILTON**, Anne, 3rd Duchess of. (To her son, Charles, Earl of Selkirk.)	1694-1703
Ms. 1032.	**HAMILTON**, Anne, 3rd Duchess of. (To her son, Charles, Earl of Selkirk.)	1704-6
Ms. 80, nos. 22-3.	**LENNOX**, Katherine, Duchess of. (To William, 7th Earl of Morton.)	1630
GD 29/1901.	**LINDESAY**, Anna. (To Sir William Bruce.)	1670-1
GD 26/13/351 & 352.	**LIVEN**, Margaret, Countess of. (To Lady Catherine Melville.)	1673
Ms. 1101, fols 75-7.	**MACKENZIE**, Katherine, née Gordon. Second wife of John Mackenzie, Advocate of Devlin. (Letters to her husband. Fols 1-8 are letters from JM to KM.)	1687
Ms. 1101, fols 83-92.	**MACKENZIE**, Margaret, née Hay. Third wife of John Mackenzie, Advocate of Devlin. (Correspondence and papers of.)	1731-52
Ms. 1211.	**MACKENZIE**, Mary. (215 letters, mostly to her brother John.)	1736-45
Ms. 80, nos. 51-3.	**MAR**, Marie Stewart, Countess of. (To William, 7th Earl of Morton.)	1604
Ms. 6409, nos. 101-2.	**McFARLANE**, ?, née Straiton, First wife of John McFarlane.	?early c18[th]
La. III. 347.	**MELVILLE**, Elizabeth, Lady Culros. (To her son, James, and Rev. John Livingstone.)	1625-31

Ms. 6409, nos. 61-3.	MIDDLETON, Martha, Countess of. (To Lord Gosford.)	1675
Ms. 6409, nos. 19-37.	MORTON, Anne Douglas, Countess of. (To Sir James Halkett.)	?1650
GD 29/1925.	ROTHES, Margaret, Countess of. (To Sir William Bruce.)	1685-96
GD 29/1934.	RUTHVEN, M. (To Sir William Bruce.)	1700-8
Adv. 29.3.12, fols 93^v, 159^v-60, 230, 240^v-242, 245, 251-3, 255.	STUART, Margaret, Countess of Lennox, née Douglas. (Letters by & to.)	1570-1
GD29/1907-25, nos. 1921/1-3.	WEMYSS, Margaret, Countess of. (To Sir William Bruce.)	c. 1685
GD 26. Section 13/ 401 (1-44).	WEMYSS, Margaret, Countess of.	1696-98

DEVOTIONAL TEXTS/MEDITATIONS

Ms. 3469.	?ANON. (Copies of John Livingston's sermons.)	1651-4
La.III.76.	?ANON. (Treatise on Devotion.)	c18th
Ms. 1032, No. 159.	?HAMILTON, Anne, 3rd Duchess of. (Unsigned and undated meditation, but the hand corresponds with the Duchess's letters in the same volume.)	n. d
Ms. 1941, fol 35.	MAULE, Marie (Marie Mar). (*?MEDITATIONS on Affliction.*)	1689

HALKETT, Lady Anne

Acc. 6112.	Letter, to the Earl of Lauderdale.	n.d.

MS. 6409.	Letter, to James Kenewy, plus receipts.	n.d.
Ms. 6407.	Four letters, includes one letter to her step-son, Sir Charles Halkett.	n. d.
Ms. 6409, no. 40.	Letter, to her step-son, Sir Charles Halkett.	n. d.
Ms. 6489.	*Meditation, including Expostulation about Praye* (also includes 'The Mothers Will to her vnborne child'.)	1656
Ms.6490.	*Occationall Meditations.*	1658/9-60
Ms. 6491.	*Occationall Meditations,* includes 'Meditations & Prayers vpon euery {seuerall} day that is ordained to bee kept holy in the Church of England'.	1661-2
Ms. 6492.	*Occationall Meditations & Select Contemplations,* includes 'Instructions to my Son'.	1667/8-70/1
Ms. 6493.	*The Widows Mite & Occationall Meditations.*	1673-4
Ms. 6494.	*The Art of Deuine Chimistry.*	1676-8
Ms. 6495.	*Jossph's Trialls & Triumph.*	1678/9
Ms. 6496.	*Meditations vpon the Booke of Jonah*	1683-4
Ms. 6497.	*Meditations.*	1686/7-8
Ms. 6498.	*Meditations on Moses and Samuel.*	1688/9-90
Ms. 6499.	*Occationall Meditations,* also includes exegesis of Nehemiah and 'Obseruations of seuerall good women mentioned in Scripture'.	1690-2
Ms. 6500.	*Of Watchfullnese, Meditations.*	1694-4/5
Ms. 6501.	*Select & Occationall Obseruations.* 'Select' observations based on John's Gospel.	1696-7
Ms. 6502.	*Select & Occationall Meditations.*	1697-8

INGLIS/KELLO, Esther

EUL Phot. 1189.	*Specimen of mother's calligraphy.*	1574
*Ms. 20498.	*Ecclesiastes and Lamentations.* (French verse with Latin dedications.)	1602
La. III. 525. fol. 8.	*Entry in George Craig's Album.*	1604
La. III. 439.	*Les Quatrains du Sieur.*	1607
*Acc. 11821.	Calligraphic Ms. (A summary of St. Matthew's Gospel in Latin.)	1607
La. III. 249.	*Vincula Unionis insulae Brittannicae id est. De Unione insulae Brittanicae tractatus secundas.*	1605
La.III.75.	*Preparation for Holy Supper.*	1608
Ms. 8874.	*Les Pseumes de David.*	1615
La. III. 522.	*Specimens.*	n.d.
La.III.440.	*Verses on the Greatness of God.*	n.d.
*Acc. 7633.	Calligraphic Ms.	n.d
Adv. 33.1.6. Vol. 20, no. 21.	Letter to King James VI & I.	1620
*Ms. 2197.	Calligraphic Ms. (Specimens of styles of writing in English, French, Italian, Latin, & Spanish.)	n.d.

LETTERS (SINGLE)

Adv.29.1.2(vi), fol. 254.	**ADAIR**, Jean, London.	1723
Adv,16.2.24A, fol. 138.	**ALVES**, Elizabeth, Edinburgh.	n.d.
Adv.29.1.2. Vol. I, fol. 226.	**ANDERSON**, Anne. (To her brother from Maryland, USA.)	1718
Adv.22.2.20A, fol. 14ᵛ	**ANDERSON**, Margaret, Glasgow. (Copy of letter to her brother.)	1733

Adv. 29.3.4, fol. 6.	**ANDERSON**, Margaret. (Wife of Patrick, Minister of Walston, née Threipland.)	1690
Wod.Qu.XXVIII, fols 94-8.	**?ANON.** (A letter concerning blasphemy, which makes reference to Bunyan and Sarah Wight.)	1698
GD26/13/498.	**ANON.** (To David, Earl of Leven.)	c. 1712
Ms. 578, no. 129.	**BENNET**, Isabella, Countess of Arlington, née de Nassau, Letter probably by.	?1704
GD 26/13/356.	**ARGYLL**, Anna, Duchess of. (To the Countess of Leven.)	c. 1675
GD 26/13/347.	**ARSKINE**, M. (To her niece Katherine Melville.)	1688
GD 26/13/26.	**ARSKINE**, M. (On the battle of Killiecrankie.)	1689
Ms. 1031.	**ATHOLL**, Lady Katherine, née Hamilton. (To her brother, Charles Hamilton, Earl of Selkirk.)	1694/5
GD 29/1960.	**AUSTIANE**, Sara of Culross.	1669
Ms. 6409, no. 128.	**BAILLIE**, Elisa, wife of Robert Wemyss of Grangemuir. (To John McFarlane.)	1719
Adv. 29.3.4, fol.141.	**BELASYSE**, Bridget, Viscountess Fauconberg née Gage.	1724
Ms. 109, fol. 6.	**BELSTANE**, Lady of.	1676
Ms.294.	**BLACKBURN**, Miss.	1747
Adv. 9.1.1(v), fol. 42.	**BOSWELL**, Elizabeth of Auchinleck, née Bruce.	1709
GD 26/13/339.	**BRAMFORD**, Clara. (To the Earl of Leven.)	1657
Ms. 975, fol. 11.	**CAMPBELL**, Anna, of Lochnell, née Campbell, then McNeill. (To the Earl of Argyll.)	1671
Adv.29.2.11, fol. 196.	**CAMPBELL**, Elizabeth, Lady of Calder, née Lort.	n.d.
Adv. 50.1.13, fol. 352.	**CAMPBELL**, Ellinor.	n.d.

GD 26/13/233.	**CAMPBELL**, Lady Henrietta. (To the Earl of Melville.)	c. 1690
MS. 975, fol. 5.	**CAMPBELL**, Margaret, Marchioness of Argyll, née Douglas, letter by.	1665
Adv.29.5.4 (ii), fol. 153.	**CAMPBELL**, Margaret.	early c18th
Adv. 29.5.4 (ii), fol.169	**CRAWFORD**, Mary Lindsay, Viscountess Garnock, née Home.	1719
Wod.Qu.XCIX, no 36, fol. 241	**CRICHTOUN**, Janet. (Letter to her mistress.)	1679
Adv. 17.1.9, fol. 221.	**DONALDSON**, Elizabeth Wife of Walter, poet, née Goffin. (To an unidentified male correspondent in French.)	1630
Ms. 80, no. 57.	**DOUGLAS**, Lady Anne, Countess of Marischal. (To William, 7th Earl of Morton.)	n.d.
Ms. 2955.	**DOUGLAS**, Jeane. (To her aunt.)	1671
Ms. 975.	**DOUGLAS**, Margaret. (To her son.)	1669
GD 26/13/478.	**DOUGLAS**, Margaret. (To George, Earl of Melville.)	1706
Adv.82.1.2, fol.114.	**DRUMMOND**, Anne.	1731
Adv.33.1.1, Vol.VI, no. 35.	**DRUMMOND**, Jane. (To her husband.)	1615
Adv.33.1.1, Vol. X No. 119.	**DRUMMOND**, Jane (To her husband.)	n.d.
Laing II.130, 3.	**DRUMMOND**, Lady Jean.	1658
Ms. 2955, fol. 40.	**DRUMMOND**, Jean, Countess of Perth, née Douglas, letter probably by.	1672
Ms. 3072, fol. 21.	**DRUMMOND**, Mary, Countess of Perth, née Gordon, then Urquhart, letter probably by.	n.d.
Adv. 82.1.1, fol. 129.	**DUNBAR**, Isobel of Burgie, née Crichton. (To her nephew in France.)	1716
Ms. 975, fol. 1	**?CAMPBELL**, Agnes, Countess of Argyll, née Douglas, letter to.	1589

Ms. 975, fol. 11.	CAMPBELL, Anna, of Lochnell, née Campbell then McNeill, letter by.	1671
Ms. 975, fols 65-70, 99	CAMPBELL, Anne, Countess of Argyll, née Mackenzie, then Lindsay, letters written for & accounts of.	1673-4, 1678
Adv.50.1.13, fol. 352.	CAMPBELL, Ellinor.	n.d.
Ms. 975, fol. 5.	CAMPBELL, Margaret, Marchioness of Argyll, née Douglas, letter by.	1665
Adv.81.1.22, fol. 42.	CECIL, Dorothy, Countess of Exeter, née Nevill.	1597
Adv. 29.1.2 (vi),	COCKBURN, Mary, Mrs.	1712
Adv. 29.1.2 (vi), fol. 250	COLTART, Margaret.	c. 1715
Adv. 33.1.11, vol. 28, no. 51.	COURCELLE, Marie.	n.d.
Adv. 80.1.3, fol.120.	EDGAR, Anna.	1732
Laing.II.651, 4.	EUGENIA, Isabella.	1628
Wod. XXV (Lii)	FLEMING, Anna.	1749
Adv. 29.1.2 (v), fol. 13.	GARDINER, Margaret, Mrs.	1709
Adv. 82.1.1, fol. 216.	GARIOCH, Margaret. (To Lord Oliphant at Gask.)	1725
Wod.Qu.XXVI, fol.120.	GARNOCK, Margaret.	1680
Wod.Qu.XXX(xxxiii), fol. 54.	GORDON, Mary. (To her son.)	1678
Adv. 82.1.1, fol. 23.	?GRAEME, L.	1694
Adv. 80.1.2, fol.158.	GRANT, Jean of Grant, née Houston, then Dundas, then Lockhart.	1696
GD 26/13/495.	HADDO, Lady Mary. (To her father, David, Earl of Leven.)	1710
Adv. 29.2.11, fol. 44.	HALDANE, Margaret.	late c17[th]
Ms. 6409, no. 100.	HALKETT, Ann, wife of James Cathcart of Carbiston. (Inventory of.)	1740
Adv. 80.1.2, fol. 42.	?HALYBURTON, A.	1679

Adv. 80.1.1, fol.135.	HAMILTON, Anna, Marchioness of, née Cunningham.	1625
Ms. 1033.	HAMILTON, Elizabeth, Lady of Orkney, née Villiers. (Letters by & to.)	c. 1708-14
Adv. 80.1.1, fol.184.	?HAMILTON, J, Linlithgow.	1634
Adv. 29.1.2 (vi), fol. 232.	HAMILTON, J, Pencaitland.	1717
Adv. 33.1.1, Vol. 3, no. 43.	HAMILTON, Jean, Lady of Robertoun (formerly Countess of Crawford), née Kerr, then Boyd, then Lindsay.	1610
Adv. 80.1.1, fol. 201.	?HAMILTON, Margaret, Daughter of Sir Alexander, of Innerwick.	1644
La.II.636, fol. 32.	HARE, Margaret.	1620
Adv. 25.3.9, fols 2, 5^v.	HARLAN, Christian, wife of John, Apothecary, Stirling, née Russell.	1700
Adv. 82.1.1, fol. 159.	HARRISON, Isabella, Lodging House Keeper in London. (To Lord Oliphant.)	1720
Adv.33.1.1. Vol. 6, No. 15.	HAY, Eleanor, Countess of Linlithgow. (To King James VI & I.)	1615
Adv. 19.1.26, fol. 63.	HENRIETTA MARIA, Queen Consort of Charles I. (In French.)	1665
Adv. 33.1.1, vol. 10, no. 106.	HOME, Lady Beatrix, of Cowedenknowes, née Ruthven.	1622
Adv. 33.1.1, vol. 10, no. 95.	HOME, Mary, Countess of, née Sutton.	1624
GD 26/13/480.	HOUSTANE, Anne.	1706
Adv. 80.1.12, fol. 95.	IRVINE, Margaret, of the family of Irvine of Saphock.	n.d.
La.I.350.	JOHNSTON, Lady.	1657
Adv. 29.3.5, fol. 41.	KENNEDY, Barbara. (To Mr James Anderson.)	1704
Wod.Qu.XXXV, fol. 332	KER, Lady Anna. (To her sister.)	1714

GD 29/1970.	**KER**, Rebecca. (To James Kenewy.)	1679
Wod.Qu.XXXV, no. 25.	**KERSLAND**, Lady Anna.	1714
GD 26/10/75.	**KINCARDIN**, Veronica, Countess of.	1693
GD 26/13/223.	**KINCARDIN**, Veronica, Countess of. (To George, Lord Melville.)	1689
GD. 29/1900.	**LAWDER**, Elizabeth. (To Sir William Bruce.)	1670
Adv. 29.1.1 (iv), fol. 173.	**?LEGH**, Mary.	c18th
Adv. 29.1.2, Vol. I, fol. 228.	**LEITCH**, Eleanor, née Anderson. (To James Anderson.)	1723
Adv.33.1.7, no. 80.	**LENNOX**, Lady Katherine. (To James VI/I.)	n.d.
Adv.22.3.14, fol. 14.	**LENNOX**, Margaret.	1572
Adv. 80.1.3, fol. 124.	**LESLIE**, Sarah.	1732
GD 26/13/353.	**LEVEN**, Margaret, Countess of. (To George, Lord Melville.)	1673
GD 26/13/353.	**LEVEN**, Margaret, Countess of. (To Lady Catherine Melville.)	1674
Adv. 23.3.17, fol. 23.	**LINDSAY**, Lady Catherine, née Lindsay.	1739
Adv. 33.1.1, Vol. 6, no. 15.	**LIVINGSTON**, Eleanor, Countess of Linlithgow, née Hay.	?1615
GD 26.13.524.	**LUNDORES**, Lady Margaret. (To David, Earl of Leven.)	1716
Adv. 25.9.13, fol. 6.	**?MACCULLOCH**, Katherine, Portioner of Kindyke.	?1601
Adv. 19.1.25, fol. 48.	**MARIA CLEMENTINA**, Princess, née Sobieski.	1725
Adv. 29.1.2 (ii), fol. 10.	**MAXWELL**, Marion, née Ellis.	1694
La.II.363.	**MCKENZIE**, Lady Anne.	1666
GD 26/8/103.	**MCNACHTANE**, Jean, Lady Melville of Monimall, née Stewart, then Leslie.	1609

Adv.80.1.1, fol. 181.	MENTEITH, Isobel, Lady of Kerse, née Hamilton.	1634
Adv.33.1.1, Vol 5, no. 98.	MONTGOMERIE, Anna, Countess of Eglinton, née Livingstone. (To her brother, 'Mr. Morray'.)	1614
Adv.33.1.1, Vol.7, no. 3.	MONTGOMERIE, Anna, Countess of Eglinton, née Livingstone. (To her brother, 'Mr. Morray'.)	1616
Adv.33.1.1, Vol. 10, no 120.	MONTGOMERIE, Anna, Countess of Eglinton, née Livingstone. (To her brother.)	n.d.
Adv. 34.2.12, fol. 220.	MORESTONE, Margaret. (Letter concerning the murder of her child.)	1632
Adv. 82.1.3, fol. 126.	MURRAY, Jane, Duchess of Atholl, née Frederick, then Lannoy.	1640
Adv. 82. [2/1?].1, fol. 53.	MURRAY, Jean of Woddend, née Murray.	1702
GD 26/13/591.	NISBET, Emilia. (To Lady Dirleton.)	1724
Adv. 82.1.1, fol. 5.	OLIPHANT, Katherine of Balgonie, née Haliday.	1654
Adv. 29.2.11, fol. 108.	OSWALD, Ann, wife of John, née McGregor.	1725
Adv. 29.1.1 (iii), fol. 180.	PEDERSON, Janet.	1731
GD 26/13/392.	PERTH, Mary, Countess of. (From her sister.)	1690
Adv. 50.4.8, fol. 56.	POWLETT, Catherine, Duchess of Cleveland, née Stanhope, then Primrose, then Vane.	n.d.
Adv.29.2.11, fol.200.	QUEEN Anne.	1704
GD 26/13/230.	ROTHES, Margaret, Countess of. (To George, Earl of Melville.)	1691
GD 26/13/402.	ROTHES, Margaret, Countess of. (To George, Earl of Melville.)	1691

GD 26/13/462.	ROTHES, Margaret, Countess of. (To Anna, Countess of Leven.)	1699
GD 26/13/395.	ROW, Elizabeth. (To David, Earl of Leven.)	c. 1690
GD 26/13/344.	RUTHERFURD, M. (To Lady Catherine Melville.)	1664
Adv.33.1.1, Vol. X. no. 106.	RUTHVEN, Beatrix. (To James VI and I.)	1622
GD 26/13/1671.	RUTHVEN, Jean.	1671
Wod.Qu.C (xxi), fol. 291ᵛ.	SCHURMAN, Anna Maria. Letter to.	1673
Adv. 29.3.4, fol. 65.	?SCOTT, J.	1712
Adv. 29.1.1 (iii), fol. 183.	SCOTT, Margaret.	1727
Adv. 80.1.2, fol.8.	SETON, Christian, Lady of Abercorn, née Dundas.	1689
Adv. 80.1.1, fol.8.	SETON, Isobell, Lady Seton, née Hamilton.	1601
Adv. 23.3.26, fol. 88.	SETON, Isabella.	1640
Adv. 80.1.1, fol. 18.	SETON, Margaret, Countess of Winton, née Montgomerie.	1605
Adv. 80.1.1, fol.144.	SHAIRP, Margaret, Lady of Ballindoch, née Dundas.	1627
Wod.Fol.XXIX, no. xviii.	SIMPSON, Marie.	1641
Adv. 29.1.1(ii), fol. 181.	SMITH, Mrs. Postmistress at Morpeth. Letter to.	1728
Adv. 82.1.3, fol. 44.	SMYTHE, Katherine of Methven, née Cochran.	1737
Adv. 33.1.11, Vol. 28, no. 24.	SOPHIA, Queen Consort of Frederick II, King of Denmark.	1590
Adv. 29.1.2, Vol. vi, fol. 231.	SPOTISWOOD, Janet, Edinburgh. (To 'Mr Iames Anderson'.)	1703
Adv. 22.3.14, fol. 47.	STEWART, Margaret, Lady of Eday & Tullos, née Lyon.	1592
Adv. 33.1.1, Vol. 5, no. 118.	STEWART, Marie.	c17ᵗʰ
Adv. 80.1.4, fol. 28.	STRATHAN, Katherine, Charleston, S. Carolina. (To the Countess of Wemyss.)	1739

Adv. 33.1.7, Vol. 22, no. 68.	STUART, Frances, Duchess of Lennox, née Howard, then Pranell, then Seymour.	c. 1622
Adv. 33.1.10, Vol. 27, nos. 3-4.	SUAREZ DE FIGUEROA, Jane, Duchess of Feria, née Dormer. (To James VI/I, with 'Reasons to be intimat to y{e} kings maiesty of Scotland whereby yt maye appeare yt his best way to obtayne ye croune of England, is to become catholyk'.)	1600
Ms. 2955.	WEMYSS, Lady Jeane. (To the Duke of Lauderdale.)	?1649
Adv. 29.1.1 (iv), fol. 169.	TRAPPES, Mary.	n.d.
La.II.638, fol. 18.	TURGIS, Elizabeth.	1653
GD. 26/13/604.	WEMYSS, Janet. (To Alexander, Earl of Leven.)	1731
Ms. 2955.	WEMYSS, Countess of Margaret. (To the Duke of Lauderdale.)	1677
GD 26/13/222.	WEMYSS, Margaret, Countess of. (To George, Lord Melville.)	1689
GD 29/1956.	WEMYSS, Lady Margaret.	n.d.
La.II.635, 24.	WHARTON, Bridgit.	1589
Adv. 29.1.1 (ii), fol. 182.	WILSON, Mrs. Letter to.	1728
Adv. 29.1.2 (vii), fol. 17.	YVOY, Magdalen, of Rotterdam, née Voorburg.	1716

POETRY

Wod.Qu.LXXXVII (xii), fol.55.	?ANON. (Satirical poem in voice of Elizabeth I.)	1622
Ms. 921, fol. 31.	BAYLEY, Catharine, poem by.	n.d.
†Ms. 2065, fol. 6r.	BEATON, Mary, Lady Boyne. (Sonnet.)	n.d.
Ms. 1706, fol. 29.	CARTER, Elizabeth, poem by.	n.d.

*Laing III. 444.	**DAVIES**, Lucy, later Hastings. (Poems compiled by or for Lucy, daughter of Sir John Davies.)	n.d.
†EUL Dr. De. 1. 10.	**DOUGLAS**, Elizabeth, Countess of Erroll. (Copy of dedicatory poems.)	1587
†EUL. De.3.70, fol. 68v.	**LINDSAY**, Christian. (Sonnet.)	c.1580
†EUL Ms 436.	**?KER**, Lady Anne. ('Lady Laudian's Lament'.)	n.d.
Wod.Qu.XXVII, no. 2, fols 9r-23ᵛ (see also Adv.Ms.19.3.4, fol. 104 (fol. 9).)	**MACKAY**, Barbara. (*The Song of Solomon & the Lamentations of Jeremiah.*)	1657
Wod.Qu.XXVII, no. 3. fols 24r-28r.	**MACKAY**, Barbara. (*Severall other poems dedicated to the Countess of Caithness.*)	1657
Wod.Qu.XXIX (iv), fol. 10.	**MELVILLE**, Elizabeth. (Copy of sonnet by.)	n.d.
*GD56/157.	**YOUNG**, Dame Margaret. (Poetry and fragments by.)	n.d.

PROPHECY/VISIONS

Wod.Qu.XXX, fols 74ᵛ-5.	**?ANON.**	c.1679
Wod.Qu.XXVI, fol. 283	**PEEBLES**, Barbara.	1660
Wod.Qu.XXXV, no. 22.	**PEEBLES**, Barbara. ('The exercise of a priuate Christian'.)	1660
Wod.Qu.XCIX (iii), fol. 50.	**J., R's** wife	1651
Wod.Qu.XCIX (iv), fol. 52.	Another copy.	n.d.
Wod.Qu.LXXII.	**LOVE**, Grizell.	1661-78
Wod.Oct.XXIX, & Wod.Qu.XXVI, fol. 219.	**SHIPTON**, Mother.	n.d.

PUBLISHED TEXTS

Edinburgh, Society of Stationers.	**ANON.** *An Exact and faithful relation of the process pursued by Dame Margaret Areskine, Lady Castlehaven, relict of the decesed Sir James Foulis of Collingtoun, against Sir James Foulis now of Collingtoun, before the Lords Of Council and Session.*	1690
Edinburgh.	**ANON.** *Answers for James Anderson and Agnes Campbell his Mother.*	1690
Edinburgh.	**ANON.** *Answers for the Countess of Weymss.*	1693
Edinburgh, John Reid.	**ANON.** *The golden island, or, The Darian song by a Lady of honour.*	1699
Edinburgh (reprint).	**FOX,** Margaret Askew Fell. *The standard of the Lord revealed.*	1667
Edinburgh, Andrew Symson & Henry Knox.	**HALKETT,** Lady Anne. *Meditations on the Twentieth and Fifith Psalm.*	1702
Edinburgh, Andrew Symson & Henry Knox.	**HALKETT,** Lady Anne. *Meditations upon the Seven Gifts of the Holy Spirit, as also Meditations upon Jabez his Request. Together with Sacramental Meditations on the Lord's Supper and Prayers, Pious Reflections and Observations.*	1702
Edinburgh, Andrew Symson.	**HALKETT,** Lady Anne. *Instructions for Youth, For the use of those young Noblemen and Gentlemen, whose Education was Committed to her Care.*	1702

Edinburgh, Evan Tayler.	**HUME,** Anna Mrs. *The Triumphs of Love, Chastity, Death, translated out of Petrarch.*	1644
Edinburgh, John Wreittoun.	**LIVINGSTON,** Eleanor, Countess of Linlithgow. *The Confession and conuersion of the right honourable, Most elect lady, my Lady C. of L.*	1629
Edinburgh, Robert Charteris.	**MELVILL,** Elizabeth, Lady Colville of Culross. *Ane Godlie Dreame*	1603
Edinburgh, Andro Hart.	**MELVILL,** Elizabeth, Lady Colville of Culross. *A Godlie Dreame.*	1620
London	**OXLIE,** Mary, of Morpeth. Lyric printed (sigs. A8^{r-v}) in *Poems by that most Famous wit William Drummond of Hawthornden.*	1656

Notes

[1] URL: http://human.ntu.ac.uk/perdita/PERDITA.HTM.

[2] While quantification of female literacy remains an area of debate, information about the development of the postal service can be found in Howard Robinson, *The British Post Office: A History* (Princeton, NJ: Princeton UP, 1948), and A.R.B. Haldane, *Three Centuries of Scottish Posts : An Historical Survey to 1836* (Edinburgh: EUP, 1971).

[3] A full listing of Halkett's manuscripts is appended to *The Life of the Lady Halkett* by S. C [Simon Couper], (Edinburgh: Andrew Symson & Henry Knox, 1701). The only extant manuscript not deposited in the NLS is Halkett's *Memoirs*, BL Add. 32, 376.

[4] See, for example, Georgianna Ziegler, '"More than Feminine Boldness": The Gift Books of Esther Inglis', in *Women, Writing and the Reproduction of Culture in Tudor and Stuart Britain*, ed. by Mary E. Burke and others (Syracuse, NY: Syracuse UP, 2000), pp. 19-37.

[5] At present, the checklist does not incorporate material in Gaelic.

Index

Printed in the United States
30411LVS00001B/64

9 781403 911810